INQUISITOR
DREAMS

INQUISITOR DREAMS

SCENES FROM THE LIFE OF

DON FELIPE DE ALHAMA DE GRANADA, ETC.,

SOMETIME SERVANT OF THE HOLY OFFICE IN SPAIN

PHYLLIS ANN KARR

WILDSIDE PRESS

INQUISITOR DREAMS

"There can, indeed, be no doubt that, amid much greed and callous indifference to justice, there were men engaged in the service who deemed themselves to be doing the work of God and that their methods were merciful...the individuals were not necessarily as vicious as the system..."

—Henry Charles Lea,
A History of the Inquisition of Spain,
v. II, bk. VI, ch. 2; v. III, bk. VI, ch. 8

AUTHOR'S FOREWORD

When I began this book, I thought it would be easy for me to understand its Catholic viewpoint, since I had grown to college age before Pope John XXIII convened the Second Vatican Council. I quickly learned that a Polish ethnic version of Midwest American Catholicism on the eve of Vatican II was a very different thing indeed from Southern European Catholicism in the decades preceding the Council of Trent! Whoever calls the Roman Catholic Church monolithic speaks from gross misinformation.

There are things in this novel, both religious and secular, which I myself would probably have thought erroneous before doing my research. To cite four examples: (1). Priests were not automatically called "Father." That title was reserved to bishops, abbots, and—by pentitents—to their own personal confessors (the use which presumably led to its present "universal" application, at least in the English-speaking world). Thus, in these pages priests belonging to monastic and itinerant orders are "Brother" ("Fra" or "Fray") like their fellow but non-ordained monks or friars, while secular priests are "Don" ("Sir"). (2). Confessions were heard in the open, often before an altar; St. Charles Borromeo (1538-1584) is credited with inventing the confessional box. (3). Wives did not automatically receive their husbands' surnames. Even in Don Quixote, written almost a century after my Felipe's time, Sancho's wife is surnamed Gutiérrez and Panza alternately, and, in the later case, Cervantes deemed it necessary to explain that that was a custom in La Mancha. (4). It seems highly unlikely that Don Felipe would have known the Sanskrit term "swastika," but he would have known the very ancient, widespread, and—until Hitler got hold of it—good symbol, probably as a "gamma-cross."

Outside of the dream sequences, in which I have purposely mixed up fact and symbolism, I have tried to be as meticulously accurate as possible. Where I have erred through forgetfulness, misplaced dramatic license, or failing to find the best reference work, the fault is my own; for the rest, I insist on pleading that no historical fictioneer can possibly be better than the research sources available.

As with the characters, so with the places: some, like Alhama, are authentic; others, like Agapida, completely fictional. The real places, though not the recorded facts of their history, have been somewhat fictionalized. A footnote in one of Lea's volumes mentions a perplexing reference to "the bishop of Daroca" in an old document, and I took this—almost certainly a scribal error—as my excuse for creating a fictional bishopric seated in that city.

This foreword would not be complete without acknowledging Gregory Remington, who made my acquaintance after I critiqued one of his stories rather harshly in print. Some of his as-yet-unpublished tales feature a Spanish inquisitor named Don Felipe. While discontent with Greg's acknowledged shallow level of research, I liked the character and traded Greg free use of some of my own characters and worlds for the chance of doing something further with Felipe.

SPECIAL ACKNOWLEDGMENT

With thanks and love to my husband, Clifton A. Hoyt, who saved this book when I might have abandoned or even destroyed it in despair after being denied a grant to help me finish it as originally envisioned.

—P.A.K.

INQUISITOR DREAMS

PART I

SAINT PATRICK'S PURGATORY

CHAPTER 1

THE DREAM OF THE FALL OF ALHAMA

He stood among mountains, feeling a wind whip through his vestments. He was vested to say Mass, but could find no chalice. Watching the chasuble's red brocade crease over his elbow, he searched for the holy vessel, moving rock after rock. Curls of ash blew past him in the wind.

"Great-great-grandfather," said a woman's voice.

He looked up. The tall woman who wore trousers and a homely face stood before him.

"Is it you?" he said.

"Me. Rosemary."

"But, I tell you yet again, you meant to address me as 'granduncle.' I am vowed to celibacy," he reminded her.

"That didn't slow down priests like your patron Alexander the Sixth."

"Who?"

She looked thoughtful. "Right. We're in February, 1482. Borja isn't pope yet. Well, let's go." She turned and set off upslope as if expecting Don Felipe to follow her lead.

He took half a step and caught himself, calling after her: "Wait!"

Already so far distant that she looked little taller than a dog, she paused and looked back.

"Who are you, Doña Rosemary," he demanded, as he should have demanded on earlier occasions, "that I should render you obedience? Some descendant of mine in a collateral line, perhaps, but that is rather reason that you should obey my authority than I yours, even were I not both priest and—"

"Shut up, grandfather. I'm an unchristened policewoman."

"Unchristened?" In his shock, he found himself within arm's reach of her. Scooping a palmful of water from the stream that ran at their feet, he leaned toward her. *"Ego te baptizo in nomine—"*

She caught his wrist and turned it, shedding its water over the mountain herbs. "Never try that again."

"That any offshoot of my family should remain unbaptized—"

"Like quite a few of your ancestors. Well, understand 'policewoman'?"

"No."

She sighed. "An officer of the secular arm of the law."

"Pardon me, Doña. I have heard of women who go to war and women who avenge their kin with the sword. But, no matter how virile the lady, I have never heard of a female alcalde."

"Times change. Maybe in your time a mere member of the civil branch doesn't have any authority over a churchman, but neither does an inquisitor have any authority over an unbaptized soul."

"An inquisitor?" he said somewhat coldly. "You mistake me for Fra Guillaume."

"No, I don't. I'm just a few years ahead of you. All right, we'll call ourselves equals. Now come on and let's see what we've got to watch this time."

Glancing over her shoulder, he saw a column of black smoke rising from beyond the ridge. "In curiosity, I will come." He emphasized "curiosity."

They moiled upward, leaning into the slope as it grew steeper. He began a pace or two at her heels, gradually closing the gap until they plodded shoulder to shoulder. "I know these hills," he observed at length.

"Recognize them, huh?"

"We roamed them as boys, Gamito, Hamet, and I…" He looked again at the smoke. Red-gold billows roiled through it, shaping themselves into something like a face. "Is it akin to that column of smoke which led the children of Israel by day?"

"Probably not."

"That is not the face of God?" He pointed.

She glanced up. "No."

Seizing her elbow, he came to a halt. She stopped also, more as though by complaisance than constraint, and stood eying him with an expression of quizzical tolerance.

"Is it, then," he demanded, "the face of the Devil?"

"Depends what you mean by 'Devil.'"

"If we are in the mountains of my own boyhood, and you know—as it appears—little if anything more in this matter than I, then, in the name of Heaven, for what purpose have you been sent to guide me?"

"The Lady God knows."

Recoiling, he made the Sign of the Cross at her.

She neither vanished nor flinched. "Maybe," she went on, "because I'll understand it better myself if I see it with you. You can go first, if that'll get us there any faster."

"I will not have you at my back."

"Funny. I don't mind having you at mine."

The smoke scowled down at them like some gigantic gargoyle in livid reds and blacks. "That *is* the face of the Evil One!" Don Felipe exclaimed, staring at it.

"Evil, yes."

"But if you are unbaptized, and the disciple of heretics, it follows that you must be damned."

She clapped one of her palms to his forehead, the other to his cheek. "Feel damned to you?"

Both her hands were cool and dry, with only a very slight workworn roughness. "No," he was forced to admit in confused relief, actually drawing human comfort from her touch.

"All right." Transferring one hand to his wrist, she pulled him the rest of the way to the top.

He gasped. At their feet lay Alhama, home of his boyhood, her walls breached, her looms smashed, her houses aflame. Her people—Moor and Jew and Christian alike—fled through the streets like panicked ants, soldiers at their heels like greater ants, cutting them apart joint by joint. The column of smoke rose from her wealth, bolt upon bolt of fine woolens and silks, rare cottons and proud brocades, all drenched with not quite enough blood to stop their smoldering away to ash.

"God! Ah, God!" cried Felipe, for the moment past caring that at his side the strange woman repeated her blasphemous "Lady God!"

She was first to recover, if by only a little. "Sorry," she said grimly. "Those are King Fernando's and Queen Isabel's troops, taking revenge for Zahara. Which must have been as bad or worse."

"Zahara?"

"Last Christmas. And that was revenge for Villaluenga in October. Maybe you've forgotten. Or else the news hasn't reached you yet. In my time, anybody interested, anywhere in the world, could learn about things like this while they were still happening. Maybe you were luckier. You only had local tragedies to cope with while they were fresh. If they happened at any distance, they were cold by the time you heard about them."

"Such things as these do not grow cold."

"If you say so. But we're still witnessing part of the glorious Christian Reconquest of Granada."

"What..." He swallowed hard and blinked. "What of my family?"

Now they stood in a street of the city, blood soaking the soles of their shoes. A small dog, once perhaps some lady's pet, came and lapped at Felipe's right heel, its tongue a tiny pink banneret flittering in and out of the ball of hair, looking like newly washed and carded wool, that was its body.

"Shoo," the woman remarked, gently, scooping rather than kicking the dog away with one foot. "Well, grandfather, you know this town better than I do."

He gazed around. Everything looked strange. This street seemed free from present fighting, except at its farther end, where conflict still raged between a Castilian knight and two women, one clumsily wielding a halberd and the other armed with meat-hook and frying-pan. All three ignored Felipe and his companion. Somewhere, a baby's wail rose, then abruptly ceased. Corpses lay everywhere, draped every window, clogged every doorway. A few seemed whole, though mangled and bloody. Many more were in pieces. The dog had already abandoned Felipe in favor of a severed, beringed hand clutching a scimitar. Over all, the smoke threw an ashy black odor that, mingling with the stenches of blood, fear, and sinful flesh, formed a fog to torture nose, throat, and lungs.

"I knew it once... Once, I knew it well. Alhama de Karnattah...my poor Alhama." Turning at last, Felipe led the way to the free end of the street.

Here he hesitated, casting about for some familiar landmark in the shambles deserted by living souls, until he glimpsed what he thought might once have been Ben-Siddim's butcher shop, which had provided his family's table with so much veal and lamb.

Thus, sometimes finding places he seemed to recognize, but more often wandering lost, he led his guide back and forth among the ruins of his native town for an interminable period. Now and then they passed near some last hand-to-hand combat, but without drawing the attention of those involved. Once, indeed, Don Felipe strove to halt a rape in progress, and once to rescue a half-grown boy from the pikes of two assailants. Each time he found himself and his self-styled descendant suddenly translated into another street, to begin the weary search anew.

"How, then," he asked after the second failed attempt, "was the dog able to lick my feet?"

She answered, "Dogs go by their own guidelines."

Privately, he could not help but rejoice whenever he saw the corpse of a Castilian invader or recognizable fragment thereof amid the carnage, although he saw that he must lock such rejoicings forever within his own breast, as disloyal alike to king, queen, and Holy Mother Church.

Eventually he stumbled on an arm that looked grotesquely familiar. Overcoming fear, he turned his head to follow the direction of the stump. His gaze met a doorway clotted with the frozen bodies of his father and elder brother.

"Here." He could say no more. The door hung in splinters. From inside the house poured screams and a few curls of smoke.

The policewoman gave his shoulder a grip of solace, muttered, "I'm sorry," and began climbing through a gap in the front wall. Numb, Felipe followed.

His brother's wife lay on the floor, staring sightlessly up, her arms still locked about the top half of her child. Its lower half lay in the far corner. Felipe had never seen this child in life; he remembered only, from his mother's letters, that it was the single one of her grandchildren to have survived the natural perils of infancy.

His mother's body lay on a bed, blood soaking the linens from the back of her head and the cleft between her legs.

In his father's study, the head had been smashed from the bust of Tully and the head of Felipe's younger brother, child of his parents' age and not yet twelve years old, thrust into its place on the marble neck.

At all these horrors, Felipe stared only long enough to comprehend the fact of death. The fullness of grief must wait, for one living voice screamed on.

At last they found its source, in the walled garden, beneath the mosaic-decorated fountain. Three Castilian soldiers were raping Felipe's only sister, while a fourth looked on laughing even as he bandaged the joint of his right thumb where some defender had managed a crippling blow.

"Serafina!" Felipe started forward, but before he could so much as throw his bare arms round her present attacker, the man, finishing, struck his hard fist to her chin with a force that snapped her neck, opening a hole at her throat.

"Bravissimo, Manuel!" laughed one of his comrades.

They left, in their coarse laughter, taking no notice of Felipe and his guide. Sinking to his knees beside his sister's body, the young priest wept.

"In all my life…" He gathered her poor body into his arms, willingly smearing himself with her blood. "Never before, except in nightmare, have I looked on the face of carnal warfare. Never have I seen it in all its bitterness!"

"Not that different from 'spiritual warfare,' is it?" Then, as though somehow to soften her words, Rosemary repeated, "Grandfather."

And, so speaking, woke him with her own dissolution beyond the touch of waking memory. He recollected nothing of his dream save that a small dog had licked his foot.

CHAPTER 2

THE NEWS OF ALHAMA

"You're wanted in the Jewry, Master," Gubbio announced, striding into the courtyard with market basket still on his arm.

Don Felipe looked up from the idle tale of Don Florindo, survivor of Roncesvalles, and the fair Zorinda that he was penning in the shade of the colonnade. "The Jewry? I hope that they do not expect us to ape their Castilian ways and go sniffing out conspiracies among our Jews of Aragon? Bad enough that we have been commanded to bottle them up in their own quarter as if infected with the plague. Do they suppose that a bishop's Ordinary has no other work in hand?" (Not that he had. Nothing, at least, that could not wait until tomorrow. Else he would not have been penning his romance of Florindo and Zorinda.)

"Rest easy, master. By my calculation, it concerns only you, not your office, still less his Eminence your noble bishop or Fra Guillaume, either one." Shutting his eyes, the Italian screwed up his face as if in the throes of concentration. "One who shall be nameless approached me in the market—"

"You mean the beautiful Sarah," Don Felipe remarked with a chuckle.

Gubbio cleared his throat. "I mean one who shall be nameless. Approached me as I stood examining these oranges—newly come from Granada, you see—to impart the information that a certain Gamaliel Ben Joseph—"

"Gamito!" The priest jumped up with a suddenness he would have scorned to display anywhere else save alone with his servant.

"Ah, so Gamaliel Ben Joseph is Gamito, is he?" Gubbio nodded, obviously unsurprised. "Who arrived in the same ship with the oranges, I would guess, and is staying at present in the house of…let me see…Nathaniel the Silversmith, if your Reverence would like a word with him."

* * * *

Castile had boasted fierce legal restrictions on her Jews since before the memory of all save the oldest persons now alive; but in proud Aragon, the law confining them to their own district was little more than a year old and largely honored without being observed. If some Aragonese Old Christians interpreted it as commanding them to stay aloof at all times from their Israelite neighbors, others did not: Don Felipe found Juan and Estevan del Quivir, two promising sprigs of one of Daroca's

Oldest Christian trees, looking Nathaniel Ben Solomon's wares over in search of a gift for their mother. He acknowledged them with a priestly blessing before following the silversmith's gesture to the upper floor of the house.

It was a comfortable, but not a pretentious dwelling. The stairs led directly into a single room large enough for three beds and, on the opposite wall where it could receive the best light from the windows, a study table reasonably cluttered with bound volumes and a few scrolls.

Gamaliel Ben Joseph stood beside the table, apparently having risen and turned to face the stairs at the sound of the newcomer's footfalls.

For a moment, the two men stood gazing at each other. Felipe felt torn between joy at beholding a friend feared dead, and pain at seeing that friend clothed in homespun so coarse that its weave was clearly visible across the length of half a room, with a yellow patch blazing on the chest and new Jewlocks framing a black beard of some half a year's growth. It did not occur to him until afterward that Gamaliel's hesitation might have been that of any Jew faced with the presence of any Christian priest—even a secular wearing little of the sacerdotal—especially one known to be associated in any way with the Inquisition, whether the ancient one of Aragon or the new one of Castile.

Felipe broke the pause, throwing wide his arms and softly crying, "Gamito!"

In the middle of the room, they met and embraced. Their friendship was, after all, as old as themselves, and each of them already a year or two past the quarter-century mark.

"Old friend, old friend," Gamito began, when he could speak. "Will you still touch me, when you have heard…"

"My family?" Felipe's grip tightened on his friend's arms. "Gamito, what can you tell me of them?"

"Little that is certain." Falling back half a pace, Gamaliel shook his head. "To have been there is not to know everything, but…we fear the worst. We know that they were all in the city—your good father and mother, both your brothers, the wife and child of your older brother, and your beloved sister, the gentle Serafina—when the Castilians came. Since the day Isabel's army breached our walls…since that day, old friend, we have seen none of your family, not one. Nor have I found anyone who has. We heard that your father's house was among those burned to the ground, but I could never return there and see for myself."

"But…" It was natural to fear the worst for those caught in a city struck by war, yet to have the fears confirmed—to know that the home of one's memories was no longer anything but blackened ashes, to find oneself alone and familyless in a single blow—and did not the Catholic monarchs pride themselves on the righteousness of their war? "But we were Catholic Christians!"

"Some Christians attempted to side with the invaders—although not, by all that I could learn, until after the wall was breached and the Castilians actually in our streets. Some may have saved themselves in that manner. Abou Aben Hassim spoke of glimpsing one of the Nuñez Calatravo brothers drinking with the conquerors during the days when our own men of Karnattah besieged the city, trying to relieve us, and the Castilians allowed water to their horses and soldiers alone, and none to us their prisoners. But among those Christians made prisoner were a few who dared complain of having offered to join the conquerors and been refused. Many other Christians fought with us for Alhama. Or so they claimed when held prisoner with the rest of us in the desecrated mosques, and I believe that most or all of them spoke truly. Almost all of those whom I met had lost family and loved ones. In the end, I fear that it had less to do with their religion than with whichever soldiers pillaged their houses. We heard that it was Manuel Urtigo and his men who sacked your father's house." Venturing to step forward again, Gamito renewed his grip on Felipe's arm. "This Manuel Urtigo is said to be a mercenary, almost a bandit, though fighting that campaign with Isabel's army. Old friend, I am sorry. I grieve with you. They were a second family to me."

"Manuel?" The name seemed to strike a flash of some grotesque half-memory—Serafina naked and screaming beneath a bloodstained ruffian, while another man shouted, "Bravissimo, Manuel!" Where the image had come from, Felipe could not think. Perhaps some shard of fear-born fantasy engendered by the earliest news, this past Lent, of the Catholic monarchs wresting his native Alhama de Karnattah from Moorish rule. He had been schooled in the caution necessary when dealing with visions and fancied visions, whether they came from God, Satan, or the fevered human brain; yet this impossible glimpse of his sister lying in her own blood, once remembered, was a sword to his soul. "Manuel," he repeated. "Manuel Urtigo. Urtigo. Manuel Urtigo. I will remember the name."

* * * *

After some moments, Gamaliel poured Felipe a cup of wine. Accepting it from his friend's hand, the priest found a chair and sat. "But you, Gamito?" he asked. "Your family?"

A spasm passed through Gamito's face, but when he spoke again, his voice was quiet. "My married sister must have died with her husband and children in the sacking of their house. I saw its ruins as I was led with other prisoners through the streets. The house of my father had the blessed fortune to be taken by Pedro Alçon de Córdoba, an honorable captain who forbade his men to harm their prisoners, or even to pluck from their persons anything except gold, silver, and jewels. But later, when the men of Karnattah tried to retake the city, they stopped up most of its springs outside the wall. That was when the Castilians hoarded whatever water they could get for their horses and fighting men, and many of us prisoners died of thirst. Among them Yousef Ben Yeshu, my father. Later still, more Castilians came to drive away our would-be rescuers and destroy all hope that the Moors might recapture Alhama. Yet this proved a blessing to the surviving members of my family, for Pedro Alçon de Córdoba permitted our cousins in the city of Karnattah to ransom us. My mother is with them still, and my unmarried sister to help nurse her. My brother took his wife and fled to Rome. I came here."

"To bring me the news? Old friend, I thank you." Don Felipe laid one hand on Gamito's shoulder. "And I grieve for your own losses, and rejoice that they were not even worse. As mine to you, yours was a second family to me."

Gamaliel covered Felipe's hand with his own. For a moment, one man seated, the other standing, both heads slightly bowed, they remained in silence.

At length, Don Felipe spoke again. "But your clothes, Gamito? Has the ransom left your family so impoverished? Your beard? The side-locks? And…the hated yellow badge? Was all this necessary?"

After refilling his guest's cup and pouring wine for himself, Gamaliel drew up another chair and sat.

"Afoot or on shipboard, I call it safer to travel through these most Catholic realms as the unbaptized Jew I am than to risk being mistaken for a relapsed converso. Better to be spat upon than court the flames. They say there have already been burnings in Castile."

Don Felipe nodded. "At Seville, after the Act of Faith a year ago this February just past. But, by our information, the conspiracy there had been actual, my friend. Not the mere bag of wind and empty rumors that most such plots dissolve into at a sufficiently forceful touch. Unfortunately, it has enabled the people to find new conspiracies in every shadow."

"Is it true that plague struck the day after the burnings?"

"I have heard that the first cases appeared before the Act, but who, now, can say for sure? Certainly plague struck at about the same time, and the people saw it as God's judgment on the conspirators. Even though one of the inquisitors was among its earliest victims," Don Felipe added wryly, "which some graceless wits might have seen as divine judgment on the other party, had the general wrath burned less fiercely against the victims of the stake."

"How is it that you have such clear news of these matters?"

Felipe almost winked. "Is it not in my interest to know as much as possible about this new, half-legal Inquisition their Majesties are trying to plant? Do you suppose I am eager to see Fernando bring it here to Aragon? where folk have done very well with the true old Inquisition since the days of the Albigensians. Do you think that I, as secular priest and bishop's Ordinary, care for the thought of these hot new hounds of Torquemada's replacing our sleepy old Fra Guillaume? who regards *me* as invigorating new blood!"

"Old friend, old friend," Gamaliel replied, shaking his head, "their Majesties may succeed. All my way here, I heard the sailors talk as if they panted for Queen Isabel's Inquisition as we prisoners in the mosques of Alhama had panted for water and food."

"Perhaps. But what is true of Castile may not hold true of Aragon. I have found that the people here take fierce pride in their own will, their own ancient fueros, privileges, and liberties. Each Aragonese noble holds himself fully equal with his king, whom he serves of his own free will, only as long as it pleases himself to do so—and when it does not, he appeals to the Justicia of Aragon and his court! As long as your people guard themselves in prudence and avoid following the example of Seville, I think you may find our Old Christians of Aragon your strongest allies in keeping this new Inquisition out of Fernando's kingdom. But as for you yourself, Gamito…I hope and believe that we shall preserve Aragon relatively safe, but…" Don Felipe thought of the new law restricting the children of Israel to their own quarters of the cities. "…were I you, I should join your brother's family in Rome, and bring your mother there from Karnattah as soon as she can bear the journey, along with your sister and cousins."

"Do you think that I have not thought of all this? Every step of the way to port, every rise and fall of the ship, as I saw, and felt in my own person, how the Castilians treat us, not only in siege and war, but… But no, my friend." Gamaliel shook his head. "I believe that the Lord calls me to remain here and do everything in my power to help my people in the times that lie ahead."

"I know you were studying to be a rabbi."

"It is a longer study, perhaps, for us than for you," Gamaliel replied with a smile that touched soft irony. "But I have also been schooled in the trials of Alhama de Karnattah."

"And so you plan to remain here with us?" Felipe raised his cup in salute to his boyhood companion. "It cheers me already to have you near."

For a time they sipped in silence, as if all the new things had been said and it was as yet too painful to reminisce about the old. Eventually, however, his wine three-quarters drunk, Felipe asked, "And Hamet and his family? Are they still in the city of Karnattah, where they went…was it in '70?"

"In 1471. Yes. I saw them twice, the time I spent in that city after we were ransomed. They have done well, as well as possible in these days." After a pause, Gamito added, "He told me that his sister Morayma is happy with her Moorish husband."

The priest replied with a fatalistic nod and the comment, "It is enough."

Why, after all, should she not be happy in her marriage?

CHAPTER 3

MORAYMA

The Moors were freer about allowing infidels than fellow Islamites into the company of their women, so that Felipe and Gamito had twice seen their friend Hamet's younger sister. Those two visions of Morayma, coupled with her brother's accounts of her, had been enough. After his second glimpse, the boy Felipe had begged his father to approach her father with the proposal of an alliance between their houses.

In wealth, the two families were equal. In social standing, comparable: if Morayma's family was Moorish in a Moorish kingdom, Felipe's was descended on both sides from some of the noblest blood of Old Spain—on one side, as family tradition maintained, from El Cid himself. It might have been argued forever which family lowered itself to the other. But the barrier of religion, although in the old ways of the kingdom of Karnattah preventing neither friendship nor good business relations, held both fathers back when it came to arranging a union between their offspring while still little more than children.

Felipe was then fourteen, and his father lost little time before shipping him off to Italy, to complete his education in that completely Catholic country. Two years later, in Rome, he received a letter from his mother which included the news that Hamet's father had wedded Morayma to a rich Moor of the city of Karnattah, where the whole family had moved. Morayma would have been fourteen at the time of her marriage.

As though sensing Felipe's emotions, in the same packet with that news his mother had sent him her own golden betrothal ring, set with a carnelian bearing the carven likeness of Juno's head, in hopes that when the time came he would set it upon the finger of his bride to be.

Not that he would ever find one to take the place of Morayma in his heart! No, nothing was left for young Felipe save to worship her as a knight his sovereign lady—the devotion that neither time nor distance could ever dim, for it depended upon the excellence of the lady rather than the fleshly hope of the knight.

Not that actual knighthood was a vocation which held great allure for young Felipe de Bivar y Aguilar, even despite his proud family name. While not sickly, he had no exceptional strength nor stamina. Neither did he feel any burning desire to dress in iron for the purpose of battering and being battered by a fellow mortal similarly armed and clad. Such sports were all very well for leather-coated boys at play with wooden staves;

but Felipe had been thwacked twice or thrice with such a mock weapon wielded over-forcefully, and he saw little honor and less usefulness in putting his excellent brain at the mercy of a true sword or mace.

Therefore, he decided upon the Church. Was not a priest in some sense a knight of God? As well as a man in the way to considerable success even in the worldly sense.

He would take orders, but not enter an Order. Being the child of a cloth merchant, he appreciated fine clothing. Being the child of a wealthy family of Karnattah, he possessed a finely developed if somewhat delicate palate, and misliked the thought of coarse diet as much as he misliked that of sleeping with any other discomfort than the inevitable mouse or bedbug. True, religious houses that actually kept their ancient rules and austerities were fewer than those that did not. But in any wild and luxurious cloister, his virtuous devotion to the lost Morayma would doubtless be put to sorer tests than he desired enduring. As a secular he could keep his independence—even, wealth allowing, his own household—along with freedom to hold himself forever pure and innocent of fleshly love, in honor of his lady.

He would be a true knight-errant of Morayma and God: that is, a secular priest.

CHAPTER 4

THE DREAM OF THE MARTYRS OF BAAL

It was on the eve of his ordination that Felipe dreamed his earliest dream of the two women.

He stood in a parched land: desert behind him, and before, and on his right hand. To his left, distant mountains. Remembering no other goal, he turned and began trudging toward them. His forward foot sank ankle deep in pale sand at every step. His thirst was great.

As the hind longs for running waters …

A hind shimmered between him and the mountains—a pure white hind framed by dry golden dust, azure sky, and the deceptive cloudlike blue of the mountains.

No, not a hind, a woman. A woman clad all in loose and flowing white, like one in mourning, or some sainted virgin. Indeed, the martyr's palm lay green in an upright line between her left arm and breast, its end resting lightly, even carelessly, in her light brown hand; and while her hair fell long and black to her waist, the sun seemed to strike a pale golden aureole from its crown.

"Felipe," she said, holding her right hand out to him. "Grandson."

"Señora," he answered, taking it, aware only vaguely that in order to do so he must have covered several paces in a single stride, this time without sinking to the ankle. "Who are you?"

"I am numbered among your distant great-grandmothers, and in life I wore the name Raymonde." Her voice was gentle and musical, yet penetrating.

"Which would you prefer that I call you: Raymonde or grandmother?"

"Either or both, great-grandson, as you will." Still holding his hand, she turned, and he found that they were already in the foothills.

The hills were almost as dry as the desert. One tiny stream trickled its way through a bed far too wide for it, where a few herbs struggled to stay green. Everywhere else, the dry brown grasses crackled underfoot like the shells of tiny beetles.

"This land has lain long under drought," Felipe observed.

"Too long. Its people have grown too desperate." Raymonde pointed upslope.

Felipe became aware of a crowd populating the mountainside, milling about like dusty sheep a little below two high points. For a moment, it seemed to him that all of them stood upon the body of a vast, reclining giantess: himself and Raymonde on one of her knees, the bulk of the crowd girdling her like a broad sash about the waist, with the two high points being her nipples, the ridge beyond and between them her chin. The belt of humanity wound up to cover one of her breasts. The other rose denuded except at the very top.

Then he saw that her nipples were a pair of stone altars, one with a mass of priests surrounding it, the other attended by a single man.

A chant rose from the priests encircling the left-hand altar. The sound swelled and intensified until Felipe felt it as a rumbling in the soles of his feet. The solitary attendant of the right-hand altar began to shout, but Felipe could not make out his words.

"Is it safe to draw nearer?" he asked of Raymonde.

"It is safe for us," she replied.

The multitude of priests were brandishing blades of various sizes, slashing their own bared arms and chests, shaking their blood upon the bloody altar offering. They might have been pelicans opening their breasts to give life to their young. Their chant had grown into a wail. Yet the offering was a mangle of dead and skinless flesh that could almost as well have been human remains as butcher's meat.

"Shout louder," the solitary man at the right-hand altar called across to them. "Your Lord is a God, and He might be sleeping, or eating, or shitting!"

"Who is that blasphemer?" Felipe demanded of his guide.

She answered gently, "Do you not recognize the first of all holy inquisitors?"

Squinting, Felipe could only make out that the solitary man's altar was heaped with as much anonymous fresh meat as was that of the multitude of priests.

"Enough!" shouted the solitary man, pointing to the sun. It rested straight overhead; lack of shadows lent the glare a cast of emptiness. The multitude fell silent, staring from their altar to his. Each of their eyes resembled a pearl set with an onyx.

The solitary man beckoned downslope, and several more men began toiling upward with waterskins and earthen jars. One by one, they emptied their vessels over the heaped altar. Gathering in great, glistering drops, the clear fluid oozed down from fiber to crimson fiber of the raw meat, stone to bloodstained stone, until it filled a trench dug deep around the altar.

"Where have they found so much water," Felipe marveled, "in the midst of a desperate drought?"

"Cannot people always provide for their ceremonials?" Raymonde replied. "Though it may mean robbing themselves and their children of food, water, and even truth."

"Now!" cried the solitary man. "Choose, O my people, which you will serve—Lord or the Lord!"

He threw wide his arms, gesturing toward both altars at once. For an instant, his open palm hovered almost directly above his own offering. Even as he jerked it back, fire sprang out upon the surface of the meat, scorching it until it writhed like something alive, shimmering down the stones, sheathing the whole erection in dancing flame. When it reached the trough, it rose in an eager crimson ring to circle altar, offering, and all.

"Was it water," said Felipe, "or was it oil?"

"Beware, great-great-grandson," Raymonde murmured. "One must always look upon these things with the eyes of Faith."

How he heard her words, Felipe was not sure, for a huge shout had risen from the mob as it surged up the left-hand hill to lay hold on the outermost priests, who offered no resistance.

The next thing Felipe knew, he stood with his guide on one side of the nearly dry brook they had crossed earlier. On the other side, the defeated priests stood, weary and disheartened but meekly proud, waiting in a long, long line that stretched from horizon to horizon. No; it did not: far to the east, it ended abruptly.

The trickle of water increased. The streambed began to fill, flowing red. Don Felipe looked again to the east. The end of the line was much nearer now—the solitary man of the consummated altar was progressing westward. Before him, the priests stood still. Behind him, they lay motionless across the streambed. He held a bloody sword in his right hand, and his garments dripped heavy with blood. One by one, he was cutting their throats.

He reached those almost immediately facing Felipe and Raymonde. So far, none of the defeated priests had offered any protest; but now one, a beardless youth, perhaps an acolyte, raised face and voice to the heavens, crying, "O Lord, O Lord, why have You forsaken us?"

The solitary man cut the youth down and moved on. At Felipe's feet, the brown grasses grew lush and green as they greedily lapped the torrent of blood.

"But what choice was this?" Felipe protested. "The Lord or the Lord?"

"Heirs of the prophet-inquisitor will translate the one title and not the other," she explained, "but 'Baal' means 'Lord.'"

"Then…have I been deceived? How is this possible?"

"When I was in the flesh," Raymonde said musingly, "I believed that this Lord of the Old Testament was hard and cruel because He had not yet learned compassion by passing through the Virgin's womb, by tasting for Himself the full measure of human pain through enduring the torture of the cross."

Felipe stared at her in horror. "Can this be? My own ancestress a heretic?"

With a sad smile, she brushed her martyr's palm across his sleeve. "All flesh is weak and liable to error."

Catching his arm away as if it had been burned, he stared at her for one heartbeat, then turned and fled.

The bloodsoaked dust sucked at his ankles, yet still he ran—though no one pursued—ran like a rabbit from the hounds. A line of pointy forest stretched between him and the distant horizon. If he could reach those firs, he might be safe…

He had reached them. He stood beneath them, panting, leaning heavily against the rough bark of the nearest tree, feeling his heart thud within his chest, wondering vaguely why he had run. Did the nightmare arise from the slaughter of hundreds of pagan priests, or from the revelation of his ancestress as martyred heretic?

Something fell on his shoulder. Raymonde's hand? But this touch was firm, far from gentle. He whirled around, to behold a homely and hard-faced woman who stood tall as a man and wore trousers like a man. For a time he wondered if she were a man. Even for a man, she would have been tall; but her long nose, strong chin, and hollow cheeks would not have appeared unhandsome.

"Call me Rosemary, grandfather," she told him. "Now come on." Gesturing for him to follow, she turned and started walking deeper into the woods.

Still numb, repeating an Ave in his mind, he followed.

The forest thickened, then thinned. Suddenly they stood at its edge, between two of the outermost trees, facing a field of herbs and gravel. Across the field, a stone church, seen from the back, blocked Felipe's view of whatever lay beyond. The shadow of its spire and cross, falling backward over the slate roof, pointed to a row of pits. How large they were he could not quite judge, but that they were freshly dug he guessed by their sharp lines and the darkness of the clods heaped up between them.

A strange machine appeared with a dull, roaring noise, sped fast as a running cat to the corner of the church, and lurched to a stop just short of the building. This machine looked like some strange and immense wagon, covered over with walls of dull-painted metal and resting on wheels that appeared to be encased in black cloth almost as stiff as wax. Yet it had moved with neither oxen, horses, nor any other creatures to pull it, but with only a little bump or proturberance at its front, windowed after the manner of certain watchtowers.

"What thing is that?" Felipe asked, coughing at an acrid stench that might have been its breath.

"We call it a truck."

Out of the church came men dressed in close-fitting black. Each bore strapped near his waist a small leather sheath curiously bulky in shape, and most of them also carried long, thin rods with paddle-like swellings at one end. All these men wore on one sleeve a band marked with a vivid gamma-cross.

The back end of the truck opened into a pair of doors, spreading like the wings of a beetle, and people filed out...an endless procession of people, men and women, children, youths, and grown folk in the pride of their strength, babes in arms and elders hobbling upon canes, all clad in strange garments: the women in gowns of many colors and little fabric, barely covering their knees; the men mostly in trousers and doublets stark in cut and somber in hue. Several of the men wore their hair in locks much like those the laws of Felipe's own time had come to pre-scribe for Israelites.

A very few people came naked from the truck. The rest paused and stripped themselves to the skin, helping the very old and very young where necessary, dropping the garments into piles. Two men armbanded with gamma-crosses emerged from the windowed front of the truck and began gathering up the piles of discarded garments, loading them back into the truck. The naked people, shivering a little in the chill morning wind, filed to the edges of the pits.

The black-clad men lifted their rods, each placing the paddle end against one shoulder and pointing the narrow end at the waiting line of naked people. Those who lacked long rods brought strange little handles out of their sheaths and pointed them instead. Small tongues of fire licked momentarily from the tips of the rods, a thunderous din enveloped all things, the first rows of naked people fell into the pits, and a faint veil of blue smoke started rising over the scene. The naked procession shuffled forward to fill the empty places beside the pits.

"Guns?" cried Felipe. "Mother of God! They are hand-held cannon!"

Again they spat quick fire. The next rows of victims fell.

"But armies should use such weapons against one another," the priest protested. "Why turn them on naked people?"

"War isn't chivalry, grandfather," his guide answered. "It's killing. Killing as much of the other side as possible, and demoralizing everyone who can't be killed right away." Watching the people fall dead into the pits, she added in a voice bereft of all passion, "And every last one of them with a story just as valid as yours or mine."

The small guns roared a third time, and more people fell, still twitching. Some of the black-garbed men sat down on the edges of the pits, aimed their tiny, hand-held cannon downward, and made them spit again and again.

"But why do they not resist?" Felipe beseeched. "With so many, even unarmed and weaponless, they might rush their enemy!"

"Or sit down and refuse to take their clothes off," Rosemary added. "Make the soldiers work harder for every corpse." She uttered the word "soldiers" as the worst of epithets. "I don't know, great-grandfather. Why did the priests of Baal just stand there and wait? I don't think I would've, but who knows?"

The truck rolled away, its roar lost in that of the guns. Another truck passed it and stopped in its place beside the church, to disgorge another crowd of people for the pits, which must be very deep. One of the black-clad men paused to yawn and stretch, as if already tired and bored with his work.

Felipe woke. Mercifully, the memories of his dream trickled away at once through the sieve that lies in the first turn of the body between sleep and waking.

He remembered only that this coming day he would receive his priesthood.

CHAPTER 5

THE ITALIAN PROCURER

The step was taken. At the age of twenty-one, Felipe de Alhama de Karnattah—or Granada, as more northerly tongues pronounced the name—now bore within himself a soul wearing the indelible mark of a priest of God and Holy Mother Church. The young man had set his hand to the plow, and there was no longer time to turn back had he wanted to.

After the momentous events of the days just past, he sat down to refresh himself a little in the wineshop of Giuliano Abruzzi. Had not our Lord Himself often eaten and drunk with sinners? Moreover, Giuliano's was a quiet place, in which a man might eat and drink alone, resting and meditating on the peaks he had scaled and the path he found suddenly before him.

His father, no doubt, would have preferred him to follow in the cloth trade that had proven so lucrative over the years. Still, the epistle over which Felipe had labored for weeks, and which he had not dispatched until almost too late for any messenger to return to him with a reply before the day of his ordination, had brought only parental congratulations and hopes that, when these troubled times for the kingdom of Karnattah were over, Don Felipe might revisit his family. His mother had even added the wish, in her own gentle hand, that her priestly son might in the due course of time officiate at the marriages of his dear sister and his younger brother.

He guessed, now, that his father had already laid the money aside for his university education, that his love for Morayma had merely precipitated the moment of leavetaking. No doubt his parents had hoped for him not only to broaden his view both of letters and of the world, but to make influential connections in Italy. He wondered...if he had come home boasting of personal acquaintance with the greatest Italian merchants and bankers, prepared to follow his father in business, would he have found his way cleared to a mature courtship of his friend's sister?

Ah, but no! They had not even thought of waiting. They had married her only two years after his departure to one of her own religion. The young priest could never have been other to her than her loyal knight, worshiping her honor from afar.

And yet, if he had been less violent in his protests seven years ago, if he had merely signified to his father a readiness to bow beneath the parental will in humble hopes for a future chance at the lady's hand...

Well, influential connections he had made, though perhaps not in the spheres his father had hoped. He remembered his last interview with Cardinal Borja, the pope's vice chancellor, whom many called the most powerful man in the Curia.

"His Holiness has heard good reports of you," the cardinal had confided, "from certain of his own onetime fellow instructors at the university."

In trained humility, the young priest might have dismissed these words as kind flattery, had not his patron gone on to name two of his theology instructors. Both were conventual Franciscans, as was Pope Sixtus himself.

They had tried to make a Franciscan out of young Felipe de Karnattah, even before they knew his intent to turn priest. Certain Dominicans as well, and at least one Augustinian, had tried to bag him for their respective Orders, so that he had already begun to glimpse the rivalries between and among all these venerable brotherhoods, with their endless squabbles as to processional precedence.

"The benefice of Nuestra Señora del Pilar de Agapida, in Aragon, is open just at present," Cardinal Borja had continued, running his long if chubby forefinger down a sheet of notes.

"Your Eminence is very kind, but I had thought to stay here in Italy. Perhaps in some small parish near Assisi."

"A man of your talents?"

"Well, then, if I were to seek a university post?"

The vice chancellor had leaned forward, slowly shaking his handsome head with its prominent nose and delicately arched brows. "Listen to me, Don Felipe. The Church can show a proud and unruly face in Spain. I know. By birth, I am a Spaniard myself. We need men there whom we can trust. It is best when they, too, are Spanish, for our fellow Spaniards—yours and mine—all too often balk at having foreign clergy sent to shepherd them. My instinct tells me that God Himself has provided you to help us in the good work of solidifying our ties with Spain. Now: in addition to the benefice of Nuestra Señora, I believe that we can find you a good secretarial post with his Reverence the bishop of Daroca."

"I am of Karnattah," Felipe pointed out. "In the kingdom of Aragon, I would be as foreign as any Italian priest."

Cardinal Borja sat back, folding his large white hands over his comfortable middle, and spoke with a companionable twinkle in his eye. "I came here to Italy a foreigner, and now I flatter myself that there are those who consider me an Italian among Italians. You have this advantage: you speak the same language they do in Aragon. Yours is a more southern form, true, but it is my observation that mere accents can be lost or, at least, overlaid."

The vice chancellor was a man of great personal charm and persuasive power. It had taken no more than that one interview, and the young priest found his entire life changed for him yet again.

So now he sat in Giuliano Abruzzi's wineshop, gazing into the goblet he turned between his hands while wondering whether, and how far, he was being used as a mere tool.

Nevertheless, as long as the work was worthy, what business had the tool to complain of being a tool? Did a true loom turn upon the weaver, or a needle shed tears over its lot in life? Did the good hammer rebel against the carpenter, or the plow against the plowman? Did not a loyal knight in arms owe unquestioning loyalty to his liege lord here on this sinful earth? And should not the priest outshine the secular knight in obedience to the voice of God as it spoke to him through his spiritual lords? Was not the length of the Spanish peninsula distance enough to worship his lost Morayma from afar, without the additional safety of the sea between? True, the work of a bishop's secretary might prove much different from that of a village pastor or a university instructor, but he would have the task of finding and approving a vicar for Nuestra Señora del Pilar de Agapida...

"Hey, my lad!" a jovial voice cut into his meditations. "Do you read the future in that cup, like a witch telling fortunes in a bowl of water?"

Felipe looked up. A tall and skinny Italian stood before him, perhaps a year or three older than himself, his once brightly-colored cap set to one side of a lean but lively face with thin lips and dark eyes.

"I am an ordained priest," Felipe answered stiffly, annoyed at this stranger's having addressed him as "lad."

"Ah! But belonging to none of the holy brotherhoods, as your fine clothes tell me. Well, your priestliness might render you all the more eager to hear what I have to say." Without waiting to be invited, the newcomer swung his frame into the empty chair at Don Felipe's small table.

Suddenly amused, the new priest told him, "Young man, you interest me strangely."

"Host me to a good cup of wine, and I promise to interest you still more."

Felipe counted out the coins, added something to the amount in honor of the generosity it behooved priests to show, and pushed the money across the table, more or less expecting the stranger to take it and never return.

Instead, the Italian got his wine and settled himself more comfortably than before.

"I am listening," said Felipe.

"Well, friend priest…" The Italian took a long drink, wiped his mouth with the back of his hand, and casually pointed at a table near the window. "Do you see that man with the pair of ladies?"

"Yes."

"Do you recognize them?"

After a moment of study, Felipe shook his head. "No."

"Not even when I tell you that the man is a fruiterer of some prominence?"

"I do not question your word," Don Felipe replied with growing curiosity. "But I fail to perceive how any of them may concern me."

"The man, no, except in so far as he is one of my own satisfied customers. Nor, I fear, should the blonde lady, with whom he is so obviously smitten, concern you. But she who dares to flaunt her tresses in their natural raven black—ah! Is she not a morsel for the very gods?"

Felipe considered her again. She was indeed a beauty. His gaze traveled over her as appreciatively and calmly as if she had been a fine marble sculpture surviving from classical times. "She is everything you say. What of it?"

"What of it?" The Italian looked slightly taken aback for a moment. Recovering, he went on, "But perhaps you think she is unavailable. I tell you, no. That lovely lady, that tempting delight, is one of my own sweet nymphs and, at the moment, our fruiterer having opted for her fellow nymph, she is free."

"By the way you call her 'one of your own,' implying slavery, I take it you are not approaching me to save her soul."

A laugh and a wink. "'Saving her soul'! As good a way as any to speak of it. And popular, I have heard, with the old hermit monks of the desert."

The young priest replied quietly, "I will not hear you slander those holy saints."

"Saints, do you call those desert fathers? Well, perhaps, in their dotage, when they had no better use for their feeble strength." Another wink. "Come, come, friend priest! Look around you. Your brothers of the cloth—both in Orders and merely ordained—your bishops, your cardinals, the Curia, the very popes themselves, one after the other… all of them understand that God has given our flesh certain needs, and that the best way to satisfy those same needs is not in a brothel. Now, look again at my lovely Isabella, there. No slave, she! Bred up gently as a lady, ready to be good as any wedded wife—better, indeed, than most wedded wives, for she will never turn shrew, nor give herself airs, nor beggar you with demands for scarves and jeweled trinkets. Priests' women know their places! 'A fruitful vine in the recesses of your home,' as King David tells us. For three ducats only—no more than that—you will enjoy her company all the rest of this day and the whole long, joyous night until tomorrow morning. After that, if you and she should come to a more permanent understanding—as I am sure is more than likely—I ask a mere five ducats a month for myself. Or, if you should prefer a nice, quiet marriage—as I know many of your fellow priests do—deal with me in the place of her parents."

Felipe looked again at the lady, then back to her procurer. "Other men, alas! would no doubt find your offer a sore temptation. But my love and loyalty have been pledged already, to a lady as good and beautiful as she is unattainable. For her sake, I have made myself a spiritual Abelard."

The Italian stared at him. "What tale is this? If you wish to haggle over the trifling little price I ask—"

"No tale, my friend."

"Then... Then why in God's name did you not say so at once? You have made me waste my time!"

"Let me speak for a moment as a priest," Don Felipe replied, allowing a bit of unction to flow into his voice. "Your time was much better wasted in talking with me, than spent in successful pandering. God made both your soul and the lady's for better things."

Still gaping at him, the Italian sat back, took another swallow of wine, and then started laughing, so suddenly that he snorted up a noseful and so violently that even the need to spew it out hardly interrupted his mirth. "So now, I suppose," he said at last, still choking a little, "you will want us both to sit down and hear you preach at us concerning our sins?"

"That sounds a profitable way of spending our evening."

"Profitable in heavenly coin only." Chuckling again, the Italian pulled out a tattered handkerchief and began to wipe the wine as best he could from his face, hands, garments, and the table. "Well, it is my bad luck. Or the malice of the gods. Friend priest, that man is indeed a wealthy fruiterer of the city, but the blonde lady is his wife and the dark one, I believe, either his sister or hers. I know them only by having seen them and asked folk about them. They know me not in the slightest. You were the first on whom I tried this pleasant little scheme, and see what it has earned me!"

"You would have taken my three ducats," Don Felipe mused, "and then slipped away at once. You would have had to enjoy the ensuing jest in your imagination only. You could hardly have risked staying to watch it."

"I would have taken your money, pretended to arrange an assignation for the pair of you, then gone to their table, paid her some such little compliment as any lady may accept even from a complete stranger, nodded in your direction, and so out the door, leaving her none the wiser and you to cool your heels at your choice of Rome's lovely fountains, or whatever trysting place you had named, from Vespers until…dawn, if your patience lasted so long."

"And suppose that I had insisted on meeting her here, at once?"

"Why, in that case I would have taken your money, played out my little dumbshow, and slipped away as above stated, to enjoy the ensuing jest in my imagination only. And now, by your kind leave…" The Italian started to stand.

The priest darted one arm forth to catch him by the sleeve. The state of this fellow's handkerchief had not escaped his eye, nor the frayed and threadbare areas that pocked his faded garments, nor the fact that the fabric had never been of the best. "Stay a moment. Dine with me, at my expense. I may try to save your soul, but I will not report you, either to the secular authorities or the spiritual."

The fellow hesitated no more than a heartbeat or two before laughing again and reseating himself. "I see I did not choose my mark too badly, after all. Enough such failures, and I could become a fat man."

Not until near the end of their meal, when the Italian seemed sufficiently mellowed with food and wine that the priest judged him reasonably likely to speak truth in the matter, did Felipe ask his name and personal history.

"Francesco di Gubbio. A scamp in my native town, a sometimes successful—and sometimes not—rogue here in Rome."

"By your leave, I shall call you Gubbio. Another San Francesco you are not. But have you considered, friend Gubbio, that your efforts might more often meet with success if they were directed in honest pursuits?"

"For another bottle of wine and a plateful of fruit and cheese, I will consider whatever you like."

It was the only meal they were ever to eat as equals. Another bottle of wine and two plates of fruit later, Felipe had not only a benefice and a secretarial post with the bishop of Daroca awaiting him in Aragon, but his own personal manservant to accompany him there.

CHAPTER 6

THE DREAM OF HYPATIA

He stood on something slippery as ice, in the midst of swirling black fog. Somewhere, a woman's voice was calling: "Grandson! Great-grandson!"

At length he discerned a brightening of the fog in the direction of her voice. Sliding his feet with extreme caution, he inched his way into the beam of light. Mist still clouded his vision, as though he swam through milk; but now, at least, he saw that the light had a source. He climbed toward that more than toward the voice, which he recognized and feared.

"Great-grandson!" she called one last time.

The fog fell away, and he found himself on the edge of a sort of raft of icy stuff, near the outer wall of some great building. The top of the wall was roughly even with his waist, but between his raft and the stonework was a deep chasm. His heretic ancestress waited at the edge of the stonework, extending her hand to him across the gulf.

He drew back.

"Will you drift?" she pleaded.

"How anchor myself to heresy?"

"Great-great-grandson! You are anchored in your priesthood, and your bishop has named you his Ordinary, to tie him with the Inquisition. Are you so loosely anchored in your own Faith that the mere touch of my hand might shake free your soul?"

The chasm was widening. His choice was to accept her help or drift back into darkness. Reluctantly, he stretched forth his arm.

She clasped it. There came a kind of soft, creeping shudder, and he stood beside her, his feet firm on the stone. Her touch was warm, human, and very gentle. Horrified in himself to find it so—should not a heretic's touch burn the skin?—he pulled free of her and stepped back.

"Beware," she cried sadly.

He saw that he had stepped too near the edge. One of his heels rested on empty air. Stepping forward again, though keeping his distance from her, he peered around.

The place where they stood was like a piazza overlooking a great seacoast city. Sunlight danced in large bright flakes on the blue water, and salt breezes blew the commonplace stenches of any great city away inland. Distant roaring, as of mobs or the sea, reached his ears; but up here all seemed peaceful.

On the other side of the piazza white smoke rose, swirling in the breeze, from a huge basin he guessed to be some roasting pit or giant incense burner. Indeed, the smell of incense teased his nostrils. Many people, most of them brown-robed monks, stood grouped about the basin. Several bent over their work at something that Don Felipe could not see. The rest chanted a strange chant, like none he had ever heard, but clearly meant for Christian rites.

He walked forward for a closer look.

One of the workers stood up, waving something above his head. It appeared to be a small white hand. He threw it into the basin. The smoke turned dark, and cheering interrupted the chant.

Now Felipe saw one tall monk, cowl pushed back upon his shoulders, standing at a pulpit raised above the burning pit.

"Bless you, my brothers!" this monk declaimed. "God blesses you, Christ and His great Mother Mary most holy bless you, for this holy work which you have done today in purifying our city of the Pagan philosopher and her baneful teaching!"

In a few steps, Felipe covered the remaining distance and gazed down between the workers. He beheld a woman's body, naked, bruised, and covered with blood. Once, he guessed, she had been beautiful, but she must have been stoned to death. One eye was gone, the other stared up blindly at nothing. Even as he watched in stunned silence, a monk hacked off her other hand and rose to throw it after the first, into the fire.

Raymonde had come up at Felipe's shoulder: he felt the brush of her inexplicable martyr's palm.

"Hypatia of Alexandria," she murmured. "By both your creed and mine in life, great-grandson, a Pagan steeped in false doctrine; yet great Christian churchmen—though not including the bishop Cyril and his toadying monks—called her friend, respected her learning, and had hopes of her wisdom. She deserves to be remembered for more than the manner of her death."

Raymonde dropped her own martyr's palm down upon Hypatia's body. A monk pushed it unseeingly aside as he swung his axe into the dead woman's elbow.

Don Felipe turned away, sickened, but as quickly turned back. "Is this fit work for monks?" he shouted at them. "The woman is dead! You have murdered her! She was unbaptized—you had no right to judge her—and yet you murdered her! At least return her body for burial!"

"And leave her soul to the good, merciful God," Raymonde added, so softly that even Felipe heardly heard her.

The rest of them paid the two no attention whatever. Instead, they listened enrapt to their preacher, who was going on:

"Yet the greater part of your pious work remains to be done! The Pagans merely deny God—the Jews murdered Him on the Cross! Have we not suffered God's murderers to live among us long enough?"

"Who is that man?" Don Felipe demanded.

"His name is Legion," Raymonde answered mournfully. "Every age has many such."

Felipe could no longer see the corpse of Hypatia. They must have burned the last of it for incense in the burner which now sent up fragrant curls as it swung, golden and clanking, in the acolyte's hands. The great church wherein they stood was a converted mosque, its Moorish architecture clear to Don Felipe's eyes. Gone were sky and seacoast, and the crowd of listeners had greatly increased in number. Only the preacher in his pulpit remained the same.

"Think of how those accursed Jews howled for Christ's holy Blood!" he ranted on, lifting both his hands. "Let it be on our heads and our children's, they themselves vowed in their shameless guilt! Is not God enraged with us for failing all these generations to root them out?"

Don Felipe guessed, "That man is not...Fray Vincent Ferrer?"

Raymonde shook her head. "It is the sixth day of June in the year of our Lord 1391, and we are in Seville, where this time the horror begins."

"Is this not why He struck our parents and grandparents down by the thousands forty years ago?" the preacher thundered, "In what man may call the Black Death, but I tell you solemnly was the holy wrath of God! Elsewhere in the world, did good Christians not take warning and drive them out then, purging the sickness with fire and sword? And we—why have we been lax? I tell you, if we purge not the vile Jews from our midst, God Himself will purge us with fire and plague to make men forget that of forty years ago!"

"His name in this age and place," Raymonde said, "is Ferran Martínez. But his words mean less than the way in which his hearers receive them."

The crowd of worshippers cheered. In that moment, Don Felipe watched them turn from congregation into mob.

"Was not Ihesu Himself a Jew!" he screamed at them. "His holy Mother—was she not a pious Jewess? Saint Joseph—the blessed apostles—"

"The king, the archbishop, the pope himself," said Raymonde, "all have forbidden Ferran Martínez to say these things that he says. He, however, claims a higher obedience to God, and continues to say them. Great-grandson, can you stop the mob where your own pope has failed to stop their leader?"

He turned on her. "They are ignorant, but you are heretic!"

And, as he turned, the roar of the mob broke upon them, overwhelmed them, churned them under as the beast with a thousand heads and twice as many feet stormed over them and out of the church to the Jewish quarter…and there was blood, fire and blood, the screams of maidens, and limbs of children flung everywhere, and Felipe screamed and half awoke.

But as he lay trembling, before all memory of the dream had faded, he dozed again. Now the great massacres of 1391 were over, and he stood in a place that he understood, though he had never seen it with his waking eyes, to be the huge new cathedral of Seville, begun in the year of grace 1402 and already, after not even a century, nearing completion. He heard a loud voice saying, "Fifty thousand killed, but hundreds of thousands baptized, to the glory of God!"

"No!" answered the preacher in his pulpit, and if he was no longer either Ferran Martínez or the monk who had led them to martyr Hypatia, he might have been brother to both. He went on, "For these were no true conversions, and in their vile hearts and behind their filthy doors these so-called New Christians remain secret Jews, more to be despised and feared than their ancestors."

Don Felipe opened his mouth to argue before the preacher could rouse another mob, and in so trying to speak, woke himself, and remembered nothing of his dream save that it had concerned the great religious zeal of almost a century ago, which had inspired the new cathedral of Seville, the great efforts of Fray Vincent Ferrer, and other noble works.

He also remembered, with a frown, that there had been mobs and massacres. But these had been akin to those of ancient times. The old Romans and Greeks had understood very well that mobs were mad beasts seizing upon any excuse for violence, and that the role of religion was only to quell them.

CHAPTER 7

SAN JUAN DE CALAMOCHA

"Here." Fra Guillaume handed Don Felipe a small book, crudely bound between two separate pieces of boiled leather. "This gives us our present work."

Taking his seat in the old inquisitor's tiny study closet (cushioned and comfortable, but barely large enough for two small chairs, a desk, and, in cold weather, a brazier), the young Ordinary opened the volume and found himself gazing at a picture, drawn clumsily but with obvious energy, of two humanlike figures and many bare trees against a darkly diapered sky. One figure, in russet cloak, had his back to the reader. The other was a monstrous, grinning creature like some misshapen ape, with oversized tusks from which poured lines of as bright a red, no doubt, as the young artist had had at hand.

Beneath this illustration were several lines of text, neither as straight nor as even as they might have been; and the wide margins were filled on all sides with scrolling vines and fanciful flowers.

Every page was so illuminated, with illustrations of bloody vigor and demons or grotesque beasts frequently peering through the marginal vinework. Don Felipe read:

> Through the dark wood I wandered, lost and alone, when one came and grabbed me by the shoulder. He had a face of great ugliness, but his smile was pleasant, although his fangs dripped blood.
>
> "Who are you?" I cried in my fear.
>
> "I am Arazel," he said. "I am one of the fallen angels, and you are a sinful man. Together, let us work our way back to heaven."
>
> He led me to a great gate, on which was inscribed, "Abandon hope, everyone who enters here." When I read this, I held back in fear, but he pulled me on, saying, "That means to abandon all hope of ever again enjoying your sins."
>
> We entered, and came to a great, empty, black plain, full of nothing. "What is this place?" I cried, and he answered, "Once it was crowded with poor sinners and fallen angels, but they have all worked their way up to higher regions."
>
> We went on, and came to a great black lake of burning pitch. Naked men were pushing hairy demons into the smoking pitch and holding them beneath the surface with big dung-forks.

"What is this place?" I cried, and Arazel said, "The first duty of damned souls, whether angels or humans, is to hurt. Their second duty is to be hurt."

He handed me a dung-fork and said, "Here. You must push me in and hold me down for seven years." I protested, "But why? You have never hurt me, and I have no wish to hurt you. Besides, it would add still more to the number of my sins." He answered, "It will not add to the number of your sins, because punishing sinners is holy work. But we fallen angels belong to a higher order of creation than you mortal humans, and moreover we fell before your father Adam was made. Therefore those of us who still remain on this level are closer to heaven than those of you who are still here, and it is your duty to hurt me, and mine to suffer. Now lose no more time, for while we have talked, half a year has passed, and you must hold me down that much longer."

Thus admonished, I pushed him in, and held him down beneath the surface of bubbling pitch. When it filled up his eyes and ears and nose and mouth, he choked and struggled, and he struggled so hard he got his neck out from between the tines of the dung-fork, so I had to stab it down through his chest and stomach, so his blood bubbled up and made dark red circles on top of the pitch, but I held him down for seven years, although the hard work and hot steam made my sweat pour down, and I could not lift even one hand from the dung-fork to wipe my face.

When seven years were over, I let him up. He blew pitch out of his nose and mouth, grinned at me, and said, "Come."

I followed him, and we came to a woodland where men and demons stood in pairs, flaying each other with iron rakes.

"What place is this," I asked, "and who are these?" Arazel answered, "This is the middle ground, and these are humans and fallen angels who have suffered their way this far."

He got two rakes and gave one to me. "Sinful man," he said, "it is your turn to suffer. But my turn has not yet come to its end, and here on this higher level we must do it to each other."

Each rake had seven tines, and the tines were sharper than swords. We raked each other, and our skin peeled up behind the rakes in great curls, and blood ran down to hide our nakedness. People are very naked indeed without their skins. After that, we tore each other's flesh away and pulled out each other's entrails until we stood white skeletons in a shambles of our own broken meat. Last, we ate each other's hearts, and were made whole again.

"Now I am completely purified," said Arazel. "But you have still to suffer somewhat more. Come."

I followed, and he led me to a great place of burning. As far as eye could see, in every direction, stakes stood high, with wood piled around them, and some of the piles were green wood, and some were dry, and some were tall, and some were tiny, and some were charcoals. Many of the stakes were empty and waiting, but many more had men and women burning at them. Demons walked through the burning-place, carrying lighted torches.

Arazel said, "In this place are the best mortals and the worst fallen angels, for the mortals have suffered their way here through the lower levels and will go on from here to heaven, but all the better demons have already gone. But these are good enough so all they must do here is light fires. You must find your own stake."

He bade me farewell and hurried on to heaven, and I saw him no more, but wandered on until I found a stake that seemed fitted to my size. It had a crosspiece, and when I stood with my back to the stake and my arms to the crosspiece, salamanders came and wound themselves around my limbs and body. They held me fast, and a fallen angel came and lit my pyre with his torch.

The dry wood blazed up and seared my skin black and crisp. My eyes boiled and burst, and while they ran in streams down my cheeks and chest, everything looked strange, as if I looked through water. I saw the green wood and charcoals catch fire at my feet, and then I was blind. The salamanders danced in their delight, for fire is their natural home. Their feet cut my flesh, and I heard my blood sizzle in the fire, but not enough to put it out, and I was roasted to ashes.

Then someone came and took me by the hand and led me on farther. There were sweet breezes, and they restored my body to me. When I could see again, I beheld a fair plain all around, as far as eye could see, and flowers bloomed, and birds sang, but still there was wailing and gnashing of teeth.

Then I saw my new guide, and he was a man, but very ugly. "Who are you?" I asked. He said, "I am King Herod, who was never baptized, and was very wicked besides, and killed all the babies of Bethlehem, and so I am still here in the lowest room of limbo."

I looked around again, and everywhere I saw people racking other people on ladders. "Who are these?" I cried.

He said, "Fallen angels are a higher order of creation than mortal men and women. Even so, baptized souls are a higher order than unbaptized souls. Here, we unbaptized must torture those of you baptized who still remain."

He summoned two others, who were Cain and Goliath, and together they bound me into a ladder so that my limbs and body were woven under and over its rungs, and the rungs were heavy and sharp. Then they bound strong ropes around my wrists and ankles, and Goliath slowly pulled at my ankles while Cain and King Herod slowly pulled at my wrists, until both my body and the ladder were lifted high off the ground, and blood ran down from every place the rungs cut into my flesh, and all my bones were broken.

Then they pulled me out of the ladder, like pulling one thread from woven cloth, and laid me on the flowery grasses, and sat and talked with me of their great desire to be baptized, until I was whole again and could go on.

Then all three of them bowed to me, because now I was a blessed soul. And Cain and Goliath clasped King Herod by the hands and clapped his shoulders, because in death we are all equals, and wished him happiness, for that now he was sufficiently purified to go on with me. We went on, and crossed a wide, quick-flowing stream, into another flowery meadow, where more birds sang and the air was sweeter than incense.

In that place were ladders laid out on trestles everywhere, and countless people bound all on top of the ladders, while other people gave them the water torture. "What place is this?" I asked, and King Herod answered me, "Here is where we unbaptized receive our baptism, and because we received it not in life, here we must receive it interiorly. But they who give it are the worst of the baptized, who are not yet ready to enter the third heaven, so you have nothing else to do."

I watched, and Judas and Ganelon came and stripped King Herod and laid him on a ladder and bound him tight. Then Judas got a great bellows filled with clear, clean water and pushed it down his throat, and Ganelon got a great bellows filled with clear, clean water and pushed it up his buttocks, and then both of them squeezed their bellows slowly, and King Herod swelled up like a bladder, and finally burst, and clear water mingled with blood sprayed over everything like a fountain.

Then they unbound his arms and legs, and his head smiled up and said to me, "Now am I well and truly baptized, and as soon as I am healed from my baptism, I must return to the first heaven and there suffer for my own sins until I am purified, but you must go on at once to the third heaven."

So I went on and entered the third heaven, but of what I saw there, tongue may not speak, only that it was glory and happiness beyond measure.

Here ends the vision of
San Juan de Calamocha
which he dreamed in
the eleventh year
of his age. AD
MCCCCLXXVI.

"It is a great pity," Don Felipe pronounced on coming to the end, "that this little work is so riddled with heretical fancies. Put it into poetry, and in certain passages it might almost be worthy of Dante, were it not for the manner in which it implies that between Hell and Purgatory, or Limbo and Heaven, there is no fundamental difference, but only measures of degree, and that salvation is freely available to the unbaptized after death, and even to fallen angels."

Fra Guillaume nodded, smiling. "It would be a very pretty work, if it were not heresy."

"Is the author truly in his eleventh year?"

"Or twelfth."

"How has he come by Saint Paul's description of the Third Heaven, of which mortal tongue may not speak?"

"Most likely from some wholesome sermon. His father testifies that the boy always pays close attention to every sermon he hears. Which is of course commendable in itself." The inquisitor's voice grew more somber. "It is a troubling case. The boy's name is not properly Juan, but Mehmoud. He himself has never been baptized, but it appears that he likes to call himself after his father or, perhaps, the Evangelist or another Saint John. His father is Juan Maria Delgado—formerly Fazoud Aben Fazoud—of Calamocha, who accepted the holy Faith into his heart and was baptized, along with his wife and his children by her, six years ago. Our young author, however, was Juan Maria's son by his concubine. Juan Maria has ceased to cohabit with her as his wife, and now she lives beneath his roof as sister only. Alas, he made it a condition of his own Baptism that, having been put away, his former concubine must have the choice whether or not to accept Baptism for herself and the children she bore him, of whom Mehmoud is the eldest living. Whether rightly or not...I seem to recall making some formal protest when the case first came to my attention...this condition was granted them, and the lady chose to remain unbaptized, along with her son and daughter."

Don Felipe studied the old man to whom the bishop had assigned him as Ordinary. Elsewhere, the episcopal courts might contend hotly with the inquisitorial as to which should judge heretics, but here in the diocese of Daroca, bishop and inquisitor seemed to vie with each other only in laxity. Thus far, the young priest's duties as his bishop's representative to the Inquisition had proved more social than onerous. At the same time, the mild old French Dominican seemed never entirely to have accustomed himself, even after decades of living and working on this side of the Pyrenees, to the free relationships among Christian, Jew, and Moslem that had existed in Spain for centuries, and still continued to exist, in friendly pockets, even despite the terrible riots and massacres of Jews in great cities not quite a century ago, and the current Holy War into which the Castilian queen had drawn her kingly husband of Aragon against the Moors of Karnattah.

"If the author of this 'Vision' remains unbaptized," Don Felipe pointed out, wondering that Fra Guillaume had not commented further on this point himself, "then his case belongs to no Catholic court, neither yours nor his Reverence the bishop's, to judge."

"That would be very true, were it not a case also of proselytizing. This manuscript was found in the possession of one of our lad's little playmates, Béatrix Cabaza, the child of a fine Old Christian family. It was her mother who brought it to Juan Maria, and he, being no longer Moor but sincere Catholic, wisely chose the Holy Inquisition as that authority to whom the matter must be reported." Fra Guillaume sighed. He would clearly rather have been dozing in the sun with some holy book resting open on his lap.

"What, then, are we to do, my brother?" Don Felipe awaited the answer in some suspense. Heretical the book certainly was; yet its author, while undeniably of the age of reason and obviously well educated, was still of tender years and, being unbaptized, might remain unaware that his work was anything more than a diverting romance drawn upon spiritual rather than secular themes.

After another sigh, Fra Guillaume replied, "The boy has been in the cell since yesterday afternoon, when his father brought him to me. Juan Maria, having passed the night, as I believe, with a business acquaintance in this town, has been waiting outside the tribunal since early morning."

Don Felipe nodded. "I believe I noticed him. A tall man of middle age, well dressed, with somewhat shaggy black brows?"

"That was he. A good man. I regret that I have not some sort of vestibule where he might wait with greater comfort." At one time, the Inquisition's Daroca tribunal had been housed in a monastery on the outskirts of the city; but for one reason or another it had been moved several times, to end, some years ago, in a few rooms beneath the arcade of a wealthy merchant's home, flanked by shops to right and left. "I had thought," Fra Guillaume went on, "that this matter might be disposed of with the minimum of formality. If the bishop's office makes no objection, we might proceed as far as a little gentle application of the first degree, and manage to dismiss our young culprit back into his father's custody as early as tomorrow."

By "the first degree," Fra Guillaume meant the threat of torture. This being in itself a form of torture, it ought not, formally speaking, be applied except in last resort, after careful consultation and deliberation. Already in a few months, however, Don Felipe had come to trust the old inquisitor as a man who would always choose the smoothest and least painful course for all concerned, who would take no step unless he judged that thereby he could end the matter as quickly and satisfactorily as possible. Better, surely, that the boy be subjected to the threat and returned home at once, than that he should remain weeks in prison, costing all the labor of a full inquisitorial investigation for what was, after all, little more than the childish romance of an unbaptized brain, based on misinterpretation of Christian doctrine.

The Ordinary nodded. "His Reverence's office will make no objection, even at this stage, to some judicious use of the first degree."

"Then I think," said Fra Guillaume, "that we may as well proceed."

They repaired to the audience chamber and Fra Guillaume sent his one assistant to fetch the prisoner. Fra Guillaume's assistant was a lay brother even older and slower than his master; the Inquisition was to call upon the bishop's resources should need arise, but as far as Don Felipe could learn the need had not arisen in this diocese for years. The young priest had time while waiting to ponder whether or not the rolls of dust round the edges of the floor had grown measurably larger since his last visit.

Once, the Inquisition had been a weapon to strike fear into the armies of Satan. The Dominicans still boasted of how, with God's help, they had stamped out the deadly peril of Albigensianism some two centuries and a half ago. How had the proud army decayed! At least here in Aragon… and only in Aragon, of all the kingdoms of Spain, had the Inquisition ever been planted.

Some attempt had been made to return Fra Guillaume's present audience chamber to the fabled black-and-white austerity of earlier ages; but here and there the black draperies were torn or moth-eaten, and in many places the white paint was already worn away, leaving the former bright colors of murals and floor tiles showing through, while the long table and chairs were at best only dark brown.

Fra Guillaume's lay brother brought young Mehmoud in and gave him a three-legged stool to sit on before the tribunal, then shuffled back to stand at the door, his hands folded into the sleeves of his coarse habit.

Looking around guardedly, with many apprehensive glances across the table at Fra Guillaume and Don Felipe, the young offender adjusted the position of his stool three or four times, hitching it minutely here and there across the painted tiles, until the inquisitor sternly bade him cease, when he finally sat still, head lowered.

"Well, Mehmoud," the inquisitor began, almost genially, "what have you to confess today?"

"Juan," the boy mumbled. "My name is Juan."

"If you were baptized, it might be Juan. Until then, it is Mehmoud."

Mehmoud lifted his head and stared back, anger struggling in his face with fear. "Then I have nothing to confess! And…and if I did…how could you listen to it?"

Don Felipe shut his eyes, grateful that the boy was directing his stare principally at Fra Guillaume. The image had flashed unbidden into the

Ordinary's mind of the boy Ihesu debating in the Temple with the rabbis of Jerusalem. Even so must the divine Child have appeared, dark-eyed and olive-skinned—all paintings and illuminations to the contrary, Felipe de Alhama de Karnattah was aware what the Messiah's true race would have been. Even so might the boy Ihesu have lifted one brown hand to push a lock of straight black hair away from His high forehead.

Yet surely the holy face of Ihesu would not have been stained, at this age of His earthly life, with tears. Surely neither His hand nor His voice would have trembled before His mortal elders. And then it came to Don Felipe that whom young Mehmoud really reminded him of was his own boyhood friend Hamet. Flooded with relief, he opened his eyes and looked again at the author of the heretical Purgatorio.

"It is not a question," Fra Guillaume was saying, "of the holy sacrament, but rather one of practical jurisprudence. Mehmoud Aben Fazoud, confess your crime!"

"My...my father is Juan Maria Delgado de Calamocha! At least I am Mehmoud Delgado de Calamocha!"

"He was not of that name when you were born. As for you, you have still the name you had then, in its entirety. Now, confess."

"It is not...If it were sinful to write visions of...of..."

"Boy," the inquisitor said harshly, "have you any conception of how it would feel in reality, to be tied to the ladder, made to swallow whole jugsful of water, dipped in boiling pitch, and so forth? Have you any idea what a single real beating with rods would be, in comparison with all these agonies when simply put in a story?"

Mehmoud seemed to shrink into himself. Face writhing as if he already felt the blows, he protested, "I put my name to it! What...what else...?"

"Confess your crime," Fra Guillaume repeated.

"Mehmoud Aben Fazoud, then! Is that what you want? Not Juan de Calamocha, but Mehmoud Aben Fazoud de Calamocha! It is mine, I wrote it, I do not hide that I wrote it, I have never hidden that I wrote it!"

"Holy Church will rejoice on the day she can welcome you as another Juan in baptized truth," said Fra Guillaume, "but today search your conscience further."

"Is it...because I used 'San'? Is that it, my lords? I should not have called myself 'San'—I renounce 'San'!"

"Good." The Dominican nodded. "It is not for any of us to sanctify ourselves in this earthly life, but only for Holy Mother Church to bestow that title, upon those whom she finds worthy of it, after their earthly deaths. But is this all that you can find it in your heart to confess this day?"

"What else? Ah, God! Is there still something else?"

Fra Guillaume sat and gazed somberly at the boy, beating one gnarled old hand against the other with regular if seemingly unthinking strokes. Don Felipe found his brain repeating the Gloria Patri. It had scarcely reached "*et Spiritui Sancto*" when Mehmoud asked again, in a desperate voice, "Can there still be something else?"

The young priest could stand no more. Dangerous though it was even to hint at the exact nature of any accusation in the hearing of accused parties, lest in their eagerness they fall into the sin of bearing false witness against themselves, he guessed that this boy sincerely did not understand wherein lay the one crime for which the Inquisition could rightfully try him. Turning to Fra Guillaume, Don Felipe said carefully, "Perhaps we should turn our attention to the person actually found in possession of the book."

"No!" Mehmoud half wailed, falling from his stool to kneel before them. "My lords, it was my fault—all mine! I gave it to her! She cannot even read yet—she only liked the pictures!"

To Don Felipe's eyes—though he doubted young Mehmoud would notice it, head down and weeping as he was—Fra Guillaume's whole being relaxed. Later, inquisitor might take Ordinary to task for his words; but not in front of the boy. Indeed, Felipe suspected, Fra Guillaume was secretly much relieved to have had the hint dropped, but not by himself. For now, he said only, "The sinner has made full confession at last. Some hours we will need for consultation as to his sentence and penance; but I think, with his Reverence the bishop's blessing, we might finish this process tomorrow. Meanwhile," he added to his lay brother, with a gentle nod toward the prisoner, "let him be returned to his cell, and see that he has broth, good bread, and I think, a little good wine."

After the lay brother had led Mehmoud away, not unkindly, Fra Guillaume turned his gaze full on Don Felipe and said, "With all respect, my honored friend, do you understand what it was that you did just now?"

"With deepest regrets, good brother, I do. And I pray that God and our Lady may preserve me from ever falling into such error again."

"Good. Then we need say no more on that subject." Nodding, the old Dominican put his hands upon the table as if to push himself up to his feet.

"What of the other child?" Don Felipe asked. "Béatrix Cabaza, was it not?"

"I hardly think we need worry about her," Fra Guillaume answered like a man who had already weighed the matter to a satisfactory conclusion in his own mind. "That her parents brought the book to its author's father shows their concern for their daughter's spiritual welfare.

Moreover, by the boy's own testimony, young Béatrix cannot yet read, and I think that the pictures alone could do her soul no injury. Without reading their names, she could not even know who King Herod and the others are meant to be."

Unless, Don Felipe thought, Mehmoud had told her his story. Close on that thought came another: that the boy had not actually named Béatrix Cabaza; that he might have made more copies than one, and passed them around to more playfellows than one.

Nevertheless, if the Inquisition itself, in the person of its experienced servant, chose not to pursue the question of how many youthful disciples or even accomplices Mehmoud's infant heresy might have gained in his town of Calamocha, who was a very young Ordinary to teach him his venerable business? Truth to tell, if Fra Guillaume preferred dozing in the sun with a spiritual book to rooting out possible juvenile heretics, so did Don Felipe.

They returned to Fra Guillaume's study and settled Mehmoud's penance over one or two glasses of sherry. Or, more accurately, the inquisitor imparted what he had already decided, and the Ordinary approved it: a reprimand and warning, to be administered privately tomorrow morning in the audience chamber; burning the book in the author's sight—both churchmen regretted this necessity, but Fra Guillaume believed that, with the permission of the house's owner, it could be accomplished on a brazier in the courtyard; and requiring the boy to abstain from all meat for a period of two months. Since Mehmoud was unbaptized, Fra Guillaume judged that such penances as prayers and pilgrimages could hardly be imposed. He had, however, an old manuscript volume of the *Tractatus de purgatoria Sancti Patricii*, which he would loan to Juan Maria Delgado de Calamocha on condition that Mehmoud make two illustrated copies, one to keep and one to return along with the parent volume.

"The Purgatory of Saint Patrick," Don Felipe mused aloud, turning its pages. "I think I have heard somewhat of this place. In Ireland, is it not?"

Fra Guillaume nodded. "At the very edge of the world. Had our Lord seen fit to put it in some less outlandish place, with fewer wild natives and discomforts of the journey, it is a pilgrimage I might have wished one day to undertake for myself."

CHAPTER 8

THE DREAM OF THE DEATH OF RAYMONDE

He was Fra Hugon, a Dominican of older days, and he sat behind a shiny black table, polished to mirror finish, in a long black room, hidden away from sun and daylight, lit only by seven, or three, or nine beeswax tapers—he could not quite determine their number—in a silver candlestick.

On the other side of the table stood Raymonde, whiter than the candles. She, and they, and the silver in which they rested were the only white things in all that black chamber; the orange candle flames and Fra Hugon's hands on the table the only spots of color. Though Dominican, his habit was entirely black.

They were alone, he and she. Some part of him was aware of the irregularity. Even when there was but one inquisitor, he should have other men present to validate the proceedings: scribe, advocate, consultor, Ordinary... Yet the larger part of him recognized the delicacy that had left him completely alone with her in this most sensitive of cases.

"You have claimed," he began, "to be my progenitrix."

She inclined her head. Part of it might have seemed grotesquely missing, so black was her hair. But a glowing aureole, much the same color and intensity as the candle flames, outlined it against her black surroundings.

"And the Pagan Rosemary—do you call her your descendant through me?"

Again Raymonde bowed her head in affirmation.

"Even knowing this to be impossible, sworn as I am to eternal celibacy?"

"Anna, Elizabeth, Sarah—had not each of them despaired of children? Had not Mary pledged herself to virginity?"

"Woman, do you not tremble to liken us to them?"

"We are what God has made us. What use to tremble before our Maker, Who knows each of us so well?"

"*I* am my ancestor, not you!"

"Great-great-grandson, we are both of us your ancestors."

"Heretic!" cried Fra Hugon, rising to point one forefinger at her. To his annoyance, it trembled slightly. "Blasphemer and heretic! Albigensian—believer in Dualism and disbeliever in the actuality of Ihesu's humanity, to the stake with you!"

Lifting her head, she looked him full in the face. "Yes," she replied, still without raising her voice, "it is always our readiest answer, is it not?"

They stood at the stake, the two of them alone. It was cruciform, with a great mound of fagots heaped around its base. Ankle deep in splintery wood, he caught her nearest wrist and set out to clasp it into one of the shackles that swung from the crosspiece.

Neither resisting nor assisting, she went on quietly, "You call us 'Cathar' and 'Albigensian' as though you were naming unspeakable wickedness. We are many sects, with many beliefs, yet you make no distinction among them, as in a few years you will make no distinction among many other offshoots of Holy Church, but call them all 'Lutheran,' as if their creeds were identical. With fire and sword, you scrub us from the face of the Earth, and think you have cleansed it forever from the threat of our mere presence among you—as in a few more years, you will no longer be able to scrub away the 'Lutherans,' for your own sins will have made them far too many for even your fires."

The rusted iron, not her wrist, gave him trouble; but at last he clamped it tight and reached, scrabbling, for her other wrist and the shackle on the far side of the crosspiece.

Her voice finally rose, sounding not of anger but of exultation. "And at last we are so many that it is impossible for any of us ever to destroy all those others who see the universe through different peepholes!"

He could not clamp the second iron. Giving up the attempt, he left her to dangle by one wrist, while he half tumbled down from the fagots and caught a blazing torch from the hand of someone who stood shadowy behind its light.

"For God is truly immense!" Raymonde sang from high atop her pyre. "Far too immense for any one creed ever to encompass! No, not though that one creed possessed all the souls in the world and all the ages of time!"

The wood was smeared thick with pitch and tallow. Fra Hugon thrust his torch deep in among the fagots, left it there, and stood back to watch the red flower blossom forth.

"And upon the Surface of this Great Immensity of God," Raymonde cried in ecstasy and triumph, "we crawl, specks infinitely tiny, visible only to God and one another, and we *must* use many religions and creeds beyond counting if we would ever glimpse even the tiniest Atom of the Essence of God!"

Then the red flower blew around her. Her garment blazed up in livid brilliance. She shrieked. Peeling away in shards of glowing ash, the remains of clothing revealed her naked body, scorched and blackened beyond any touch of lecherousness, with widening red cracks like fresh wounds spurting more and more blood into the fire. Unquenched, the flames closed in again. A sound of hissing and stink of charred meat filled the air. Exhausted with pain, Raymonde fell limp against the stake, her arm stretched taut in the single wrist iron. In one shocked moment, he saw that she was not weeping: rather, her eyes were melting. The strained joint of her wrist gave way. She slumped into the red flower, her hand alone—little more than bones trailing strips of burning flesh—left balanced on the shackle, first finger pointing like a candle straight up to Heaven.

Aghast at what he had done, for he had never till now looked upon death at the stake, he turned to see who had handed him the torch. It was himself.

CHAPTER 9

THE HOLY CHILD OF DAROCA

In the year of grace 1483, on the afternoon of Easter Sunday, after a search of almost two days, little Estevan del Quivir was found at last, dead, in one of the small caves near Daroca.

He had been covered with half a sheet of torn linen, and below it he wore only one soiled strip bound round his waist and upper legs to cover his shame. His feet and the palms of both hands were crushed and broken as if nails had been pounded clumsily into them and yanked out again with desperate brutality. Deep rope burns circled each small wrist. The crown of his head showed lesser wounds, as if from thorns.

Many of those who spread the report spoke of the look of unutterable peace upon his face, the scent of otherworldly perfume that filled his cave, the golden aureole surrounding his slim young body. At six years of age, Estevan del Quivir instantly became the martyred Holy Child of Daroca.

To many of Old Christian blood it seemed obvious at once who had authored this martyrdom. Who were widely known, everywhere in Europe throughout these Christian centuries, to have used little Christian children in their sacrificial rites? thus joining themselves to the guilt of their fathers who had murdered God's Holy Son. Did not their Passover fall at this same season? (It had in fact fallen two weeks earlier that year, but Old Christians paid little attention to the actual date, and New Christians said nothing to betray any knowledge of their former creed.)

And had not poor little Estevan often gone with one or both of his older brothers in their rash expeditions to the Jewish quarter of Daroca, especially to the shop of Nathaniel Ben Solomon, the silversmith?

Estevan had attended the long Good Friday service in the cathedral. Both his brothers, Juan and Luis, testified to that, as did their good friend Pedro Choved, and many others—more came forward hourly—who remembered seeing the lad already marked with his holy smile, if not yet with the clear golden aureole of sainthood. Being the best of Catholics, Don Martin del Quivir's household made their fast complete on Good Friday, and retired silently and supperless to their bedchambers immediately on returning from church. Next morning, Estevan had been gone from the bed he shared with his older brothers.

Nothing—not the disappearance of King Fernando himself, which God forbid!—could have been permitted to stop the sacred ceremonies of the holiest triduum in the year. Processions, blessings, the great Easter Masses, all went on as usual; but many among the servants, relatives, and friends of Don Martin del Quivir's family, even to the missing boy's father and one of his brothers—the oldest boy, Juan—would have non-attendance to confess before their next Communion. Estevan's mother, good Doña Sancha, knelt trembling and pale, one hand upon the shoulder of her son Luis, throughout all the Easter Masses, obviously throwing her entire strength into prayers for her missing boy.

The discovery of Estevan's mangled body made it clear, to those good and pious Old Christians who knew so well the falsehood and wickedness of all creeds not their own, especially the Jewish, that Hebrew sorcerers, calling on Satan to keep the older boys fast asleep, must have spirited the child out of his bed in the dead of Good Friday night. This increased the city's terrified outrage.

Gubbio brought the latest news to the bishop's household as they sat at supper in the evening of Easter Sunday. "My reverend masters, a crowd is gathering at the gates of the Jewish quarter. They say that Doña Sancha has cast the silver brooch her sons bought for her from Nathaniel the Silversmith into the fire."

Don Felipe found that he had started to his feet at his servant's words.

The bishop looked ponderously from servant to master. "You, my son Felipe?" he asked, the calm of a lifetime's experience in his voice. "Would you wish to put yourself in the way of the mob?"

For a moment, their eyes met. Trapped between self-preservation and old friendship, Don Felipe replied, "No, your Reverence, no more than Jeremiah wished to serve the Lord as prophet." Pleased at the steadiness of his own voice, he added, "Nevertheless, Justice imposes certain demands on us."

His Reverence nodded. "Then go. But remember, my son, that you speak for us, and that it is as grave a matter to be overhasty in judging innocence as in judging guilt."

Don Felipe made his bow to the bishop, signaled his servant to follow, and took his departure, Gubbio at his heels. Not until they were in the street did the Italian produce a boiled egg and crack it.

"From the bishop's table?" Don Felipe inquired with a glance.

"I saw plenty there," Gubbio responded, "and a belly needs fuel in times like these."

"Indeed. What else did you take for your own needs, out of the plenty that you saw there?"

"A hand-loaf and a fig or two." Having eaten the egg in two bites, Gubbio reached again into his pocket. "What great difference, master, whether I take my share of the table scraps now, when I feel the need, or later? A fig for you?"

"Argued like a true philosopher," Don Felipe observed dryly, pretending not to see Gubbio's wink. "But is this a time for pleasantries? Has the alcalde been summoned?"

"How could he remain unaware of what is happening?"

"How can many things come to pass? Go and make sure that he has been summoned."

Swallowing his mouthful of fig, Gubbio imitated his master's bow to the bishop and turned in the direction of the alcalde's house. To do him justice, he ran at his utmost speed, and he was fleet.

Somewhat restraining his own steps, as befit the dignity of bishop's Ordinary, and to avoid arriving out of breath, Don Felipe hastened toward the Jewish quarter.

Although it was but twilight, torches already flowered above the heads of the crowd around the gates. Mere half-completed piles of masonry, doorless as yet, the great posts rose like pretended but nonexistent fortifications in some nightmare of invasion. With his grandparents' tales pounding through his head—those great massacres they had heard of in their youth, fifty thousand killed in the terrible year of 1391 alone, when so many cities of Castile, Valencia, Catalonia, all those Christian kingdoms to Karnattah's north, drenched in the misdirected piety of overzealous preachers—Don Felipe suddenly saw Daroca's new gates as serving less for the isolation of her Hebrew inhabitants than for their protection, and regretted that the workers had been too long in finishing their task.

At any moment, the mob might burst over that intangible barrier and set to work with fire, steel, and stone. What mystery held them in check thus far? Ah—the good alguazil Manrique de Dios—Don Felipe glimpsed him now, standing wide-legged and watchful, holding his wand of office in one hand and his drawn sword in the other. So his Honor the alcalde had been notified, and Gubbio sent on a superfluous errand. But it needed only one single soul more zealous than the rest to step forward shouting about God's honor and glory, and the entire mob would surge across the line to take holy vengeance for Estevan del Quivir and save their remaining children from similar fates.

Every instinct of self-preservation ordered Felipe de Alhama de Granada to hang back, avoid notice, slip away and denounce this thing from a safe distance. Yet he was ordained priest and bishop's Ordinary. Who would be safe from a religiously motivated mob, if not he? Who else could hope to turn them back from their purpose, if not a man armed with ecclesiastical authority? Bitterly regretting that he had not Gubbio at his side to perform the office for him, Don Felipe cleared his throat and proclaimed his own "Make way!"

To his gratification, the alguazil caught sight of him and took over the cry, even as the outer fringe of the throng began to obey it. The Ordinary pushed through the crowd relatively unhindered, save by the stenches of fear and garlic.

Reaching the front, he spied a fair-sized stone waiting for the masons to fit it into the gatepost, and signified with a gesture that he wished it placed as his platform from which to address the crowd. Two or three men at the front understood his desire and hurried to obey, thus heartening him further. Stepping up onto the hewn stone, he spread his hands and cried,

"My people! In the voice of your bishop, I command you: Go to your homes—or to your churches—fall upon your knees, and pray! Do not mar the young saint's entrance into Heaven with your own violence!"

"Justice!" shrieked a woman's voice from the back of the crowd, and a man's took it up: "We want justice!"

"Justice shall be had!" Don Felipe shouted back. "As your bishop's Ordinary, I promise you that the Holy Inquisition—"

"What, old Fray Potbelly?" shrilled the voice of a second woman, earning a little ragged laughter.

Manrique de Dios stepped forward and raised his wand of office, shouting: "I tell you again, even now my companions are arresting the foreign Jew and his host!"

"They are all murderers! All of them!" screamed a voice so hoarse it might have been either man's or woman's, and another added, "Will you jail every Jew in Daroca?"

The alguazil answered, "They will all be held fast in their own quarter until this matter is sifted through."

"And then burned!" "Burned or hanged!" "To Hell with them all now at once!" Three shouts, coming almost simultaneously, raising many more shouts and a general loud mutter, like heavy seas on rocky shores.

"Hear me!" Don Felipe shouted above it. "Hear the voice of your bishop!" As they fell grumblingly silent, he hurried on, "You have lived side by side with these people for many years! Have they ever been known to do such a deed among you? Why now—"

One of the anonymous voices cut in, "That foreign Jew!"

"Stop!" The Ordinary raised his hands higher. "We, your priests, have studied their faith more deeply than is permitted to any of you! For we must know in order to combat. A false faith, yes, and riddled with many errors, but—mark this and mark it well!—*nowhere does it allow the sacrifice of children!* Indeed, from the days of Abraham down to our own, all Jews everywhere have ever and always been most strictly *forbidden* to harm or kill any human child!"

This speech, at least, they heard through; but as he paused for breath, someone shouted, "What of God's own Son?" At the same time, a clod of earth sailed out of the mob and struck Don Felipe on the shoulder.

Catching his resolution with difficulty, he pointed a slightly trembling finger in the direction from which he thought the clod had come, and shouted, "In striking me, you strike your bishop! In striking any ordained priest, you strike at God Himself!"

"Does God defend murdering Jews?" came the response from somewhere in the crowd.

Thank God and our Lady, thought the priest, that all these cries came from several different throats. Had it been always the same voice, the mob would have had its leader, its spearhead. "In striking out at God," he told them, "at God as represented by the lawful authority He has appointed over you, you make yourselves worse than the boy's murderer—than the boy's *as yet unknown* murderer! You place yourselves on a level with the damned archrebel Satan!"

That seemed to cow them a little. Or perhaps—he saw by glancing round—it was the appearance of Gamaliel Ben Joseph and his host Nathaniel the Silversmith, in chains and surrounded by four of the alcalde's soldiers, that caused the breathless silence.

It lasted for only seconds before the muttering started again, with waving of torches and movements as of gathering missiles.

Brandishing both wand and sword, the alguazil shouted: "Clear our way!"

"Justice!" shrilled the woman near the back.

"Justice?" Don Felipe shouted back. "You shall have justice! Yes, you shall all have justice indeed! You have heard of the new Inquisition your king and his Castilian queen have brought, under the pope's own authority, into her realms to the south! By your own actions, you shall bring it here as well—down upon your own heads! No more old Fra Guillaume, whom you should shudder to insult, as you should shudder to insult any of God's anointed servants—but harsh strong men, stern and fierce in their righteous calling, men who will know well how to ferret out each and every one of you who raises hand or voice against your bishop's authority here tonight, men who will have less mercy on the baptized Christian than on the unconverted Jew—for to whom much is given, from him much more will be expected!"

That held them back...long enough, at least, for the soldiers to get their prisoners through. Don Felipe could not help looking at Gamito, who never turned his head, never met his glance. The Jew was more prudent than the Christian, in refusing to betray their old friendship by even the slightest sign to the sharp, suspicious eyes of the mob. Nathaniel Ben Solomon, however, turned his frightened face toward the priest once or twice before the group of prisoners and guards rounded a corner and disappeared from sight.

It required another half hour, and the arrival of more soldiers to guard the Jewish quarter, before the last of the crowd finally dispersed, ending the immediate danger of riot and massacre.

* * * *

Don Felipe sought out Fra Guillaume that same night, to find him dozing over books and wine in his study closet. The single candle, although of wax, cast too little light for the younger man's eyes, let alone old "Fray Potbelly's," to have scanned the letters of tiny print swimming over the quarto pages. Don Felipe guessed that the open books were for show...though for whose benefit? That of the angels?

"We must—You must demand authority in this case, my brother!" the Ordinary began after minimal formalities of greeting.

"How can I, friend? They are unbaptized Jews, are they not?"

"And for that very reason, the secular arm will make short work of them, hoping to stave off general riot."

"Well?" Fra Guillaume hiccuped softly. "Would that not be better than to see all our poor Jews slain in a body?"

"But they are innocent, my brother! Is it not acting the part of Annas and Caiaphas and Pontius Pilate, this allowing of two men to be slain even to save the multitude?"

"Young priest, young priest." Sighing heavily, Fra Guillaume shook his head and swallowed more wine. "Even admitting your argument, we can do nothing. We must leave this thing to the secular arm. I know— most of the city knows, and it is hardly to your credit—that this Gamaliel Ben Joseph is your friend. But he remains unbaptized, for all that he is your friend and you his. Over the unbaptized, neither the Holy Inquisition nor the bishops' courts can claim any jurisdiction, unless there is some question of proselytism, and there can be no such question here. This is murder, pure and simple. Ritual or not, and even if it is some false ritual, it is theirs alone, as long as they were never baptized. We can do nothing."

Dismayed to hear even Fra Guillaume seemingly ready to consider the thought that Jews might have done it, Don Felipe suggested, "We could find two or three New Christians, and arrest them. That would make it apostasy, giving us the right to investigate, and allowing Gamaliel Ben Joseph and Nathaniel Ben Solomon to be released."

Again Fra Guillaume shook his head. "Quiet your young blood, my friend. Not only would such a trick be more unjust than allowing your friend and his host to suffer, it would never cause the secular arm to release them. We would simply widen the net, make new victims to join them. And do you accuse me of playing the part of Annas and Caiaphas?"

"But you could hold them for a year or two, then quietly release them…"

"Do you truly think that this furor over our new little Holy Child will die away as quickly as that?" The Dominican gave a great belch and rubbed his middle as if it pained him. "Or that old Fray Potbelly is likely to outlive it? Our Lord alone knows who is likely to replace me here! No, friend, leave them to the secular arm and let us not make an evil matter still more evil."

"But…"

"Moreover…I grieve to point this out to you, my friend…but can you truly be sure of the innocence of this Gamaliel Ben Joseph?"

Finding his breath, Felipe protested, "Never once, brother—never once, in all my boyhood years in Alhama de Karnattah, where we lived side by side, Christian and Jew and Moslem mingled together—never once did the Jews ever do such a deed! If not there, why here?"

Fra Guillaume rubbed his tonsure. "It may mean nothing save that the Moors, in their own realm, could keep their Jews under tighter rein. Go home, my friend, and leave it in God's hands and the alcalde's. We can do nothing."

Don Felipe rose shakily to his feet. "I can appeal to the Justicia!"

The inquisitor shrugged. "As you will, provided only that you attempt no further demands of poor old Fray Potbelly. You may, perhaps, even find the Justicia willing to hear your friend's case. I would not, however, do anything more to remind either him or the people that Gamaliel Ben Joseph is your friend. A word to the wise… Now go, Felipe, and leave me in peace. This is, after all, a holy night."

* * * *

Holy night or none, it was far from peaceful for the bishop's Ordinary. Sporadically he would succeed in calming his soul, reach the jumping-off place into sleep…only to have the prickle of some flea startle him awake with thoughts of how much worse the bed vermin must be where Gamito lay this night. In some secret cell of the alcalde's, surely; for Rodrigo de la Paz, being a reasonably just magistrate, would not risk two Hebrew prisoners in the common jail, among Christian cutthroats, now when mob feeling ran so high.

Don Felipe reached the dawn of Easter Monday haggard and heavy with vague guilt for suffering in luxury while others suffered in hunger and filth...his guilt all the heavier in that he would not willingly have traded his luxury for their squalor and discomfort. He made an unaccustomed attempt to read his Divine Office, but laid it down when the words danced meaningless and dry between his eyes and his brain. He heard the day's first Mass, and it woke no devotion, but rather parched the desert of his soul still drier. He sat to break his fast, and might as well have still eaten the hardest of Lenten fare, for all that he took double the sauce.

As he rose from table, thinking to seek out the alcalde himself in the time remaining before High Mass, his servant brought him word that someone waited to see him.

"Who is it, Gubbio?"

"One Fray Bartomeu, the priest of Santa Maria near the north gate. Franciscan, by his habit. You may remember his face, master. As for his name, I had to ask it myself. He begs to see you in private."

Don Felipe sighed. "Cannot it wait?"

"Master! Do you ask a simple layman to judge on the urgency of priestly matters? I suspect, by the set of his round old shoulders, that he may want you to hear his Confession."

"A Franciscan? Confess to a secular?"

Eying the table, Gubbio made one of his Italian shrugs. "Yes, that is strange to me, also. Why come so far, and then stop short of the bishop himself? Well, I may be mistaken."

"I will see him at once," Don Felipe decided. "In my closet." Pretending not to observe his servant pocketing a sausage, the young priest passed into the little room, smaller even than Fra Guillaume's, that served him for study and rare private audiences.

Fray Bartomeu arrived without loss of time—an elderly monastic, creased of face and comfortable of waistline. God grant, thought Don Felipe, that he has not come seeking to draw the bishop's office still deeper into their everlasting Franciscan squabbles between Conventuals and Observants! Not at this time... Aloud, he courteously requested his visitor to be seated.

The Franciscan sat, appeared to ponder for the length of an Ave, and said at last: "I would make my Confession."

Thinking that once again Gubbio had guessed shrewdly, Don Felipe asked, "Shall we go into church?"

Fray Bartomeu shook his head. "Not at this time. Not with the hour of High Mass fast approaching, and the place crowded."

"As you will."

"Shall I begin?"

Felipe thought, Yes! old man—begin and end and let us be done with all this! Aloud, he said courteously, "Whenever you are prepared, brother."

"I last confessed on this Saturday morning just past, to prepare myself for the holy feast. On Saturday afternoon…" Fray Bartomeu's voice fell still lower… "Pedro Choved came to make his Confession to me, insisting that we go far apart. Little thinking that so young a lad could have any sin on his soul but what any man would only smile to overhear by accident—in my religious duties, I had not yet heard of his little friend's disappearance… My lord, young Pedro confessed, weeping, that he had helped his friends Juan and Luis del Quivir to murder their brother Estevan!"

"Wait." It is not easy to shock a father confessor—but this… "Why? How could Satan move them to such a deed?"

"It began innocently enough, by Pedro's account. They thought only, in youthful piety, to re-enact our Lord's Crucifixion, and make a shroud, such as they had heard of from pilgrims. They nerved themselves to inflict that grievous pain by meditating on the piety of their intentions. They did not expect Estevan to die. Even when they uncovered him, the first time, and found him cold beneath the cloth, his brothers could not believe it. He would rise, they still insisted, between Holy Saturday and Easter Sunday, as our Lord rose, and this time he also would imprint his little shroud."

"My God!"

"Pedro himself seemed half convinced, even making his Confession, that the miracle would yet come to pass. He saw their sin, but still expected the miracle."

"I…see… What penance did you give him?"

"I told him there could be no spiritual absolution in such case until he had confessed to the secular arm as well. As far as I have heard, he has not done so. He protested at once to me that it was not his sin alone, that he could not put his friends in danger of law along with himself. I insisted that his absolution was dependent upon his confession of the crime to the alcalde, although he might choose to accuse only himself, as if he had acted alone. Still, he seems to prefer keeping the whole, unpardoned burden of his guilt, rather than bare it to the secular arm."

"But…when did they do it?" Don Felipe asked, remembering in bafflement that the family had gone directly from church to bed on Good Friday, and missed their youngest son already upon rising before dawn on Holy Saturday.

"They did it on Good Friday afternoon, thinking it as holy a ritual as that enacted in every church. My lord, does this not add heresy to murder?"

"It does," Don Felipe replied abstractedly. "But...but all these witnesses who have come forward with their tales of seeing Estevan and his brothers in church on Good Friday afternoon?"

"The children themselves—Luis, Juan, and Pedro—began that tale, saying they had been there together, although apart from their families, and Estevan with them. They meant to avert any doubt or suspicion that must have risen out of their absence, but Pedro himself seemed filled with wonder that others should have seen them, too. I think he believed it to be a sign that in some spiritual sense they were indeed all present in church, and that the miracle would indeed come to pass. Even now that Estevan has been found still dead, his killers may think it a sign that his sainthood lessens their guilt."

"It remains mysterious," said Don Felipe. Somewhere, deep within his head, a strange, brusque voice—a woman's?—seemed to say: Never trust your eyewitnesses. Tell people what you think they should have seen, and their memories change to order.

Neither recognizing this voice nor understanding its message, he ignored it and more or less accepted the apparitions as some miracle resembling that of bilocation. Was not the child still a holy saint, even though martyred by fellow Catholic Christians? The Ordinary went on, searching every aspect, "They thought to make a shroud, you say? A holy relic, like that of our Lord?"

"Their cloth was at first too large for the child. Half of it served to cover him. When they found him dead beneath it half an hour after they had laid him out, they tore away the part that was all bloody from his wounds, and left the clean second half over him, thinking to have their shroud more clearly imprinted when the miracle should come to pass on Holy Saturday night."

For some moments the two men sat silent, Don Felipe's mind groping through a maze of terrible images in search of further questions. At last he told his penitent, "I can find nothing in your actions to condemn, my son."

"Should I not have given the boy our Lord's forgiveness without condition?"

"No. In such a matter, the condition you attached was right and commendable."

Several more reassurances, a few peccadillos of the Franciscan's own to justify penance and absolution, and Fray Bartomeu finally took his departure, leaving his young father confessor to grapple alone with the revelation.

If only it had come to him in any other way! The initial horror of this thing—four Christian boys playing piously at crucifixion until the chosen one died—had at first banished thoughts of Gamito and Daroca's other Jews, their danger and what this truth would do in their behalf...if only it could be made public!

And that it could not. Told in sacramental Confession, it was knowledge imparted by the conscience-ridden soul directly to the Lord Ihesu. Only within another Confession could it be shared, as the Franciscan had shared it. Outside this sacramental conference, both Fray Bartomeu and Don Felipe were strictly forbidden any claim to possess this knowledge in their own persons. The secret belonged to God and Pedro Choved. Young Pedro alone, as the original penitent, had the right to reveal it... the duty to reveal it, if he obeyed God's voice as transmitted through Fray Bartomeu. And if the boy had gone to another confessor, gained absolution without Fray Bartomeu's condition? Or if fear for his body outweighed fear for his soul? In any case, if he had not come forward yet, it seemed unlikely that he ever would. That left it to God, Who might reveal it through miracle... And why would God so bestir Himself now, when He had not done so to save or revive little Estevan?

Lives hung upon this secret. Innocent lives, lives unjustly maligned. Among them, the life of one of Felipe's earliest friends, his last remaining link with boyhood, one who had survived the horrors of Alhama's capture and hardships of the journey north from Karnattah, one whose family and whose people looked to him for support and comfort. And Felipe de Alhama de Karnattah must forget as man what he had learned as priest: the knowledge that could save Gamito, might yet prove essential to save all the Jews of Daroca.

Ah! sweet Mother of God! if only I had stayed in Italy!

After a long time he rose. Like one stunned, he understood that High Mass would be almost over. He had missed it. No matter. Possibly men and women had seen him there, as they had seen the Holy Child and his companions on Good Friday. As though half drowning in dense fog, he made his way alone to the tribunal and sat waiting for Fra Guillaume's return from church.

The Dominican reached his small lodging aglow with a tranquility that would have been natural after High Mass during this holiest triduum of any other year, but today seemed out of keeping with the city's mood. "Felipe, my friend!" he greeted the Ordinary in mild surprise. "Do you not dine with his Reverence the bishop?"

"I have had information, brother," Don Felipe replied, now on his feet. Somehow, in the fog that had choked him, mind and soul, since Fray Bartomeu's Confession, he found that his decision had been formed. "Secret information, from an anonymous source, concerning a case of suspected heresy."

The old inquisitor heaved a sigh. "On this, of all days! Well, dine with me, and we will speak of it after our midday sleep."

"It is a matter of some urgency. I believe that it concerns this matter which has inflamed the city against our Jewish brethren."

Fra Guillaume seemed to ponder for the space of a Gloria, then smiled and shook his head. "My friend, my young friend. You have yet to learn that there is no matter so urgent that it cannot wait until after dinner and digestion. Does not the Apostle himself instruct us to take a little wine, for our stomachs' sake? We will, however, cut our rest a little short, so as to look into this, whatever it is, without too much delay. Until then, as you value your health and mine, not another word."

There was no help for it. Not for our Lord Himself in Person, Don Felipe thought, would Fra Guillaume have broken his iron rule of allowing no serious talk over meals, nor would he have omitted his nap afterwards. As for the younger man, he ate and drank only as much as necessary to escape comment, and felt even that small amount knot his stomach like a chain of lead as he waited, in forced idleness, for the Dominican to have his fill of dozing.

He turned the pages of a small volume, pretending to read; but his conscience thrust itself between his eyes and the print as if every serif were a thorn, and if ever he were aware what author it was whose work he gazed at, he immediately forgot it.

And yet, he kept repeating to his conscience, how does God work, in the daily course, if not through human beings? How can I know but that God, Whose secret this is to keep or to reveal, chooses to reveal it, not through miracle, but through my weakness—that I have been predestined, like Judas Iscariot, to commit grievous sin that greater good may come of it?

At last Fra Guillaume snorted, woke, and gently shook himself. "Now!" said he. "Let us go where we may more fittingly examine this information that you bring."

They went into the audience chamber, which served Fra Guillaume's tribunal also as council room. Toeing aside one soft lump of dust, Don Felipe mused briefly upon an audience chamber in stark black and white, awesome in its unfrayed cleanliness, where no flocks of dust lambkins grazed the floor; and a council room completely separate, with warm hangings on its walls and cushions on its chairs.

Feeling less like a bishop's Ordinary than an unfortunate under investigation, Don Felipe moved his chair opposite that of the inquisitor, sat some moments hesitant to broach the matter he had been fretting to speak of since making his decision, and finally, beneath Fra Guillaume's mildly expectant gaze, began:

"My witness—who claims the strict rule of secrecy—saw three young lads heretically re-enacting our Lord's Crucifixion upon a fourth boy, this Good Friday just past, near the cave where Estevan del Quivir's body was found."

It gave him some satisfaction to see that even an experienced and sleepy inquisitor could still on rare occasion be shocked. Fra Guillaume's eyes first widened, then blinked. His hands, clasped before him on the table, tightened until the knuckles turned pale.

At length the Dominican asked, "Did your witness recognize these lads?"

"One definitely: Pedro Choved."

"And the others? Were they truly Estevan del Quivir and his elder brothers?"

"So my witness thought."

The old man drew a long breath and splayed his fingers over the dusty wood of a table left always in place. His nails whitened as he pressed down, holding his hands steady. "This...would change the aspect of the case. Holy Mother! I am not sure that Estevan even merits the title of martyr, if this can be proved."

"How willing or unwilling was the victim's involvement, who can say?" Guessing at Fra Guillaume's thoughts, Don Felipe shook his head. "No, brother, in my humble opinion, we need not worry ourselves over the cultus that will inevitably grow up around our Holy Child. Whoever actually killed him, they who reverence him as martyr surely do so in all orthodox good faith. But must we not investigate this case of his brothers and their friend?"

"Certainly, certainly." The heaviest of sighs. "The witness came to you, my friend. Let the bishop's court investigate this case."

No! thought Don Felipe. I cannot act alone—I am known to be Gamito's friend. And to perjure my soul yet again, in repeating, as if I had the right to repeat it, what came to me under the Seal of Confession...

Aloud, he argued, "Think, Fra Guillaume! If you should fail to represent the true Inquisition in examining such a notorious case as this, will we not give them one more pretext for forcing their new Castilian Inquisition into our diocese...into Aragon?"

The old inquisitor pondered slowly, sighed again, and nodded. "You are right. It was, perhaps, for this very hour that our Lord put me in this place. But…you will act with me?"

"To do otherwise, would be to turn my back upon God." Uttering these words, Don Felipe half expected God to strike him dead for compounding sacrilege with hypocrisy. But no—had He not left Judas to hang himself?

"Well!" Fra Guillaume leaned on the table for support as he got to his feet. "If we are to look into it, we must do so quickly. Let us go at once."

* * * *

The merchant who owned the house wherein Fra Guillaume kept his tribunal had among his servants a former soldier, one Luis Albogado, still strong and sturdy in his sixtieth year. This former soldier the merchant had placed at Fra Guillaume's disposal whenever the Holy Inquisition should need a man at arms in Daroca, which had not happened for many years. Attended only by Luis Albogado, inquisitor and Ordinary made their way to the house of Don Enrique Choved's widow. No more than a Gloria after Albogado's announcement of "A matter of Faith!" accompanied by his three firm raps, the door was opened by a young maidservant, wide-eyed, pale, and breathless, who immediately shrank back like a frightened fawn out of their way. Poor creature, thought Don Felipe, our errand cannot touch you…except as it touches this entire household.

The widow of Don Enrique stood midway down the stairs. "Fra Guillaume," she acknowledged, inclining her head to the inquisitor. "Don… Forgive me, my memory does not hold many names. Who in this sad house has sinned against our Holy Faith?" Her glance went in the direction of the poor maidservant, as much as to say, "If one of my servants… my servant no longer!"

Don Felipe took it upon himself to step forward and answer the widow as gently as possible in so stern a matter. "Doña Beatriz, we have cause to suspect your son, and him alone in this house."

"My son Enrique is in Granada, fighting his king's holy war against the infidel Moors."

"It is your younger son, Pedro, whom we have cause to suspect."

Pressing her lips together before speaking again, she answered at last, "If guilty of sinning against our Faith, he is no longer his father's son, nor mine."

"He is still God's son, Doña," Fra Guillaume told her, in a voice between mercy and sternness, "and he has still a soul, which must be saved at any cost."

She descended the stairs and stood to one side. "Save it, then. He is on the floor above us."

They went up, Luis Albogado leading and Don Felipe, as the younger priest, next. Pretense it might be, as if a bodyguard were needed against a ten-year-old boy; and yet this ten-year-old boy was under grave suspicion of having taken part in the heretical murder of a friend.

They found Pedro sitting on the floor between bed and window, staring up at the intruders, a bowl of nutmeats, pile of whole nuts, and two or three heaps of broken nutshells surrounding him like toy fortifications.

Luis repeated the dread words: "A matter of Faith!"

The boy leaped to his feet, dropping his knife and the nut he had been holding, as if his guilt consisted of shelling nuts on Easter Monday. Knife and nut fell with a clatter, the nut rolling across the floorboards to catch in a knothole near Don Felipe's toe.

"Remember, Pedro Choved," Fra Guillaume intoned, "that our first concern is for your immortal soul, and that He Whom you must fear is not us, but God, and God alone, Who sees all. Bear ever in your mind that it is worse than useless to lie to the Lord our God, and answer the questions of your bishop's Ordinary as if you were already answering God Himself upon the Day of Judgment."

Wondering when it had been decided that he should be the one to do the questioning, Don Felipe began, "Well, Pedro, is this your room, where you sleep?"

The child nodded.

Don Felipe said to the former soldier: "Search it thoroughly. I will question the suspect in the courtyard."

"Yes, my lord. What should I search for?"

Exchanging a glance with the inquisitor, the Ordinary replied, "Perhaps Fra Guillaume will deign to oversee your findings."

"If you fail to discover anything here," Fra Guillaume added, with—Felipe thought—some relief, "we must see the rest of the house searched as well."

Nodding, Luis laid one hand heavily upon Pedro's shoulder and delivered him to Don Felipe, who received him with a hand upon the other shoulder and conducted him downstairs, past his mother's frown, to the courtyard below.

Here they stood in silence, facing the fountain, while Don Felipe repeated two Paternosters in his mind. At last he said, "Look at that water, Pedro. It ought to remind you of your holy Baptism."

The boy said nothing.

"Not that you can remember the actual event," the man went on, "but you know, by virtue of having been taught, what an indelible mark of grace was bestowed on you that day."

A slight tremor seemed to pass through the little body. That was all.

"Are you not deeply ashamed to have so blotted out and disgraced the holy purity you received that day, as God's sacred gift to you?"

Still Pedro said nothing.

"Speak, boy!" Felipe exclaimed in exasperation and bafflement, shaking him by the shoulder.

"Sir," the boy answered dully, "what do you want me to say?"

"It is for you to confess! But know this: your sin did not pass unseen."

"Who saw us?" He must finally have panicked, to blurt it out like that.

"The One Whose displeasure you ought to fear above that of any earthly court. God, Who sees all things!" (Even as He sees my own sin at this moment, the priest thought heavily, His Holy Mother help me!) He finished aloud, "This is not to say that you went unseen by mortal eyes, as well."

"No!"

Don Felipe drew a deep breath. What was one more lie in comparison with the sin already on his soul? "Your accomplices have already confessed."

"No! They would not! Never!"

"Confess, Pedro Choved, or it will come to the torture."

"No! Not here! Not in Aragon! Our fueros—"

"The fueros of proud Aragon mean nothing before the sacred duty of the Holy Inquisition!" Don Felipe said with mock assurance. "Do you know what torture is, boy? Do you know what it is to cause another human creature cruel and deliberate—"

"No!" Breaking away from his grip, Pedro fled across the courtyard—to come face to face with his mother, who had just entered on that side. Hands tight on the silver cross she wore round her neck, she frowned down upon him without speaking. Turning at bay like some hunted animal, he cried, "We were all in church! Together! Everyone saw us!"

"Do you know what it is to hear screams brought forth by the work of your hands?" Don Felipe continued, seeing his advantage and—hardening his heart for Gamito's sake—relentlessly pursuing it. "Do you know what it is to see the face writhe up beneath your ministrations? To feel the warm blood—"

"No! No! No!"

Heavy footsteps interrupted them. The inquisitor's bodyguard appeared, followed by Fra Guillaume. In his left hand, Luis Albogado held before him half of a linen sheet, thickly stained with blood.

* * * *

"I do not understand," Gamito remarked, some weeks later and some distance beyond the town, "why he kept the bloodstained sheet."

"They still hoped, I believe," Felipe replied, stroking the neck of his mule, "that the Holy Child's blood would form into his image. In any case, whether or not they hoped for a miraculous shroud, they had the true relic of a martyr."

The two friends were effectively in private, as they had not been since before Passover. Having chosen Zaragoza as his destination, Gamaliel Ben Joseph, the "foreign Jew," had ridden forth from Daroca alone except for Don Felipe, who brought only Gubbio and Luis Albogado to attend him. The Italian, for once showing some deep sense of delicacy, was hanging behind, engaging the former soldier in a conversation of their own, near enough to guard their master but not to overhear him talking.

Gamito rode another moment in silence before adding, "But why hide it so carelessly?"

"Ah, my friend! For Estevan's brothers to have kept it, knowing that their house would surely be searched as matter of course even while the boy was still merely missing—that would have been to hide it carelessly. As for keeping it in the bottom of Pedro's chest, how could they expect blame to fall anywhere else than upon your people?" Don Felipe spoke with a heart made all the heavier by the secret knowledge that, had it not been for his own actions taken upon information given, received, and given again under the strict Seal of Confession, the boys would have been safe in their expectation. "Even those children themselves," he went on bitterly, "knowing their own guilt, saw nothing wrong in allowing the blame to fall on Jews! This is not the world as we knew it under the infidel Moors of Karnattah, old friend."

"I fear," said Gamito, "that it will grow worse yet. We may live to see more such massacres as those of our grandparents' days."

"And you, Gamito? Would it not be better for you to join your brother and his wife in Rome?"

The Jew shook his head. "I will not abandon my people as long as need remains here."

"There are still those who cling to their belief that you caused the Holy Child's death, who refuse to believe in the guilt of his brothers and their playfellow. Rumor may point you out even in Zaragoza."

Gamito shook his head. "It is a large enough city, I hope, for me to live quietly in its Jewish quarter, unseen by any save my own kind."

"And if our monarchs force Aragon to accept their new Inquisition?"

"Old friend," said Gamaliel Ben Joseph, "I no longer so greatly fear the Inquisition. Is it not thanks to your Inquisition that I am free? No, it is the mob that I most fear now, and not the Inquisition that holds it somewhat in check."

Far back though his servant and the former soldier were, Felipe lowered his voice. "Then never allow yourself to be baptized, Gamito—not, at least, without feeling true conversion in your heart," he added, prudent even in their privacy. "And never, even if asked, speak a word concerning your beliefs to any Christian, for that might be called proselytizing. Avoid these things, and you should remain safe even from this new Inquisition."

Gamito nodded, and they rode on.

Not that the investigation of local inquisitor and bishop's Ordinary had been enough, Don Felipe thought with some anger. No, it had been necessary after all to appeal to the Justicia on behalf of Gamaliel Ben Joseph and Nathaniel Ben Solomon. The Justicia was a man able to weigh evidence, and pardons for both Jews had come, along with a document ordering the Christians of Daroca to keep the peace and withhold hasty judgment as regarded their Hebrew neighbors. Alas, not even this had crushed out the earliest opinions concerning the death of Estevan del Quivir. Nathaniel the Silversmith had already traded his house for mules and taken his family across the mountains to France. Certain others of Daroca's Jews, even though never accused by name of this crime, had followed his example.

Another half hour, and Gamito said, "There is the inn where two of my brethren from Zaragoza are to meet me. Farewell, old friend. Peace be with you. I shall not risk either of us by writing letters."

Swallowing hard, Felipe brought himself to say, "Except in need, Gamito. If need should press you, let me know of it."

Because of the servants behind, they ventured nothing more, save that halfway to the inn, the Jew turned back briefly and gave the Christian a single wave of one hand.

Felipe returned it, then sat and watched until Gamito reached the inn. His friend would never know how much he had sacrificed—the peace of his own conscience, perhaps the very salvation of his soul—for the sake of friendship and justice.

Gubbio and Luis eventually came up to him and sat in silence, awaiting his pleasure and meanwhile leaving him to his own thoughts, which had turned back to the three boys: victims, in some sense, of his own sin. Especially was Pedro Choved his victim. Merely pointing to a door and naming it as that of the torture chamber—an irregularity which shamed Fra Guillaume's with the Moorish lad Mehmoud Aben Fazoud into insignificance—had sufficed to bring from young Pedro, already broken in spirit as he was, a tearful admission at last, complete with the names of Estevan's older brothers. Neither of them, however, had confessed to anything. Seeing his friends' resolve, Pedro had refused to ratify his admission. Without public confession, there could be little use in so much as offering the young killers to the law's secular arm. Nor, to Felipe's secret relief, would Fra Guillaume even hear of holding a consultation on resorting to any degree in more regular fashion, let alone of attempting to find a laborer for the manual work attendant on exercising the long-disused inquisitorial privilege here in Aragon.

The ecclesiastical arm still had power to judge guilt and assign some penalty, even without confession. All three boys had been sentenced to make the pilgrimage to Santiago de Compostela, the last mile on their knees, as soon as they should either find sponsors to accompany them, or be old enough to go by themselves. In addition, Pedro Choved's mother had disowned and turned him out by her own act. Don Felipe hoped that their souls, at least, might be saved.

Blinking tears from his eyes, the Ordinary turned Castaña—his favorite little mule of the bishop's stables—motioned to his attendants, and started back toward Daroca.

CHAPTER 10

THE DREAM OF THE DRAGON

He stood on the shore of a wide, dark water, its surface like glass reflecting the stars. No, not the stars; those ruddy reflections came from an opposite shore so far distant that its torches, if torches they were, looked no larger than the flames of candles. That distant shore was an island, or so he guessed by the way it appeared to lie across the wide path of moonlight on the glassy water.

From the island, he heard faint music...hymn music, he might have said, but for its happiness, like a satyr's hymn to Spring. Well, and why should a hymn not be happy? Had not the Lord Ihesu Himself eaten and made merry with sinners?

From the shore behind him, Don Felipe heard...not a sound...but a silence, great and menacing, like the silence of an army massing. He looked around. He saw nothing, still heard nothing—save a single, muffled cough. Shivering, he turned back. Now he had to blink against the moon's pathway, so brightly it shone after the dark into which he had just been staring.

From downstream, the prow of a small boat entered the glittering ripples. As it drew fully into the moonpath, Felipe saw that a figure stood in its stern, upright and willowy, clad in flowing robes that shone dark against the moonlit water yet pale against the island lights. A lady alone in a little barge, like a fay from some romance of Arthur of Britain.

Slowly, the barge drifted around to glide toward Don Felipe. Now the woman faced him, and he saw that she was Raymonde...Raymonde, come back to life. A faint nimbus trailed from her like cool smoke from a censer.

The prow touched shore at his feet. Joy in meeting him seemed to overwhelm all other emotion in Raymonde's eyes as she extended one fine-boned hand. "Great-great-grandson!"

"Great-great-grandmother! Am I forgiven?"

"For which of your sins?" She seemed amused.

After a moment, he remembered. "Why, for your death!"

"Many times great-grandson, that is rather for you to help forgive, than to be forgiven. Now, come."

Stepping unquestioningly into the boat, he accepted her hand. He would have kissed it, but she turned it, twining her fingers with his, then lowering her arm so that they stood with hands clasped like two innocent children.

"Pay me no homage," she reminded him gently. "To the good God alone is homage due."

"Do we not pay God homage in offering due honor to those whom He has set above us?"

She smiled. "And in what way has God set me above you?"

"In making you my ancestress, and in sending you back, in His great mercy and your own, despite my part in your death, to act as my guide."

"Did Virgil, though a condemned Pagan, become Dante's superior in guiding him through Hell?"

"In so far as God gave Virgil to Dante as guide and teacher, I would say yes, for the time that they were together, the Pagan poet held authority over the Catholic one. But you, my grandmother many times great, surely I see you in glory! Surely at the last you were saved through the flames, as I was lost through them; and you have come this time to show me glimpses of salvation and happiness."

Her smile grew sad. "The people of this island call it their New Eden; but Eden is not Heaven, and no expanse of water can stop enemies forever in the material creation."

Now they stood upon the island, even though, looking back, he could recollect neither crossing the water nor stepping from barge to shore. He regretted his lapse. Floating up the moon-laid path across the water, while engaged in edifying conversation with his glorified ancestress, ought to have given him a memory to cherish like the mustard seed of great price.

"The New Eden?" he repeated. Almost at their feet, a man and a woman, both naked, were furiously coupling. Felipe could avert his eyes from them only by staring at Raymonde.

"And they call themselves the Adamites," she replied. "Each one as innocent of sin, in their own conception, as Adam and Eve before the Fall."

"But, without true Baptism, none of us can ever return to that lost innocence. Have these people been baptized?"

"Great-grandson, where does true Baptism lie: on the head, or in the heart?" Averting her own eyes from the act of bestial innocence, she tugged at his hand to lead him on.

Overgrown with trees and wild shrubs, the island bore little resemblance to Don Felipe's imaginings of Eden. It did not lack a certain crude and unkempt beauty, for the torchlight made some trees and shrubs glow in ruddy outline against the dark sky, and elsewhere moonlight lay a heavy coating of silver on every leaf and stem it could touch. But where were the gardens, pastures, and flocks that should have fed these Adamites?

"What do they eat?" he asked at last.

"They go in groups to the mainland and gather what they need from the stores of their neighbors. Sometimes they knock down or tie up a neighbor who complains. The neighbors liken it to a fierce dragon devouring the countryside."

"Still, it is undeniably sinful."

"By both of our creeds—yours now and mine when I walked in the material world—this people's entire Faith is deadly sin."

She brought him to the island's heart: a village of bowers, thatched tents, and crudely wattled huts, bedecked everywhere with curling vines. In the grassy mud of its plaza sat a large circle of chanting people. More people danced and gyrated in and out of the circle, weaving back and forth in paces and patterns matched to the chant, dancers continuously changing places with chanters according to some order that Felipe could almost make out. Here and there someone, usually elderly, wore a flowing garment; but most of the people went naked to the skin. They were of all ages and both sexes, and in the center of the circle three pairs lay coupling to the half sacred, half profane rhythm of the song.

"My God!" ejaculated the priest. "Can this be their idea of Eden?"

"As it would have been, they suppose, for all of us if not for Adam's Fall."

"Ah, happy Fall!" Yet even as he quoted the Easter liturgy, Don Felipe felt some part of himself throbbing in time with their chant, some impulse that made him ache to tear away his own garments and join these strangely innocent sinners. "How many of them are there?"

"About three hundred now. All the survivors of Jan Žižka's first inquisition on their sect."

"An inquisition on them, yes. Pity that it bore so little fruit. Yet this name—Jan Žižka—I seem to recollect, and not as that of one who bore any legitimate authority to head an inquisition."

"The captain of the Taborites, that group of Hussites who believe the others still too close to Rome."

"How deeply God has planted the impulse to purity in our breasts!" Don Felipe mused. "That it should still survive even among heretics, seeking to purify their own heresies."

"Their own?" his ancestress replied. "Or someone else's?"

Beneath their feet, the ground began to quake as with the thunder of an army's heavy march. A fanfare of brassy horns rent the air. The Adamites seemed to pay it no attention.

"Joshua at Jericho," Raymonde remarked, sounding in that moment more like Rosemary.

The Adamites had neither town wall nor tower to fall at the sound of the horns, but suddenly one of their bowers blossomed into flame, followed next instant by another on the opposite side of their grassy plaza. On every hand a great warcry smothered the sound of chanting, though the lips of the Adamites continued to move even as they sprang to their feet and from somewhere produced weapons.

"Come," said Raymonde, tugging her descendant into the nearest hut. From outside, he had thought it small and miserable; but, blinking around at its interior, he found that it approached the palatial, with a baffling complexity of chambers opening one into another, furnished with fine things and poor ones mixed at haphazard, lined with cupboards containing books he longed to investigate. At first he supposed that the illumination enabling him to see all this glowed forth from the books. Then he saw that the cupboards—indeed, the very walls around them— were afire.

Pulling back a Samarkand carpet, Raymonde stamped once on the earthen floor. A section of it dropped away beneath her foot, revealing a ladder. It looked steep, ill-balanced, and rickety, with several rungs broken or missing. Yet to remain above would be even more perilous, especially now that the walls were ablaze; so he followed her down.

"The dwelling above us," he asked as they descended. "How could it be so large?"

"To hold the souls of those dwelling within."

"And contain so much treasure mingled with the dross?"

"Love still abides, even in the heart of what others call heresy."

They reached the bottom. He found it slimy underfoot, yet Raymonde led the way through it without soiling her white hem. Roots, large and tiny, hung down everywhere from the tunnel's crumbling ceiling. Small underground birds and moths—some of shining loveliness—flitted among them. Here and there in the muck at their feet gems shone gently, some of them large enough to form stepping stones. At length they came to another ladder. This one seemed more solid than the first, and he followed her up with relative ease.

They emerged behind what remained of a smoldering bower. Its skeleton, mottled charcoal black, ashen white, and ember red, framed Don Felipe's view of the battle. At least half the Adamites lay dead and dismembered. The rest—men, women, and children—fought on desperately, some with true weapons, others with stones, torches, and cooking implements.

Brave they were, but Eden-naked against soldiers armored in boiled leather, chain, and even plate. Nor had the Adamites any cannon or musketry, while from one side Felipe saw a Hussite war machine—an armored wagon drawn by armored horses and filled with armored gunmen—advancing on the battle.

"Alive," he protested, "they might make restitution to those whom they have robbed."

"Do you not believe in spiritual restitution, great-grandson?"

The war machine reached the plaza. Now it seemed to be a thing of whirling blades, before which limbs and heads flew, trailing arcs of blood. Satan's own fountainworks it appeared to Don Felipe. He turned his face away.

When he looked again, the war machine was gone. In its place lay a high, tumbled mound of naked corpses and fragments of flesh. Taborite soldiers, many of them bleeding but mostly whole, ringed the mound on three sides, leaving on the fourth a clear view for the priest and his guide, of whose presence they seemed unaware.

A huge captain strode forward. Felipe knew him to be Jan Žižka himself, for the Hussite commander stood three times larger than his men, like some great saint or angel towering above ordinary souls in a painting.

The giant turned his head toward the mound of death. One of his eyes had been drained away through an ancient scar, and the other was milky and sightless; but his face showed displeasure as stern as if he saw everything. "Have you *all* disobeyed my orders?" he thundered. "Have you not left me *one* alive?"

The mound began to quiver, then to heave. Like ants, the Taborite soldiers clambered over it, hurling broken flesh away until they had cleared it all off into a wide circle of smaller heaps.

Beneath that mound, one living pair, man and woman, had lain the entire time in each other's arms, still coupling as though oblivious to the destruction of their little Eden around them.

Dragging them apart, the soldiers looked expectantly to their commander. "Save me the man," said Jan Žižka. "Woman's tongues are quicker to deceive."

Immediately a soldier lopped off her head.

After a short flight, it fell and rolled to Don Felipe's feet. He stared at it in shock. All had happened so quickly that neither lover had yet recovered from the daze of finding themselves pulled roughly apart. The woman's eyes blinked twice, her lips parted a little as if to speak, and then she closed her eyes as though with one last great effort of will, and lay frozen for the Final Judgment, bloody and yet strangely beautiful in death. One could have thought her another martyred saint.

Her lover, having regained his worldly senses, sent up a piercing cry. Don Felipe thought it consisted of her name, wailed over and over. But he could not quite understand its syllables, and this increased his own grief.

"Why, then, did Jan Žižka demand survivors," he asked Raymonde, "if not in some small token of mercy?"

The man's screams turned from wails of grief into cries of pure animal pain.

"For information only," Raymonde replied in grief.

Refusing to look again, Don Felipe protested, "What further need can there be for information after the entire sect has been condemned and executed?"

"Perhaps to justify the act," said Raymonde. "Although there are those who value information above all else, for its own empty sake. Even now, I call this one more trap of the material world."

He began to ask in which world they stood at that moment, and, asking, awoke baffled, supposing that his sleep had been dreamless.

CHAPTER 11

VOICE IN THE WILDERNESS

During Holy Week in the year of our Lord 1484, a voice began to cry in the wilderness north of Daroca: a ringing voice of middle pitch, coming from the throat of a man of middle height and sufficient leanness to suggest appropriate fasting. The dirt on his face, arms, and ragged garments made it difficult to be sure of his age. He carried himself very straight, and harangued at vehement length, at first to some few shepherds and passing muleteers but, as the weeks rolled on, to increasing audiences.

Always he appeared within two or three hours' walk of the town of Calatayud, coming and going with no announcement of where or when he would speak next. He seemed to appear in some place or other on every Catholic holy day and most Sundays, but on Christian working days he showed himself only rarely, and then always in either the morning or the evening twilight, and close to the town. He spoke against two things: the Holy War in Granada, and the new Inquisition that King Fernando and his Castilian queen were seeking to force into Aragon.

Almost all the Aragonese opposed this new Inquisition, Old Christians as well as New, Catholics as well as Jews and Moslems—many Catholics, indeed, still more strongly than Jews and Moslems, for the baptized had far more than the merely circumcised to fear from either Inquisition.

The Holy War was another matter. Most Christians considered it as pious as any Crusade of olden times, especially distant as it was on the far southern side of Spain. By his utterances against the Royal Inquisition, this new prophet could have belonged to any of Spain's three religions; and the dirt upon his garments and person seemed more appropriate to a Christian than a Moslem holy man. But his harangues against the invasion of Granada, taken together with the times of his appearances, seemed to mark him as Mohammedan; and soon he came to be called El Santon—El Santon de Aragon, to distinguish him from that more famous santon who had for years gone about Granada prophesying doom to his fellow Islamites.

"We, who are as good as you," ran the pledge of the Cortes of Aragon to their monarch, "take an oath to you, who are no better than we, as prince and heir of our kingdom, on condition that you preserve our fueros and liberties; and if you do not, we do not." Among these ancient liberties of which the Aragonese were so proud and jealous, freedom of speech stood high. El Santon de Aragon sometimes met with heckling and argument, for his auditors, many of whom were Christian and favored the war, also had freedom of speech; but he went otherwise unmolested, growing in popularity as the Royal Inquisition waxed ever more and more menacing.

The previous autumn, Fernando and Isabel had gotten yet another document from Pope Sixtus, this one a bull appointing Fray Tomás de Torquemada as Inquisitor General over Aragon and her neighboring kingdoms of Valencia and Catalonia. Not until the following spring did Aragon's Cortes accept this fiery zealot of the king's Inquisition, but when they did, Fray Tomás acted with all speed in appointing two creatures of his own—Fray Gaspar Juglar and Maestre Pedro Arbués—his new inquisitors for Zaragoza. Their haste became unseemly. As El Santon's cries to the south of that great city rose in desperation, Fray Gaspar and Maestre Pedro held their first Act of Faith on Monday, the tenth day of May, 1484.

On Thursday, the thirteenth day of May, a broadsheet appeared on the doors of every church and public building in Calatayud, more than two days' journey on foot from Zaragoza:

CONTREFUERO!

Contrefuero! Send forth the cry to keep Liberty alive!

They have fashioned a new weapon in their war on Holy Granada, a weapon to fill their coffers with plunder wrested from their own Jewish and Moorish subjects in kingdoms at peace, even as it sets every Christian against every Moor and every Jew. They have bought from their pope a new inquisition, one in which they themselves, king and queen, will name the inquisitors! No longer will it be the bishop of Rome who gives us men to keep the Catholic faith pure and well-washed with confiscations and penances: now it will be the king himself—this same king who gave us his bastard son, not yet grown to manhood, for archbishop of Zaragoza—who will name his own creatures and tools as inquisitors to burn us, plunder whatever wealth we possess, and leave our widows and orphans beggars in the streets! Is this what Christ Himself would have commanded?

Already fires burn in Castile. It is already three years ago that flames licked high around the victims of Seville. Their screams rose to Heaven, mingling with the wails of that wretched, beautiful woman who betrayed them to their death. Their skins blackened and burst, their bones were broken and raked into the earth, and from their ashes rose the plague, God's own judgment to scour the unhappy city that had watched them suffer. Its victims lay piled in every street, among them Fray Alonso de Hojeda, he whose preaching had sown the seeds of Inquisition in the proud and merciless heart of the Castilian queen. And yet, not reading aright these signs of the times, even as Heaven's judgment abated, they raised their stakes once again and renewed their search for human fuel.

Like pestilence over the land, they have spread it into all parts of Castile. And now, not content, they would force it into our own country, our free and ancient Aragon, against all fueros, against even our own ancient inquisition! By license, as they claim, bought from the pope, they would replace the pope's own inquisition with this new one of their own. Can this be the Will of God? That so-called holy child of Daroca, did it not prove that he was murdered this year just past by fellow Christians? Why, if not to fuel false fires of hatred and fear against unoffending but prosperous Jews? That night when the Christian mob hunted down one wretched and impoverished Moor, tearing him to pieces for daring to steal their golden pyx and consume the wafer they call the body of that Lord who Himself lived in poverty and preached mercy to all people and commanded that his flesh be eaten—what inflamed that mob, if not their monarchs' cruel intolerance?

Fernando and Isabel are called pious and noble for seeking to purify their lands by depopulating them of so many good and useful subjects. But in truth, in thus impoverishing their lands, are these monarchs not looking to swell their own princely treasuries?

Already on this tenth day of May just past have his majesty's inquisitors in Zaragoza, Fray Gaspar Juglar and Maestre Pedro Arbués, acting under the pious and benevolent blessing of the boy archbishop, their king's young bastard, held their first solemn Act of Faith, penancing four unfortunates and robbing them, in Christ's name, of their hard-earned property. This Act was held, these victims penanced, although no Edict of Grace had ever been read, no Term of Grace ever granted, not so much as a single fortnight expired since the appointing of the royal inquisitors! How much longer before Fray Gaspar and Maestre Pedro light their fires and begin burning victims to the greed of the boy bishop's royal father?

Catalonia still holds out: having refused to send deputies to swear allegiance to the king's sacrilegious inquisition this January past, our Catalan brothers cling to their own pope-appointed inquisitor of Barcelona. Our own Teruel holds out, shutting fast her gates against Fernando's new inquisitors sent through his creature Fray Tomás, falsely called inquisitor general of Aragon as well as of Castile—forcing them into the unhappy town of Cella, fighting their excommunications and interdicts with counter-excommunications and counter-interdicts—as if it were man and not God who held all power of salvation or damnation!

Rise, Zaragoza! Follow brave Teruel! Rise, Aragon! Follow the examples of Catalonia and your own most noble Teruel!

Good Justicia, awake! Awake, and call your people of Aragon to arms:

CONTREFUERO!
Send forth the cry to keep Liberty alive!

Almost immediately upon its appearance, rumors flew naming El Santon de Aragon as the author of this call to arms. The following morning, Friday the fourteenth day of May, the people of Calatayud's nearest neighbors, Ateca and Daroca, awoke to find copies of this same broadsheet on the doors of their churches and public buildings, where they promptly flocked to read and hear it read for themselves.

The copy tacked to the great door of Daroca's cathedral did not long remain in place. Before midday, the bishop having already perused it, his Ordinary sat studying it with Fra Guillaume in Daroca's tiny and so far untouched tribunal of the ancient Papal Inquisition.

At length the old inquisitor raised his head with a heavy sigh. "I can find in it only the one heresy."

"The one, however, is enough," Don Felipe responded with reluctance.

"Enough…if the author is a baptized Christian. But I suspect, by these words, 'they call,' that he is not." Fra Guillaume heaved another sigh, whether at the enormity of the heresy, or at its appearance in any statement directed against the new Inquisition, his companion could not have said.

"Proselytism?" the Ordinary guessed.

"How? See how immediately he follows it—whatever his own creed—with unimpeachable praise of our Lord? No, to read in this any attempt at turning Christians from their Credo would be to torture the words beyond measure. Our author actively preaches against two things only: the war in Granada and this new Inquisition. In both these areas he is free, so far as Holy Mother Church officially concerns herself in matters of the Faith, to win others to his way of thinking. Unless he is indeed baptized, we have no case."

"Nevertheless, we have grounds for looking into this matter. And, my brother, we must do so. We owe it to the true Inquisition."

"We do indeed." Another sigh. "But where to begin?" The old inquisitor could have retired quietly into one of his Order's houses long ago, and might perhaps be wishing in his heart that he had done so before this present storm broke over their heads, making retreat cowardly. As it was, with a strong arm to lean upon, Fra Guillaume stood willing to do his best throughout the crisis.

This strong arm Don Felipe was ready to provide, both for his bishop and for himself. Secretly, the young priest applauded El Santon for opposing the war in Karnattah. That war had, after all, cost him his entire family, good Catholics all, slain by mercenaries who could be Christian only in name.

Manuel Urtigo. He turned that name over and over in his heart every night. Or had done so until…Gamito had given him the mercenary's name, and for the sake of Gamito and his people Felipe had himself committed sin and sacrilege that must be worse in the sight of God than even Manuel Urtigo's murders. (Nor had he ever confessed this sin. In part, he feared that no confessor would grant him absolution; in part, it seemed monstrous so to use the same sacrament he had so grievously abused. Also—though he denied this thought whenever it leered like a demon out of the depths of his conscience—having himself broken the Seal of Confession, he had conceived a damnable distrust of his fellow priests, even to the point of wondering if Fray Bartomeu could possibly have come to him with young Pedro Choved's confession knowing the bishop's Ordinary to be a friend of the Jews and desiring him to break the Seal and bear the guilt.) Nevertheless, little more than a year later, he found that sometimes an entire day, sometimes even an entire night, could pass without thoughts of the probability of his own damnation, while the name of Manuel Urtigo still floated to his lips with evening prayers.

But, no matter what pride a country might take in her freedom of speech, there remained certain opinions less than prudent for certain lips to utter. Not only was Felipe de Granada a servant of Holy Church, he was also, now, an orphan, thrown back upon his benefice, his salary as bishop's Ordinary, and such monies as remained with his Italian bankers. Seeing the necessity of a certain amount of worldly advancement, if only for the sake of his tender digestion and the soft bedding without which sleep would have been impossible, he chose to keep his opinions concerning their Majesties' Holy War locked within his own heart.

Opposing the Royal Inquisition was another matter. His Reverence of Daroca himself, along with most bishops everywhere, opposed it. Having borne the earliest responsibility for judging heretics, bishops were by long tradition jealous of inquisitors. Hence the ruling that inquisitors could officially do nothing except in the presence of a bishop's representative. At one time the inquisitors of Valencia had held unique permission from the archbishop of their city—Cardinal Borja, Don Felipe's own patron, who was frying more important fish in Rome—to act without episcopal representatives; but already in 1481 Borja had seen the coming storm and revoked that rare privilege, requiring the Valencian inquisitors henceforth to do the very little that they did only with his own concurrence as granted through his episcopal vicar-general in Valencia. Borja being possibly the most powerful man in Rome after Pope Sixtus himself, Valencia had felt emboldened to keep the king's new inquisitors barred outside the city gates since January—a circumstance that, had the author of the broadsheet known of it, he would surely have included along with his praise of Catalonia and Teruel.

Don Felipe spent the rest of that day and much of the night turning over plans for investigating this case, the best of which he discussed with Gubbio. Next morning, however, he found the problem solved for him when one Jaime González presented himself at the bishop's house.

This Jaime González was a thin lad nearing eighteen, who had walked to Daroca from Calatayud, where he was apprenticed to Maestre Micer the printer. He had set out on Friday, slept along the way when benighted in a field, and, upon reaching Daroca, come straight to the bishop, not being sure where else to go or whom else to see. His master had decided already on Thursday to send him, soon after the first copies of the Contrefuero were discovered in Calatayud. Both Maestre Micer and Jaime believed the printer's other apprentice to be El Santon de Aragon.

Don Felipe himself escorted Jaime to Fra Guillaume's tribunal, where he told his story at greater length. His fellow apprentice, Juan Calamocha, a year or two the older, was a dark, serious, hard-working young man who would rather think alone than drink with friends. He laughed freely, but rarely, and then over ironies that his companions often failed to see until he explained them…and sometimes not even then. He had a ringing voice of middle pitch, as El Santon was said to have—although neither Jaime nor Maestre Micer had ever seen El Santon—and on this past Wednesday, waking early after his midday nap to hear his press in operation, the master printer had gone down into his shop to find Juan at work with a companion who kept his face in shadow or otherwise hidden. Juan had explained that he sought only to better his skills, that he had bought paper with his own money instead of spending it for drink or gaming, and that what he printed was a sheet of love sonnets which he hoped to sell secretly to amorous young men. When berated for showing a stranger the mysteries of printing, he had accepted his master's rebuke in all meekness, but replied that he had already set his copy late the night before and shown his friend only as much as absolutely essential to provide the needed manual assistance, and that only after swearing him to secrecy. Next day the Contrefuero had appeared, and small irregularities in certain letters proved it to have come from Maestre Micer's press.

"Juan Calamocha," mused Don Felipe. "The name has a familiar sound to it." But so much was only natural, Juan having been a favorite name from the days of the Apostles, and the town of Calamocha lying about as near Daroca to the south as Calatayud lay to the north.

In kindly tones, Fra Guillaume asked the lad, "And is your fellow apprentice a baptized Christian?"

"If not, your Reverence, I do not know it. He goes to Mass on Sundays and workdays too, and I have never seen him eat meat on Friday or Saturday." After a moment's thought, Jaime added, "But I have never seen him eat pork at all, nor take Communion, even at Easter."

Fra Guillaume tapped the heretical passage in the Contrefuero and nodded. "It is past time, in any event, that we should make a visitation to Calatayud."

Truth to tell, it was so many years past time for Fra Guillaume to make a round of inquisitorial visitations anywhere that more heads than one or two might have wondered whether the Daroca tribunal even enjoyed authority to make such visitations, were it not that Aragon's old Papal Inquisition had probably never before been as popular as it was now. It had come suddenly to be understood as a kind of bulwark, however feeble, against the Royal Inquisition. Don Felipe had even heard the opinion that if Castile had only had its own Papal Inquisition from olden times, her queen could never have brought in this outrageous new one.

So far, Fray Tomás de Torquemada and the king's other newly appointed inquisitors had left the Daroca tribunal alone in its obscurity and inactivity. Thus, Fra Guillaume still had comparative freedom of action. Now, in the twilight of his service in the world, with the bishop's young Ordinary to assist him, he rose to the occasion with more energy, perhaps, than he had shown in half a century. As for Don Felipe, he had his secret conscience pricking him to offer what amends he could in the service of God and Holy Mother Church.

Between them, they were able to inspire their servants to make the necessary preparations with all dispatch. They set out at once after early Mass on Tuesday, the eighteenth of May, in a party of nine men—Fra Guillaume and his lay brother; Don Felipe, Gubbio, and a fresh-faced new Dominican scribe, Fray Pablo de María; the old former soldier Luis Albogado and three stout familiars—all mounted either on horses, asses, or good mules. Don Felipe rode the good little mule Castaña; she moved in a pleasant amble that left his stomach capable of holding the small feast with which the alcalde and other notables of Calatayud, forewarned first by Jaime González and next by the bishop's messenger, welcomed the inquisitor and his retinue upon their arrival late in the day.

So eager was his Honor the alcalde to fight the Royal Inquisition by assisting the Papal, that he provided them space in the town hall, with lodging for the churchmen and Gubbio in his own house, for Luis and the familiars in houses of his personal friends. After taking Wednesday to settle into these temporary quarters, Fra Guillaume and Don Felipe were particularly scrupulous to have the Edict of Grace read aloud on Thursday at every Mass in every church of Calatayud. Thus they pointed their disapproval at Fernando's new inquisitors, who had not had it read at all in Zaragoza, thereby rendering their Act of Faith on May the tenth, and the royal will that sanctioned it, of very questionable legality in proud Aragon.

Maestre Micer de Calatayud, the printer, who had actually appeared among the alcalde's welcoming officials, but been told to wait with his case until the tribunal was settled to begin its holy work, presented himself promptly on Thursday morning—the words of the Edict must still have been fresh in the mouths of the priests in some churches. He repeated substantially the same account he had earlier sent through his younger apprentice, of how he had first discovered Juan Calamocha printing his sheet during siesta hour eight days ago, believed it to be mere love sonnets until its appearance on church doors next day, and then decided at once to send Jaime to the proper authorities in Daroca.

"Can you so much as guess at the identity of that young man whom your apprentice had assisting him?" asked Fra Guillaume.

Maestre Micer, a thin and bespectacled man past his half-century mark, with hair still thick but almost entirely gray, and a comfortable bulge at his middle bespeaking the good meals of prosperity, shook his head. "That one kept himself well in shadow. I thought no more harm of it than that he feared to be seen meddling in mysteries of a trade not his own. Perhaps he is a stranger to me, come from Ateca or another place. He may even be go-between for El Santon and my poor Juan."

"We had thought," Fra Guillaume observed, "that you suspected Juan Calamocha himself of being El Santon."

The printer shrugged cautiously. "So indeed he may be. Or we could be mistaken. Who knows? But if El Santon is someone else, Juan may not have understood what he set into print. This happens to us, your Reverences. We come to see what we print only word by word, letter by letter."

"I know very little of your mysteries," Don Felipe put in, "but still it seems strange to me that he could do so much before you found him out. When he set his copy into print the night before, did you not glimpse his light? And where had he kept this paper purchased with his own money?"

"Juan has always been a good, quiet lad, one who works hard. Not like Jaime. Jaime..." Maestre Micer tapped his own forehead. "Jaime can muddle things sometimes, but I had no one else to send to your Reverences. Juan, I never had reason to worry about until now. As for his paper..." Another shrug. "He must have kept it with my own store. Even now, I trust him to have kept our accounts in all honesty."

"And you did not so much as glance at what he was printing, to see that it lacked the form and shape of sonnets?" Don Felipe persisted.

"It was still in my press, your Reverence. Hidden, you understand. And my eyes…" Maestre Micer removed his spectacles, held them up in one hand while blinking at the churchmen. "They are no longer sharp. I had no interest in young men's sonnets, no cause to doubt my good apprentice Juan. I admit I was surprised that he should put his hand to such sonnets, but still his industry seemed to me in itself commendable. We must print what people will buy, not always what we ourselves would like to print. I have sometimes thought that this may be the reason we come to pay so little attention to the sense of the words taken all together."

Fra Guillaume nodded. "Well, urge Juan Calamocha to come to us in his own person. Remind him of the Term of Grace. At present, even if he himself should be the author of this sheet, he may obtain pardon and mercy merely by confessing his guilt to us."

When the master printer had left, Don Felipe observed to Fra Guillaume, speaking softly so as to exclude their new scribe from the council, "Maestre Micer knows, and has long known, more than he admits."

"Of course, of course," the inquisitor replied quietly. "But is it worth our while to press him at this time? We have no evidence that Maestre Micer is other than a faithful son of the Church, and the people's good will is more important to us in this present crisis than the name of one accomplice in the printing of a document which contains, among many words of value, a single heretical statement."

They waited. Others came. More came to accuse themselves than to report their neighbors: word must have spread that the Papal Inquisition, as represented in the person of the mild old French Dominican, was indeed lenient and merciful, where the Royal Inquisition was not; and honored its promises, where the new Inquisition did not. Yet not enough came to save the tribunal from long intervals of waiting in idleness. Fear must be abroad that the new Inquisition would win out, after all, and absolutions gained from its predecessor might prove worse than useless, becoming so many hands pointing out whom to prosecute anew.

Perhaps it was this fear which prevented Juan Calamocha from being among those who presented themselves to Fra Guillaume.

At last, after three days of waiting in vain, Don Felipe went himself late on Saturday afternoon to the printer's shop. He went alone, with only Gubbio to attend him; nor did he name his destination to Fra Guillaume before setting out, saying only that he wished to walk after his hours of sitting. To idle view, he would have seemed merely a stroller with some thought of purchasing a book.

Maestre Micer de Calatayud, apparently less fearful of thieves than of spies, had divided his shop. Stepping in from the street, Don Felipe found himself in a rather narrow room where long shelves held piles of printed books awaiting purchasers and bindings. From an inner room came the sound of voices. Wrapping his churchly dignity closer about him, the priest bade his servant wait for him and penetrated the secrets of the inner room.

He found Maestre Micer showing both apprentices some secret of the mystery of their craft. The master printer looked up at him with a trace of alarm, but said simply, "Your Reverence, welcome to my shop." Jaime González, also recognizing the bishop's Ordinary, followed his master's lead and stood in silent attention.

By the look in the older apprentice's eyes, like that of some animal captured in a trap, Don Felipe saw that this lad recognized him also. A few moments of returning Juan Calamocha's gaze, and the priest understood why his name had seemed familiar from the first. The boy of twelve was still visible in the youth of nineteen.

"I wonder," Don Felipe began, ostensibly addressing Maestre Micer, "if your shop might have on hand any copies of the *Divina Commedia* of Dante Alighieri of Florence?"

"In which language, your Reverence?"

"The original. I have studied in Rome, and the great Florentine himself abhorred translations."

"It is unfortunate," the printer apologized uneasily, "that few of the people for whom I usually print are so blessed. The *Comedy* was among the first works I printed, it is long ago now, but only in a Castilian rendering. I believe some few copies may still remain, but your Reverence might find it poor stuff."

"Well, let me read a little and judge for myself. I should think one of your apprentices would be able to find it for me, would he not?"

Jaime González started forward, but his master, showing better comprehension, stopped him with one arm. "Juan, please attend his Reverence."

Keeping his eyes lowered, the older apprentice wove his way through the workaday clutter surrounding his master's press and silently accompanied Don Felipe back to the outer room.

Gubbio was hunkered on the floor, idly rolling dice against himself. At Don Felipe's nod, he touched the dice to his head, returned them to his pouch, and slipped outside to continue his wait.

Still without speaking, Juan Calamocha stooped to one of the lower shelves and fetched up a sheaf of pages, which he presented to Don Felipe, his gaze never rising higher than their hands.

He had found it with little or no trouble, and the pages were already cut. "Have you yourself read this work?" the priest inquired in normal speaking tones.

The younger man nodded.

"How did you find it in comparison with your own vision, Juan de Calamocha?" Don Felipe did not raise his voice. "Or are you still, in the sight of God, properly called Mehmoud Aben Fazoud?"

The apprentice shuddered violently. No doubt he had guessed on Don Felipe's entrance that the Inquisition remembered him, but hope must have been growing within his soul as long as the Ordinary postponed his move. Don Felipe felt a pang of remorse. He had meant to be tactful, not cruel.

"Sir," murmured the apprentice, "how...if I were to make you my confession?"

"It is what we have hoped. Come on Monday to Fra Guillaume, and, under the Terms of Grace—"

Juan shook his head. "No—I meant...my Confession. Here. To you. Under the Seal." He could not have known how his words tore into the priest's soul.

Yet Don Felipe answered steadily enough, "That, and much else, hangs upon whether you are indeed Juan or still, correctly speaking, Mehmoud. It is of vital importance, young man: Have you or have you not yet received the sacrament of Baptism?"

For a moment—a moment in which Don Felipe seemed to feel his own heart suspend its beating—the apprentice hesitated. Then, at last, he ashamedly shook his head.

The priest released his breath in a long sigh. "Then neither I nor any other Christian priest can hear you in sacramental Confession, for reception of all other sacraments depends upon reception of the first. As God's loyal servant, I must urge you most vehemently to remember that death may take any of us at any time, and to put off your salvation no longer. But, in a worldly sense, your unbaptized state gives you certain purely legal advantages. The Holy Inquisition does not presume to judge unbaptized souls."

"You judged me seven years ago," the youth protested, lifting his head for the first time in a sudden show of courage.

"We judged you, not for writing down your childhood vision, but for giving it to your Christian playfellow. Doing this was in some sense proselytism and rendered you liable to the Inquisition, as you would not otherwise have been. Now, this Contrefuero of yours contains what would be, from a Christian pen, the gravest of heresies; but we find that we cannot call it proselytism, since you do not ask your readers to join with you in denying the Real Presence of Christ in the Most Holy Eucharist, but only in resisting the false Inquisition and certain bloody warfare."

"I do not deny the Real Presence!"

"Do you deny authorship of the Contrefuero?"

The apprentice stared back into the priest's eyes. Reading honest surprise, Don Felipe guessed that Juan—or Mehmoud—had let the damning words slip out in the heat of composition, and truly forgotten their presence in the midst of what must seem, to him, his broadsheet's weightier matters.

He shook his head. "It is mine. I wrote it. I am proud to have written it and tacked it up for our people of Aragon to read."

"Well, if you should print it again, remember to omit these few words: 'the wafer that they call.' It would be best, indeed, to omit any passage dealing with any Christian sacrament. And, while your words about our Holy Child of Daroca are neither false, as far as they go, nor tainted with any heresy, they seem likelier to lose than to win certain Christians over to your stand in these other matters. Also, no matter whose is the guilt before God, it is the secular arm rather than the spiritual which lights the actual fires."

Looking astonished to find the priest more ally than persecutor, the apprentice nodded.

Belatedly, Felipe remembered another point or two. Late as it was to ask, he went on, "And are you 'El Santon,' or is that prophet the man who helped you print your Contrefuero?"

"No, but he is unbaptized, too. And I am El Santon de Aragon. For lack of a better."

Don Felipe nodded. "Take care, then, that you say nothing which could be understood as trying to win the Christians among your hearers away from Holy Mother Church herself, and you will be safe enough, at least from the true Inquisition. And, for the sake of our good Fra Guillaume, you might come to us again on Monday and repeat what you have told me." Should he add that they had deeply regretted the necessity of burning Mehmoud's little book seven years ago? No, best not lend the youth too much encouragement. "I think," the priest added, finding the Castilian *Commedia* still in his hands, "that I will buy this book. I know a binder in Daroca who will clothe it nicely."

While the apprentice wrapped the pages in clean cloth, Don Felipe returned to the press room to assure Maestre Micer and his second apprentice, with a few words and payment for the book, that as far as the Papal Inquisition was concerned, the matter of El Santon's Contrefuero was as good as settled, and all in this house could rest easily.

When he came back to the outer room, he found Juan—or, rather, Mehmoud—standing still as a board, his face ashen and his stare fixed. Mutely, he handed over the book in its wrapping. His hands trembled.

"Rest easy in your mind, my friend," the priest reassured him. "Our ancient Inquisition plays no tricks. I have asked you to present yourself merely in order to settle Fra Guillaume's mind."

The apprentice shook his head, but seemed unable to bring forth words.

"Well, then, you need not come at all," Don Felipe added. "I shall settle his mind myself." Touching the youth's shoulder as in fellowship, he took his purchase and stepped into the street.

"Your Loftiness missed a piece of news just now," his servant greeted him.

"What is that, Gubbio?"

Lounging against the wall, Gubbio dug at his teeth with the ivory pick for which he had spent part of his earliest wages in Don Felipe's employ. "Fra Guillaume will likely have heard it already," he went on, speaking around the toothpick. "It seems by the gossip of the street that the crier appeared before his Honor the alcalde's house scant moments after our setting out for Maestre Micer's shop."

"This must be a momentous scrap of news," Don Felipe observed, "for you to draw out its telling in this manner."

"I flatter myself that I am no such unmannerly lout as the ruffian who came bawling it out all down this street, so loudly I marvel that you did not hear it with your own consecrated ears."

"I was with the printer in his inner room just now. We heard nothing," Don Felipe replied. But, he thought, Juan—El Santon—must have heard; and as he remembered the lad's expression, cold fear squeezed his heart.

Gubbio carefully put his toothpick away. "Fray Tomás de Torquemada's new breed must be finding Zaragoza ripe for the harvest. Fray Gaspar Juglar and Maestre Pedro Arbués have announced a second Act of Faith for…let me see…the week after next, on the third day of June. This time they promise a burning or three."

"My God!" Don Felipe whispered. "Two Acts within a month? …El Santon has shown himself a prophet in truth!"

He turned and went back inside the shop. Mehmoud, or El Santon, or Juan Calamocha, by whatever name God might know him, stood exactly as before. Not even he could have foreseen that his warning, "How much longer before Fray Gaspar and Maestre Pedro light their fires," could be fulfilled so soon as this.

"Catalonia and Teruel do not stand utterly alone." Don Felipe spoke not too loudly, but without preamble, and more as if addressing the room itself than its only other occupant. "Valencia too holds out. Since January, the city of Valencia has barred her gates against Fernando's royal and foreign inquisitors, pointing proudly to her ancient fueros that allow Valencians by birth and them alone to hold office in their native land."

With a single glance at Mehmoud's face, to see that his words had impressed their meaning, Don Felipe quit the shop for good.

Within the week, more copies of El Santon's Contrefuero appeared. This second printing altered not a word as to which arm lit the actual fires; but it omitted all reference to Pyx, Blessed Sacrament or the Holy Child of Daroca, and it added Valencia's bravery to that of Catalonia and Teruel.

On the third day of June, the royal inquisitors, those creatures of Tomás de Torquemada, relaxed two men and the effigy of one woman to the secular arm for burning. By then hotter fires of the spirit were already ablaze throughout Fernando's kingdom. And who was to say, Felipe de Alhama de Karnattah mused in his most secret heart, that Gaspar Juglar and Pedro Arbués were themselves less worthy of the stake than were those whom they had sent there?

CHAPTER 12

THE DREAM OF THE DEATH OF PEDRO ARBUÉS

He thought at first that he stood in a great, vast cave. Slowly he saw it to be a cathedral. Almost he seemed to know it, yet where one atom of time brought a wisp of near-recognition, the next blew it away again like the smoke of incense before strong wind.

This much was clear: its floors were bare as though swept by that selfsame wind; its columns wide and distant; its arches incredibly high; its vaults lost to sight. Which was perhaps as it should be. A cathedral's vaults ought to merge with Heaven, ought to touch the seat of God's infinitude—that same infinitude which the sanctified building and the holy sacraments enacted therein funneled down into humanity. But here and now, in the starkness of this night, those high vaults might as well have touched blank emptiness, draining desolation rather than grace down from above.

Had not God rained fire and brimstone down upon Sodom and Gomorrah? And yet were not brimstone and fire the proper adjuncts, not of Heaven, but of Hell? But this place was cold, its stones colder than winter, its air colder than lonely death.

How, Felipe began to wonder, could he see as much as he saw? It was surely moonless night, for not even the windows themselves, which ought to be stained glass—pale faces of saints clothed in rich colors—could be seen anywhere beyond the columns; and the votive candles created only little caverns of light that illuminated nothing beyond their own stands, making all the rest seem darker yet.

He became aware of a sound high overhead, faint at first...how long it might have been going on before he first noticed it, he had no idea... but then suddenly enlarging, approaching, rushing over him with a roar that winked the candles out. A crash resounded from far in front of him, causing the whole structure to shake. Then, silence.

"Great-grandfather," a woman's voice said out of the silence.

He turned and saw her standing beside a column, her trousers and short tunic almost the color of the stone. "Rosemary," he acknowledged. "What place is this?"

"Some people might call it Plato's Cave."

"What sound was that a moment ago?"

For answer, she stepped forward and lifted her right hand, which held a long tube of metal with a knob on one end. He supposed it to be some sleek kind of mace, though the way she bore it implied no threat. But it was no mace. It was a strange, flameless torch, as he saw when she caused the swollen end to send a beam of white light forth to the far end of the aisle.

On the dais where the high altar should have been, a statue stood instead: a Virgin Mary of the Pillar, wielding her rosary like a whip.

Rosemary led the way forward. Don Felipe followed close at her side. The cold beam of her torchlight shortened with their progress, closing in on the dais.

Across its steps, at the feet of the Virgin, sprawled a dark bundle. Step by step, as Felipe approached, he saw it to be a corpse. Streams of blood ebbed from it over the stones; splotches of blood bespattered the statue's carven skirts. The head of the corpse lay at a painful angle, its neck half severed, eyes staring in blank surprise beneath the edge of a steel cap.

"Who is it?" whispered the priest. "The English bishop Thomas Becket?"

Shaking her head, she pointed her light at a few links of chain mail showing beneath the edge of the murdered man's vestment. "We're in the cathedral of Zaragoza."

"Zaragoza? But—"

"It doesn't always look like this. We're seeing its spiritual truth right now."

"Then this man is..." Don Felipe tried to study the dead face, distorted and bloodsmeared in the murk of the ghostly cathedral. "Not their Majesties' new inquisitor from Castile?"

Rosemary nodded. "San Pedro Arbués. Rome gets around to canonizing him in 1867, but the Church never acts especially proud of him outside of Spain. Not like Becket."

"My God! Who assassinated—martyred him?"

"A few desperate Jews and judaizers."

"No! Ah, no! Poor fools! Why make such a move as this?"

"Had their backs up against a wall full of nails," the woman replied, quietly grim.

Don Felipe looked from her face to the Virgin of the Pillar. He believed he saw a certain resemblance.

"But this will turn the people against them!" he protested. "The last resistance will crumble, and we will have this new Inquisition thrust down our throats even here in proud Aragon, whether we wish it or no. It could not have turned out better for their Majesties if—wait! Is it not more likely that this is the work of the royal court, plotted so deeply that the right hand knew not what the left was doing, disguised so as to cast the unhappy Jews into odium?"

"Lovely thought, grandfather, but history says judaizers killed Arbués. Becket was the one with the good luck to have a king blamed for his martyrdom. If it's any comfort, at least this time they hit directly at one of their enemies. Another five centuries, and people who get desperate enough for justice are going to murder anyone they find handy."

Her words made still less sense than this martyrdom of the inquisitor from Castile. Could they not have seen that to kill Maestre Pedro Arbués was but to lop off one of the hydra's heads so that nine more would grow in its place? Looking again at the corpse, Felipe saw new miters springing already, like the tiny caps of new mushrooms, from the stones watered by the martyr's blood.

"But wait!" he cried. "When is this to happen?"

"Even as you watched," the woman answered sadly, her voice so much more gentle that he jerked his head round to look at her again.

She was no longer Rosemary, but Raymonde.

CHAPTER 13

THE COUNCIL OF FAITH

"Adsumus Domine, Sancte Spiritus..." Fray Junípero began the prayer, the others bowing their heads and joining in their voices to implore the blessing and guidance of God upon their day's work. Six grave men, sitting in quiet dignity around the long table with its pitcher of water and tray of wafers intermingled with dried fruit.

"...in Nomine Tuo..."

Six grave churchmen, facing what for them was a morning's work, but for the subjects of that work, pain or release, death or life. And for one of the six churchmen... Ah, God, have You truly delivered my ancient enemy into my hands? Or is it Your holy will to test my poor honor?

"Veni ad nos..."

Fray Junípero de la Sangre Sagrada, Spanish Dominican of the strictest observance, senior inquisitor for Daroca and all her environs, according to the new order thrust upon the people of Aragon by their king and his Castilian queen. Incorruptible, upright, and zealous—sometimes, it might seem, overly zealous—in his efforts for the glory of God, Fray Junípero would hear of no other refreshments than water and wafers to sustain the Council in its dry labor, with a few figs and raisins as grudging dispensation to the less austere among his fellow laborers.

Don Guillen de Valderrobles, who had replaced Don Felipe as ordinary to his grace the bishop of Daroca. Of middle years, round face, and little ambition, Don Guillen seemed manifestly content to take his ease at the apex of his mortal career. As much as a middle-aged Spanish secular priest could resemble an aged French Dominican, Don Guillen resembled his near namesake Fra Guillaume (who had retired, following the triumph of the new Inquisition, to his motherhouse beyond the Pyrenees, there to die within a few years in comfortable odor of sanctity).

And Don Felipe de Granada, still secretly bemused at finding himself Fray Junípero's fellow inquisitor for Daroca and her environs. Surely, he might have refused King Fernando's appointment, which had taken him by surprise after his steadfast, if quiet and prudent, protests against bringing the Royal Inquisition into Aragon. Had the monarch wished to enlist one more former foe into the ranks of his friends and allies, or had Fernando even been aware of Felipe's opposition? And had it been some idealistic thought that he might help temper the new Inquisition in its most fiery excesses that prompted Don Felipe to accept the apointment, or had it been the secret worm of guilt driving him to condemn himself to the long penance of sitting in inquisitorial judgment on his fellow offenders against divine and churchly law?

"Esto salus et suggestor et effector judiciorum nostrorum, Qui solus cum Deo Patre et Ejus Filio nomen posides gloriosum...."

Here, also, their chosen consultors, one jurist of Canon Law and two learned students of theology:

Fray Juan de la Misericordia de Dios, Dominican theologian, Fray Junípero's creature though outwardly resembling him in little, being silver-fringed around the tonsure to his principal's black-fringed prime, and having obviously indulged in all the dietary privileges and dispensations to which his venerable age entitled him—already, half furtively, he was eying the fruit. Yet if his body was soft and wrinkled, his theology was not.

Fray Clemente de María, wiry and vigorous, his eyes appropriately closed in full concentration upon the prayer. It was he, ironically, whom the uninformed eye might pick out as the most fiery ascetic, after the senior inquisitor himself, at that table; yet Fray Clemente's formation in the wise old order of Saint Benedict led him to forgive much, understand more, and seek always for balance. He had been Don Felipe's candidate for this table, against whom Fray Junípero could find no sufficient grounds for exclusion.

And Fray Roberto de la Sagrada Familia, sportively called "The Silent Franciscan" for thinking more than he spoke. He was their jurist, a studious conventual of moderate frame and late middle age, the ordinary's nominee to this Council of Faith.

"...ut in sinistrum nos ignorantia non trahat, non favor infectat, non acceptio muneris vel person' corrumpat..."

The senior inquisitor had proved himself, time and again, ever and always to prefer the harshest way, whereas the ordinary favored leniency in almost all cases. I have but to follow Fray Junípero's lead for once, thought Don Felipe, and Manuel Urtigo suffers in this life as well as in the next—the murderer of my family enters Hell through the most fiery of mortal gates! Let me but vote with my fellow inquisitor, and it matters not which way Don Guillen casts his vote. The simple majority of us three, no matter how our consultors may vote: that, until such time as the Suprema may clearly direct otherwise, is the rule we follow, in accordance with the wisdom of his eminence our bishop of Daroca. And, while the consultors' votes may sometimes sway Don Guillen's opinion, they never sway that of Fray Junípero, and they need not sway mine.

"...ut hic a Te in nullo dissentiat sententia nostra, ut in futuro pro bene gestis consequamur premia sempiterna. Amen."

The opening prayer was over, and the Dominican theologian reaching for a date with one hand even as he finished crossing himself on forehead, lips, and chest with the other.

Ah, God, am I to serve You as instrument of vengeance, or of mercy? Which way, for this man—this murderer, this "Scourge of Axtilan," this Manuel Urtigo—lies justice? It was the question with which Don Felipe's secret heart had wrestled since Manuel's accusers had first brought the case to the Holy Inquisition.

Fray Clemente poured water for himself and held the pitcher poised, with an inquiring look at his patron. A beam of sunlight piercing the glass vessel cast small spangles of rainbow like divine largesse over the table. Finding his mouth dry as sawdust, Don Felipe nodded and held forth his goblet. The well in the courtyard of Don Feliz de Sarmiento y Tobogo de Luna gave clear, delicious water—water befitting everything else in this fine, modern house which the wealthy merchant had in his piety turned over to the Holy Office—water much more grateful, to Don Felipe's tongue, than the lead-piped stuff of certain great cities.

There were other cases to discuss before that of Manuel Urtigo. Among them that of the unfortunate printer Maestre Juan de Calamocha, or Mehmoud Aben Fazoud as he might still properly be called, once again under investigation.

"First," said the senior inquisitor, "we must consider the case of Doña Jeronima de Mesquita y Valderrama, accused of wilfully and contumaciously cleaving to the heresy that fornication is no sin."

"This is no heresy, as such," said Don Felipe's Benedictine. "It is merely grievous error and mortal sin."

"It is heresy!" roared Fray Junípero.

"It is mortal sin, pure and simple," the Benedictine threw back quietly but stubbornly. "The Inquisition has no right to hold this woman imprisoned for…it is the fifth month now, is it not?"

"How carefully he keeps count of the months!" Fray Junípero's sleek Dominican put in. "Can our esteemed colleague be among those men who mourn Doña Jeronima's absence as deeply as she mourns theirs?"

Don Felipe kept his thoughts neutrally to himself. Even though she had tried to seduce him (at least, so he supposed), no doubt in some attempt to buy her freedom (and yet she was notorious, and he—he flattered himself—able enough to draw women's attention had he so chosen), Doña Jeronima meant little to him. The lady was lovely, but in his heart and body the inquisitor remained true to his lifetime love, the lost Morayma.

After a cough, the ordinary observed, "It is true that Doña Jeronima makes no secret of her error—"

"No secret!" exclaimed Fray Junípero. "Why, man, she propagates and dogmatizes the heresy broadcast, among all who will listen!"

"No heresy!" Fray Clemente repeated. "Sin and error only—a matter for her confessor, not for the Inquisition!"

"Heresy!" Fray Juan shot back. "Arrant, wilful heresy!"

"Error," argued Don Guillen. "Error born of the royal tolerance of brothels. If you would stamp out this particular so-called 'heresy,' persuade your king to outlaw the free sale of love and end the popular confusion between what is moral and what is merely allowed."

Fray Juan snorted. "Next you will tell us that this error springs from the prophet Daniel's taking the part of the seductress Susanna against her victims!"

Remembering Doña Jeronima's smile, her soft nudge and furtive wink, Don Felipe inquired, "Did not our Savior Himself take the part of the adultress against those who would have stoned her?"

"He did not take her part!" thundered Fray Junípero. "Beware of imputing sin to our sinless Lord! He simply ordered that the first stone be cast by a man without sin." The senior inquisitor's aspect suggested that, had he himself been present, he would unhesitatingly have hurled that first stone.

The Benedictine protested, "The sins of the flesh are the sins of beasts: unthinking, and our Lord stands always ready to forgive such. Whereas heresy is a sin of the mind—"

"Such creatures as La Doña Jeronima," said Fray Junípero, "use the sins of the mind to justify those of the flesh. They wilfully make the mind into the slave of the body. This woman is a heretic, and her sin is heresy!"

"Fray Roberto," the ordinary asked his jurist, "what is your opinion?"

The Fransciscan cleared his throat, smiled, and said, "The woman is guilty of mortal sin and grievous confusion. To win salvation, she must be absolved and corrected, but both these tasks are matters for her confessor—assuming she does not seduce him first—and not for the Holy Office. My brothers of the Inquisition, do you not have work enough, and more than enough, with true heretics and relapsos? I vote that this woman be set free and a confessor found for her whose age and sanctity place him beyond temptation."

"I cast my vote with that of Fray Roberto," the Benedictine said at once.

"And I," replied Fray Juan, glaring at his fellow consultors, "vote that this is notorious heresy, and the woman belongs to the Holy Office by right!"

The consultative votes were cast, with no power unless to sway the opinions of the principals...and in this case, as in so many others, the minds of both inquisitors and ordinary were already made up. By Fray Junípero's expression, he understood in advance that he was defeated. The ordinary voted this proposition to be mortal sin only, because his reverence of Daroca, like all bishops, was determined to keep jurisdiction over such sins from the Holy Office as long as possible; and Don Felipe voted Doña Jeronima to be no heretic, not because she had smiled at him (of which he said nothing), but because he agreed that the Holy Office could best serve God by limiting its area of endeavor, like a lens concentrating the rays of the sun. A pretty argument; but, by the frown which the senior inquisitor cast along with his own fruitless vote, Fray Junípero once again regarded his colleague as a Ganelon, a Judas, and far more culpable than the ordinary, whose vote was mere loyalty to his bishop.

"As to the case of Ximèn Ximenès of Tafalla," Fray Junípero went on, with a disgruntled show of laying aside the documents relating to the lady and picking up those relating to the rogue, "will you also argue that the crime of impersonating a holy inquisitor is mere mortal sin and no matter for the Inquisition?"

Their memories needed little refreshing on the facts of the case, nor were these facts in any dispute. Ximèn, a wandering rogue, had accosted one Doña Alvara de Santillon y Cortilla with the claim that neighbors had accused her to the Holy Office but that he, as an inquisitor of high standing, would bury the whole matter for a certain trifling consideration. Being an elderly widow of prouder name than fortune, of cleaner conscience and greater trust in her neighbors than the scoundrel credited her with, and of sublime confidence in the purity of her own, if not her late husband's, Old Christian blood, the lady had informed him she had nothing to fear from the Holy Office, and then sought it out herself to report him.

"It is not heresy, as such," opined the Benedictine, "and yet by its very nature, I think we must agree that it belongs to the Holy Office to penance."

"Indeed," said Don Felipe, "for it may well be said that we were its intended victim, equally with Doña Alvara. If this rogue aimed at her purse, he aimed tangentially at the Inquisition's good name."

"The only question, then," Fray Juan said, munching a date, "is how to make this scoundrel refund the money, when he has none, and how further to penance him, for example and public edification."

"He has no money that he has told us of," Fray Junípero said darkly. "So far, God alone shares the secret of whatever funds he may hold hidden elsewhere, to make the Inquisition house and feed him at its own expense."

"For our own expense," said Don Felipe, "we must lay the money to his charge until repaid, and hope. But for Doña Alvara, since she wisely gave him nothing, I do not see how we can force him to repay her."

"She gave him no money," said the ordinary. "He has, however, cost her somewhat in reputation, grief, and time."

"The time of an old busybody of a widow!" Fray Juan snorted.

"Time that she might otherwise have spent in prayer," Fray Clemente rebuked the Dominican. "To judge by her fearlessness when threatened, Doña Alvara doubtless prays much and often."

The senior inquisitor said, "Too great piety in a lay person is in itself matter for suspicion."

"Let be Doña Alvara," Don Felipe said, thereby undoing any redemption he might have won in Fray Junípero's eyes by agreeing that the Inquisition should have the punishment of Ximèn Ximenès. "She is an Old Christian of blameless repute—which can scarcely have been scratched by the rogue's assault, uttered as it was privately; and she showed little grief in reporting him."

"Nevertheless," declared Fray Junípero, "in wholesome penance, he must repay the sum he tried to exact!"

"Then let him repay it to the Holy Office," Fray Juan proposed, with a comfortable glance at the senior inquisitor.

"It cannot hurt to add it to his charge," Don Felipe agreed. "Moses did succeed, by God's grace, in striking water from the rock, though he had to strike twice."

"You have wilfully misread the passage," Fray Junípero told him with a scowl, but Don Felipe paid it little attention, for thinking that, had he himself not saved his servant from a life of roguery and vagabondage, it might well have been Gubbio standing where Ximèn stood.

"That," nodded Roberto, "with two hundred lashes and a sentence of, say, five years in his majesty's galleys, should make of Ximèn Ximenès a sufficiently colorful example for the coming Act of Faith."

So it was agreed, the vote quickly taken with not one dissenting voice, and the Council of Faith moved on to its next subject.

"Francesca Cascajo," said the senior inquisitor, glaring around the table as fiercely as though he had not had his will in the case of Ximèn the impersonator. "She is under grave suspicion of heresy on the following grounds: that she soaks meat in water before cooking, and fries in olive oil rather than honest lard; that she has been witnessed cutting the lump of fat from a leg of mutton before cooking; that she is known to have refused on at least three separate occasions to eat pork, and once to have refused the gift of a rooster found dead of natural causes; and that she openly slices bread with the edge of her knife turned away from her body."

If Don Felipe's servant had somewhat in common with the rogue Ximèn, Felipe himself had somewhat in common with Francesca Cascajo. He pointed out, "She has correctly identified all of these charges save one, and explained her actions as springing from the delicacy of her digestion and, in the instance of the dead rooster, from a personal experience in her youth of falling seriously ill after eating a capon found dead of unknown causes."

Fray Junípero snorted, but before he could speak, Felipe's Benedictine put in,

"There is no heresy in these actions in and of themselves. They are merely signs and indications that there *might* be heresy in the household."

Fray Junípero demanded, "Did not our Lord Himself, in the vision He sent to his first vicar, command us to eat all meats?"

To Felipe's astonishment, his colleague's fellow Dominican, speaking around a mouthful of raisins and dates, said, "He declared all meats clean and worthy to be eaten. He did not command every good Christian to eat all these meats at all times. Else every Order that practises abstinence—indeed, the general rule of abstinence for all Christians on certain days—would fall under suspicion." Fray Juan would probably never have requested such a luxury as dried fruits at this solemn conference, but he obviously knew how to avail himself of what he found set before him: already the plate was half empty.

Don Felipe pointed out, "Francesca Cascajo has never, in all her months in our prison, refused to eat boiled pork, and both those two times that she left fried pork untasted, she also failed to finish the rest of the meal—fruit, cheese, gazpacho, even bread and cake—pleading the distress of her stomach and showing certain signs that she spoke truth."

"They are clever, these heretics!" said Fray Junípero. "The Devil knows how to teach his servants subtlety."

"It was a subtlety, then," Don Felipe argued, "that eluded our own physician, who pronounced the woman distressed in fact, and directed that she be fed on porridge and certain herbs for several days. For myself, I am satisfied of her innocence."

"And the charge that she did *not* identify?" demanded Fray Junípero. "Are you also satisfied that her habit of cutting bread with the knife turned away from the body is another sign of *innocence*?"

"So did my own mother turn the blade away from her body when slicing bread," Felipe replied steadily. "And the reason for this was because once in youth, when cutting the common way, by accident she cut open her left breast. I myself saw the scar when she suckled my younger brother. Small doubt that Francesca Cascajo failed to identify the charge because to her this habit is so old and innocent a precaution that she understands no harm in it."

"So your own mother had a scar upon her breast!" the senior inquisitor returned sarcastically. "Let us have this Francesca stripped for torture, then, and see whether she also has a scarred breast!"

"And if she does not?" exclaimed Don Felipe. "Will you work the pulleys yourself, with your own hands and arms and back, as you did upon that poor wretch Fidenzo?"

"If necessary in the work of God!" Fray Junípero shot back. "For lack of any competent and willing torturer, I will! By God! In Castile there would be no difficulty finding workers for the field!"

In Castile, where torturers were trained to work for the civil courts, which was forbidden in Aragon by ancient privilege.

"But why did she fail to identify this charge, along with the others?" asked Fray Juan. "Was it not mentioned in the last Edict of Faith?"

"She cannot read," Fray Clemente, who seemed himself to have read the case more carefully than had his fellow consultor, reminded Fray Juan. "And she missed its public reading—which absence she dutifully if mistakenly listed among the charges—due to nursing her sick husband."

Don Felipe said, "For the details of that edict, she relied upon the very neighbor who accused her of the irregularity with the knife."

"She had three accusers," Fray Junípero grumbled. "And named only the other two as personal enemies."

"Scripture itself," said Don Felipe, "counsels us to caution before passing judgment upon the word of a single witness."

Fray Clemente asked, "This woman comes of Old Christian family, does she not?"

"So far as can be proven," Fray Junípero grudgingly admitted.

Fray Roberto, the jurist, spoke. "I see no reason to proceed even as far as the threat of torture. Let us emulate our Lord in His mercy rather than His justice, and suspend this case with no further action. You can always reopen it should the woman indulge in any suspicious actions not related to her diet."

That did not end the argument, for Fray Junípero was like an angry dog with a bone it would not relinquish willingly to anyone. When at last he admitted the vote to be taken, even his own fellow Dominican voted simply that Francesca Cascajo appear in the coming Act of Faith and be made to abjure *de levi*, while Fray Clemente voted along with the jurist for immediate suspension of the case and release of the prisoner. Don

Felipe hesitated in his mind, for the woman was far from young, and abjuration *de levi* would at least put a more final period to her present case than would mere suspension. Yet it would also leave a blacker mark against her name, so when the ordinary voted for suspension, Felipe did likewise, outflanking the senior inquisitor for the second time that day.

Had they uncovered in Francesca Cascajo's bloodline any ancestors converted from the creed of either Moses or Mohammed within the last century, it would have gone less gently with her. Moreover, Don Felipe reflected, having been thwarted of two public examples for the next Act of Faith would render Fray Junípero all the more ferocious concerning those cases yet to be discussed.

As far as touched the brigand Manuel, Don Felipe had yet to determine in his own mind whether to use or oppose the temper of the senior inquisitor—whether to accept the chance for revenge that God might be offering him on a silver platter, or to resist what could equally as well be diabolic temptation and preserve his own honor.

But between the earlier cases and Manuel Urtigo's came that of the hapless printer of Calamocha.

Whether he was still in God's eyes Mehmoud Aben Fazoud, Don Felipe did not know—thus far, he had given his name simply but stubbornly as Maestre Juan de Calamocha, and meekly but stubbornly refused to voice or pen any speculation whatever upon his own case. No doubt his earlier experiences with the Papal Inquisition had given him a certain caution of the Royal...but perhaps also, Don Felipe feared, a less than justified confidence in his present chances to escape once again relatively unscathed.

Following the completion of his apprenticeship with Maestre Micer de Calatayud, he had returned to set up his own printing shop, partially funded by his father, in his native town. The elder Juan Delgado de Calamocha, while ever both honorable and loving, had begun to fail in health, and could say with certitude only that his son had never, to his knowledge, received the sacrament of Baptism in or near their town of Calamocha—whether he might have received it in Calatayud or elsewhere during his years as apprentice, the father could not testify.

This time, the witness against Juan-Mehmoud was a printed pamphlet from his own shop. Ostensibly a lampoon upon certain abuses of royal power and injustices in secular courts, it would have held no interest at all for the Inquisition but for one passage, called to Fray Junípero's attention by a courtier of King Fernando, in which Saint James, showing the unnamed narrator a place of burning, asked how mortal men dared suppose that their fierceness mirrored the temper of God, or that whom they condemned to brief fire on earth, the merciful Christ would condemn to eternal fire in Hell.

In this passage, the senior inquisitor of Daroca saw heretical dogmatizing, for which the author, baptized or not, could himself be burned. Thus, it became even more important to ascertain the exact nature of the printed words than the sacramental estate of their author.

"I suppose there is no doubt," Fray Junípero's fellow Dominican remarked, reaching for the last dried date, "that printer and author are indeed one and the same?"

There was no doubt in Don Felipe's mind: he saw in the pamphlet the zeal of El Santon's *Contrefuero*, joined with the imaginative power, matured now, that he still remembered from Mehmoud's youthful Vision of San Juan de Calamocha. For the moment, however, the junior inquisitor remained guardedly silent.

"Fray Pablo," said the senior inquisitor, referring to the tribunal's notary (not now present, for the Council's freedom of discussion) "has drawn up a complete list of all the authors named in works from Maestre Juan's press. All, without exception, are either long deceased or, so far, of unquestioned orthodoxy. It is unlikely that the printer himself has penned every pamphlet from his shop, but he has named for us none of the anonymous providers of fodder for his press. In his continued silence on all matters touching his own situation, we have no choice but to hold him equally guilty, if not identical, with the author."

As his senior paused for breath, Don Felipe put in, "I have it on the word of Maestre Micer de Calatayud, a printer of unquestioned loyalty to Holy Church, that in the mysteries of their craft printers often concern themselves so thoroughly with the texts they set letter by letter and word by word, as to lose all sense of the meaning of the whole."

Fray Junípero retorted, "They must read and understand these texts before deciding to print them!"

"Not necessarily," Don Guillen replied. "An author may bring his manuscript to the printer, along with the required sum of money, and the printer, being hard pressed with work and desirous of payment, may set it into print without first reading it."

"Maestre Juan did not scruple to set his imprint to it," said Fray Juan.

In almost the same moment, Fray Clemente asked, "And what of printers who set books in Latin and Greek without themselves knowing these languages?"

"For them," Fray Junípero declared, answering the Benedictine rather than his own creature, "they must rely on the guidance of orthodox scholars, and be held accountable for any heresy they may print through failure to obtain the same."

Don Guillen muttered, "That is arguable."

Seeming not to notice the ordinary's words, Fray Junípero continued, "But the pamphlet before us is in the vernacular, leaving its printer no cover of excuse whatever! Even assuming that he is not also its author—and, if he is not, he must be made to tell us who is!"

"First," said Don Felipe, "we must ascertain whether or not the words are truly heretical—"

"Can anyone question—" Fray Junípero began.

But for once Don Felipe continued his own speech without deferring to his senior's interruption. "It is, after all, a mere lampoon on the secular power, with never a word touching upon the spiritual."

"Can anyone question," Fray Junípero demanded, "that the author intends this burning-place as a slanderous reflection upon our own Holy Office?"

"I can question it," said the ordinary. "On grounds that the Inquisition burns no victims, but rather protects them as long as she can from the vengeance of the secular arm, always and ever begging it to temper justice with mercy when at last she has no other choice but to relax them."

The jurist nodded. "It is the State that tears out the weeds. The Church merely relinquishes them in sorrow and grieving."

"But, my brothers in Christ," said Fray Clemente, "I have sifted this passage, pondering it deeply and prayerfully, with close attention to all the works in our library, and, for myself, I find in it no heresy."

"It reeks of heresy!" cried Fray Junípero.

"Hear me out, brother," the Benedictine insisted. "True, put into the mouth of Saint James, and naming God and Christ directly, these lines are certainly intended in a religious sense, and as such have no place in a secular lampoon. As for the proposition itself, rash and scandalous it may well be, even impious, and, possibly, ill-sounding. But heretical in the strictest sense, no."

"I call it blasphemous, schismatic, insulting, and, at the least, savoring of heresy if not actually heretical," Fray Juan said around a mouthful of raisins.

"Blasphemous it certainly is not," Fray Clemente argued, "for in no way can these words be construed as an insult to God or Christ. Insulting to king and queen, justicia, secular judges, and various other officials it undeniably and intentionally is—many of them even by name—and it is true that they are good Christians; but, in context, the insult is aimed at their secular authority and not at their religion."

"You will at least admit schismatic, savoring of heresy, and erroneous, will you not?" Fray Junípero demanded, tempering his wrath with sarcasm.

"Not without first settling the question of whether there is any heresy here at all," Fray Clemente insisted. "And I repeat: for my part, I find none!"

"It is blatant apocatastasis," said Fray Juan. "For which Origen was condemned by the Council of Constantinople."

"Origen was condemned for various points," argued the Benedictine, "but not for the belief that all would eventually be saved. Else the great Jerome himself, as well as Gregory of Nazianzus, Titus of Bostra, and my own namesake Clement of Alexandria would likewise have been condemned."

Fray Juan frowned. "Condemn Jerome, and we risk calling the Vulgate itself into question."

"If this devilish opinion were to be tolerated and broadcast about like good seed," cried Fray Junípero, "we would soon have each man and woman freely committing every sin they pleased, on grounds that God condemns no one to Hell!"

"We would still have the fear of the secular arm to hold them in check," said Don Felipe.

Fray Junípero snorted his opinion of the fear of the secular arm.

Fray Clemente said, "It is for that reason I admit the proposition to be rash, scandalous, impious, and—possibly—ill-sounding. The opinion that God will, in the fullness of His own good time, bring all souls unto Himself, even from out of the depths of Hell, is hardly a leaven that any prudent person would wish to see widespread throughout the bread of Christianity as a whole. Nevertheless, privately held by souls of sufficient learning, prudence, and piety, it is not in itself heretical."

"And do you call publishing it in print either private or prudent?" Fray Junípero exploded. "Or do you credit for one moment this printer and author as a soul of sufficient learning, prudence, and piety to thumb his nose at the holy wrath of God?"

The ordinary, who had been examining a copy of the lampoon, observed, "He does not actually deny the just wrath of God or the existence of Hell. He merely remarks that no mortal ferocity can adequately mirror the justice of God, and that God need not necessarily condemn to Hell the identical individuals whom man condemns to the stake. To question either of these propositions would put us in risk of presuming to know the mind of God, which presumption is in itself mortal sin."

Fray Junípero persisted, "But mere presumption is not the deadly sin of heresy, nor does it imperil—as this heretic does—the salvation of the whole people!"

Fray Clemente threw up his hands. "Ask the author what he intended! As for the printer, it is my opinion that condemning him would imperil your own salvation."

Fray Junípero returned to his alternate weapon of sarcasm. "Indeed! And might we have your kind permission to question the printer as to the identity of the author?"

"That much," said Fray Roberto, "might be permissible. But only to the second degree. The nature of the offense does not merit going further, even to ascertain the identity of the author."

"It may be heresy," exclaimed Fray Junípero, "and you say its nature merits nothing more than showing the man the implements of torture?"

"It may or may not be heresy," the jurist replied quietly. "The element of doubt is too great to justify proceeding to the more extreme measures."

"We have difficulty enough," Don Felipe pointed out, "finding men both able and willing to apply torture in any degree." He looked directly at Fray Junípero. "It is hardly fitting that an inquisitor should work the pulleys or tip the jug with his own hands!"

"And I tell you," the senior inquisitor thundered, "that when there is work to be done for the glory of God, then be damned to these human notions of 'befitting' and 'dignity'!"

Finding his hands on the table as if to help push himself to his feet, Don Felipe looked around at his fellow churchmen, beginning with the ordinary. "My brothers in Christ! What would the Suprema say to this?"

"And what would the Suprema say," Fray Junipero demanded before any others could speak, "to the fact that this heretic whom you would obviously coddle has twice already been under investigation by my doddering predecessor of the ancient Inquisition, with the able assistance—I might better say connivance—of Felipe de Granada himself, then ordinary to his reverence of Daroca!"

With conscious care, Don Felipe relaxed his hands and removed them from the table, feeling his palms damp. What hours must Fray Junípero have spent in sifting through the all but uncatalogued archives of the ancient Inquisition of Daroca?

But the eyes of the four other men around the table had all turned from his senior to himself. Drawing a deep breath, the secular priest explained, "It is true enough, so far as it goes. The first instance took place when this man was still little more than a child, and had written a childish romance of Heaven and Hell, which he had unthinkingly shared with a Christian playmate. Being unbaptized and uninstructed himself, he had embellished his tale with certain erroneous details. His playmate, however, understood only the illuminations, in which there was nothing unorthodox. We burned his book and committed young Mehmoud, with such penances as could be applied, back into the authority of his father, a good and stern man." (Thank God, Felipe thought, that we burned that book! and pray there were no other copies to stray by mischance into the hands of this fierce zealot whom God in His mysterious purpose has set here to serve the Holy Inquisition.) "The second instance," he went on aloud, "occurred when the man was an apprentice. Still unbaptized and imperfectly instructed, but aflame with the hasty zeal of youth, he let slip a few words of heresy into what was, in its essence, a political protest." (Tread gently here: some copies of the *Contrefuero* might still exist, if not in actuality then in the memory of witnesses.) "At that time, he came forward himself for pardon under the Terms of Grace."

Fray Junípero sneered. "And so, in the wisdom of tired old Fray Potbelly and a raw, unschooled lay priest, you gave the notorious El Santon a free pardon and permitted heretical dogmatizing to go unchecked!"

"He reprinted his sheet at once and redistributed it without the offending words," Don Felipe protested. "As for my own education, true, it was shaped by no one monastic order, but I studied in Rome herself, under teachers drawn from many Orders, and I was made priest under the patronage of no other than his Eminence Cardinal Borja, now Pope Alexander the Sixth!"

For a moment, no one spoke. Then, at length, Fray Roberto said, "I think, in light of this printer's history, it would be permissible to go so far as stripping and binding in order to make him reveal the authorship of the present lampoon and whether or not he is himself baptized now. As far as that," the jurist emphasized, glancing at Fray Junípero. "No farther. Surely you can find men willing to do that much, without sullying the hands of an inquisitor."

The ordinary nodded. "In that light, I would cast my vote *in conspectu tormentorum.*"

And so the vote was taken, Don Felipe siding with Don Guillen to make the majority that would stop Fray Junípero from further argument, and comforting himself with the hope that Mehmoud-Juan, who had once written so imaginatively of hellish torments, might draw salvific experience from coming so near to earthly ones.

At last they reached the case Don Felipe had most ardently desired and dreaded: that of Manuel Urtigo, murderer and brigand, called "The Scourge of Axtilan."

"Accused," Fray Junípero reminded his fellows, glaring around at them, "of denying the omnipresence of God, the virginity of Mary, and the existence of Heaven and Hell alike; of speaking scandal of both churchmen and holy inquisitors, and of invoking demons for the purposes of currying their favor and paying them the honor due to God and

God alone. Well, brothers? God knows we have few enough examples so far with whom to honor Him and edify His people at this coming Act of Faith!"

Don Felipe drew a deep breath. Much though he had prayed for God's guidance in this very matter, he hardly knew himself—perhaps because of his own grievous and hidden sin—what words were about to issue from his mouth. "This man has named as personal enemies all of his accusers save one."

"And that one his own loyal lieutenant in banditry!" shouted Fray Junípero.

The ordinary observed wryly, "His entire village of Axtilan accused him, and he listed his entire village among his personal enemies."

"Except his lieutenant and dear friend Enrico Carranza!" Fray Junípero insisted. "Enrico's testimony ratifies all! Whom else are we to credit, if not a close comrade in arms of the accused?"

"No one, perhaps," said Don Felipe. "The very uniformity of the charges bespeaks conspiracy!"

Fray Roberto nodded. "Or, at the least, strongly suggests it."

Fray Juan, who was filling his goblet with water, gave a grunt. "Or, possibly, the simple truth."

"I find some difficulty," the Benedictine said, "in comprehending how the same individual can both deny the existence of Hell, and invoke demons."

"He may have invoked the demons in mockery," Don Guillen suggested, "to demonstrate that they would not appear. This would somewhat reduce his sin."

"It would not!" said Fray Junípero. "It is also heretical to make light of these matters!"

"Properly speaking," the jurist put in, "to deny the existence of Heaven and Hell does not necessarily entail denying that of God and the Devil."

"And where, then, would he have God to live? seeing that he also denies God's omnipresence!" Fray Junípero exclaimed, not apparently aware that he might be undermining his own argument.

"I believe," said Don Felipe, "that when the laity say that there is no Heaven and no Hell, what they actually deny is that they themselves have eternal souls to go to either place."

"Which is the heresy of the Sadducees!" Fray Junípero shouted in triumph.

Having finished the last of the dried fruit, Fray Juan reached for a few wafers as he said, "There can be little question as to the slanders he has uttered against men of our holy cloth."

The Benedictine eyed the Dominican as if counting the crumbs on his habit. "But did he utter them against us as priests and clerics, or did he utter them against our merely human failings?"

"Against us as priests and clerics," Don Felipe admitted in all fairness. "That, at least, is what I make of his words as reported to us. But, again, they are reported with so great a uniformity as to suggest conspiracy, and the man has in fact named his accusers as personal enemies—"

"Except his lieutenant!" repreated Fray Junípero. "Do not forget his own lieutenant, Enrico Carranza!"

The ordinary, who had been scanning the written record, observed, "Concerning the virginity of Mary, at least, Enrico Carranza's testimony does not quite agree with that of the other villagers. They testify to hearing Manuel on two separate occasions declare that her Child was Joseph's son, begotten on her before marriage. Enrico testifies to hearing his captain say, 'I wish that I had had the chance to get that Virgin with child—I would have shown her Blessed Highness what it is to lie with a real man!'"

At the mere repetition, for council purposes, of such words, every man present crossed himself. Don Felipe, however, did so with different thoughts, perhaps, than those of his fellows. Would Manuel Urtigo have left even the Blessed Virgin Mary alive to bear his bastard, Felipe wondered, remembering the rape and murder of his own sister Serafina almost as clearly, it seemed somehow, as if he had witnessed it with his own eyes and not merely heard at second hand from Gamito's lips how it had been this same brigand and his band who sacked his family's home, none of its occupants ever being seen or heard of again.

Drawing another deep breath, for the remembrance of his murdered family had shaken him even after all these years, he said, "Who can blame the villagers of Axtilan for wishing to rid themselves, by any means, of this scourge in their midst? Yet if in order to do so they have indeed manufactured heresies to put in his mouth, then the crimes of which he is truly guilty are not the crimes which it lies within our own sphere to judge."

How simple, in God's mercy, it had suddenly become! I, too, am Manuel Urtigo's personal enemy. Therefore, by the very rules of the Holy Office I serve, I am forced to judge him innocent of heresy!

"And what of Enrico Carranza's testimony?" cried Fray Junípero.

"'Et tu, Brute?'" Don Felipe quoted as if to prove his education. "How do we know but that Enrico Carranza is the trusted viper whom this man has been cherishing, unsuspected, in his bosom?"

"You cite profane authors," Junípero hurled back, "wisely fearing to cite holy ones!"

"True!" Felipe cried, his own voice rising. "I will not call Enrico Carranza Judas or even Ganelon, for Manuel Urtigo is certainly neither Ihesu nor even Roland! But neither can we judge him a heretic, by the very mass and uniformity of the charges against him."

Hands on the table, Fray Junípero rose. "No more can we allow such notorious and blasphemous heresy to go unchecked and unpunished! Brothers, we dare not *fail* to judge this man as the heretic he so notoriously is! We dare not fail to relax him to the secular arm!"

To see the flames leap up around this man, curl his blackened flesh away layer by bloody layer, melt the fat from his scorching bones—and if for some reason—to prove his courage?—he stayed stubborn to the last, refusing the mercy of strangulation before the fire was lit... Don Felipe had never attended the place of burning, never witnessed these executions with his own eyes; but, to see Manuel Urtigo suffer, he would gratefully make an exception. Half praying that in the case of his family's murderer Fray Junípero would prevail, Felipe rose to face the senior inquisitor and argue: "If this man's guilt were beyond question, I would agree. I, too, would call it both infamous and destructive of public morals to permit such heresy to go unchecked. But the very circumstances of the case call his guilt into question!"

Beetroot red, Junípero argued, "It is better to prune away the yellowing leaf than to lose the entire plant to the blight!"

"Our Lord Himself commanded that the weeds be allowed to grow alongside the good wheat until the harvest!" Don Felipe replied. "My brothers! Can the Holy Inquisition afford to lose its name for justice by pursuing a man unjustly accused? Dare we make the Holy Office a laughingstock by allowing a conspiracy of false charges to prevail?"

"Enrico Carranza's testimony ratifies all!" Junípero insisted, seizing the documents and shaking them in Felipe's face. "Do not again argue as you argued in the case of the woman Francesca Cascajo!"

Fray Roberto coughed and said, "At the least, this man must be given the chance to purge the evidence against him."

In the breathing space that the jurist's words provided them, first Don Felipe and then, more reluctantly, Fray Junípero resumed their seats.

Don Guillen said, "If it were not for the testimony of his own lieutenant, I would say, on behalf of his excellency the bishop, that Manuel Urtigo should be quietly released and his case dismissed. As it is, I agree that he must be allowed the opportunity to purge the evidence against him and, since it seems highly unlikely that he could gather enough witnesses for a compurgation, it must be the torture."

To pay him back, at least so far, for Serafina's pain and the others, Felipe thought, I would work the pulleys and pour the water myself!

Yet he swallowed his heart down and said sarcastically, "And must we condemn the inquisitors to sully their own hands with this work, for lack of any other men both willing and able to do it?"

"*In conspectu tormentorum*, then," Fray Roberto suggested.

There was further heated discussion, but at last it came to the vote.

"*In conspectu tormentorum*," Fray Juan said, belching, "and relaxation when he confesses."

"*In conspectu tormentorum*," Fray Clemente echoed. "But no farther."

Fray Roberto nodded. "*In conspectu tormentorum*, and let that be enough to purge the evidence of the single witness he has failed so far to identify."

The merely consultative votes being cast, those that weighed began with Don Guillen, who said cheerfully, "*In conspectu tormentorum*."

And so it came to the younger of the two inquisitors.

If I were to reveal how grievous is my own personal enmity to this murderer, thought Don Felipe, I might win abstention from the vote. Junípero will surely cast his voice for torture to the highest degree, or even immediate relaxation, and the vote would be split. Thus, it would go to the Suprema, and, for worse or better, Manuel Urtigo's fate would be out of my hands. And my fellow inquisitor, who already has innumerable grievances of his own against me, would at least lack this additional one. Yet can I without adding to my guilt in the eyes of Heaven trust Manuel Urtigo's fate to the Suprema? How if I were to vote for immediate dismissal of the charges? The vote would split three ways, the case would still await the Suprema's decision, and Fray Junípero would harbor an even deeper grievance against me. But can I without open blemish to my honor reveal at this stage what Manuel Urtigo has done to my family, after breathing no word of it until now?

He could no longer postpone his decision. With a deep breath, he said, "*In conspectu tormentorum*, and no farther, and let his own silence or confession seal it."

Glowering at his junior, Fray Junípero said: "It will be his silence, then. Can any of you truly think that the mere threat will loose the tongue of a man who in Castile would say even in the unchecked torture chambers of the secular courts, 'It is as easy to be silent as to sing'? I honor my own conscience and my duty to God by voting for immediate relaxation!"

But Don Felipe's vote added to that of the ordinary had already defeated the senior inquisitor. Fray Junípero did not stop scowling all the rest of that day.

* * * *

When brought in and told that he was to be taken to the place of torture, Mehmoud Aben Fazoud fell on his knees and confessed that he had never received Baptism. "It is all that I ask, my lords!" he went on, half babbling. "To be baptized and instructed in the Holy Faith of Ihesu!"

"Had you no chances before now?" Fray Junípero demanded in cold sarcasm.

"To be baptized, your reverence, many! But to be both baptized and instructed in the true Faith—no! Your reverence—reverences—I did not wish to besmear the Holy Faith in ignorance, not knowing what I did!"

"That much," Don Felipe murmured to his fellow inquisitor, "considering the state of Church and clergy today, could well be true."

Fray Junípero frowned, but nodded and agreed, however reluctantly, that the threat had already served its purpose with no need to proceed further.

Manuel Urtigo, however, listened with knees as unbent and frown as fixed as if he had been chiseled from stone. His scowl, indeed, matched Fray Junípero's own for depth and ferocity, so that, looking at them, Don Felipe privately thought they could have served one of Italy's sculptors as models for Satan and Lucifer. And, as the senior inquisitor had predicted, the brigand's stony resolve showed not the slightest crack when the effort reached the utmost allowed by *in conspectu tormentorum*, though he moved his gaze between Junipero and Felipe, scowling equally at both.

At the next Council of Faith, it was voted, despite Fray Junípero's grumbling, to have Mehmoud Aben Fazoud baptized wth proper sponsorship and placed six months in a monastery for instruction and penance. The great argument was the choice of monastery; but, with Don Guillen's acquiescence, Felipe brought the decision to Fray Clemente's house of Benedictines.

As for Manuel Urtigo, it was finally decided—Junípero determined to make him a spectacle in the one way remaining, and Felipe conquering his own secret distaste with great effort—that, in order to prove the justice of the Holy Inquisition and warn all persons against seeking to rid themselves of their enemies through the sin of false witness, he should be shown off at the coming Act of Faith as one exonerated and cleared of all charges, a true and loyal son, for all his merely mortal failings, of Holy Mother Church.

CHAPTER 14

THE DREAM OF THE MANTICORE

Mountains, gray and brown beneath the brightness of the day. Between two buttress-like folds of mountainside, a cleft of black shadow; and, standing just within that shadow, yet still where sunlight limned her clear as a candle, a white-robed woman bearing a wax taper in her uplifted left hand and a martyr's palm in the crook of her left arm. Raymonde.

She smiled and extended her right hand. Becoming aware of himself, he caught hold of it.

Gently, she drew him after her into the shadow, which he now saw to be the mouth of a deep cavern. The rock beneath their feet vanished from sight: it was as though they trod on nothingness, their lower legs paddling air while their bodies from the knees up floated in a bubble of candlelight, downward, ever downward along a broad, slow spiral. For a great time, black nothingness closed them in, held back only by the flame of Raymonde's taper. Then, for the first time, the flame flickered, and Felipe started as some huge shape, like a strange, bony fish, loomed and lunged past the very edge of the light.

"Take no alarm," said Raymonde. "They are dead these forty thousand years. They are but pictures now."

The cave wall closed in upon their left, and, with it, a long row of further shapes—some recognizable as horses, bulls, and deer; others like nothing ever glimpsed outside whimsical illuminations and outlandish bestiaries.

"Dead before the world's creation?" Felipe whispered. "Whose eyes could glimpse, whose hands picture them?"

"Before this our world ever came to be," his ancestress murmured in reply, "amen I say to you, it already was."

She lowered her candle. As its light moved down the wall, a hand came into view…the shadow of a hand, dark against an outlining cloud of whitish paint. A maimed hand: the thumb and three fingers showed clear, but the middle finger had been lopped off clean at the knuckle.

"What is this?" Don Felipe inquired.

"The scholars who find and study these," she replied, "will offer many theories."

They proceeded downward. More and ever more shadow-hands appeared on the wall, some few whole but most lacking one or even two fingers. In the candlelight, they waved back and forth… No, it was not the wavering light that made them merely appear to wave, they were waving in fact, the hands of a vast mob, cheering and jeering like storms in the mountains or waves against rocks.

It was the pious mob of yesterday's Act of Faith. For here, coming toward Don Felipe and his guide, was the procession, penitents and their sponsors—no one, by God's grace, for the stake—that far had they prevailed against Fray Junípero—although Ximèn Ximenès already rode his donkey, stripped to the waist and with the gag in his mouth, bearing his two hundred lashes.

And here, almost face to face with Don Felipe, Juan Delgado de Calamocha, who had been Mehmoud Aben Fazoud, in his penitent's sanbenito, with Lopé Cabezo beside him as sponsor, bearing the lighted candle.

But what was this? Juan's sanbenito painted with flames, and on his head the miter of one marked for relaxation to the secular arm?

"No!" Don Felipe observed to his ancestress. "Great-grandmother, I have caught you out in a flagrant lie!"

"Not all truth lies in mere accuracy," she replied, "nor is the strictest accuracy always truth."

He glanced at her sharply, for although the words were Raymonde's, the tone had sounded like that of Rosemary. But no, it was still the Albigensian who stood tranquilly at his side.

"Stop!" cried Juan Calamocha.

Staring into his face, Felipe beheld the stake reflected in his eyes. The inquisitor turned to look for it, and saw only the painted cavern wall on one side, the festively bedecked square of Daroca on the other. He turned back, to find the condemned man kneeling before him, arms upstretched in supplication.

"I am unbaptized!" El Santon went on in his ringing voice. "I have never been baptized!"

"Why, then, have you awaited this moment to reveal the true state of your soul?" the inquisitor asked him.

Without rising from his knees or lowering his arms, Mehmoud winked and dropped his voice from the declamatory to the merely conversational level. "It must be seen how I am forced to accept that which I have always desired. Otherwise, I lose the mantle of Moorish santon."

Felipe sighed. "You play a dangerous game, my friend. Beware lest the many brands you strive to juggle fall at the end into a pyre about your feet."

"I will take that chance," El Santon replied, crossing his arms over his chest and bowing his head so that the damning miter tumbled off.

Lopé Cabezo had disappeared: Don Felipe now held the lighted candle in his left hand, a cruse of holy water in his right. Nevertheless, he made one last attempt. "Mehmoud Aben Fazoud, Holy Mother Church does not demand that you put yourself within her discipline."

"My reverend lord, it is what I myself desire."

Shutting the eyes of his soul to his own unworthiness as priest, Don Felipe poured the water and spoke the words that transformed Mehmoud Aben Fazoud into Juan Delgado the younger in truth, then gave him the candle and bade him begone from the procession.

Grinning broadly, Juan stripped off the condemned penitent's sanbenito and left it lying empty on the path while he leaped naked from the ledge and disappeared among the people thronging the crowded square below. The rest of the procession, which had bottled up patiently behind him, burst back into its reverent upward shuffle. Raymonde again took hold of her descendant's hand and guided him downward, holding him steady against the tide of the procession until it was past and the two of them walked alone on the path.

But now when he looked at her, she was indeed Rosemary.

He tried to draw back. She gripped his fingers more tightly and said, "Great-great-grandfather, come on."

"I have guessed what this means. She shows me scenes of the past—you, of the future."

Her grip loosened, though for a moment only, as she seemed to ponder his statement. "Huh. I'd have called this one the luck of the draw, but you could be right. From your current point of view, anyhow."

"And she has just lied to me concerning the past. Mine was not the hand that poured El Santon into the Church, and in many other details, also—"

"We do the best we can, considering what we've got to work with! If you think you people do any better with your expert consultants and so-called Councils of Faith, just stay here and choose your own nightmare."

Humbled, he let her lead him along.

The town and its plaza had vanished, and now there was only darkness to the one side of the path. To the other side, the cavern wall showed its paintings more clearly than ever, for in place of lamp or candle, Rosemary carried some strange new lantern of the future, that cast a steady and unflickering radiance in all directions at once from a glasslike bubble at its top. Fewer and fewer animals appeared among the paintings, and more and more outlines of hands, usually lacking one or more of their fingers.

When next he looked, maps had appeared among the hands. Maps of Greece and Rome and the Holy Land...of Italy and Spain...of northern

Europe and distant Britain…of the Irish coast at the northwestern edge of the world…then Ocean…Ocean with the far Azores, and then nothing more, nothing but the expanse of waters flowing on one side down the cavern wall and rising on the other side in a great, dark tide engulfing the narrow path below their feet, rising to their knees, their waists, their chests…yet Rosemary strode along ignoring the tide, her light shimmering up greenly through the waves, while against the weight of water Felipe strove to match her pace…lands and rumors of new lands beyond the seas?

But now a last creature came down from the wall—a huge beast, no longer painted, larger than horse or bull—as gigantic, Felipe thought, as the elephants might be—with the bulk of its body in its brown-maned forequarters and great, shaggy, broad-nosed, short-horned head—

"It is the Manticore!" he cried, without knowing why.

She shook her head and grunted, "American bison."

Manticore or bison, the beast ploughed past them, parting the waters in a great swathe that spread until Felipe found the earth once again firm and dry beneath his feet.

A large fire burned in the center of the space, several smaller fires around its circumference. The ceiling, too, had fallen, so that it seemed now to be little more than a man's height above Felipe's head, and ribbed with thin beams. From these beams, here and there about the central fire, depended several nearly naked young men, swaying freely from ropes attached to skewers thrust through the flesh of either chest or back shoulders. Chest or back, the strips of muscle and sinew, following the skewers up away from the weight of the suspended body, had drawn out to incredible length. Half a dozen wildly contorting figures surrounded each sufferer, mocking and jeering, prodding with shafts, even driving into weak arms and legs further skewers, from which they hung additional weights.

"What form of terrible strappado is this?" the inquisitor exclaimed. "God and the Virgin! You have brought me into Hell! You are showing me the Inferno itself!"

She shook her head. "Coming of age, early Native American style."

"But…it is such torture as even Fray Junípero would blush to demand!"

"Sure about that, are you? Maybe you should check with the victims. These lads all want it. They're going to take great pride in the scars. Badges of manhood."

He made himself look again at the unfortunates, this time observing the passivity with which they hung…one might at first suppose some of them already dead. "Are they drunk into stupor?"

"Three or four days of fasting, sweat lodge, and sleep deprivation. Enough to make most of us Vanillas see visions even without the climactic nonsense."

Don Felipe pondered. "There are those who say that the innocent welcome torture as the final means to prove their innocence, and the guilty who refuse to confess welcome it as their means of winning free despite all weight of evidence and witness."

"Amazing, the excuses different societies find for hurting and getting hurt. Watch out!"

The great beast—bison or manticore—reappeared, lunging back through the cavern to butt its huge shaggy head against one of the dangling bodies. The victim jerked and stiffened. His human tormentors stood back, one of them pointing upward. The beast tossed its head as if to ravage the sufferer with its horns.

The thongs of flesh, already grotesque in their tortured length, strained yet further. With a wet wrenching that Felipe seemed to feel above his own left nipple, one stretch of skin and sinew pulled apart. For the space of half a *Gloria*, the victim dangled by a single strand before it, too, parted, letting him drop crumpled to the hard-packed earth.

The manticore-bison snuffled at him for a matter of heartbeats, then trampled him beneath its hooves in making its departure. The painted humans clapped hands to one anothers' shoulders and melted away, perhaps to join the demonic groups around other sufferers. Don Felipe found his hands pressed tightly to his own chest.

"Don't break your heart for him," Rosemary said dryly. "He just had a Great Vision. The greatest. It's all over now but the chopping."

"And he wished for this? They all of them wish it?"

"The way martyrs wish it."

"No!" Don Felipe shook his head. "Never tell me the holy martyrs desire their pangs! It would rob them of meaning."

"Huh! What about your flagellants?"

"All the value—all the heroism—of their sufferings lies in the fact that they *are* sufferings. That which is desired cannot be suffering, or there is no meaning in the word."

She snorted again. "Don't tell me that a darn lot of your so-called martyrs didn't goad their so-called persecutors into doing them in!"

"If suffering were their goal, they would have sought Hell rather than Heaven. My ancestress Raymonde did not seek damnation!"

"*Our* ancestress," Rosemary replied. "Are you saying that Raymonde found salvation in spite or herself, or admitting that she counts as a holy martyr?" While he hesitated wordlessly, she went on, "Besides, I never said *all* of them goaded their persecutors. Though the ones who did, didn't make things any easier for the ones who didn't."

"God knows His own," Don Felipe said at last. "Out of all nations and peoples."

"Righteous minds!" she said in disgust, less as if answering him than as if following her own thoughts. "If you call them 'holy martyrs,' you say they've won Heaven with their sufferings, and if you call them 'criminals' and 'heretics,' you justify torturing them to death as 'giving them a wholesome foretaste of hell.'"

"In the hope that it may bring them to repent even at the eleventh hour and save their souls."

The young man who had fallen to the ground began to prise himself up to his hands and knees. He moved slowly and heavily, as though under great weights, yet he shone with the radiance of an aureole.

"It is—" Don Felipe blinked. "But it is El Santon!"

As if continuing their argument without interruption, Rosemary queried, "The way you save their consciences by torturing confessions out of them?"

"But Juan Calamocha has never sought to suffer! He confessed at the first degree—"

"In my day, if people want this kind of experience, they usually have to pay for it in special brothels."

"You must have many criminals walking free, in your day."

"We still manage to cage up our share of innocent parties," Rosemary replied with unmistakable bitterness.

"But…" Puzzlement squeezed his brain. "You condemn persons without ratified confessions from their own mouths?"

She made her curious grunt of affirmation. "We don't need confessions. We can get 'Guilty' verdicts with circumstantial evidence and biased juries. Or vice versa."

It seemed that the bison-manticore had returned, this time thundering through or over Felipe himself with the shock of Rosemary's last revelation. Indeed, indeed, the farther times unrolled from the Age of Gold, the worse history became! And yet…and yet…when had been the Age of Gold? Certainly not in the days of Abraham and Moses, or there would have been no need for Covenant or Promise…but not in Christ's own day, either, for was He not crucified for the sins of His executioners—not only all the rest of humanity, but they who with their own hands actually fashioned and raised the Cross, as well! Nor yet in whatever pre-Adamite society Albigensian and Pagan had brought him to glimpse in this dream, for as the thunder of the great beast passed once again, leaving him to his surprise still on his feet, he saw that the young sufferer—El Santon or not—had crawled to a painted man who sat crosslegged beating a drum. The sufferer stretched one hand out upon a rock at the drum-beater's knee, extending the middle finger. One hand continuing to beat his drum, the painted man picked up a stone blade and severed the finger with a thud that woke the sleeper.

For some moments, he lay awake listening for a repetition of the strange noise and wondering why he had dreamed of shadowy hands with one or two fingers folded down out of sight.

CHAPTER 15

THE CANON OF EYMSTADT

This latest Act of Faith, Don Felipe felt, had cost him more, almost, than it had the official sufferers and penitents. Three afternoons later, doubts and fears still chased one another through his soul, with far greater disturbance to his siesta than the burning crimson flashes which clouds chasing one another across the face of the sun marked on his closed eyelids.

Ah, good father, dear lady mother, beloved sister Serafina and all the rest of you, my family, my family...did I do well in letting the chief of your murderers walk free, when crushing him would have required no more of me than allowing my confrere to have his way? But I am a priest doubly tainted...trebly, in that my own sin, so much greater than that of any heretic whom we sentence, lies concealed in the deepest, most secret pit of conscience...

"Lord, my lord!" came Gubbio's voice. "Still snoozing? The market has been abustle this past hour."

Opening his eyes, Don Felipe regarded the Italian. "Surely, Gubbio, you exaggerate."

"Your Holiness thinks so? Be sure I do not exaggerate when I tell you I bought us this for the price of a cabbage." Gubbio dropped into his master's lap a leaf-wrapped lump, the size of a man's fist, of that Moorish confection Felipe had loved since boyhood but tasted more and more rarely as the years went on.

Felipe cocked a brow at his servant. "From the same market as yesterday's dinner? Gubbio, my Gubbio, I rejoice that I am not your confessor!"

"Rejoice at whatever you please! That market shows greater charity than our fellow Christians in trading with the servant of a servant of the Holy Inquisition, and not even our longest-faced brother questions the beef and mutton he deigns to eat when not fasting, as long as it is tender enough and sauced with sufficient bacon to prove its piety. So everyone is well pleased, from market to table, and if it still naggles at your reverend conscience, here is a trifle to distract your Sanctity." Producing a letter from his doublet, the Italian touched it quickly to his head before dropping it into his master's lap almost on top of the sweetmeat.

It bore the seal of Rome.

"I am sure," Don Felipe said, laying it down again on his lap in hopes that his servant would not see the slight trembling of his hand, "that the bearer did not simply chance upon you there in the market."

"And if he had? Who should trust one another better than a pair of Italians in a foreign land?" Grinning, Gubbio shook his head. "Your Generosity still being at siesta, our pious servant of the Holy See decided to trust me, with my certain privileges, to bring him back whatever reward you see fit to offer him for his dangers and inconveniences."

"Tell him," the priest replied carefully, "that I shall reward him generously, but all in one lump sum, tomorrow. This message will beyond doubt require an immediate reply. Now go and see to the man's feeding and lodging."

"Fed, he is already." Gubbio cast another look at his master, saw that Don Felipe was not about to open the missive in his presence, and yielded with grudging grace. "We will see to his bed for the next night or two."

Felipe closed his eyes and sat back, as if the epistle waiting in his lap were a less important thing than his broken siesta. Not until he had heard Gubbio's footfalls safely retreat did he venture another look.

In truth, this letter was anticipated—long awaited in something between eagerness and trepidation. God willing, it might contain the answer to Felipe's request of 1492.

Anno Domini 1492. That ill-fated year—although as a good Catholic Spaniard Felipe de Alhama de Granada must hold locked within his own breast, alongside the secrets of his great sin and his ancient hatred of the murderer Manuel Urtigo, his true emotions at the fall of Karnattah to their Catholic majesties of Aragon and Castile and at those same majesties' final pious expulsion of every unbaptized Jew from all their domains.

Like a sign from God to brighten that dark year with its long, doleful processions of Abraham's children filing to the seaports at the end of July, Don Felipe's old patron Cardinal Borja had been elected to the papal throne. Among his earliest acts had been the welcoming of all such rejected Spanish Jews as chose to make Rome their refuge—among them, Felipe dared pray, Gamito.

In his own congratulatory missive to the new pope, Don Felipe had reminded Alexander VI, as Cardinal Borja now was, of his own efforts in the field where his patron had placed him, by pledging to continue them. At the same time, he had hinted his readiness to undertake some farther-ranging service, some errand to France, perhaps, or even to the ever-restive and troublesome Germany, which might enable him to offer further proof of his loyalty and also increase his knowledge, thus improving his labors at home.

(And also, though this he hardly dared subvocalize even in his own heart, provide him the chance to discharge his poor conscience in Confession to some obscure and anonymous parish priest, far from both Spain and Rome, and preferably having more bastards at his knee than Latin in his head.)

There had, of course, been much to occupy the new pope during the first five years of his reign—wars and rumors of wars; the French king's attempted invasion of Italy; the need for papal arbritration of property rights in the newly found lands beyond the ocean... Yet now, at last, his holiness had remembered one relatively obscure yet loyal satellite helping bind the unruly Spanish church in allegiance to Rome.

Remembered him to grant his request at once, or to bid him continue his service in patience and obedience? Anxiety casting out dread, Felipe finally broke the seal.

The pope's dictated words were formal, yet to his relief Don Felipe drew from them a sense that his patron had forgotten neither him nor the conversation that had determined his life's course, all those years ago, by placing him here in Aragon. In words doubtless duplicated, with small variations, to satellite after satellite, his holiness said in effect, "Well done, thou good and faithful servant: continue thy loyal labors in the field wherein I have placed thee." But after this, in words that seemed tailored to Don Felipe alone, the pope added that a certain mendicant canon, formerly belonging to the Augustinian house of Eymstadt of the Congregation of Windesham, had lately brought to the papal attention a matter of ancient abuse and imposition, involving blatant superstition and quite possibly simony, long practiced upon the simple in a diocese of Ireland: namely, this canon claimed that the Purgatory of Saint Patrick was no more than a fraud. Considering the ancient fame of the site, Alexander wished to make some further inquiry before ordering it to be shut down; and, on Saint Benedict's admirable principle that a change of labor was as good as a rest, he proposed sending his good and loyal servant Felipe de Nuestra Señora del Pilar de Agapida de Aragon as legate to accompany the said mendicant canon back from Rome to Ireland, there to serve as the pope's own eyes and ears in the matter of this so-called Purgatory.

The so-called Purgatory of Saint Patrick, long renowned as a sure place of visions...if not, indeed, of actual visitation to that world beyond the grave! How many travelers' accounts had been written of it through the centuries? True testaments, or fabulous odysseys akin to those of Dante and—the inquisitor smiled, remembering—of young "San Juan de Calamocha"? Difficult, sometimes, to say for sure. And what of the middle ground?—pilgrims whom that site at the very edge of the world had inspired with dreams of a nature so luminously visionary that they afterward wrote them down in the sincere if misguided belief of their actuality.

Well! Ireland might no longer lie at the very edge of the known world, but among its simple priests Felipe de Granada y Aragon could surely find one sufficiently obscure and unlettered to serve the purpose of his spiritual salvation.

* * * *

Two decades and three changes of pope seemed to have made less difference in the Eternal City than Felipe would have expected; almost, he felt, he could still name some of the cows at their placid grazing, recognize certain of the scavenging swine by their markings. He felt the days of his youth heavy about him here, clinging close as a woolen cloak to his shoulders, while at the same time such changes as he saw served to encrust that cloak with the stiff weight of his own encroaching middle age. He would not again see forty! What had become of all those high spirits and higher ideals of his youth? Our Lord's solemnly ordained priest-knight—stained with such mortal sin as must have cost him his Lady Morayma's favor forever if she had not been lost to him already— now wasting his years away with the tedious minutiae of combing other souls' lives for hidden heresies! And to what use or purpose? Saving a few poor, sinful bodies here and there from the zealous excesses of a Fray Junípero or the harsh judgment of the secular arm which saw heresy as treason not only against Heaven but against the state as well…and all the while remembering, with every decision rendered and every punishment decided upon, the condition of his own soul before the judgment seat of God. When had Ihesu ever addressed mere heretics as "whited sepulchers"?

Meanwhile, finding the holy city as much as ever a haunt of unholy knavery, Don Felipe rejoiced that he had prudently left his Italian servant at home to care for his properties in Aragon, well removed from the temptations of earlier years.

Although he could not avoid an inward chuckle of regret on meeting the canon of Eymstadt. Gubbio's moist, warm, earthly humors rubbing against this canon's cool, dry, celestial ones must surely have provided ample entertainment for the longest journey!

The canon was staying in an Augustinian house far too reformed for the comfort of the secular priest's body, spirit, or digestion. Don Felipe elected to remain in the home of one of the pope's favorite cardinals while completing his arrangements for the mission. The canon, professing himself ready to depart at once, raised a thin brow and cited

Ihesu's words to the Apostles to "carry nothing" for their travels; but Don Felipe—already weary from the trip across Aragon, Catalonia, and the Mediterranean to Rome, and facing a far longer and more arduous journey to Ireland, cited the duties of a guest to his host and the need for a papal legate to furnish his mind with certain additional study of precedents and analogous situations, which could be done only here in the libraries of Rome. Diplomatically, he forebore to point out that his future traveling companion had already enjoyed a considerable respite from the road while presenting his case to the pope's penitentiary.

Emerging from a visit to his Italian bankers, Don Felipe thought he felt the wickedness of the city brush his own person in the form of a young cutpurse. Catching the boy by one scrawny arm, he pulled him face to face and demanded, "Well, lad, do clerical purses make thieves the best pickings, here in Rome?"

"Not a thief!" the boy protested, anger seeming to war strangely with terror in his countenance.

Without loosing his hold, Don Felipe groped one-handed for his purse and found at its top a folded paper that had not been there before. Intrigued, he drew it out and worked it open. It was scribed with the name of a certain house in the Jewry, and the words, "Come as if buying." Years fell away as Felipe recognized the hand.

Nodding, he released his young captive—who promptly dodged into the crowd—and made his way to the Jewry, rejoicing that the lad had found him alone: having spent much of the morning at his researches, he had given the old familiar and former soldier, Luis Albogado, whom he had brought with him as manservant in Gubbio's place, an errand elsewhere.

Half an hour later, Felipe found the building. Even as he began to investigate the shops of its arcade, he caught sight of a familiar figure standing at the far end. No sooner had he opened his mouth to call a greeting, than Gamito nodded and vanished into his shop.

Wondering, but slowing his steps with an effort, Don Felipe proceeded to the spot where he judged his friend had stood, and entered in his turn. It proved to be a tiny pawnshop, a place of antiquities and modernities, velvets and brocades, books and musical instruments, all cleanly stored in such a manner as to show without ostentation. Felipe's old friend sat behind the small counter, studiously turning the pages of a book after the Hebrew fashion, left to right.

"Gamito!" Felipe exclaimed.

The other looked up with an almost imperceptible shake of his head. Glancing at the door as if through his visitor, he said, "Your Reverence mistakes me for someone else. But if you please to come closer, I may have some trinkets here to interest you."

Stepping to the counter, Don Felipe lowered his voice in deference to his friend's obvious wishes. "I have mistaken no one. My God! Gamito, finding you answers my most heartfelt prayer!"

"And mine," Gamito murmured, rising from beneath the counter, where he had bent to retrieve a small coffer. Placing it on the surface between them, he opened it and said more loudly, "If it is antiquities your Reverence seeks, I can offer a fine denarius from the time of the second Caesar, or even an obol from Plato's Athens, though this last has been with me but two days past its promised time of redemption."

"I will look at them both, and at anything else you may care to show me, but why this secrecy? Has the city's spirit of intrigue infected even you, Gamito? Or is there truly some need, some danger—"

"None of which we know," Gamito murmured reassuringly. "No, we have been made welcome here, by both his Holiness and our own Roman compatriots. But a Jew learns caution. Overmuch caution, perhaps— even, at times, a caution that may seem ludicrous to a free Gentile—but our fathers had been welcome in Spain for many generations, and now there is talk that this same pope who welcomed us is about to honor Fernando and Isabel officially with the title of 'Most Catholic,' for their Christian charity in exiling us."

"Among other deeds," the priest added, "including the glorious re-conquest of Karnattah, with its rape of our beloved Alhama." Hearing the bitter notes in his own voice, he added, "But his Holiness must tread a razor's edge of diplomacy, Gamito, if he would keep any control at all over rebellious Spain. And, for the sake of that God Whom we both worship, let there be no more talk of 'Gentile' or 'Jew' between us two!"

"Do you chide me," his friend inquired, "for the pains I have been at to protect your name among your own kind?"

Taken somewhat aback, Don Felipe pondered a few moments before answering slowly, "No, old friend, I thank you. These are not the habits I have learned in Aragon of late years. There, I ventured not even to inquire of the banker where—and if—your letters of credit had been presented, lest my interest should be known to concern more than my own newly acquired properties. Being in Rome again, I seem to breathe once more the freer air of my youth. It may have made me reckless."

Over the coffer of antiquities, Gamito's forefinger found the back of Felipe's hand and rested there for a heartbeat or two. "As Spain made us cautious," he repeated softly. "If your pope walks the edge of a razor, so do we—and, I think, a sharper razor than his! But I thank you, old friend. Your purchase of our property—at a price more than fair, when so many other good Christians were fattening themselves upon our need—and payment in letters of credit upon the Fuggers, rather than in specie which we would have needed to smuggle from the country with great risk of confiscation, made this shop and our livelihood from it possible."

"I rejoice in your welfare," the priest said sincerely. "And all of you are safe?"

"All of us, although the exodus from Spain nearly killed my dearest wife, who was big with our firstborn. No blame to you, my friend, and Heaven's blessing upon those few who laid aside their Christianity, at great risk to themselves, long enough to offer us a little help along the road."

"No, Gamito, theirs was the true Christianity, the mercy which our Lord enjoined upon His followers—but you see, I say to you, here in Rome, things that not even a holy inquisitor would dare say aloud in the Spain of Fernando and his Castilian queen!"

"Perhaps you should not whisper them even in Rome. Who knows what Christian ears may overhear, what side of the razor's edge your pope may land upon when he falls?"

"I will buy both obol and denarius for a visit with you in your home, where we may talk more freely than even here."

"Felipe, both coins are yours for my great pleasure in seeing you again, but appear to haggle a little while longer. I think it safest to converse quietly here, rather than that any eyes should glimpse you seeking out a Jewish household."

"I have already set inquiries in motion for you and your family. Of all people in Rome, I judged my bankers best suited to the task. But how could even they have worked so quickly? That lad slipped me your message on my way out of the bank."

"My brother saw you at the wharf on your arrival."

"Truly? I did not see him."

"Thinking it more prudent that you should not, he stayed hidden in the crowd. He was there to collect certain merchandise for the good man who lodged my mother and sister when first they fled here to join my brother's family. As for the boy, he is a street urchin, but recommended by an acquaintance who has found him trustworthy on errands of a delicate nature."

Felipe sighed. "Have you ever thought, Gamito, that this 'New World' beyond the ocean may offer your people a second Promised Land?"

"But you frown, my friend," said Gamito.

"No—it is nothing—only some vague fancy of having once seen something of the sort in a dream. Long ago...very long ago, if, indeed, it ever occurred at all." Unable to plumb his memory for further details,

Felipe shrugged it off and went on, "But see here, Gamito. Why, when I have already begun inquiries for you through the Fuggers, should I not visit you in your home?"

"Bankers, even Gentile bankers, can guard confidences very well."

Better, perhaps, than Spanish priests! Don Felipe reproached himself on two counts, remembering both his great sin and his own failure to question his bankers in Aragon concerning the whereabouts of his Hebrew friends. "But I am forming a resolution: invite me into your home, and upon my return to Aragon I will enter into correspondence with you through my bankers." Seeing his friend's hesitation, he added, "If need be, I shall pretend an effort to convert you, mixed with sufficient pious sentiments to satisfy prying eyes. You will know how to crack through them for the true meat of my letters."

"I will, indeed!" With a low chuckle, Gamito accepted the handclasp Felipe offered over the antique coins. "You will find us a stubborn family, Felipo, and very difficult to convert, but any letter you dare send will be welcome for its own sake. Ask for us in the street of the fishmongers."

* * * *

By the time all preparations for the mission to Ireland were completed, leaving no further excuse for delay, Don Felipe had enjoyed no fewer than three visits with his old friend. By going quietly but not furtively, he felt that he had attracted little if any comment; and the late hardships suffered by the Hebrew family while still in Spanish lands had in no way impaired its cooking.

They queried each other about their third boyhood friend, but Gamito had learned no more than had Felipe about Hamet and his family. They could but hope that the Moors were safe somewhere and living in comfort, Morayma with the husband to whom she had long ago been married, and Hamet, perhaps, with his own little harem.

(Not even to Gamito would Felipe speak of his love for the lady lost to him forever. How could he speak of it, even to God, without remembering the great sin with which he had dishonored his devotion? He cringed to think how Morayma would have viewed his secret disgrace; for, while her people might not understand the Christian sacraments, they had their own strong sense of honor and religion. As things stood, she might never have so much as suspected Felipe's adulation. It was better so.)

Nevertheless, two of the old comrades had reunited, and when they parted again, it was with promises to maintain contact with letters exchanged through the bankers.

* * * *

Those letters must wait, of course, until Don Felipe was back in Aragon; or, at least, until he had parted with the canon of Eymstadt, who was likely to lend him scarcely enough peace and solitude to read his Office during what small leisure the rigors of travel might allow.

Their party was small, very small. His holiness insisted that two Roman guards accompany them in addition to the old soldier Luis Albogado, but agreed, after raising one fine if heavy eyebrow briefly at Felipe's failure to bring along a Spanish chaplain, that legate and canon might provide each other as well as their three men-at-arms with the comforts of Mass, Confession, and holy counsel when required.

Don Felipe had neglected to bring a chaplain along with him precisely because of his deeply private plan to unburden himself to some chance-found parish priest far from either Spain or Italy. Life was uncertain, especially upon a journey to the end of the civilized world, and the canon of Eymstadt would be preferable to the demons of Hell; but, granted time for any other choice whatever, Don Felipe would as soon have made his crucial Confession to the inquisitor general of Spain—Fray Tomás de Torquemada himself—as to this educated Augustinian zealot who had deliberately abandoned the cloister with its library for the austere hardships of life as a mendicant friar.

Who seemed, moreover—to his companion's discomfort—already to suspect that some heavy weight lay in Don Felipe's soul. The first day that they stood side by side aboard the ship from Rome to Narbonne, the secular priest began, speaking in the one language that both clerics understood, "Tell me of your experience at this place called Saint Patrick's Purgatory."

"Was not my report among such papers and documents as need required you to study there in Rome?"

"It was," Don Felipe agreed mildly, "but spoken testimony, for which written merely substitutes, is always to be preferred."

The canon stared at him with piercing pale eyes and said in tones just barely on the right side of civility, "Is this your training as inquisitor?"

"In part, it is my experience—rather than training—but in larger part, it simply follows Holy Church in her ancient wisdom, which advises Scripture to be imparted and expounded orally wherever and whenever possible."

With this, no churchman who had chosen the itinerant life could well argue. After a moment, the canon coughed, turned his gaze to the waters of the Mediterranean, and said bitterly, "I found it all lies, imposition upon popular credulity, and blatant simony."

"You must explain more fully, and in proper order."

Again the stare that seemed to pierce through Felipe's body into his soul. "Do you interrogate me in your capacity of inquisitor?"

"I serve Holy Church as one of her inquisitors," Don Felipe answered, remaining calm with some slight effort, "and it is for that reason, among others, that his holiness has named me to this our present mission. But I question you in your capacity of accuser and witness, not as one himself under suspicion."

"Well and good! You have enough of them to suspect, hypocrites and simonizers all, every last one. When first I came to Saint Patrick's Purgatory, and thought myself at my goal, Terence—in their own language, 'Turlough'—Maguire, who is prior and presider of that so-called ancient holy place, claimed to require consent in writing from his bishop before permitting me to enter. All part of their fraudulent game, as I finally came to see, but meanwhile behold me duly seeking out his Excellence Cathal Og MacManus, whose servants treated me in my poverty as so much dirt. Does this befit those who claim to serve our Lord, poor as He was in His earthly life?"

Privately musing that the canon's tone betrayed as much contempt for the bishop's servants as they could possibly have shown him, Don Felipe shook his head in sympathy and prompted his informant, "But they finally admitted you to see Bishop Cathal?"

"They thrust me prone before him with jeers and mockery. And he—this high churchman boasting his true service to our Lord—demanded money for his written consent to enter his saint's Purgatory!"

"On what grounds?" inquired Don Felipe.

"On grounds that such was his due from any who entered that place of supposed vision and pilgrimage! But in obedience to our Lord, Who commanded His disciples to carry no purse in their travels, I had no money, and even if I had, I would not have dared to pay, on account of simony and its contagion. So at last, yielding to my long arguments and tears of devotion, his excellency vouchsafed me his letters of admission, but sent me to his highness Nellanus MacGrath, secular prince of that territory, on grounds that I must have his permission as well."

"Perhaps amicable cooperation," Don Felipe mused, "or perhaps unseemly truckling to secular authority."

The canon indulged in a sneer. "Ah, it was amicable cooperation! Completely amicable cooperation between spiritual arm and secular—both at work to reap profit from pious deluded pilgrims. For what does his highness demand of me, but money! Enough money to have made up for his churchman friend what I had refused to pay there."

"But eventually you prevailed upon Prince Nellanus MacGrath, also, without rendering payment."

"Without payment of money, but with long payment of tears, pleading, argument, and even threats—pointing to his excellency's permission, gained without coins. So back at last I returned, with both their letters of admission, and on reading them, what does Prior Terence demand but money in his turn, as 'customary payment'?"

"It is unfortunately true," Don Felipe observed, "that without alms, no steward can long maintain any shrine in this imperfect world. Does not Saint Paul himself command us not to muzzle that ox which treads our grain?"

The canon snorted. "It is one matter to collect alms offered in free generosity, as much or as little as their givers can afford, and another matter to fix some certain sum and call it 'customary,' as if God's grace could be purchased for any set fee. That is what I call blasphemous simony!"

"You call it well," Don Felipe conceded. "Yet, for all that, this prior may have been guilty of no more than thoughtless adherence to long custom as convenient guide. He did admit you finally, did he not, without payment?"

"Oh, aye, he admitted me, more grudgingly than freely, even deigning to hear my Confession and give me Viaticum—as if his mouth were worthy to grant absolution, or his hands to fondle our Lord's sacred Flesh—"

"Such sacraments," Don Felipe protested with a secret cringe, "remain equally valid, no matter any individual priest's state of soul."

"That is matter for debate," the canon replied, his own opinion evident in his tone of voice. "In any case, thus prepared and fortified—in all good will on my own part, at least, if not on that of this prior—I followed him to that deep pit they call Saint Patrick's Purgatory, into which his sacristan lowered me by rope, along with bread and one small flask of water, and left me therein all night in perfect comfort, expecting demons and visions in plenty and never seeing as much as one!"

Musing on the degree of aceticism that could refer to the bottom of a deep pit, presumably hard, very probably damp or rocky or both, perhaps too narrow to lie down in at length, with no other amenity than bread and water, all for the length of an entire night, as "perfect comfort," Don Felipe asked—he was hardly sure why—"Did you not even sleep, and suffer dreams?"

"None!" the canon said decisively.

* * * *

The canon would have traveled afoot from Narbonne to Bordeaux. Indeed, Don Felipe would scarcely have felt surprised to see him, for all his stubborn humility, try setting his foot upon the sea. When, on reaching port, the Spaniards and Italians turned their attention to finding mounts, the mendicant grumbled,

"You secular priests pride yourselves on taking no vow of poverty."

Felipe responded, "Would you delay our mission?"

"I would have set out at once upon your arrival in Rome. Afoot, wherever there is land, as our Lord and His disciples traveled."

"Not even with His miracles could He always impress every authority to do His will. We bear such orders as men may not receive willingly, even from his holiness. Would you have us appear to their eyes in less dignity than befits papal emissaries? Moreover, there are our men-at-arms to consider."

"Does this mean you are in full agreement that that place of fraud and superstition must be closed?" the canon demanded eagerly.

"I shall neither agree nor disagree until after personally inspecting Saint Patrick's Purgatory and judging for myself whether or no it is worthy of credence and pilgrimage."

"You will agree! You will not—you cannot—fail to see their imposture for yourself! At least let me run afoot beside you."

"And make us appear hard-hearted, as well as slowing our journey? Whereas," Don Felipe added with a wink, "riding, you will save your breath for arguing with me."

At last, still under protest, the canon was persuaded to ride a mule, as the one mount which none of the Evangelists described as sanctified by the touch of our Lord's posterior. He breathed no word of protest against the horses chosen by Luis Albogado and the two Italian bodyguards, as befit their soldierly status; but he seemed to look askance at his clerical companion for perferring an ass, named by Matthew, Luke, and—arguably—Mark as the breed upon which Ihesu rode into Jerusalem, John alone remembering a donkey. Though the canon kept his glances veiled, Don Felipe renewed his resolution to make Confession to this man only in case of absolute and dire need.

* * * *

The prior of the small Benedictine house of Notre Dame de la Charité, where they passed two nights between Marmande and Bordeaux—the canon insisting on full observance of the Sabbath whenever possible—was an ardent scholar of all visions and accounts of the afterlife, those of Saint Patrick's Purgatory included, and seized the chance to discuss it as eagerly as Don Felipe and at least two of their three men-at-arms (one Italian making no comment either way) seized the excuse to rest a day from travel.

"So," the prior asked plaintively, "there were no demons at all?"

"None at all," the canon returned with the merest hint of smugness, as if he enjoyed having the advantage of superior knowledge over a man of higher religious authority, but at the same time possessed enough grace of conscience to repent his enjoyment.

In his own disappointment over the lack of demons, the prior seemed to take no notice of his guest's attitude. "And no fires?" he went on.

"As I understand our friend's situation that night," Don Felipe put in, "one or two small fires might have been welcome, whether fed by burning sinners or some less exotic fuel."

Both men looked at him, the canon frowning very slightly. After a moment, the prior inclined his head deferentially and said, "Whether poor sinners actually fuel those flames with their own souls' substance, has long caused me confusion. All in all, I think not, for damned souls must survive to burn forever, and souls in Purgatory must survive to pass on, in due course, into Heaven; and therefore it must be their sins alone which burn away, or, for Hell's eternal fire, some other fuel, which 'dies not, nor is ever quenched.'"

A little uneasy at his own levity, considering the perilous state of his soul, Don Felipe offered his goblet to be refilled with good French wine, poured by the young lay brother in attendance, and agreed that the prior's argument was sound. He might have discharged his conscience to this courteous old Benedictine, but for his secular's shyness of any Order; as inquisitor, he understood mistrust, even enmity, between Orders for what it was…but, as ordained mortal, he was not immune to feeling it himself.

Turning again to the canon, their host went on, "Yet not every visitor even to Saint Patrick's Purgatory has been blessed with glimpses of what awaits our souls after death. Perhaps our good God had some reason for withholding them from you, to your own salvation?"

The canon emphatically shook his head. "For one whose desire was as ardent, prayers as fervent, and soul as carefully tended, our Lord could have had one reason only: to use me as His tool for unveiling this simony in all its fraudulent superstition."

After suffering his companionship across the Mediterranean and much of France, Don Felipe had little doubt that the canon of Eymstadt was as sincere, pious, and clean of life as his words implied. Between this canon and himself, it was less a question of Order versus secular vows, than of personal humors as discordant as vinegar and burgundy.

* * * *

Midway between France and Donegal, when Don Felipe lay below deck cocooned in a hammock, he woke from a dream that a great storm raged around their ship and he was the prophet Jonah, to find that it was true—at least in so far as concerned the storm. The very sides of the vessel shook with each crack of lightning and crash of thunder, while waves dashed against the planking as though fierce to free their brother laplets of bilge water within, and Felipe's own stomach, for all its emptiness of prudent fasting, groaned along with the general tumult, in no way soothed by the swinging and jerking of his hammock.

Return to sleep seemed impossible; yet as he lay listening to the din of sea, storm, and sailors shouting above him in their unfamiliar tongue, in his suffering he began to feel that the other part of his dream was true as well: that he was indeed Jonah, fleeing in his guilt from the wrath of an angry God—that he could even understand the sailors' foreign speech, and they were already casting lots to learn what sinner among them had brought so much divine wrath down upon their voyage.

Confess, he thought. I must find my fellow traveler and make my Confession! For death seemed very near, if not from the storm itself, then from the distress in his own poor body…and yet, crippled as much by this same distress as by fear of those rough sailors above deck, he lay during swing after swing of the hammock, adding no movement of his own to its already violent motion, but beginning vaguely to fancy it a gallows on which he swung…when he heard voices almost in his ear:

"According to his own belief, great-granddaughter, he should confess."

"Great-grandmother, that's all crackerjack."

Trying to sit up, Don Felipe tumbled from the hammock. At first, he had feared they were sailors come down to seize him. But no, the voices had been women's—at least, one of them, the softer one—though already his alarmed mind was letting go of what, exactly, they had said.

Once knocked from his hammock, he groped his way to the hatch and climbed, hand over hand, ignoring sickness and bruises alike—everything but the old, festering ache in his conscience. The canon, he must find the canon of Eymstadt, it was time and past time to make his Confession.

Finally on deck, he found himself in a great, boisterous grayness like dawn, although, with the heaviness of the clouds, it might have been midday. Like Peter sinking into the water and calling on Christ Ihesu, Don Felipe began shouting for his companion, clinging in desperation to shroudline, railing, whatever seemed secure, never daring to relinquish one handhold until he had found another, straining his eyes against wind and rain in his efforts to locate the canon.

He spied him at last, huddled head to head with Luis Albogado. Luis! thought Felipe. He, too, is making his Confession—and to this foreign mendicant rather than to me. As is wise…does he guess as much, or was it merest proximity in need? Like my own need—had they tried to wake me before now, and failed?

But what sins could the faithful old familiar have on his soul, to need any great time confessing? Don Felipe looked about for the nearest way across to them, prepared to lurch toward a handhold just beyond his grasp...

When a sailor, as he supposed, walked past him and remarked, in clear if strangely accented Spanish, "Irish priest at the mast, great-grandfather. Your choice."

Squinting forward, Felipe saw that there was indeed a man tied to the mast—so the storm was truly as desperate as it seemed to him—and this man was making the sign of absolution over a sailor. It was half the distance to the mast as to the canon.

As the sailor kissed his confessor's hand and turned away, Don Felipe thrust himself forward. A wave swung the deck up to meet him—sprawling, he reached out and found himself clutching the Irish priest—who had told him this was an Irish priest?—by one ankle. After lingering long enough to put the end of a rope in the papal emissary's hand and help him into a somewhat more secure and less undignified position, face to face with the native cleric, the sailor returned with freshly washed soul to his work of striving, with God's will, to help save the ship.

Don Felipe had seen this Irish priest boarding at Dublin, but supposed him some petty tradesman. Small and lean, though with the smile of a well-fed uncle, he had settled among his ragged compatriots laughing and joking in their own language—Felipe remembered thinking that but for their strange tongue and their laughter, the mendicant canon of Eymstadt might have preferred their company to his own for its simplicity and poverty. No tradesman, then, but a priest? Obviously a secular, by his garb and the silvering red hair now rain-whipped across his face; obviously Christlike in his ability to eat and drink with sinners and as it appeared to share poverty with the poor; and obviously beloved and valued, to be tied already to this mast against the storm's worst, while the papal emissary and his party were still left to their own devices.

"I beg pardon, brother," Don Felipe began in Latin, half-shouting to be heard through the storm. "I did not know of your priesthood."

Replying with a rush of words in his own language, the Irish priest ended by seizing Don Felipe's hand and kissing it.

"You did not reveal your priesthood to us," Felipe continued in Latin.

"...Holiness...I have...Latin, little," the Irishman faltered, with bad case endings. "Little Latin. Latin, little."

Beneath a prayer of relieved thanks to the merciful God, Don Felipe said in his slowest and most careful Latin, "I would make my Confession."

His green eyes wide despite the rain, the Irish priest crossed himself hastily. "To me?"

"To you, my father."

"Lamb of God who take away sin world's have mercy us!" At least the Irish priest seemed to have enough Latin for some appropriate approximation of the liturgy.

So Don Felipe de Alhama de Granada y de Nuestra Señora del Pilar de Agapida, inquisitor of Daroca de Aragon, confessed at last, there on the deck of a small ship buffeted by the fury of the Irish Sea, burying the most mortal of all his sins amid a hurried litany of lesser and commoner offenses. There could hardly be even the pretense of whispering, here in the shriek of the gale, but he did somewhat drop his voice from time to time, including the time of the crucial words. In no way could the distant canon of Eymstadt have overheard, and no one else aboard was likely to have any better grasp of Latin than the little Irish priest, who seemed to understand the vital words of absolution and blessing in their meaning but not, by the way he uttered them, in their grammar and syntax.

Curiously, it appeared to Don Felipe that the storm began its abatement from the moment of his absolution.

* * * *

"Look with care," Don Felipe instructed them. "This is that same, identical 'Purgatory' into which you caused my companion to be lowered?"

"It is," Prior Terence Maguire replied, uneasily shifting his weight from foot to foot.

Don Felipe moved his gaze to the canon of Emystadt, who nodded sullenly and agreed, "It is. Never could I forget this place."

During the last days of the journey, the canon's gloom had seemed to deepen almost hour by hour, from the time he had glimpsed the papal emissary huddled in sacramental Confession with the Irish priest. "He was nearer," Don Felipe had explained, "and I saw you already occupied in hearing our own people's Confessions." But no excuse would soothe the canon, who repeated that his papal holiness had meant them to act as each other's chaplains, and apparently read in Felipe's dereliction some portent of doom to his own purpose. This doom he must have come to fear more and more as Don Felipe refused to take monetary advantage of his status as papal representative, but smoothly and quietly paid every sum suggested by prior, bishop—or, more properly, acting episcopal vicar general, as Cathal Og MacManus proved to be—and the MacGrath who ruled as secular prince of this area. "But you seal their simony with papal approval!" the canon had cried, and kept shaking his head whenever the emissary tried to reassure him, "I merely put their custom upon trial."

Now Don Felipe peered down the well, or pit. Meditatively, he dropped a pebble. It struck bottom quickly, and with a comforting dry sound.

"But, your Excellency," Prior Terence whispered, bending as close to him as respect allowed, "this entrance is for paupers! It is but one of several entrances to our fine Purgatory of Saint Patrick, and your Excellency is surely no pauper—"

"It is this entrance I will use," Don Felipe replied with tranquil authority. "Are not paupers as precious as princes in God's eyes? But let all things be done in order," he added aloud, for the canon's benefit as much as the prior's. "Tonight and tomorrow I will fast. Tomorrow evening I will make Confession—to this good priest whom his holiness has assigned me for chaplain on this pilgrimage—and take Communion from his hand and no other. Thus prepared, I will pass tomorrow night in this same pit."

It might have been better to spend three or even four days in preparatory fasting, according to certain ancient precedents Don Felipe had found; but he mistrusted this Irish weather to hold dry for so long, and rain would certainly increase such natural discomfort as he expected to prove the Purgatory's sole ordeal.

CHAPTER 16

THE DARK MAN OF THE PURGATORY

He knew that he had fallen asleep only by his sense of awakening. Awakening in discomfort: he felt himself lying on a sharp-runged ladder, his limbs tightly bound, his head seeming to be on a strict level with his feet. He thought that, beneath the prickles of a woolen blanket, he was utterly naked.

Opening his eyes to a wash of ruddy light, he verified his conclusions on all points, in so far as he could do so with only his head free to move. By the absence of any restraint round head or neck, as well as the level plane of his body, he guessed that at least he need not fear the water torture.

The well seemed far deeper than he remembered, and far smoother, its polished sides soaring up and up in the glow of the unseen lamps, until his vision met a small crescent moon gleaming all but invisible near what must be the top.

He turned his head. His first impression was of demons so genially fantastic as to suggest grotesque interbreedings, not only with beasts, but even with such things as clocks and wheelbarrows. Eventually he determined that beneath the images lay three straight walls; he assumed that a fourth, behind him, squared the enclosure.

"Good evening," a masculine voice to his left said pleasantly.

Don Felipe looked again. A dark man of uncertain age perched there on a high stool, holding a lute in his lap. Unless he had appeared since the inquisitor's first glance in that direction, Don Felipe must have mistaken him originally for one of the painted figures. True, they were grotesque and the dark man was not; yet his black hairline touched exaggeration in its retreat to either side from a central point that seemed to reach a third of the way down his pale forehead, and the lute shone richly polished and decorated against clothing so black as to mask its cut and style.

"Good evening," Don Felipe replied in courtesy. "By what title and name shall I address you?"

"Why employ any?" His hands like ivory against the black of his attire, the man brushed a long chord from his lute, charging the air of the entire chamber. "What need have two entities alone to address each other by any label?" he went on. "Nomenclature is a convenience when three or more gather together. If you will, kindly glance up."

Don Felipe did so. The tiny crescent had moved a minute distance to the left. As he watched, it moved back an equal distance to the right.

"As for titles," the other added, "'When I was a child, I thought as a child. Now that I am grown, I have put away the toys of a child.'"

"Do you suggest that blood, honor, chivalry, authority both spiritual and temporal—all things implicit in titles—are mere toys?"

"How much use did Jesus Himself have for titles?" the dark man replied, not only giving the Holy Name a curious pronunciation, but failing to incline his head on uttering it.

"So might a mere mortal argue," the inquisitor replied, maintaining the tone and spirit of friendly debate, "who could claim neither title nor any other personal distinction of his own. Our Lord, being God, was and is and ever shall be so high above us that human tongue could never complete the litany of His titles and dignities. How, then, could He have demanded the respect that was His merit, and yet have time to finish His great and necessary work in our imperfect sphere? Yet the mortal who scorns all titles as toys, not only rebels against due authority, but sets himself by implication upon a level with God."

"Cast your gaze upward again," the other suggested.

Obeying, Felipe noted that the crescent appeared larger.

"Teresa of Jesus, also," the dark man mused, "complained of titles as so much needless baggage. Will complain, perhaps I ought to say."

"What Doña Teresa is this?"

"A native of Avila, born a few years from where you are now. She purifies the Carmelites of Spain, and comes to be named a Doctor of the Church."

"A female Doctor of the Church?" Don Felipe closed his eyes for a moment, the better to marvel at God's work in His creation. "What a glorious society we are shaping, after all, in which the women will grow as theological as the men!"

"I wouldn't be too quick to claim credit for the Great Teresa, were I in your place. Fortunately for her, she dies before your Inquisition plunges its fangs into her."

Struck by sudden suspicion, Don Felipe began intoning the words of exorcism at the dark man.

Clearly recognizing the Latin formula, its target shook his head. "Those words," he remarked, "are proof only against Satan and his creatures."

"And are you not one of them?"

"Not so far as I am aware, although of course my present function might justify your surmise."

"Yet you dare to suggest that the Holy Office prosecutes true sons and daughters of the Church."

"Does it not?" The man in black sounded more amused than argumentative. "Are not your own theologians in process of charting the virtuous course for a good and true Catholic accidentally arrested by the Holy Office? Are they not determining that such a person may never, upon pain of sin, utter a false confession, not even to escape torture, nor to gain the mercy—available to any genuine heretic—of strangulation at the stake prior to consumption by the flames?"

Whatever this dark man might be, he seemed well informed. "Not all of us are so strict on this point," Don Felipe explained. "In any case, the reward of such a soul will be great in Heaven."

"In any case, the tide of posterity would quibble with your choice of the word 'prosecute.' 'Persecute' will come to be considered the more natural and appropriate term for your activities."

"By enemies of Holy Church?"

"Oh, by Protestants and good Catholics alike. By the way, have you glanced up lately?"

Felipe again looked up. The crescent had grown definitely larger. Now it seemed the size of a melon, and its swing had apparently widened. "A type of pendulum, is it not?" he inquired.

"Precisely."

"And these 'Protestants' you mention—who and what are they?"

"Ah! Pardon me. In another few decades, a rebel theologian of north central Europe will spearhead the largest and most enduring split in Christendom since that of the Eastern Orthodox. I believe that in your lifetime you will generally refer to these new believers in all their diverse subgroups as 'Lutherans,' after the abovementioned rebel theologian; they will come, however, to be called collectively 'Protestants'—*id est*, protesters against the Church of Rome."

Some vague, dim memory brushed Felipe's awareness of someone murmuring plaintively, "We are many sects with many creeds, yet you make no distinction." Unable to chase the memory down, he sighed, still watching the pendulum. "More heresy?"

"Heresies *en masse*, many of them as hotly at odds with one another as with Popery itself. Although how 'heretical' they are in the sight of God remains hidden from all but the angels."

"And you?" Felipe went on, returning his gaze to his interlocutor. "Are you true angel, or fallen one?"

It was the turn of the man in black to sigh. "As human as yourself, although my dates fall some centuries after yours. The rules of chronology change considerably in eternity."

Don Felipe felt his lips twist in a smile as he inquired, "Would you have me imagine you another descendant of mine?" ("Another"? What an odd question! He could not think why he had asked it.)

"As you please. It might as well be true as not. With half a millennium or so falling between, give or take a few hundred years any individual might turn out to lie somewhere or other in almost any other individual's family lines. Again I must beg that you pay more than academic attention to the pendulum above you."

This time Felipe saw that it was large as a scimitar, and close enough to make him turn his head in following its swing. He observed, "I lie in its path."

"It is also as sharp as a scimitar," said the dark man, apparently reading Felipe's thought. At a chord from the lute, the curved blade stopped at the height of its swing, to hang poised in midair. "The irony," the dark man went on in tones of wry amusement, "is that certain of my friends and well-wishers would have called *me* the one who ought to lie on that slab, rather than the one controlling the mechanism."

"Am I not, then, dead already?"

"What great difference would it make? Do not Dante and long tradition both opine that the soul after death is lent a provisional body with which to experience any appropriate pleasures or pangs?" Brushing another chord, the dark man set the pendulum in motion once more. "I can, at least, offer you one choice. Shall I flick the blanket from you, or would you prefer to feel the blade shear through the cloth for a pass or two before touching the skin?"

Don Felipe shook his head. "No. What else is this but the fourth degree of torture prolonged? Never have I held that the pains of Purgatory were other than immediate and direct."

"Why, man, what species of suffering is exclusion from the Beatific Vision, if not mental and emotional?" Pinching a fold of the blanket near Felipe's chin, the young man—for now he seemed young, although at closer range silver could be seen in his hair—questioned the priest with his eyes.

Again Felipe shook his head.

The other released the blanket and stood back, remarking, "Moreover, can you rest assured that you *are* in Purgatory? Saint Patrick's or anyone else's?"

"Are we not?" Tears filling his eyes, Felipe tried to crane his head for another direct look into his executioner's face, but the dark man had moved too far back. "Have I not, then, found absolution?"

"Oh, you have found *absolution*, in the strictly formal sense of the word. But have you found *forgiveness*?"

The blade, majestic in its unhurried immensity, grazed along the top of the blanket, fraying the threads. Felipe felt a moment of shame upon realizing that he had winced.

"Why?" he demanded. "Why *this*? Where are the fires, the smoking ground, the burning lake, the great wheel?"

"Would you truly prefer any such sensationalism as others have envisioned here to your present fine suspense?"

"I was..." Felipe paused, baffled. "...prepared for that, if for any vision at all."

"Some minds might hypothesize," the other told him, "that this is the meet and fitting punishment for your vocation. You see, the world will come to take it as a truism that you inquisitors, as a class, were inhuman monsters who delighted in creating exquisite and ingenious new tortures—such as this very device of the pendulum."

"*What?*" Not even Fray Junípero had ever proposed any new tortures—difficult enough finding men to apply the old ones!

"Oh, yes. In time, the Holy Office will become a favorite bogy for romancers to employ as an excuse for scenes of sensational agony. I blush to own that I myself, although knowing something of the truth, rather preferred the lurid fantasy."

"Will Holy Mother Church then grow so weak, her enemies so strong?"

"Why, certain respected Catholic scholars of unquestionable personal orthodoxy will be among the most enthusiastic promoters of your 'ingenious torturers' image. Is there not a loyal Catholic opposition even in your own time? Have not you yourself, in part and on occasion, subscribed to the sentiments of this same loyal opposition?"

The pendulum returned, fraying a few more threads and, Felipe thought, his nipples. Catching back a gasp, he tried to see whether or not there was blood on the blade. When he unclenched his teeth, it was to protest: "Is this Divine Justice, to punish one of God's servants for lies that future ages will tell concerning his work?"

"As to that," the other replied, sounding for the first time embarrassed, "it may seem presumptuous, but I cannot help wondering whether the choice of this particular mechanism is less for your benefit than for mine. I suspect that the Purgatory in which you find yourself may in fact be my own."

"Indeed? For what sin?" Even as he uttered the question, Don Felipe was not sure why. Mere custom, when he lay here at the farthest pole from his own state in life? Some blind wish to strike a counterblow?

"Man," his tormentor answered in a voice gone harsh and stern, "*who has appointed* you *my confessor?*"

The blade crashed down, and there remained only dark silence.

CHAPTER 17

"A MATTER OF FAITH"

Having availed himself of the opportunity to visit the great shrine of Santiago de Compostella, Don Felipe thought to pay a pastoral visit to the small parish of Nuestra Señora del Pilar de Agapida, which he had yet to see despite the monies it had been feeding into his purse, through his personally chosen vicar Don Osorio Fadrique, for two decades.

The canon of Eymstadt had taken his leave in Ireland, after kissing Don Felipe's ring in respectful gratitude for pronouncing that the Purgatory of Saint Patrick should indeed be closed. (The dark man might have been demon—despite his protests to the contrary—or merely dream; in any case, the papal emissary had judged his own experience far too much at odds with every other vision he had ever learned of in connection with that place or any other holy site, either to reveal it or allow it to stand in the way of seeing the pit filled in and the pilgrimages stopped.)

The two Italian guards had accompanied him to Compostella for the genuine and undoubted pilgrimage. Then they, too, had kissed his ring before taking ship back to Rome, carrying with them both Don Felipe's report to his holiness and a message to Felipe's own bankers. In the latter he had double-enclosed his first epistle to Gamito.

Left with Luis Albogado as his only attendant, Felipe had considered returning to Aragon by way of the Bay of Biscay; but it was good to be on dry land again. They had met rough seas twice on the voyage from Ireland and, while neither of these storms had proven as menacing as that one between Dublin and Donegal, he had nowhere felt as endangered on land as on water. Shipboard might be the smoothest and easiest means of travel for some—though Felipe preferred the rolling of leather saddle to that of wooden deck—but they had met neither robbers nor rockfalls nor raging rivers in French or Irish lands, so what should threaten them here in Spanish? where they did not even need Latin to communicate, but Luis could speak as easily with tradesman or muleteer, as Don Felipe with bishop, abbot, or scholar. In each tribunal town, moreover, they would gather two or three sturdy local familiars to accompany them as far as the next tribunal, staying with them in monasteries and, once, a good and convenient inn along the way.

Shortly before turning off for Agapida, they rested in a Dominican house near the shadow of Borja castle, home of his own patron's ancestors, which Don Felipe hoped to see either before or after visiting Nuestra Señora del Pilar.

"Will your Reverence join us for Matins and Lauds?" the prior asked him.

"For Lauds and early Mass, I will be honored to join you," Felipe replied. "But travel is rigorous. Let me plead that fact as my excuse for begging to be allowed to read my Matins alone before bed, and slumber through yours."

"As secular priest, your Reverence needs no excuse." The prior smiled and summoned a brother to lead Don Felipe to his guest cell.

Luis Albogado and their two current companions had been bedded down, as usual, in the guesthouse for visiting laymen. Don Felipe had never felt difficulty in sleeping alone in one small room, with the door shut fast. This was to prove as well for him in years to come.

In the middle of the night he woke slowly, from a dreamless sleep, to the sound of loud, heavy knocks and a voice calling, between those knocks, "Felipe de Granada! Open!" And then, clear as the trumpet of Doomsday, the dread words: "It is a matter of Faith!"

But I am myself an inquisitor! he thought, and then: This is Fray Junípero's doing—I have pushed him too far! And then: So this is what it is like for all those others.

END OF PART I

PART II

THE LAST ACT OF FAITH

CHAPTER 18

THE DREAM OF THE TRIAL

He stood in a forest of massive black trees, their trunks straight and stubby where the branches had been lopped off almost as far up as eye could see. By the blocking out of certain stars and parts of the full moon, he could tell that leafy boughs still remained at the woods' very top.

When he looked again, the moon was crimson. Then it vanished completely. He walked in darkness…save that a faint glow limned the trees, which had become smooth as columns chiseled from stone centuries ago.

Far, far in the distance, he spied a patch of light. It seemed to surround a statue of Our Lady of the Pillar, with the body of San Pedro Arbués lying at her feet. He walked toward it. At first a column obscured it from time to time, forcing him to grope his way around; but eventually the columns formed a long, straight aisle to the lighted patch.

As he approached, he found it to be no statue. Rather, a white wall draped with the banner of the Inquisition. In front of the wall and beneath the banner a table, covered with white cloth, behind which sat two judges. Both in black and white robes that resembled, but were not, Dominican habits. Both women. Rosemary and Raymonde.

He attempted to hasten his steps. The ground clung to his feet like pitch. For what seemed a very long while, he came no closer. Then, suddenly, he stood directly at the table's edge, facing them, his fingers splayed before him on the white cloth.

"Great-grandmother," he greeted Raymonde.

"Your name?" said Rosemary.

For a moment, he could not remember it. At last he replied, "Felipe de Alhama de Karnattah."

"Alhama de Granada," Raymonde repeated, inscribing it on the cloth in gold letters.

"Age at time of arrest?" Rosemary went on.

"Forty-two."

"Present age?"

"Fifty-one."

Raymonde looked up from her writing. "How can you be sure?"

"I have kept careful count of the days. Day by day, every morning, another mark on the first leaf of paper I requested. It is nearly filled now. Soon I must request a second sheet for the purpose."

"Have they never in nine years asked why that leaf was never returned?" Raymonde inquired.

"More than once, and each time I have produced it for examination. I have never made a secret of keeping my own calendar. It is permitted. Twice, indeed, my jailor has kindly corrected a small lapse on my part, due to illness."

"Nine years," Rosemary repeated. "Shameful! And you the inquisitor of Daroca. Why have you failed to bring your case until now?"

"I was but the younger inquisitor."

Raymonde nodded. "The accused shows seemly modesty."

"He shows laziness and incompetence," Rosemary growled, looking straight at Don Felipe. "Well? Do you solemnly swear to tell us the truth, the whole truth, and nothing but the truth, and never reveal anything that happens here to anyone outside?"

"This is not the full and proper form of the oath, great-great-granddaughter," Raymonde murmured.

"On your stack of Bibles or whatever! Sorry, great-great-grandmother, I don't have much patience with crackerjack and red tape."

"Before God and His Holy and Ever Blessed Virgin Mother," Don Felipe said, "I do solemnly swear."

"Good," said Rosemary. "Where's that fiscal?"

A dark-haired man whom Felipe almost recognized appeared: at first merely a face floating among the shadows, his black robe detaching itself from the surrounding gloom only as he stepped forward. "Your Honors, I answer your summons fully prepared to publish the evidence."

"The publication?" cried Don Felipe. "I protest! Is this not rather the time for the accusation?"

"You should have thought of that before you let nine years slip by," Rosemary told him. "Now we've got to squeeze things together."

The fiscal produced a book from his sleeve, laid it on the table, and let it fall open, seemingly at random. "Article One," he declaimed, pointing a small glass wand at the top of the left-hand page. "During the year of our Lord 1497, the accused did express to one Gamito Ben Joseph, formerly of Alhama in Granada, more recently of various cities in Aragon, and currently resident in Rome, an unconverted and unregenerate Jew with whom the accused has long maintained an unholy friendship and was then most scandalously visiting in the pope's own city, the sentiment and opinion that if God had indeed guided Admiral Colón to a hitherto unknown world beyond the ocean, it might be a new Promised Land divinely designated for the safe refuge of the unconverted children of Israel."

To his confusion, Don Felipe saw that the volume was printed: all the charges against him set down in fine print on pages from a press. "That God guided Don Cristóbal Colón across the sea to those lands," he stammered, "who could dare to doubt?"

Rosemary demanded, "Would you rather have seen the 'New World' Pagans converted to Judaism than Catholic Christianity? What do you call that, if not heresy?"

"Who are you to judge me of heresy?" he shot back, anger for a moment getting the better of good sense. "You who call yourself my descendant, do you not boast of being an unbaptized Pagan yourself?"

"That's right." Slowly, she stood, seeming to grow from her chair like a plant unfurling its stem to rise straight and tall, ever taller, until she stared down directly into his eyes. "And if you want us to help you get your defense in order, great-grandfather, you'd damn well better take this seriously."

"Article Two," said the fiscal, moving his pointer down the page. "In or about the eighth month of the year 1482, the accused did accept wine from and drink the same with the said unregenerate Jew, Gamaliel Ben Joseph, in the house of one Nathaniel Ben Solomon, a Hebrew resident in Daroca, where the said Nathaniel Ben Solomon practiced the trade, forbidden to his people, of silversmith."

"I admit the act, but deny any ceremonial or heretical intent. I drank in simple friendship, in the relief of seeing a boyhood neighbor, feared dead in the siege of Alhama—"

"So," Rosemary cut in, "you admit friendship with and fautorship of heretics?"

"Gamito can be no heretic! He has never been baptized."

Rosemary replied, "Did you ever try badgering him to let himself be baptized?"

"Alhama," Raymonde said softly. "Would you have preferred that their Catholic Majesties had failed to capture Alhama?"

"I would have preferred that my entire family—good Catholic Christians all—had not been murdered in that capture—"

"'Good Catholic Christians,'" Rosemary mimicked him, "and yet friendly with Moors and Jews. You'd like it better if Granada was still Moorish, wouldn't you? If the Glorious Reconquest had never happened?"

"Their Catholic Majesties bear no blame for the death of my family," he answered stiffly. "Not only was it a misfortune of war, but the entire blame lies at the feet of Manuel Urtigo, soldier in war and bandit in peace, and his followers."

"By his own admission," Raymonde mused, writing on the table-cloth, "my descendant kept company with Jews and Moors in his youth and later."

"As did all of us in Alhama in those years!"

The fiscal remarked, "One could repeat the hoary argument about following the rest of the lemmings over the cliffs, if the allusion is not too cryptic for your milieu." Moving his pointer to a paragraph mid-way down the right-hand page, he went on: "Article Three. In or about the year of Grace 1497, the accused did willfully connive and conspire to have set free, with unmerited exoneration and signal honor, the said Manuel Urtigo, suspect of gravest heresy, on pretext that all the wit-nesses were personal enemies of the said Manuel Urtigo, soldier in war and bandit in peace."

"You can't wiggle out of that one," said Rosemary. "Your whole Council of Faith witnessed it."

The fiscal protested, "Madame Judge, I had been laboring under the impression that we were never in any way to intimate the identity of the witnesses."

"Lady God! That time it was obvious. He'd have seen it for himself."

"Why did you do this, great-grandson?" asked Raymonde. "Manuel Urtigo is the murderer of your family. Would you have taken your re-venge by seeing his immortal soul damned to your Hell forever for lack of effort to wean him from his errors?"

"I… In all honor, I argued for him as I trust I would argue for anyone arrested on such biased testimony. It was my honest conviction that his crimes were not such as belonged to the Holy Office to judge or punish."

"In other words," said the fiscal, "you desired his arrest and punish-ment by the secular arm. You considered the Holy Office too merciful a fate for him, the more particularly as it threatened to save his soul."

"Hoped the hard-working secular authorities would eventually mop him up for you, huh?" Rosemary echoed the fiscal's point.

Raymonde said in tones of gentle protest, "I think it more likely that our kinsman hoped for the chance somehow, someday, to take his own vengeance."

Rosemary shook her head. "Too long a shot, too little concern for other people, letting a mad dog like Urtigo loose on society again. How-ever you slice it, what our kinsman did smacks of something or other damnable."

"Article Four," said the fiscal. "By the testimony of many witnesses, the accused does not consume pork, lard, ham, bacon, trotters, head-cheese, or anything else appertaining to swine."

"Agreed," Felipe said wearily.

"Article Five. On the evidence of many witnesses, the accused changes or causes his servants to change the linen, both of his personal apparel and of his table, on Fridays and Saturdays."

"Agreed."

"Article Six. Many persons have borne witness that the accused habitually lights waxen candles and lamps filled with perfumed oil on the eve of the Sabbath according to Hebraic reckoning, that is, on Friday at or about twilight."

"Agreed."

"Article Seven. Diverse witnesses have testified that the accused habitually washes his hands before meals and upon arising each morning."

"Agreed."

"Article Eight. We have it upon the reliable evidence of numerous witnesses that the accused instructs his cook to fry, sauté, baste, dress, and otherwise prepare his meats, pastries, breads, eggs, olla-podridas, and other foods with olive oil rather than lard."

"Agreed."

"But you must not simply confess to everything, great-grandson," Raymonde put in. "You must either refute the evidence, or beg for mercy."

"Preferably the latter," said the fiscal. "In fact, as your advocate, I cannot urge you strongly enough to enlarge upon your confession and throw yourself on the mercy of the court."

Some dim awareness of the irregularity of these proceedings stirred in Don Felipe's mind. "*You* my advocate? You cannot be my advocate— you are my prosecutor!"

"Things have changed while you were inside, great-grandfather," Rosemary said sternly. "We've had to do some streamlining."

"I refuse an advocate!"

"That is no longer a permissible option, Don," the fiscal replied. "I fear that you are 'stuck' with me."

"Are you not grateful, great-grandson?" said Raymonde. "In my time, we were denied both advocate and fiscal. Our inquisitors of old played all these parts in one."

The fiscal began again, "Article Nine."

Felipe whirled on him. "You cannot continue the accusation after introducing my advocate!"

Rosemary stood and pointed at both men. "Go on, fiscal," she ordered in a voice that echoed as though through some great cavern. "Hit him with it."

On the banner of the Inquisition behind her, the cross of tree trunks with their limbs lopped off close to the bark was changing before Felipe's eyes into a living tree. Staring at it, he waited in cold silence.

"Article Nine," the fiscal repeated. "During Eastertide in the year of our Lord 1483, for the sake of the aforementioned Gamito Ben Joseph, a Jew, and others of that unredeemed persuasion, the accused did sacrilegiously break, twist, trample upon, and defy the solemn and sacred Seal of Confession, to the great and everlasting scandal of the entire Church."

For a moment, Don Felipe could no more speak than if the toca were already engorging his throat. It had come at last—the doom he could not refute. He had confessed it sacramentally and been absolved in the forum of conscience, but what did the innocent absolution of an all but unlettered Irish priest weigh in the scales against the unpardonable sin? He tried twice to swallow, while the tree on the banner put out new green branches reaching to the far ends of the table. At last he seized the book of the accusation and riffled through it wildly, searching for the printed charges, able to find only heretical propositions scattered with woodcut prints of demons and fornicators.

When inner pressure had stretched him to the point of a waterskin about to burst, he cried, "It is my enemy who has done this! Fray Junípero has instigated these charges and bribed and suborned all the witnesses! It is Fray Junípero de la Sangre Sagrada, who hates me for my efforts to bridle his bloodlust!"

"You idiot," Rosemary said, grimly calm. "Why the hell didn't you put that statement where it belonged, at the beginning of the trial? It's too late now." With her left hand she beckoned to the fiscal, and pointed her right at the tree behind her.

Now its branches had separated from the trunk and hovered over the ends of the table like disembodied green wings, while the trunk, once more stark and lopped, had become a stake rising from a high mound of dry faggots.

"Liar!" Felipe shouted back at her. "Liar and Mother of Lies! You call me your ancestor! Would you utterly ruin your own chance of birth by destroying my flesh still virginal?"

"Remember your own Bible," she snapped, snatching the book from his hands. "'God is able out of these stones to raise up ancestors to Rosemary.' Burn him!"

The fiscal seized his arm.

"You cannot!" Don Felipe repeated, wrenching free. "Is this not another dream?"

"*All* that we say or seem," the fiscal replied, catching his arm again, "is but a dream within a dream."

"I know you now!" Pulling free again, Don Felipe fell back and stared at him. "My God! I know you now—you are the demon of Saint Patrick's Purgatory!"

"For my own weak sins and failings," the other acknowledged, reaching once more for Felipe's arm. "Punily though they loom beside your own towering misdemeanors."

"But this cannot be!" the inquisitor stammered as he strove to elude his tormentor both bodily and verbally. "*You*, I have never forgotten when awake, but *they*—" motioning with one arm at the two women—"I never, outside my dreams, remember!"

Rosemary looked at Raymonde. "Still hasn't caught on, has he?"

"Grandson, great-grandson," Raymonde explained gently, "whenever you see either or both of us, it is no more than partially a dream."

"Never its mysteries are exposed," the fiscal remarked, chaining Felipe to the stake, "to the weak human eye unclosed. And thus the sad soul that here passes, beholds it but through darkened glasses."

The great, leafy wings to right and left swung back and forth, fanning the faggots into flame. As the fire touched his knees, Don Felipe screamed and woke.

* * * *

He lay a long while awake on his pallet, staring into the dry darkness, wondering if anyone had heard his outcry. Perhaps not. What had seemed in his dream a full-throated shout had shrunk as the effort woke him into a mewling whimper. As for the rest of the dream, he remembered that it had had to do with his trial—assuming he was ever to have a regular audience—and that he had rehearsed before unknown and faceless judges the same list of charges he had reviewed over and over in his mind. Never on paper; it would hardly have been shrewd to allow his enemy any glimpse into his planned defense, and such leaves of paper as he requested had gone for the most innocent of calendrical calculations and pious platitudes. He would not even write down what he had decided to state at once, when and if the time came, as the probable causes for his arrest and the charges he might explain away—although he seemed to recall that, in the dream, he had strangely declined to offer his planned explanations and refutations for those very offenses.

The dark man of the Purgatory had been in the dream, that much he recollected. Chaining him to the stake at the end.

As for the fire, that must have been the brain yielding to a moment of idle panic. The Holy Office would never relax nor publicly penance one of its own inquisitors, for fear of scandal. It might, eventually, sentence him privately to conventual reclusion—then, at least, he would have the

Sacraments again—but for several years now he had suspected that they would simply let him die while awaiting audience, leaving his disappearance forever ascribed to some unknown accident on his last return from Italy. For himself, he believed that he had ceased to care. He worried only, from time to time, about his servants. Gubbio, if left free, was well able to shift for himself; but *had* they left him free, or arrested him also?

CHAPTER 19

THE TRIAL

At last, one April morning in the year of Grace 1509, Don Felipe found himself, somewhat to his own surprise, on the defendant's tripod in the formal audience chamber.

It had changed but little since last he sat on the judges' side of the table. He recognized the same white tablecloth, neatly mended now in a few places by some pious and presumably feminine hand; the dark backs of the inquisitors' chairs, their carved wood quietly agleam with long polishing; the black tiles of the floor, showing scarcely more wear than a dozen years ago; and the clean white of walls and ceiling, which might have been recently repainted. The banner of the Inquisition, he thought, was a new one: its embroidery seemed brighter and finer than that of the old. Possibly done by the same hand that had mended the tablecloth.

Also new, at least to the inquisitors' chairs, were both his judges. Fray Cipriano de la Santa Cruz, his prematurely silver tonsure looking only slightly sparser and his round face seeming to have grown rounder instead of more lined, had been fiscal in Fray Junípero's time; and in Fray Cipriano's colleague Felipe thought he recognized Don Julian Herrera de Parmiento y Seveda. It was conceivable that the scholarly old hidalgo had been widowed and taken the cloth; but, seeing that his simple black garb resembled the habit of no religious order familiar to Don Felipe and that his hair, though thinner, showed no sign of tonsure, he more likely belonged to the small new wave, already underway before Felipe's arrest, of capable or influential laymen raised to the inquisitorship.

Where, then, was Fray Junípero? Dead, jubilated, or moved to some other tribunal? Was it conceivable that he had achieved a place on the Suprema?

The little scribe, Fray Pablo de María, looked no more changed than the tablecloth—a little older, a little less fresh, but otherwise the same as ever. He might have been sitting in his place every moment of the last twelve years, moving only to dip his pen, draw it across his paper, and take new sheets as necessary from time to time.

"Well, well, Don Felipe," Fray Cipriano began pleasantly, "we had better follow regular procedure. Do you solemnly vow, in the presence of God and His Ever Blessed and Holy Virgin Mother, to tell the truth, entirely and exclusively, within these walls, and to guard lifelong silence about everything that happens here, revealing none of it at any time, neither by act, word, nor sign, to anyone outside?"

"I do solemnly vow."

"Good." Fray Cipriano nodded. "Please be so good as to state your full name."

"Felipe de Bivar y Aguilar, also known as Don Felipe de Nuestra Señora de Agapida."

"Your age?"

"Fifty-three."

"The town or other place of your birth?"

"Alhama de Granada."

"Occupation?"

"The Church." As they well knew, but let all things be done properly, following regular procedure. "From 1475 until 1485 I served briefly as secretary and afterward as ordinary to his Reverence the bishop of Daroca. From 1485 until my arrest, I served, by appointment of his Majesty King Fernando, as inquisitor here in Daroca. I also hold the benefice of Nuestra Señora del Pilar in Agapida. And, most recently, I served Pope Alexander the Sixth as legate in the matter of Saint Patrick's Purgatory, so called, in Ireland."

"Length of time since your arrest by the Holy Office?"

"Eleven years and, unless my count is somewhere at fault, one hundred and sixty-two days."

Don Julian leaned forward and spoke for the first time. "One cannot help but wonder why, in all those years, you never sought an audience yourself."

"I assumed that my greater profit lay in patiently abiding the tribunal's due process and meanwhile searching my own soul, as it were in the desert, not unlike the hermits of old."

Fray Cipriano nodded. "And what have your meditations led you to recollect, assume, or suspect of the reasons for your arrest?"

Don Felipe took a deep breath and cleared his throat. "I believe that Fray Junípero de la Sangre Sagrada came to feel great personal enmity toward me, growing out of our disagreements, as fellow inquisitors of Daroca, concerning the best or most proper way to conduct various cases. As, for instance, those of Mehmoud Aben Fazoud, also known as 'El Santon de Aragon,' and subsequently received into Holy Mother Church as Juan Delgado de Calamocha the younger; Hermía Corchuelo the reputed witch; and especially Manuel Urtigo, called 'The Scourge of Axtilan,' on whose case Fray Junípero and I clashed rather bitterly. I also more than once rebuked Fray Junípero for personally handling the instruments of the torture chamber, which handling I interpreted as contrary to the wishes of the Suprema and ill-befitting the dignity and sanctity of the inquisitorship. Of certain innocent appearances I may, during the normal course of my life, have been guilty—as, of occasionally declining pork, bacon, and foods fried in lard, for the sake of my digestion, which is somewhat delicate; of lighting oil lamps or waxen candles on Friday as on any other night, for the sake of my eyes in reading; of changing or causing my servants to change my linens, whether of bed, table, or my person, whenever I judged them soiled, even if this should chance to fall on Friday or Saturday; and of washing my hands whenever I saw them in need of it, which may have been more often than seemly in one of my vocation, but my over-fastidiousness results rather from the sin of luxury than that of heresy. I acknowledge, also, a taste for dishes prepared with olive oil. I learned this taste when a student in Rome, where such foods are commonly consumed by good Catholic Christians with no thought of heretical taint, and where likewise I met my servant Francesco di Gubbio, to the best of my knowledge a faithful Italian Catholic, who often prepared such dishes for me at my instruction. I have partaken of pork, bacon, and lard with great pleasure whenever my digestion seemed capable of them, and all the other things I have always done with no regard either of the day of the week or of mealtimes. Nonetheless, all this would have given Fray Junípero, as a powerful personal enemy armed with the senior inquisitorship, material from which to fabricate charges; and his opportunities would have been ample to suborn witnesses by means of threats and bribery, particularly during my absence as papal legate in the matter of Saint Patrick's Purgatory."

Fray Cipriano, who had been fondling the sheets of paper before him, took advantage of Felipe's pause to ask his colleague, "Well, Don Julian, what is your opinion? Do we need to call in the fiscal and go through the whole rigmarole in Don Felipe's case?"

"It is my humble opinion," Don Julian replied gravely, also looking over the written leaves, "that this case has already consumed more time than it ought to have done, and other business presses heavily upon us."

"Agreed." Nodding again, Fray Cipriano proceeded to end the audience.

It was on Don Felipe's tongue to protest the irregularity. Was he not to have a sight of the new fiscal? Where was the formal accusation, where his own advocate? He had not so much as named those whom he suspected Fray Junípero of suborning, let alone been asked to name witnesses for his defense. Yet, with an effort, he kept silent, hoping that the very abruptness of his treatment, coupled with its geniality, told in his favor.

His patience had its reward. A single week passed before he walked out of the secret cells an honorably acquitted man. Eleven years, one hundred sixty-two days, and a single week.

The story to which he had sworn was that he had at last, after long delays, come home from the edge of the civilized world, arriving during the hour of siesta. If no one could swear to have seen him enter town, neither could any swear that no one else had seen him. All papers in his case, if not already irretrievably lost in the confusion of the secret records, would—he suspected—be destroyed, for it must never become public scandal that the Inquisition had tried one of its own inquisitors. Outside the tribunal (for he doubted that the Suprema itself had ever been notified of his arrest), only Junípero's corrupted witnesses would know; and, if ever they dared blab, what would their word weigh against that of the inquisitors?

So changeless, so immutable had Don Felipe's life seemed for so many days, months, and years in the secret cells, that he was bewildered for a time, blinking at the transformations in his suddenly enlarged world like that man born blind who, healed by Ihesu, had at the outset seen his fellow human beings as though they were trees walking about.

That Fray Junípero was dead came as little surprise. Neither did the manner and hour of his death—a blood vessel bursting in his brain during a Council of Faith, scarcely a month before Don Felipe's own trial. That both Queen Isabel and her first inquisitor general, Tómas de Torquemada, had likewise passed from this world into the next caused the newly freed man some surprise but less secret grief than he found it prudent to show in public. Far more painful was the news that his patron, the good Pope Alexander VI, had gone to his heavenly reward in the year of Grace 1503, and no doubt found his bliss marred, in so far as enjoyment of the Beatific Vision could be marred, by the spectacle of his old enemy Giuliano Della Rovere reigning in his place, as Pope Julius the Second of that name.

Several years before his death—very soon, in fact, after Felipe's own imprisonment, and on the eve of the new century, in the same year that saw Spain's release from her first inquisitor general, 1498, Pope Alexander had finally been driven, as even the best-meaning must sometimes be driven by the pure force of events, to purge the world of that violent reformer Fra Girolamo Savonarola of Florence. Much more commendable than the fiery Italian monk was another young reformer, Desiderius Erasmus of Rotterdam, whose *Handbook of the Christian Soldier* was sweeping Spain, along with the rest of Europe. Don Felipe made it one of his earliest acts of freedom to purchase a copy.

Neither Gubbio nor any other of Felipe's servants had ever been either arrested or personally inconvenienced by the Inquisition in any way beyond the quiet necessity of inventorying the household goods, which burden had fallen chiefly on Felipe's personal secretary Don Martin de Villaréal. The Italian proved to have been managing his master's properties with considerable worldly wisdom: maintaining regular employment in various fetch-and-carry capacities for the Holy Office, Gubbio had regularly used its pack trains, with their inquisitorial immunity from the customs, to smuggle valuable goods back and forth between the various kingdoms of Spain; and, should other markets temporarily fail him for various of these goods, he was not above selling them himself in the Inquisition's own shop, quietly bringing them in on such days as he manned the place, to stock alongside the items legitimately confiscated from condemned heretics, pocketing the price of his smuggled goods when they found buyers and calmly carrying them home again when they did not.

"Gubbio, my Gubbio!" Don Felipe repeated, shaking his head. "How I rejoice that I am not your confessor!"

The Italian replied, "Would your Severity have preferred your prison bill to rest unpaid? But here is an opportunity you may prefer for your glory and our increased profit, all sanctified in the sight of God."

What the servant held out to him was a letter from King Fernando himself, now ruling his dead wife's kingdom of Castile as regent for their widowed daughter Juana, called "La Loca" on account of her increasingly obvious madness. Fernando offered Felipe de Alhama de Granada the post of chief inquisitor of Córdoba. Although to all appearances the king himself believed, along with the multitude, that Don Felipe had simply been long delayed on his journey, the former prisoner could not but suspect that Fernando's desire to appoint him to this post might have worked along with Fray Junípero's timely decease to hasten his own release.

But why this pressing search for a new inquisitor in Córdoba? How could laborers be found lacking for this particular part of the field?

Shrewd questioning of Gubbio, Don Martin, and others eventually revealed to Don Felipe that Córdoba's last chief inquisitor had been a monster—Diego Rodrigues Lucero, called "El Tenebroso" in ironical wordplay. Under Spain's second inquisitor general, one Diego Deza, whose term of office Don Felipe had entirely missed but whom many hinted had been even more to be dreaded than his glorious predecessor Fray Tómas, El Tenebroso had held Córdoba for years in a grip of terror and torture, actually going so far as to make a public spectacle of arresting and imprisoning that saintly archbishop, Fernando de Talavera, whom Isabel had given Granada as if in an effort to heal the wounds she had herself inflicted.

Now the king had found a third inquisitor general in Cardinal Gonzalo Ximenes de Cisneros, whose desire for just reform had manifested itself by forcing El Tenebroso into retirement on half pay. Hence, both King Fernando's need for a replacement, and his difficulty in finding one.

Don Felipe spent as long as he dared in pondering the problem. But, as he considered what temper unhappy Córdoba must be in after suffering so long under a man scarcely worthy to have been a Nero, let alone a holy inquisitor; what humors must predominate at present in her long-suffering people; and what wounds must fester there, he felt himself unequal to the task, and joined the list of those who respectfully, and with many polite expressions of regret, declined his Majesty's appointment.

Indeed, Felipe asked himself, as he had asked himself over and over during the days and nights of his imprisonment, ought he not of his own volition request retirement on half pay? The Holy Office was but one aspect of a generous Church who held out vocations almost without number to her clerical members. Might he not take up residence in that parish of his own, which he had never yet seen? Might he not, now that his old Spanish-born patron was gone, return to Italy and fulfill his youthful dream of a pastoral office in that country? Might he not even conquer his prejudices and turn monk, now that so many of the monastic houses were being returned to their original purity?

Even as he began his first letter of the new century to his boyhood friend Gamito, searching for phrases to explain his long lapse without violating the further vow of silence imposed on him, the question hammered at Felipe's thoughts of why he should remain bound to that same Inquisition which had so treated its own faithful servant.

CHAPTER 20

THE DREAM OF THE STARWALKER

It seemed to be night, yet such a night as he had never known. Great, stark cylinders stood at regular intervals, like huge candles, along the broad thoroughfare, each silver cylinder capped with a light brighter than twenty full moons. It was the length of two Aves before he saw how steadily these lights shone forth in their greenish glow, for mist or smoke wove about them constantly in ever-changing swirls. He coughed—the swirls were acrid.

Beyond the cylinder lights, above them, below them, and all around, windows seemed quietly ablaze, as if the city were illuminated, but with lamps far brighter than any of his own time. And what a city it was! The windows stretched above his head in many banks and rows, until the buildings themselves, which he finally made out in their dark outlines, seemed each one taller than the Tower of Babel. Not immediately around him, but somewhat in the distance, he saw lights along the lower levels that flashed softly dark and bright again with curious figures limned in many pale colors.

Turning to examine the other direction, he found Rosemary at his side.

"Welcome to Valparaiso," she said dryly.

"Valparaiso?"

"Valparaiso, Indiana. Heartland of North America—the New World, to you. This is what it'll be in 1924 C.E.—sorry, A.D."

"How can mankind inhabit this place?" He coughed again. "The air itself is thick and tastes of some foul acid."

She sniffed appraisingly. "Gasoline inside city limits."

From this direction he saw in the distance, as if it stood on a low ridge, what he sensed must be some cathedral of the future, with a great, round tower at one end, rising in pleats of stained glass from the ground to twice as high as the rest of the building. Illuminated from within, it seemed athrob with enough holy beauty to compensate for the reeking squalor immediately about him. Lifting one arm, he pointed at the tower.

She nodded. "Big media evangelist there tonight. Holding what he calls an 'ecumenical tent revival.' Some tent, huh? Look in here."

She led him into one of the buildings. They ascended two flights of stairs, soft with thick but frayed carpeting, drenched in some strange, all-encompassing, shadowless twilight that showed every cobweb, roll of dust, and chipping of the paint. At last they stood in a passageway of straight lines and sharp angles, before a plain brown door. Insubstantially, they passed through without opening it.

Eleven people sat in a circle on the carpeted floor, some cross-legged, others with legs folded beneath their bodies. They wore short and brightly colored tunics over trousers or long skirts. Many had scarves tied round their heads, and most wore at least one or two pieces of jewelry. All had their eyes gently closed, and expressions of peace on their faces. Many had scarves tied round their heads, and most wore at least one or two pieces of jewelry. All had their eyes gently closed, and expressions of peace on their faces.

In the center of the circle was a small mound, flat on top and entirely draped with pale cloth, on which a colorful pottery mug, filled with water, rested between two thick wax candles. They provided the room's only light: to Don Felipe's eyes, it looked far more natural than the false illuminations of town and stairway. Incense filled the air, some fragrance unfamiliar but grateful to his nostrils. To his eyes, the sides of the room appeared crowded with furniture and more cluttered than any alchemist's study, but within the circle all was open and tranquil.

One of the men, lean and bareheaded, with some few white strands in his dark brown hair, began to chant. Low, calm, and resonant, his voice pervaded the room. First he himself, then several others, finally all of them swayed gently from side to side. Though no one came near it, the water in the mug rippled slightly. Don Felipe sensed some Power here; and, while part of his mind acknowledged that he ought perhaps to decry it as heretical, his awestruck soul could not recognize it as evil. Had not Ihesu Himself said, "He who is not against you, is with you," "By their fruits ye shall know them," and "If Satan were divided against himself, how could his house stand?"

Rosemary said, and even her voice was for once soft and tinged with brusque awe, "Starwalker Jones Silverstairs. Yes, I always heard he liked keeping it simple."

Don Felipe whispered, "Who are these people?"

"Wiccans. Neo-Pagans. Witches, if you like."

"But...I see no sign here of the Devil. This is surely no Black Mass...?"

"The Black Mass was a Christian invention. Shh! Listen."

He became aware of low, rumbling sounds, vibrant in the floor beneath his feet.

Rosemary pointed out the window. He had not noticed it before. Now, he marveled at its expanse of clear glass, the length of a man's arm across and twice as high. Still marveling, he peered out, and saw all the city lying like a vast, dark beast beneath its thousands of garish lights.

The building with the tower of stained glass rose above all the other lights, direct in his view. It seemed much nearer than it had outside. He sensed it pulsing, throbbing—almost, he could hear its preacher declaiming, its congregation responding. He asked, "What does the evangelist tell them?"

"Another Ferran Martínez," Rosemary replied. "This one's targeting witches."

The bottom of the tower vomited forth many tiny figures, like ants or strange wasps bursting in one mass from their nest.

"Not all of them," Rosemary commented. "Thank the Lady, it wasn't all of them. Estimated twenty percent of the total attendance that night."

How many, then, must have been gathered there, in that cathedral of the future? No more than one fifth of them spewing themselves out… he had seen many entire villages inhabited by fewer people than there were in this new mob. And it moved with paralyzing speed. Even as he guessed at its numbers, it had come halfway—and it was coming straight for the house of the witches.

Who were crowding at the window now, neither ignoring nor heeding himself and his guide…rather, treating them as merely two more bodies in the general alarm. "The Christians!" "They're coming!" "The Fundos!" "Gods, what did he tell them this time?"

"Sisters and brothers!" cried the man whom Rosemary had called Starwalker. "Stand not on the order of your going, but go! Quickly and softly. Melt in. Go with the Lord and the Lady—blessed be, and may we gather again!"

They began leaving at his first words, and were entirely gone only heartbeats after he finished. Then he himself, after one glance around, went out, neither hurriedly nor slowly, and shut the door with care behind him. Last of all, Rosemary, having held Felipe back from the general rout, led him through the closed door, down the steps, and back out upon the hard, clean black street.

Wide though it was, the mob was choking it at one end. At the other, scant paces ahead of Felipe and his guide, two witches held back, one of them a young woman, staring with anxious eyes at their leader as if waiting for him.

"Go!" he told them, his voice low and urgent.

"Starwalker," asked the young woman, "will you—"

"Go!" he repeated. "Split up! Melt in! Don't worry about me."

"*There!*" someone bawled from the mob, and another voice added, "That's him! There's the Right Arm of Anti-Christ!"

"Starwalker—" began the young man who had lingered.

Something small and hard—stone or brick?—hurtled out of the mob and struck the young woman's forehead. She staggered. Her companion seized her arm and ran, all but dragging her along. As though to shield them, Starwalker sprang between them and the mob, half turning to face it. They were close, too close to outrun—

One of those dread explosions made by handguns of the future shook the street. Starwalker stood for an instant, eyes already glazed, and then fell. The back of his head was gone in a mass of blood and soft brains.

The explosion and sudden death stopped the mob, but for no more than a few atoms of time. Someone shouted, "Praise the Lord! Now let's cleanse the whole damn nest!"

Screaming and frenzied, they surged through the street like maddened bulls. Most of them ran around or over the corpse, kicking and trampling but otherwise giving it little attention. When the greater part had passed on in pursuit of other victims, however, some few lingered as if eager to dishonor the body.

All this while, Rosemary had held Felipe back in a doorway. Now, without warning, she sprang forth and stood over the martyr's corpse, glaring at those dregs of the mob. "No!" she screamed. "Lady God! Not this time!"

Don Felipe held his breath. In the usual pattern of these visions, he and his guides could only witness, without affecting events in any way. Yet, for once, the rabble held off. Whether they saw her or not, some sense of her seemed to cow them: they shrank away from their victim, leaving him alone as they pelted after their comrades like dragon scales trying to fix themselves once more to the monster's body.

"They never caught the others," Rosemary said. "Silverstairs was the only casualty this time." Felipe saw tears rolling down her mannish face. They shocked him more, almost, than the violence. In silence, he watched her kneel, gather the corpse into her arms, and rock back and forth over it pieta-like, unconscious of self in her grief.

For some time, she seemed unable to speak further. At last she said, "One of my grandfathers was almost with Silverstairs that night. At the last minute, he decided to stay home with my grandmother, help her nurse a bad cold. My other grandparents were over *there*. They could've been in the mob. I don't know. I never asked. Never will ask."

Don Felipe laid one hand on her shoulder. The name "Great-grand-daughter" almost came to his lips. Almost, not quite. He had no children. He was both celibate and, in his fifty-fifth year, still virginal, still faithful to his half-forgotten love. All his life, in dream after dream, this woman of the future had lied to him.

Yet even she, it appeared, could grieve. Perhaps she herself was only mistaken, not malicious. Wordlessly, he squeezed her shoulder in a way that would have befitted a grandfather with more "greats" than anyone should remember.

CHAPTER 21

OUR LADY OF THE PILLAR

So this, thought Don Felipe, is the benefice that has given me income so many years—my only income, excluding what Gubbio used of his own questionable earnings to maintain my household and myself, all that time I lay in the secret cells.

They first caught sight of Agapida from the top of a low rise, looking more across than down into an expanse of not quite fertile land, mostly pasture, with some planted fields visible around the distant huddle of stone buildings, too small a village for more than the single church, Our Lady of the Pillar, standing like an ageless guardian angel between the tiny dwellings and the still more distant castle. Don Felipe guessed that both church, castle, and the greater part of the houses had stood here unchanged since before the Synod of Toledo, an unbroken link with the Visigothic past. The whole value of this site may have been military, yet its present appearance suggested that, as a fortress, it had never really been needed. Unlike that once far more prosperous stronghold far to the south, Alhama de Karnattah, this village might never have been sacked, its people never forced to crowd inside the castle walls.

Why have I never visited my own church until this day? his thoughts continued. It brings my boyhood back to me. Why has it required my duty as inquisitor to bring me here, when my duty as incumbent of the benefice would have sufficed?

"Here they come," Gubbio observed.

True enough, a line of dots was threading its way to the village out-skirts. Already Don Felipe could hear their chant, make out the fine, blur-topped pole that would be his parish's best processional crucifix.

He had seen all of it before, not in every place of his visitation, but in the greater number of them. The welcoming procession, planned no doubt from the hour of learning that the Holy Office would visit this town, set into motion by the arrival of the familiar sent on ahead of the inquisitor's main party, and designed to demonstrate a holy zeal and reli-gious fervor that might or might not mask secret failings.

"Come," Don Felipe said. "Let us see how near to town our mounts can meet them."

Don Enrique de la Santa Cruz rode forward, unrolling the inquisito-rial banner that his merits had earned him the honor of bearing before the holy inquisitor. Both fiscal and scrivener rode a little behind Don Felipe, with him as the apex of their triangle. The remaining three familiars followed in single file, and Gubbio brought up the rear, leading the pack animals along. Don Enrique and the two Juans rode horses; Don Felipe, his fiscal, and the last familiar good mules; the little scrivener Pablo de María—who, pleading overwork in the Daroca tribunal, had followed Don Felipe into the tiny and obscure one of Ainsa when King Fernando appointed him to its solitary inquisitorship as if in pique at his refusal to accept the Córdoban post—had his little donkey Rosita; and Gubbio, the latest in his line of trusty asses. Don Enrique's horse and Don Felipe's Blanca were pure white, with a certain degree of fine stuff in their trappings. Even dusty and somewhat travel-worn, the inquisitor's party made a fine short procession of its own.

They met nearer the village than the rise, for the village procession moved afoot, save for two men on horseback—in one of whom Don Felipe recognized the familiar he had sent in advance—and one man on a mule as gentle as any the inquisitor had ever seen, chosen no doubt for the rider's age and infirmity. The younger of the two local riders proudly bore a banner showing two fiery swords crossed on a field of vair. Obviously these two were Don Alfons de Monsecore y Tequilador de la Castel de Agapida, and his son Don Gaspar. Their attire would have proclaimed their rank even had they, like their people, come forth on foot, as members of the local nobility sometimes did in such processions.

The acolytes and choir boys, of course, preceded them all, led only by their immediate shepherd, Don Felipe's vicar, Don Fadrique Osorio. At first glance, Don Felipe was shocked to see the lean young new-made priest whom he had named to his church, after one brief interview so many years ago, grown corpulent and waddling as though unaccustomed to even the exercise of walking. In so poor a countryside, pastoring so underfed a flock, where had Don Fadrique found food to wax so luxuriously fat?

Beware, inquisitor, Don Felipe reminded himself, of seeing thine own weaknesses in others. Would you yourself not have grown equally large by now, if not for that same weak and too often delicate digestion which provided one of Fray Junípero's charges against you? Gluttony is in itself no more heretical than abstinence.

Half a dozen men in the castellan's colors came with the choir, bearing the church's prize possession—the statue of its patron—on her garlanded litter. So that, thought Don Felipe, is Nuestra Señora del Pilar de Agapida. If her gilding was shabby in places; if there were chips in the carved sword she held, her hands resting on its hilt while its point bit down into the serpent at her feet; if the choristers' white linen surplices showed considerable fraying and more holes than quite seemly—still, all these defects became visible only at close range, while their singing remained as clear and sweet as at a distance, and the incense grew sweeter, because stronger.

If the nobles were a little shabby in their attire and trappings, it was less so than their villagers and no more so than the inquisitor's party itself, after its weeks of travel from place to place. What most struck Don Felipe was the fact that, while the two he guessed were Don Alfons and his son came mounted, their attendants walked. Usually he had found either all the people of rank coming humbly on foot, or the dons and duennas riding as well as their lords and ladies.

The nearer they came, however, the more Don Felipe read age, even illness in the older lord's countenance and the manner in which he bore his body. Don Alfons might be too feeble to walk, and his heir perhaps too proud—or too considerate of his senior's pride—to move afoot beside a mounted parent.

Behind the people of the castle came the villagers, affecting but not entirely achieving seemly orderliness…yet a large group at the very rear, following a strange little gap between them and the others, proceeded with a solemnity to match that of the choristers and outshine that of both castle people and commoners.

Looking more closely, the inquisitor observed that this rearmost group seemed entirely blackhaired and dark complexioned, that a few more bright colors appeared in their clothing and a little more jewelry about their persons, than was the case with the other villagers as a group.

Casting his mind back, he found an old memory, from before his time in the secret cells, of one of his vicar's very rare reports. In it, Don Fadrique had mentioned that some of those wandering Christians of Lower Egypt, who claimed to be on penitential pilgrimage for succumbing temporarily to Muslim ways, were attempting to settle in Agapida—what, if anything, should be done about them? Don Felipe had directed him to give them all the spiritual assistance they sought, and be thankful for anyone who actually sought it, a thirst which was all too hard to find in these days of waning fervor.

He barely had time to notice the Egyptians—if that was who they were—before his attention was called back to the formal ceremonies of being welcomed and brought in honor to a feast spread in the village square.

It was not much of a square, nor much of a feast. The Agapidans had done their best, but their village clearly served as market town only for its own locals and the very immediate vicinity. Appraising it, the inquisitor privately rejoiced that Acts of Faith were no longer to be held along the visitation route, but exclusively in cities housing permanent tribunals.

Wondering whether it might not have been better for them to hold this feast in the castle, Don Felipe suddenly felt some twinge of guilt at deriving part of his own income from these people.

At length, near the end of the meal, he turned to Don Fadrique on his left and inquired, "Where are the rooms you have cleared for us?"

A strange, stifled expression crossed the vicar's face as he began, "Your Excellency..." and fell into an awkward pause, staring to Don Felipe's right.

The young lord, who stood there between the inquisitor and Don Alfons, proud to serve them as cupbearer, took the word. "Let us offer you the hospitality of our castle. Your chambers have been swept and strewn with fresh flooring, you may have my father's own hall for your courtroom, and all the resources of our own torture chamber will be available to you."

"Oh?" Don Felipe studied the gleam of the young man's eyes, the glint of his white teeth. "You have a torture chamber, have you?"

"An ancient one," muttered the older lord, the eager stripling's father. "Long disused...long shut up and forgotten..."

"Opened again!" his son protested. "I have seen to its cleaning myself, in preparation for your holy visit."

"And the men to operate the equipment?"

"We will provide them!" Don Gaspar assured him with all the ready confidence of youth. "I will... If necessary, I would be honored to serve the Holy Inquisition in that office with my own hands."

"I would not ask you to bloody your noble fingers with such menial work," Don Felipe answered, making an imperfect effort to keep disgust from sounding in his voice. But for the secrecy that lent the Holy Office one of her most effective tools, he would have informed this over-zealous whelp that executioners and assistants to administer torture were not so easy to find, especially here in the northern kingdom; that, when pressed into service, they were more likely than not to prove bumbling at their task, which clumsiness had all too often resulted in heinous and unsanctioned crippling of the defendants under investigation; and that torture was never to be administered until after full and careful discussion and voting on each individual case by the Council of Faith—which certainly never, within the jurisdiction of any conscientious tribunal, took place on the site during a visitation. In any event, what of those ancient fueros of which Aragon was so justly proud? What business had any private torture facility, in no matter how ancient and noble a house, not to have been destroyed long ago beyond any chance of restoration?

Turning back to his vicar, he resumed, "We have much to do in the morning. Your people may celebrate into the night, if they will; but, as for ourselves, we will soon wish to retire. Again I must ask you, where are we to rest, where do our work?"

"But...your Excellence..." Don Fadrique protested, still looking over Don Felipe's shoulder as if appealing to the young hidalgo, "my housekeeper, poor woman, lies sick abed. She could not serve your Excellence—she has not been able to cook nor clean the house during all this last week. Don Gaspar has offered you rooms in his father's castle, rooms far more spacious and suitable than any I could provide."

"The castle itself—" Don Gaspar began again.

Don Felipe cut him off with a wave of his hand. "It is too far removed from the village."

"It rules the village," the young lord answered stiffly.

The inquisitor replied, carefully measuring tact into his speech, "My friend, I do not for one moment question that your father and you understand the art of secular government. But neither is it for you to question my knowledge of how best to carry forth the work of the Holy Office. Experience has taught me that more souls are saved and heretics discovered when we locate ourselves closer among the people."

Old Don Alfons made one of his rare contributions to the discussion. "Summon Don Sagesse."

The younger man looked surly, but bowed his head and beckoned a page. Bowing in turn, the page made his way to one of the lower tables, a little apart from the others—the table of the Egyptian pilgrims, if so they were—and spoke to the lean brown man of late middle age who sat at its head. Though at some distance, Don Felipe had already observed that the table manners of these people compared favorably with those of the other locals, even of the castellan's petty courtiers at his own table. Now he noticed the delicate care with which the Egyptian rinsed and wiped mouth, mustache, and fingers before rising to follow the page back to the head table.

After a glance to right and left, as if to reassure himself there had been no mistake, the Egyptian approached the head table and made a low, graceful bow to the inquisitor and his immediate companions.

"Your Reverence," murmured the frail old lord, "allow me to present Don Sagesse Labaa, count of the Calé, as they call themselves."

"Don Sagesse," the inquisitor acknowledged, with a courteous inclination of the head. "Your Grace."

"Your Reverence." The man whom Don Alfons called "Don" and "count" even while seating him at the lower tables among the peasantry made another bow, so dignified as to show respect completely unmarred by either the obsequiousness or the half-hidden hatred the inquisitor met more often than he liked.

Well pleased so far with the count of the Calé, Don Felipe inquired, "Your Christian name is French, is it not?"

Don Sagesse smiled, displaying a broad expanse of slightly crooked but very white teeth. "Your Reverence, our pilgrimage has been long and difficult. I was born in French territory. Those of my people who had the good fortune to first see day on this side of the mountains are proud to have been christened with Spanish names."

The inquisitor nodded, briefly eyed Don Alfons and his son, and cleared his throat. "Well, Don Sagesse, we were just discussing where I am to set up residence and offices for myself and my people during this visit. By my host's choosing to present you in the middle of that same discussion, may I guess that you can offer an opinion in this matter?"

"Indeed, your Reverence," the Calé count replied with another slow bow. "Something less than a mile to the north of the village, the nearest mountains crowd close, with many snug small caves in their folds. When first we came to this place, my people pitched their tents and began to build their houses among these caves, and found the site so pleasant that we live there still, a generation and more afterwards, partly under roofs of our own raising, partly in the fair sunlight, and partly in the cool warmth of our mother the earth. We have room and to spare, your Reverence, and upon hearing that the question had arisen, having taken council with my people, I most humbly offer accommodation in our poor quarter of Agapida, if so be that by any chance you should deign to choose it."

The inquisitor nodded. "Your Grace, I may well do so."

Sucking in his breath, Don Gaspar exclaimed, "Your Reverence! These Calé are vagabonds and outcasts!"

"I have seen no such evidence," Don Felipe replied, leavening his voice with a touch of gentle reproof. "On the contrary, the face they have shown me thus far disposes me to think well of them, and to thank them for offering the hospitality which my own vicar, whose office it should be to house us, seems inclined to withhold."

"Your Excellence…" Don Fadrique stammered, his heavy face flushing deep crimson. "If you insist…of course we must do what we can… but it would be much more seemly—your Excellence would find it so much more comfortable, more convenient, in the castle…"

"Where rooms are prepared and ready for you," Don Gaspar repeated. "Our torture chamber—"

"We will remember that," Don Felipe promised the young lord, "should any need for it arise. Until then, before making our final decision, we will see for ourselves what the Calé offer us so kindly and generously."

"Kindly?" cried Don Gaspar. "Generously? Your Reverence, have we not offered our castle with greater kindness and generosity than can ever lie in the power of penniless knaves and outcasts?"

Less to spare the hotblooded son than the ailing father, Don Felipe applied a double thickness of velvet glove. "If they are penniless, that in itself makes their generosity nobler than that of the wealthy can ever be, as Christ Ihesu Himself taught us in His comment upon the widow's mite."

"What widow?" Don Gaspar demanded, glaring about as if seeking to make his own example of any such poor widow.

Don Felipe cast a searching gaze upon his vicar, who immediately shook his head and spread his hands helplessly, as much as to say: I have taught them all of the Gospels that it befits them to know—can I be blamed if they refuse to listen?

"And if your Reverence fears that our townspeople will not come to the castle to report on heretics," Don Gaspar went on fiercely, "be sure they will be far less likely to find their way to the camp of these filthy rascals who call themselves Christians and pilgrims! At least the castle has people of its own to bring you reports of sin and heresy."

"I do not doubt it," the inquisitor remarked.

"While as for these Calé, they are the very ones who should be cleansed from our land!"

The Calé count eyed him with proud anger, but remained silent and dignified.

"Remember, young man," said Don Felipe, "that the Holy Office frowns as sternly upon false witness as upon heresy itself. If you slander these people, we will hope that you do so only in error and not in malice. If you speak truly, where better for us to find it out for ourselves than among their own dwellings?" Standing up to indicate that he would hear no further argument, Don Felipe bestowed a smile on the lord of the Calé.

Lifting his head slightly, his attitude seeming to blend relief and respect, gratitude and the offer of friendship, Don Sagesse returned the smile.

* * * *

The Calé quarter pleased Don Felipe well. That it lay half a mile from the rest of Agapida made it seem more like a neighboring village than a new section of the old one; but, if poor even for this region, it was cleaner and sweeter-smelling than most places of human habitation he had known since his boyhood.

The few houses were not entirely impressive, seeming imperfect imitations of the older Agapidan constructions. Don Sagesse himself still dwelt in a tent, pitched before a double-chambered cave that lent him and his family additional space for living and storage. Don Felipe soon selected this for his temporary tribunal. The foremost cavern would provide an excellent interview room, its atmosphere suitably somber and tinged with mystery; while the rearmost chamber could be used for any prisoners he might need to hold. The count of the Calé stated that he would be honored to give up his own bed to his reverend visitor, and Don Felipe saw no reason to question his sincerity. Gubbio would sleep, as usual, within call of his master; and the rest of the inquisitorial party would be quartered here and there with other Calé families.

Only half of Don Felipe's men complained within his hearing:

The little scrivener Pablo de Maria had a great appetite, and his complaints ceased upon his first Calé meal.

The grievance of the well-born familiar Don Enrique de la Santa Cruz ran deeper. Coming directly to the inquisitor, he complained that he was accustomed to rest where the company best suited his rank and birth.

"The old castellan," Don Felipe pointed out—sympathetically, as befitted Don Enrique's loyal service—"is clearly too ill to play host, and I mislike the looks of his son."

Don Carlos Cascajo, the other gently born familiar of the party, who had ridden ahead with word of their coming and thus seen more of the castle people at closer hand, agreed with Don Felipe. "There is something unwholesome in the air of that place," he said. "I feel it could well be what has settled in the humors of Don Alfons and made him sick. There is also, to a lesser degree, something unwholesome in the air of the village. For myself, I prefer the air in this quarter, encampment of outcasts though it is called."

His testimony, and the deference with which the Calé treated their guests, finally laid Don Enrique's complaints to rest.

The fiscal, Fray Giuliano de la Trinidad, had another concern. While he made no complaint of the place for living and working, he did come to his master with certain private reservations regarding the manners of their hosts. "Your Excellence, is not their great and scrupulous cleanliness in itself grounds for suspicion? Why, they even keep separate basins for washing their hands and their garments!"

Don Felipe sighed. His fiscal was young, and learning. God grant he did not learn too much from those who scented relapse in every fresh-washed shirt. "In and of itself, Fray Giuliano, love of cleanliness is no particular proof of secret adherence to the Law of Moses. A person can enjoy being clean, and yet remain as good a Christian as Saint James. You may trust my word in this matter: I grew up neighbor to Jews and Moors—I know that there is much more to their practices than mere cleanliness. Or even than abstinence from pork. I commend your vigilance in the observing of detail, but habits of washing and diet must always be weighed in combination with other evidence, never used by themselves as grounds for suspicion or arrest."

The fiscal looked confused, as well he might be by the discrepancy between Don Felipe's words and the actions of too many of his fellow inquisitors. (As who should know better than Felipe himself?) Nevertheless, having learned nothing if not obedience to his immediate superior, the young Franciscan bowed his head and accepted the penance of living and working, for the time, in comparative comfort.

The last source of discontent was Gubbio, and his misgivings were most difficult of all to quiet. "You have made an enemy of that green shoot at the castle, my Don," he muttered that night while heating Felipe's wine, "and I give the old lord another six months at the longest."

"You have never told me, Gubbio, from which university you hold your degree in medicine."

The Italian grunted. "No more do I hold a university degree in statecraft, but a man hardly needs one to guess that being enemies with the castellan could prove less than convenient when one holds the churchly benefice in the same lord's village."

"I should not worry about that, old friend. Whatever Don Gaspar may feel toward me after today, or I toward him, my vicar has obviously snuggled his way well under the young lord's wing."

"Aye, that vicar of yours." Gubbio snorted. "Does my memory miscarry, or is our Don Fadrique Osorio de Nuestra Señora del Pilar de Agapida something less and quite a bit more than that earnest young priest of the highest morals we set in place here thirty-three years ago?"

"So long as that." Don Felipe sighed. "The total lifetime on this earth of our Lord. How years speed on when one has been…abroad for fully one third of them! Well, my friend, which of us remains the youth he was so many years ago?" The inquisitor chose to overlook his servant's use of the plural in mentioning who had appointed Don Fadrique. Possibly Gubbio had tactfully meant to lighten the responsibility for setting this unworthy fop—no, Felipe reminded himself, we do not as yet *know* anything of real gravity against him—to shepherd his own flock of simple Christian souls.

"Some of us," Gubbio was saying, "wear our old garments better than others. I am far more nearly the man I was when a stripling, only, I flatter myself, a little wiser, a little shrewder."

"Wiser, I question; and greater shrewdness than was yours already in youth would be difficult for any man to acquire. Somewhat greater familiarity and even looseness of tongue when alone with your master, that I grant."

"Hmmm. And if I may make so bold as to measure your Excellence, the years have considerably improved you."

"Who would not return from so long a pilgrimage with a sense of coming back to life?"

"I would have said," the Italian suggested, "calmer and quieter. Less easily tempted to any act of foolhardy heroism."

Don Felipe thought, As when I imperiled my own soul to save Jewish lives. He could remember no other grounds for his servant's present veiled caution (unless the servant were aware that the letters taken to and received from his master's bankers sometimes concealed private correspondence with Gamito). "Well, well," he replied mildly, "I hope and pray that the years have not stolen too much of my youthful ardor in return for this greater calm and prudence you see in me. As for Don Fadrique and young Don Gaspar, we will do our work both warily and very watchfully."

* * * *

Next morning they published the Edicts of Faith and of Grace, proclaiming it the duty of all good Catholic Christians to report any suspicions of their neighbors and promising benign mercy to all who would admit their own questionable doings within thirty days, which was customary, although three times as long as Don Felipe planned to spend here. After reading both edicts aloud at Mass, with all due solemnity, Fray Giuliano posted them on the door of Nuestra Señora.

Then, having slept upon Don Gaspar's argument that the villagers would hesitate long before trudging out to the Calé settlement, the inquisitor spent that day in the church itself, along with his fiscal and scrivener, waiting. And waiting. For informants who did not come.

It was not that this had never happened before, as Don Felipe knew from his years of accompanying Fray Junípero on visitations, and from talking with fellow servants of the Holy Office. Occasionally a small and close-knit community would refuse to tattle on any of its members. Faced with such a situation, he himself would choose to do as his old mentor Fra Guillaume would doubtless have done, and bless the hamlet for its love and Christian charity. Had not Saint Paul himself admonished the Church that charity covered a multitude of sins?

More often, however, the Edicts of Faith and Grace brought in a spate of gossip so obviously petty and malicious that the inquisitor and fiscal, having nodded over it gravely in the presence of the informant, could dismiss it after, at most, one interview with the accused and a parting sermon to the parish as a whole regarding the spiritual dangers of scandalmongering.

Don Felipe would have guessed Agapida to be more the second type of village than the first. Yet no one came.

Moreover, Don Gaspar, in his misplaced and mistaken eagerness to put some dubious ancient facilities of torment at the service of the Holy Office, had all but promised informants from among the castle people. Yet still no one came.

"His young lordship may, in some fit of pique, have forbidden them to come to me," the inquisitor remarked late that afternoon.

"If so," said the fiscal, "he himself may well merit investigation for obstructing the Holy Office in its pious work."

"Let us not act hastily," Don Felipe replied. "I prefer no accusation at all to false or empty ones, of which I rather fear our lordling is preparing all too many against the Calé, intending to flood us with them after allowing us some few days to stew in idleness. My impression is that he imagines himself a great manipulator, does young Don Gaspar de Agapida. Tomorrow, however, we wait in the cave, as I originally planned."

Fray Pablo said nothing, gently snoring as he was with hands folded over his honest belly and writing implements piled neatly at the foot of his chair.

* * * *

Don Sagesse Labaa had a niece, a darkly handsome woman of about thirty, born in Agapida and baptized in its church, being named Pilar after Nuestra Señora. Orphaned, widowed, and childless, she lived in her uncle's tent almost as if still a young girl, although Don Felipe could see that she was accorded a certain affectionate deference, in keeping with her maturity and experience. She it was who served his supper.

On the morning that followed the day of publishing the edicts, she came to Don Felipe in the outermost cavern.

"Father," she addressed him carefully, after making her reverence to all three of them, "I wish to make my Confession to you."

"I am not your father confessor, Doña. That would be your own parish priest, Don Fadrique Osorio. Nor have I come to hear sacramental Confessions."

"You are also the true priest of Nuestra Señora, are you not?"

"I hold the benefice, true. Nevertheless, it is Don Fadrique, my vicar, who stands to you as parish priest and father confessor."

"There are reasons, Father, why I do not wish to confess to that one, ever again."

Don Felipe exchanged a glance with his fiscal before turning back to the lady. "In that case, Doña, are you sure that it is a sacramental Confession you wish to make?"

"It is," she answered in a calm and steady voice. "I have not washed my soul for several years. I would seize this chance to bathe it clean."

"I see. Perhaps you would prefer that we went to the church, as the place best befitting the sacrament?"

She shook her head, causing her lustrous black hair and light veil to ripple a little, her gold earrings to send forth a tiny, bell-like clicking. "I would prefer here, in my uncle's cave, among my own people."

"I will hear your Confession," Don Felipe decided, directing Fray Giuliano and the little scrivener, with a glance and a nod, to leave them alone.

Fray Giuliano looked back shrewdly and inquired, "Shall we retire to the far side of this cavern, your Excellency?"

Don Felipe would actually have preferred it; but the cavern was small. Trained brothers of unquestioned piety though they were, he desired as little chance as possible of their accidental overhearing; his own ancient fall from grace had made him exceptionally scrupulous about the secrecy that must surround the Sacrament of Penance. "Wait outside," he answered. "I shall want you to prevent anyone else from entering."

With yet another long glance, the fiscal left, drawing Fray Pablo out with him by one sleeve.

"Your last words," Doña Pilar said softly, her dark eyes fixed on Don Felipe's. "You meant them in honor and innocence?"

"In all honor and innocence." He met her gaze steadily. "My companions remain within call, as do your uncle and the rest of your people. You have only to raise your voice at need, but there will be no need. Doña, my sole concern is for the sanctity of your Confession."

"Not every priest is so honorable."

He sighed. "Do you think we of the Holy Inquisition suppose otherwise? Do you think that my fiscal and even my scrivener have failed to understand the full implications of your refusal to confess your sins to Don Fadrique?"

"How else could I have said it? To catch you alone, at any other time, would have looked still worse to *gadje* eyes, would it not?"

"'*Gadje*'?"

She hesitated, as if searching for words to explain. "Foreigners," she said at last. "Strangers. Other people."

"Such as the other folk of Agapida?"

"You will leave again, Don Felipe," Pilar told him. "You will leave, and bit by bit, small sin by small sin, my soul will grow dirty once more. But your vicar will still be our priest, well enough to sing the Mass—when he remembers to sing it—to marry people, baptize their children, and bury them when that time comes. I would not make him more my enemy than he is now. What your fiscal and your—scrivener?—may do with what they have already heard, I think that I cannot be blamed for that, pressed as I am."

"They have guessed, Doña, but even so, all that you said before the three of us remains insufficient for drawing up an accusation. Other interpretations *could* be placed upon it. Gossip might even say, however improbably, that *you* had dark designs upon *my* virtue."

"My own people would never say that. They know me, as I know our customs."

"I do not doubt this. I merely point out that you have not given us enough to shape into a formal accusation. Nor can anything you tell me under the Seal of Confession be so used. Indeed, to deliver any charges you may have against Don Fadrique to me as part of your sacramental Confession would render it all the more impossible for me to act upon your testimony to the relief of my parish. Doña, let me beg of you now, at once, if you have charges against my vicar, bring them to the Holy Office as a formal accusation."

She stood awhile in silence, as if stirring his words through her brain. "The Seal of Confession, Father," she said at last. "Does it not bind me, also?"

"No. It does not. The penitent is the one person who remains free to repeat all that passes in Confession."

"The priest's words and deeds as well as my own?"

He nodded.

"This is not what Don Fadrique has told us."

"If my vicar told you other than what I have just told you, that compounds his sin. But you must report it to us formally, outside the Seal of Confession, before we can act upon it."

"Ah! So I remain free to speak of it—all of us to whom he has done it remain free to speak of it?"

"'All of you'?"

One lock of hair had escaped from beneath the side of Doña Pilar's veil to tickle her left cheek. Lifting her long-fingered hands to tuck it back, she explained, "I suspect that there are many of us whom he has used so—or tried to use so, for I will tell you, Father, here where there would be no need to hide it were it otherwise, that he did not succeed with me. Nor, I think, with other Calé, for it is many years now since any of us have gone to him to confess our sins. Yet some of the villagers still confess to him, and once he excommunicated Isabel Garate for a year, for telling her husband what had happened when she went to confess. Don Fadrique said in his sermon, when he excommunicated her, that it was for lying slander, but even if it had been true, it would have been a greater sin for her to reveal anything that happened in Confession."

"Wait!" said Don Felipe. "Your parish priest, my vicar, has taken it upon himself to excommunicate one of his flock? And for no other sin than slander?"

"For myself," Pilar replied, "I do not think that it was slander. I think that Isabel Garate spoke truth, but he must punish her for breaking the secrecy of Confession, to keep others from speaking. And now you tell me that she had the right to speak of it, after all."

"Doña, you *must* make formal accusation of these things!"

Once again she stood pondering. "And if I do this, and no one else does, what then? With Isabel Garate, he merely excommunicated her for a year, and no one else suffered anything. With me... I am Calé, and he and our lord Don Gaspar might make all my people suffer for my speech."

This woman, Don Felipe thought, marveling, has already in her thirties as much shrewd caution as it has taken me more than half a century, and eleven years of that in prison, to learn. Aloud, he assured her, "It is true, Doña Pilar, that in such cases the Holy Office can rarely act upon a single accusation, for Scripture admonishes us that there must be at least two witnesses. But I myself will preach a sermon this Sunday to tell all the people here the truth concerning whom the Seal of Confession actually binds and whom it does not bind. And at worst, if no one else comes forward to accuse him, your report will lie privately buried in the secret records of the Holy Inquisition. I promise you this, Doña. If we cannot accumulate evidence enough to remove an unworthy pastor, then he himself need never know of our efforts. And, again at worst, as his benefactor I hold the right to remove him myself, stating no reason for it, and replace him with a better."

After another moment of thought, Pilar nodded slowly and knelt before him. "I will do as you ask, Father. But later. First, if you will, I would confess my own sins to you. Mine, not his. His, I will save for my formal accusation."

* * * *

She must have spread the word among her people, for within two days five more Calé women and—to Felipe's horror—one young boy came into his cave to make formal accusation against Don Fadrique Oso-rio. The boy's charge involved outright rape at about the age, as nearly as he could state his own age, of six. Three of the women, like Doña Pilar Labaa, stated that the priest had failed in his assault on their virtue; Don Felipe did not press the other two for exactitude on this point, but simply accepted as much as they chose to reveal in the presence of his fiscal and scrivener, to whose curiosity he afterward made it clear that they were to assume, if the erring pastor had indeed succeeded, it was without the women's own will or consent. In any case, the Inquisition was to protect these witnesses and guard their privacy with as much strict care as it protected and guarded all its other informants. Neither their own people nor Don Fadrique—especially not Don Fadrique—was ever to know from any servant of the Holy Office the identities of any of his accusers. Although, Felipe began to fear, Don Fadrique would prove able to name them all simply by naming every woman and too many boys in his flock.

No Calé of either sex or any age came to the Inquisition with charges of any kind against anyone else and, after preaching his sermon that Sunday, between the statues of Saint James and Our Lady, the inquisitor made it his habit to pass his mornings, from Mass until dinner, waiting in the church. What he had told the villagers about the Seal of Confession, how it bound only the father confessor and any third party who might chance to overhear, while the penitent himself or herself always remained free to speak of it to anyone else at any time, bore fruit: Isabel Garate brought him her accusation immediately the next day, and by midweek three more village women added theirs.

Pablo Savarres, the husband of Isabel Garate, brought another charge: "This priest has his own woman. Yet he wants to make free with ours, as well."

"His own woman?" asked Fray Giuliano.

"His so-called housekeeper. Beatrix de Córdoba."

"Beware, man," Don Felipe told him sternly, "of bringing us mere idle slander. The Holy Office knows how to punish sins against the Eighth Commandment."

"The Eighth Commandment, your Reverence?" the informant asked, humbly enough. "Which is that?"

"Has your priest not taught them to you?" Fray Giuliano asked in turn, his voice betraying some shock. Already, as priest, Fransciscan, and fiscal, he had encountered too many parish priests barely able to mumble through their Latin with bad pronunciation and worse comprehension, who could hardly have named the Seven Deadly Sins, still less the Ten

Commandments, without much hesitation and long pauses; but Don Felipe had told him of choosing his vicar, so many years ago, as much for Don Fadrique's apparent learning as for his apparent piety.

Eyes turned down, Isabel Garate's husband muttered, "Yes, he teaches us...when we are little children...and I remember well enough what they are, but I forget their numbers."

The inquisitor breathed a sigh of qualified relief. "The Eighth Commandment, Pablo, is that one which forbids us to bear false witness against our neighbor. By 'neighbor,' as our Lord Himself taught us, we are to understand any and all of our fellow human beings."

"False witness, your Reverence? Beatrix de Córdoba has borne him three sons and a daughter, and is lying abed big with yet another of his getting. All Agapida knows this! One of the brats died, and Don Gaspar has taken the other three into the castle while you are here."

Don Felipe nodded slowly. "Have you ever heard it said that your priest married this woman openly and publicly?"

The informant looked as though, if not for whose presence he was in, he would have spat. "Beatrix de Córdoba is his whore, not his wife."

"So. Well, then, Pablo Savarres, I must tell you, this matter of your priest keeping a concubine is not in itself heretical, and therefore does not fall within the business of the Holy Inquisition, as does the matter of abusing the sacrament of Penance. Nevertheless—not as inquisitor—but as holder of the benefice of Nuestra Señora del Pilar, and thus the immediate superior to whom Don Fadrique must make account, I thank you for bringing this to my attention. As inquisitor, I ask if you can tell me in what manner Don Fadrique gave you cause to complain, regarding your wife?"

"The holy devil tried to rape her when she went to him to confess her sins!"

"And how do you know this, Pablo Savarres?"

"How do I know it, your Reverence? Am I not her husband? Did she not run home to me with tears running down her face, and tell me all?"

Don Felipe thanked him again and dismissed him with the admonition that he might be called upon to repeat his testimony at another time.

When they were alone once more, Fray Giuliano observed, "His testimony agrees with what the Calé woman told us concerning the manner in which Don Fadrique's attack upon Isabel Garate became known."

"My thought exactly," Don Felipe agreed, twitching not so much as one corner of his mouth at the bound his heart took upon the fiscal's reference to the niece of Don Sagesse Labaa. "It may turn out that my inquisitorial duties will suffice for removing this man from my parish, with no need of my personal jurisdiction over him."

* * * *

Whether Don Gaspar had indeed planned all along to leave the Holy Office a few days in idleness before feeding it with whatever local suspicions could be garnered, or whether Don Fadrique observed those who entered his church as the Inquisition sat there, and applied to the young lord in some attempt to point inquisitorial attention elsewhere, that Tuesday and Wednesday saw a small press of other informants, from castle and village both, armed with tales and suspicions, mostly of the Calé.

Many charges concerned such matters as presumably stolen chickens and suspected illicit love affairs between laypeople. Dolores Banet and Beatrix del Sol had torn each other's hair in a quarrel over one of the castle squires; Manuel Cardoza had knocked Vicenzo Oblaño unconscious for borrowing his donkey halter without permission, and so on and so forth. All such complaints were naturally discarded at once. Don Felipe directed his fiscal to file all the rest, the ones which did touch upon matters of the Faith, very scrupulously, knowing that, unless brought forth again immediately, they would safely vanish amongst the mess of other, similar documents.

Some few he glanced into immediately. Where two or more informants agreed, especially if they seemed unconnected with each other—in so far as any member of so small a community could be called independent of any other member—he and Fray Giuliano read their reports through a second and third time. In half a dozen cases, they sent their familiars to conduct the accused parties to Don Felipe's afternoon tribunal in the Calé quarter. Each time, the accused guessed at once, either exactly or closely enough, why he or she had been summoned. Several identified and explained the incident—washing a soiled shirt on Saturday, forgetfully eating bacon on Friday, and so on; the others guessed and named their accusers as personal enemies. Only one of this class of cases involved a Calé.

Fray Giuliano was young and earnest enough still to worry a little over Don Felipe's custom of hearing such cases on the spot and closing them without further ado. The putative irregularity seemed to bother him less in this place, however, than it had in other villages, where there was no such young lord as Don Gaspar offering the castle prisons and panting to put the ancient torture chamber back into use. Don Felipe needed to remind his fiscal only once that in no way could their own secret cells of Ainsa house so many accused persons for all the months that full investigations would have required.

"I think," Fray Giuliano replied on that occasion, "that we may need one of our cells, at least. May we not?"

"I think it very likely," the inquisitor agreed.

As for little Fray Pablo, he scrivened away as usual, making no comments and—Don Felipe suspected—thinking as few thoughts as possible upon the matters he set down with so much obedient diligence between his stifled yawns.

* * * *

And yet, had it been only the niece of the Calé count, had all those other women and at least one young boy not also been involved, had it been only Doña Pilar who had tempted Don Fadrique, all innocently and unintentionally, with the swell of her bosom beneath the bright if much-mended bodice and shawl, the curve of her neck above its silver necklace, golden earrings dangling against the faint hollows of her brown cheeks, her dark, dark eyes and that lock of black hair with one silver strand that escaped the bounds of her colorful coif from time to time…had it been this woman alone, Don Felipe might have understood, even compassionated—though never condoned—his vicar's weakness.

Catching this thought in his brain, the inquisitor whipped it away with images of Christ's Passion and *mementes mori*. Yet it returned. *Mementes mori* would not long remain in the mind of a man still so newly released from the secret prison (whether it were living tomb or second womb), and thoughts of the Resurrection, dangerous to his present state because of the throbbing they did nothing to quiet, sprang more readily into the perpetual Easter of his soul than more wholesome meditations on the sufferings of our Lord.

At length he remembered the lady of his youthful devotion, his lost Morayma, and attempted to smother the new feelings beneath thoughts of her; but the old memories were too old, too long and successfully buried, too far on the other side of that great barrier between his youth and his maturity which more than a decade of total, solitary imprisonment had left scored across his life. The ancient devotion, the chivalric loyalty that had so long served him as armor against the fleshly weaknesses which beset priests, like other mortals, on all sides, and to which he had seen so many clerics so gleefully succumb, he finally felt trembling beneath the unconscious assault of a woman—no longer entirely young—but who had not yet been born at the time he was forced apart from his boyhood love.

Other women had tempted him throughout a life already long; he would not have been human had they not. Rarely had the temptation lasted beyond the time of actually being in the woman's presence. Yet other women had danced through his thoughts, waking as well as sleeping, during his imprisonment. Frequently faceless, they had been no more to him than pimples popping up from the festering restlessness of the secret cell. But never, never since boyhood, could he recall that any other woman had haunted his thoughts so persistently and perpetually; and now, beside this woman of the Calé, even Morayma faded to the dim memory of a childish ideal.

Prudence dictated that he should avoid all further contact with Doña Pilar, but to shun the niece of his host would have betrayed the duties of a guest; and for this excuse to continue glimpsing her, exchanging scraps of polite conversation with her, accepting food and drink served by her hand, he felt profound gratitude.

And Doña Pilar trusted him. He had appealed to her to help him right the wrong, and she had complied by arming him with the first formal accusation against Don Fadrique Osorio. Fighting his own temptation in the only way remaining, by plunging himself into his holy work, he took his fiscal, scrivener, the two Juans and, for sniffing, Gubbio—and paid Don Fadrique's house a visit on Thursday morning, while the priest was in his church saying Mass.

No servant opening to their knock, the familiars had to force open the door. The house was not deserted, however: scarcely had the party entered, when a woman's screams assailed their ears.

The screams came from above. Fray Giuliano bounded up the stairs first, his young legs leading Don Felipe's by no more than two or three steps, the familiars following. In the upper bedroom, they found the woman abed indeed—in the act of giving birth, with one midwife to attend her.

Don Felipe retained sufficient presence of mind to ask, "Beatrix de Córdoba?"

Both women stared at him. In the eyes of the one giving birth, he beheld such horror as he could not even remember feeling in that most awful moment on the way between Santiago de Compostela and Daroca when he had heard the dread words, "A matter of Faith," directed against himself.

The midwife was a woman whose skin suggested some mixture of African and Moor, as her dark eyes suggested strong anger mixing with her natural fear. "Yes, Beatrix de Córdoba is her name!" cried this woman. "And mine is Teresa La Negra, and you are the Holy Inquisition, and—with your pardon—the business the good God has set on her cannot wait, even for you!"

"It is for you to pardon us, Teresa La Negra," Don Felipe replied, courteous as knight addressing noble lady. "Neither you nor Beatrix de Córdoba is under any present suspicion of heresy. We will leave this part of the house alone for now."

He herded his party back to the ground floor. At the foot of the stairs, the fiscal observed softly, "The explanation could still be innocent."

"True," the inquisitor agreed. "He could have been providing the unfortunate woman shelter for herself and her offspring by unknown fathers, and Pablo Savarres could have brought us mere slander."

"But the sworn testimony of ten women and one boy would seem to render the most obvious explanation also the likeliest."

"Even were it otherwise, is it not part of a pastor's duty to avoid, so far as possible, any appearance of slander?"

Meanwhile, the little scrivener had found a doll and Juan de Torla a toy horse, seemingly left behind when the older children were hidden among those belonging to the castle. Even more damning, Gubbio looked twice around Osorio's study, went straight to the oaken press, opened it, lifted out two books and three folded garments to uncover, at the bottom, cards, dice, and several bags of jingling money.

"All this," Fray Giuliano exclaimed sadly, "and he has made his house into a gambling den as well!"

"And with small children beneath his roof," Don Felipe added.

"I marvel," Gubbio put in, "that he could find players willing to come to him, trying as he seems to have been to cuckold every man in his flock."

Of course the Italian spoke in jest. Gamblers always came forth, ready to play at every opportunity. Don Fadrique Osorio was far from the first parish priest they had found also serving as master of a gaming house—deplorable, but hardly heretical.

But they had all they needed without the cards and dice. Bidding Gubbio bury them again in the chest, Don Felipe settled down with his men to wait.

In a few moments, Don Fadrique returned from saying Mass. He stepped into his house, saw the Inquisition, and crumpled even before Don Felipe rose to utter the words of arrest.

Upstairs, the newborn infant began to cry. Its wails did not appear to hearten Don Fadrique in any way.

* * * *

As it turned out, Don Fadrique Osorio was the only prisoner the Holy Office claimed in Agapida. Don Felipe recognized his priesthood, however dishonored, by appointing the hidalgo Don Carlos Cascajo as one of the two guards to escort him back to Ainsa. As Don Fadrique's other guard the inquisitor named Micer Garcias; these two familiars got on well together.

He could easily have had one or two more nobly-born familiars from the castle. Don Gaspar showed himself ready to turn the rack with his own hands on some unfortunate if by so doing he could win appointment as familiar to the Holy Office—but then, Don Felipe suspected that Don Gaspar was eager to set his hand to any such work even without additional incentive. The inquisitor ignored the castle, however, and selected replacements for Cascajo and Garcias from among the villagers, naming Pablo Savarres and a strong young man called Ernán del Río. He would have liked to make familiars of some Calé men, but Don Sagesse smilingly declined the offer on behalf of himself and all his people. "I fear," he explained to his guest in private, "that already we have made no friends with his young lordship, by housing you here when you could have gone into his castle."

"Friend, that choice was my own."

"And deeply have you honored us, my lord."

"Consider this: being named familiars would benefit you. The Holy Inquisition protects its own."

Still Don Sagesse shook his silvering head. "If you will name Don Gaspar your familiar, then we also will take pride in accepting this great gift. But, I beg you, do not give him further cause to envy us."

"It is your choice, my friend. In any case, you will have time to reconsider. I will be back."

Filling Don Fadrique's place cost the inquisitor more pains than replacing the familiars. Again, the castle had two chaplains available, but the old lord's confessor seemed as feeble as Don Alfons himself, and Don Felipe would as willingly have left his former vicar alone as trusted the young lord's confessor in his place.

At last he turned to his trusted fiscal. "Will you suspend your career in the Holy Office, at least for now, to serve God, myself as your immediate superior, and this unfortunate flock by acting as their new shepherd?"

Fray Giuliano bowed his head. "Obedience before all. But which does your Excellence need more, a good vicar or a good fiscal?"

"Sorely as I shall miss your services as fiscal, at the moment I and my benefice have greater need of a vicar whom I can trust. A new fiscal I can find at the nearest monastery."

"That would be Nuestra Señora de las Nieves," Fray Giuliano pointed out, "and they are Dominicans."

"Curb thy Franciscan jealousies, brother. The Dominicans, too, have proved themselves capable of serving the Holy Office with some small competence. Remember: my fiscal I will have constantly under my eye, but my vicar I must be able to trust at a distance."

Fray Giuliano's eyes suggested that his superior, being a secular priest, could never understand the vital importance of distinguishing among the various Orders. But he quickly blinked and nodded. "Write the appointment, Excellence, for I may need it to prove my authority in Don Gaspar's face, and I shall place it upon my head and wear it in my heart for however long you see fit."

"Take heart, good brother! I intend to pay Agapida another visit within the year—if not as inquisitor, then as holder of the benefice."

And as ardent admirer, his heart added, of one dark-eyed lady of the Calé. The moment his head recognized this thought, it tried to smother it, but neither very successfully nor very enthusiastically.

"Remember, also," he added, half sportively, half to cover the silent clamor of his own heart, "that to eat meat on a day of abstinence is no evidence of judaizing if the meat is pork."

"Have no fear, your Excellence. I shall not attempt to serve two masters at the same time. I shall not be pastor and inquisitor both!"

CHAPTER 22

THE DREAM OF THE ILL-CLAD LADIES

He stood atop the high bell-tower of the Alcazaba, the very nose of the Alhambra, looking down over a city which was and was not the great Karnattah he had twice visited as a boy. He understood the reason for its strangeness when he saw Rosemary standing beside him.

"Yet it is not entirely as strange as I might have expected," he mused. "The Río Darro still flows through the city, like a thread of shining silver. The neighborhood on our right shows that they have respected their promise to the Moors; and they have respected the Alhambra itself."

"Look behind you," said Rosemary.

Obeying her, he gasped to see that much of the Moorish wonder of the modern world had been knocked away to leave a ragged, gaping hole.

"Charles V decided to build himself a new palace right there," Rosemary explained, "and then died before finishing it. They'll make another effort pretty soon. We're in 1610 now."

The bell began to sway, but its tolling sounded less like a bell than like the cry of a muezzin wailing his call to worshippers who could no longer either hear him or spread their carpets for prayer.

"And that," Rosemary added, jerking her head at the destruction to the Alhambra, "makes a fair symbol of how they've honored their promise to the Moors."

"I had forgotten." Sighing, he turned to gaze again at the city.

"This time we aren't here to see blood, anyway," said Rosemary. "Just symbols."

All about the city stood women clad in sanbenitos—heavy, garish, the garb of penitents on their way to an Act of Faith. At times these women seemed of ordinary size, so that it was wonderful how clearly he thought he saw them; at others, they seemed to tower above the highest roofs, so that they could hardly have taken a step without crushing anyone beneath their feet; and there were moments when he thought it was not the single city of Granada that spread out before him, but all the kingdoms of Spain.

"Churches," Rosemary explained with a nod.

"They are our churches?" Looking more closely, he saw that each of them wore, not a single sanbenito, but layers upon layers of them one atop another, weighing each lady down like so much lead. Most of the women here wept like Rachel in Rama. A few of them, here and there, laughed. "It is this accursed new custom of hanging the penitents' sanbenitos in their parish churches," Don Felipe cried, "to the perpetual disgrace both of them and their descendants!"

"'Unto the thousandth generation,'" Rosemary said dryly. "Exodus, somewhere near the middle of the book. I did my homework."

"'Unto the thousandth generation,' was God's promise of His mercy. Punishment was to be inflicted only unto the third and fourth generation."

"That was Yahweh's idea, not the Inquisition's. Not that it'd make much difference to mere children and grandchildren."

"You are Pagan," said Don Felipe.

"I honor Divinity in my own way. Which isn't by clogging holy places up with souvenirs of alleged heresy."

A man wearing rich vestments recognizable as those of an archbishop in times of celebration could be seen now, striding joyfully toward one of the women—the tallest lady in Karnattah, who stood directly in Don Felipe's line of vision, wearing on her head a crown with the inscription, "Ave Maria." He remembered the tale he had heard, and been forced by his Christianity and priesthood publicly to applaud, of the Catholic captain who, creeping into the besieged city one dark night during the Glorious Reconquest, had nailed a banner with these words to the door of the mosque that had stood on that spot in Moorish times. Sure enough, by squinting hard, he could see blood still trickling down the woman's brow from the Castilian captain's nails. The banner, indeed, resembled Christ's crown of thorns.

"You had said this time we would see no blood," he accused Rosemary.

"Symbolic blood only," she replied.

"My bride!" the man in archiepiscopal vestments cried aloud to the cathedral-woman. "Strip thyself! He grants his permission!"

"Archbishop Pedro González de Mendoza," Rosemary explained with a nod. "'He' being Inquisitor-general Sandoval, who just consecrated him and gave permission to move all those sanbenitos out of the cathedral."

"Archbishop consecrated by inquisitor general!" cried Don Felipe. "It is as though the Holy Office were establishing itself as papacy of the Spanish Church!"

But bells and laughter drowned out his words. Not only the bell beside him, but every bell, so it seemed, in all the city was pealing with joy, as the cathedral woman raised her head, her tears turned to laughter, and began to strip garment after sorrowful garment from her body, flinging them this way and that.

Half of them fell upon a church-lady in the old Moorish neighborhood to Felipe's right, who knelt weeping to arrange them over those that already burdened her down. The rest fell to a woman who stood—Felipe thought somewhere to his left—and she gathered them up and waved them above her head, dancing and exalting before draping them upon her shoulders.

Everywhere he looked, they were all laughing, both the cathedral who disrobed herself until she stood straight and unbowed in her simple shift of stainless white, and all of those who did nothing save witness; but none rejoiced more exuberantly than she who gathered up half of the discarded sanbenitos, and none still wept save she upon whom the other half fell.

"Who are these?" Felipe asked his guide.

"San Salvador in the Albaycin," said Rosemary, nodding to the weeping one, "who has to take the Moriscos' sanbenitos. And Saint James, who gets to keep those of the Judaizers, and who happens to be the Inquisition's own local church."

The cathedral-woman spread her arms, and the new archbishop rushed into her unencumbered embrace.

"But why?" cried she of the Albaycin, and in her voice Don Felipe seemed to hear again the wail of the muezzin and the accusing tones of an El Santon. "Why cannot we hurl them into the sea, bury them in the earth, burn them in a pyre, unburden ourselves of them completely? Why cannot we all stand as pure and unfettered as his Grace Mendoza's own bride?"

"Lest the world forget!" the Inquisition's local church crowed in reply. "Because we must never forget! The world must never be allowed to forget!"

"Why the hell not?" Rosemary grumbled.

The bells pealed more loudly yet, and Don Felipe awoke, hardly knowing whether to rejoice or to mourn, nor why he might wish to do either.

CHAPTER 23

THE OLDEST SACRAMENT

The priest's house was far otherwise than it had been during the residency of Don Fadrique Osorio. No more toys, cards, nor any other traces of either women, children, or gamblers. Of even such luxuries as were permissible under God's Law, few enough could be found in Fray Giuliano's habitation, and those few had been allowed to remain from Don Fadrique's time, no doubt for the sake of visitors. The closet in which Fray Giuliano himself slept had been converted, as Don Felipe saw with a glance, into as near a semblance as possible of a monastic cell according to the strict rule.

Clean and well kept, that the house was indeed. "Isabel Garate serves me as housekeeper," Fray Giuliano explained, "with her husband to assist her. They come on Mondays, Tuesdays, Thursdays, and—to cook only—Sundays."

On Wednesdays, Fridays, and Saturdays, no doubt, the Franciscan indulged to the limit his taste for fasting; Don Felipe hoped he got himself at least one meal on each of those days. Today being a Wednesday, the older priest was glad he had brought his own good cook Diego Sos, along with his personal secretary Don Martin de Villaréal, two guards, and of course Gubbio. This time there was no question but that they would stay in the vicar's house.

Surprisingly, this life seemed to suit the strict Franciscan. He looked happier and healthier, if very slightly thinner, than when he had served the Holy Inquisition as Don Felipe's fiscal.

"How do you find pastoral work?" Felipe questioned his new vicar as they walked in the courtyard.

"I find it better, perhaps, than befits me. I had some trouble, at first, with those who had fallen into the habitual sin of gambling in this house. And the castle is a great thorn in our side—because of young Don Gaspar, I should explain. Poor old Don Alfons, his father, must be as sure of Heaven, I think, as any man in this life, but neither he nor his personal chaplain has strength to preserve much more than their own virtue. Still, all in all, it is good work. Most of the flock seem to trust me." He hesitated before going on: "Indeed, I fear that your Excellence had best find someone to replace me soon, before my soul grows too attached to Agapida."

"You do not believe that your true vocation might lie here?"

"My vocation lies in the cloister, your Excellency," the Franciscan answered, regret in his voice. "Or in the Holy Office, if obedience to my superiors places me there. Here...I am too much my own master."

"Your Blessed Poverello was a friar, not a monk," Don Felipe pointed out. "As I remember the story, Saint Francis preached directly to the people whenever he could. And the work of the parish comes first. Without a healthily nourished Christian people, there would be nothing for the Holy Office to defend."

"All this is true," the younger man argued, "and yet it is also true that my own first allegiance was conventual."

"As to that, perhaps we should inquire whether this area might prove suitable for a Franciscan house," Don Felipe said, and was rewarded by seeing new light in his vicar's eyes.

"I had scarcely dared hope..." Fray Giuliano murmured, "...but, with your Excellency's support...already I know of two Agapidan lads who appear called to the Franciscan way of life, and three or possibly four girls and women—would it be premature to contemplate a sister house?"

Gubbio interrupted them, coming into the courtyard with a message. "Your Reverence is summoned to the castle."

Don Felipe stood still, contemplating his servant. In Gubbio's mouth, this summons seemed, to say the least, high-handed; yet Gubbio's own prejudices might have colored it. "I am summoned by whom, and for what reason?"

"Heresy, I gather," the Italian replied with a yawn. He often yawned when hungry; and dinnertime approached. "It must have become urgent when they heard of your arrival."

"Heresy?" Relieved—he had feared that old Don Alfons might have need of some stronger priest than his ancient chaplain—Don Felipe turned inquiringly to his vicar.

Fray Giuliano spread his hands and looked perplexed. "I know of no such pestilence among my flock. Unless it is another complaint about the Calé. As far as I am aware, no new matter for complaint has arisen since we investigated them together when you visited Agapida as inquisitor, but discord, alas, still continues between the Calé, the castle, and certain of the villagers."

For a moment, Don Felipe stood and pondered. He disliked truckling to cruel young Don Gaspar, and yet if the Calé were concerned... He had intended to visit them again in any event—if on no other pretext, to try persuading Don Sagesse once again to accept appointment as one of the Holy Inquisition's familiars...and there was the Calé count's niece, the lady Pilar.

That dark-eyed, slim-fingered presence had haunted his thoughts, through the months since his first visit here, as no other woman had ever done—no, not even Morayma…whose face he feared he would no longer recognize even had her portrait been painted at the age she was when he saw her, no more than twice or thrice, all those years ago in Alhama de Karnattah.

If the Calé were concerned, it would be good to learn as much as possible, to be able to warn them. "Tell the castle's messenger," Don Felipe instructed Gubbio at last, "that this time I am here, not as representing the Holy Office— else I should have forewarned them and expected the customary welcome—but simply as holder of the benefice of Nuestra Señora del Pilar, come to examine the welfare of my parish. I have brought with me neither colleagues nor records of the Inquisition, and can officially perform none of its business. Nevertheless, as a favor, I will come to the castle this afternoon, after dinner and siesta, and hear whatever they have to say to me."

* * * *

He took his personal secretary, his two guards, and the ever-inquisitive Gubbio, leaving his cook behind in the vicar's house, happily preparing supper.

Don Gaspar could have done Don Felipe the courtesy of meeing him and his party in the castle courtyard. Instead, they saw no one save pages and servants until they stood in the chapel, whence they had been ushered with bowing deference, but the offer of not so much as a cup of cold water.

"I wonder," Don Felipe murmured to his secretary, "if Don Alfons knows of even our presence in Agapida, let alone of my summons to his castle."

"I doubt it," Gubbio grumbled, overhearing.

At least they had not long to wait before Don Gaspar made his entrance. A slim woman of medium height accompanied him, one white hand resting as lightly as its encrustation of rings would allow on the crook of his arm. Her gown appeared cut from the same bolt of crimson brocade as Don Gaspar's own doublet, and her hair showed golden beneath her black veil.

"My young lord," Don Felipe addressed him, taking one step forward. "Why, of all the offices and withdrawing-rooms your father's castle has to offer, have we been brought here to the chapel?"

As if ignoring his question, Don Gaspar said: "My lady, allow me to present the venerable inquisitor of whom I have told you. Doña Violante, his Reverence Don Felipe de Nuestra Señora. Don Felipe, the most pure and excellent Doña Violante de Raíz y Silvestro de Barcelona."

"Doña," the priest replied with a stiff nod. It was not lost on him that Don Gaspar had presented him to the lady, and in such a way as to emphasize the greater importance such an introduction presumed to be hers. Her sex rendered it difficult to challenge this presumption without violating the rules of chivalry, and yet Don Felipe suspected that Violante de Barcelona was neither more nor less than her consort's leman. He repeated his initial question.

"Why, what more fitting place than the chapel," Don Gaspar countered with a show of innocence, "to entertain a priest inquisitor come upon a matter of holy business?"

"I have not come here today as a priest upon the business of the Holy Inquisition, but as a gentleman paying another gentleman the courtesy of a requested visit."

"Ah," Don Gaspar said with a mock sigh, "that we could all shed our skins so lightly! Of course, there is no need of your servants to remain kicking their heels here. We could set out wine for them in the great hall."

"I choose to keep my men with me," Don Felipe replied. "Nor have I myself either the need or the desire to hear you while fasting. Let us all go together to your father's great hall."

Don Gaspar hesitated a moment, then smiled and bowed. "As your Reverence wishes, so be it."

The great hall was little if any improvement on the chapel. Where the former had been small, bare, and cheerless, the latter was large, echoing, and equally cheerless. Where the former had been reasonably clean save for its layer of dust, the latter was strewn with rushes that smelled of moldy decay, and three of the tables had been left upon their trestles between meals. Where in the chapel one might, with effort, remember the physical Presence of God, in the great hall one could sense only the hollow echoes of worldly vanity. Still, Don Felipe had carried his point, and that meant something. Sampling the sherry Don Gaspar caused to be brought for him and his secretary, and deciding it was good enough to accept without complaint, but not to merit compliment, he waited for Don Gaspar or Doña Violante to broach the matter Gubbio had guessed lay behind the summons. Give them the satisfaction of inquiring about it himself, he would not; if they did not speak of it now, he was determined to treat his coming here as a mere visit of courtesy.

Lingering some paces away, Gubbio and Don Felipe's two guards drank ale, ate hard little pears, and muttered with some of their host's soldiers of rolling dice, but did not bring any forth. Gubbio, of course, would have one ear as much as possible on his superior's conversation, even more than Don Felipe had half an ear on his servant's while waiting for his host to say something of moment.

It was the woman who first let her mask slip. "Don Felipe," she said at length, "is it true, or is it not, that to tell fortunes is heresy?"

"Sometimes it is," he answered warily, "and sometimes it is not."

"But in any case," Don Gaspar thrust in, "it is always forbidden, is it not?"

"It is not smiled upon by Holy Mother Church. We are speaking, you must understand, only of actual prognostication of future events. Astrology as it is used to treat illnesses and understand character is of course permitted."

Violante de Barcelona drew her breath in sharply. "Well! There is a woman among the Calé who tells people's fortunes by tossing beans down into circles she draws on the ground."

"Indeed?" Don Felipe responded quietly. "Has she promised you long life and many children, Doña?"

"Do you accuse me of such sin, your Reverence?" Flushing, Violante darted a glance at Don Gaspar.

The young lord's lips twitched as though he relished such jests even when aimed at his mistress, but he spoke chivalrously enough. "If this is how your Reverence pleases to treat all your informants, small wonder so few of them come to you."

"Enough come to keep my humble branch of the Holy Office well occupied. But again I remind you, Don Gaspar, I am here this week, not as inquisitor of Ainsa, but as simple beneficiary of Nuestra Señora del Pilar de Agapida, come to see to the affairs of my parish and nothing else."

"And when will your Reverence return on the affairs of the Inquisition? Does time hang so heavily upon you that you prefer to make many trips where one might serve? Or is the work of the Holy Office, which you yourself call of such vast importance, to be set aside for the concerns of one humble parish? Do you intend to come back to us at all, if it means investigating your beloved Calé on charges of heresy?"

With cold care, Don Felipe set his sherry down, barely tasted, upon the unwiped table, and looked Don Gaspar in the eye. "Are you yourself so competent a steward of your father's castle, that you dare cast stones at any man devoted to the service of Holy Mother Church? Learn your own business first, my young lord, before venturing to question that of anyone else. And, the next time you invite guests, I would advise you to set out a better vintage for them. Esteban! Ramon! Gubbio!" he called to his men, as if they needed to be alerted beyond what their own ears must already have told them. Then, turning to his secretary, "Come, Don Martin, let us end this profitless visit."

The secretary, ever his master's loyal shadow, set his glass down beside Don Felipe's: the level of liquid in both glasses was even more identical than when they had been poured. Esteban de Sotra set his mug down upon the board with a force that caused some of ale to slosh over. Ramon Armiento actually emptied his into the floor rushes—a gesture Don Felipe would not have suggested, but would not censure. Only Gubbio took another hasty swallow or two before relinquishing his mug and following the others from the hall, ignoring the threats and imprecations Don Gaspar hurled after them.

Once safely out of the castle, the secretary leaned over and murmured to his master, "I fear that your Excellence has made an enemy."

Don Felipe sighed. "I fear, Don Martin, that the enmity began with my first visit to Agapida, and that Don Gaspar, not myself, began it. He is unworthy of his father, his family, and his rank. I fear he will prove both a scourge to his own country and a thorn in the side of the kingdom."

They arrived back at the vicar's house half an hour before Fray Giuliano, who had spent his afternoon visiting a sick parishioner. After hearing Don Martin's account of what had happened at the castle, the Franciscan said gravely, "Then your Excellence has learned very little of this new cause for complaint, not so much as the woman's name?"

"They will have aimed their shaft as high as they could," Don Felipe replied. "I can scarcely believe they mentioned only one and not half a dozen." But, he thought, who was that one? It could not conceivably be the count's niece...could it?

"And yet I wonder," said Fray Giuliano, "if they know any names. As little commerce as I have observed between castle and Calé, Don Gaspar's woman may have consulted only some gossip from which names had vanished before it reached her guileless ears."

That such a man as Fray Giuliano should call the young lord's female companion "woman" rather than "lady," and employ sarcasm when mentioning her ears, trumpeted his estimate of her character more clearly than if he had preached a sermon. Don Felipe nodded, and turned the conversation into another channel. Only, he wished he had not left before learning whether or not Violante de Barcelona had any name to offer him.

The answer came shortly before supper. Two messengers from the castle appeared at the vicar's door with a letter which they insisted on delivering directly into Don Felipe's own hand.

"Who has sent this?" he asked them, failing to recognize the signet impress in the sealing wax.

"My lord Don Gaspar," replied the less surly-looking of the two messengers.

Don Felipe deliberately omitted touching the letter to his head in token of respect, but opened it at once. It read simply:

"The Calé woman who tells fortunes with beans is Bonté Labaa, sister to that man they call their count."

It was unsigned, but he suspected it was from Violante's hand, penned quite possibly at the insistence of her lover. Rejoicing that he had not placed it upon his head, and even more that the woman whom it named was Bonté and not Pilar Labaa, he refolded it, told the messengers, "Say to those who sent this that I shall act upon it or not, as seems to me fitting," and sent them on their way the wealthier by a florin.

"That seems overgenerous of your Excellence," Don Martin protested mildly.

"Perhaps," Don Felipe answered his secretary. "But I wished to prove that my attitude toward their young master and his leman does not arise from mere stinginess."

Later that night, while putting him to bed, Gubbio grumbled, "I wish you might take it into your head to prove that your attitude toward your faithful servant had no stinginess at its root."

"Gubbio, Gubbio! Is not all I possess equally yours, by your own regard if not by mine? As you demonstrated so ably during my long absence."

"Yes, and as well for all of us that I stewarded your goods so ably and loyally, is it not?" the Italian answered without a blush.

For long intervals that night Don Felipe lay wakeful, his body athrob with tingles of anticipation; and yet whenever he slept, it was deeply and sweetly.

In the morning, he took only his secretary and his vicar with him to the Calé settlement, entrusting Gubbio with whatever marketing their cook might request—a secure way to occupy the Italian, since he shared whatever dishes that excellent New Christian man of the kitchen Diego Sos prepared—and leaving Ramon and Esteban at their own leisure. Let whoever served as Don Gaspar's eyes and ears in the village report back to him that the priest of whom he would make a tool trusted the Calé enough to visit them without the personal guard he had brought when visiting the castle.

The morning was beautiful—surely as splendid as that day on which God created Adam and, after seeing him labor at naming every animal, drew Eve from his side to be his fit and matching companion. Fifty-five years Don Felipe de Granada might have lived, yet his soul sang like that of a man less than half his age. Every birdsong, every breath of fresh breeze, sank into the fertile soil of his heart and caused fresh flowers of happiness to spring forth. It was as if only now, after all these months, was he truly and fully emerging from the long slumber of eleven years in the secret prison; and the need to maintain outward dignity added a spice of something like mischief to his secret joy.

He found the Calé quarter echoing his own sense of rebirth. In the short time since his first visit to Agapida, they had already added two more dwelling houses to their isolated outgrowth of the village, and were at work upon replacing the tent before their count's own caverns with antechambers and porticoed forecourt in wood and stone. Soon the entire colony would have real roofs to cover their heads.

"My friend!" Sagesse Labaa welcomed the churchman and his party with a grave bow, but honest pleasure dancing in his dark eyes. "And our dear Fray Giuliano, and…I think we have not yet met this good man?" he added with another bow.

"Don Martin de Villaréal, my personal secretary." Allowing one of Labaa's grandsons—Pablo, he thought—to help him off his mule Blanca, Don Felipe embraced the count. "My friend! And how have you found my new vicar? Can you speak as highly of him as he does of you?"

"We could not desire a better shepherd for our souls. But come! Of course you will dine with us. Will you not? And enjoy my garden for a little while before we take our food!"

Glancing beyond Don Sagesse, Felipe saw Pilar standing in the unfinished doorway. She flashed him one smile, half gracious and half bashful, before vanishing again into the new construction.

Don Felipe and his companions followed their host through the same doorway, a large number of the welcoming party trailing at their heels. They emerged in a crude but enthusiastic little courtyard, alive with sun, flowers, and fresh beginning.

The niece of Don Sagesse was even now reseating herself at an embroidery frame. Felipe crossed the courtyard to look respectfully over her shoulder. "What do you make, Doña Pilar?"

"It is an altar cloth, Don Felipe," she answered quietly. "I have no more shyness of going into the church, these days." Lifting her head momentarily, she gave him another quick smile. "My soul rejoices to see you among us once again."

In that moment he made up his mind, in so far as it had not already been made up, that, whatever the accusation against this lady's kinswoman might involve, it would never become a case for the Inquisition.

Calixta Aranse, the young wife—if Don Felipe's memory served—of Pilar's brother Iago, picked up a spindle that lay nearby and held it toward the visitors like an offering. "And my wool will go into a set of fine new vestments, your Reverence...good Fray Giuliano."

There followed half an hour of being shown and admiring all these people's work before they returned to it: Hernani, Fernando, and Iago Labaa, Sagesse's son and two of his nephews, raising the last of the wooden columns into place; his brother-in-law Florello Montagnard—husband of the accused woman—painting bright designs upon those already in place; the count's daughter Margarita watching over the older children as they tended the little kitchen gardens and beds of flowers; the younger children running merrily about in pursuit of their small games; Calixta at her spinning; and Doña Pilar, like the calm eye of the happy bustle, at her embroidery. Felipe could not rid himself of the impression that even so must Mary often have sat in the heart of the blessed household of Nazareth.

At last he was able to draw Don Sagesse apart, the two of them retiring into the cavern which only months ago had served the Holy Office as audience chamber. "Now that we are alone, Don Sagesse, I must ask whether you spoke truly concerning Fray Giuliano, or whether you spoke as prudence dictated in his presence."

The Calé looked puzzled. "But, my friend, I spoke truly. Why should you doubt? He is a young man, but good, kind, and earnest. And, I think, happy to be so, and to be here leading our souls."

Don Felipe nodded, well pleased to have his own belief confirmed. "You understand, my friend, it was my duty to ask. Don Fadrique, too, had been my choice to represent me here. I had to be sure that this time I had chosen a worthy vicar."

"Ah! This time you chose very well indeed." Don Sagesse grinned happily. "That other one...I remember when first we came here...I think that he could show two faces, although to us he showed always the bad one."

"If it should ever happen—*ever*—that Fray Giuliano show a worse face, whether to you or, in so far as you can observe, to any of Agapida's other people, you must send me word of it at once. I rely on you for this, Don Sagesse," Don Felipe repeated.

"I will not fail you, our best of friends. And now, should we not return to my garden?"

Shaking his head, Don Felipe laid one hand on the count's arm to restrain him. Deeply as he regretted this next step, it must be taken, if only because in order to counterattack, he must know more about Don Gaspar's ammunition. "There is one other matter, my friend. An accusation of fortunetelling has been brought against Doña Bonté, your sister."

Don Sagesse stood still, his dark face suddenly haggard. "You cannot tell us who says this?"

No Seal of Confession guarded the affair, and Don Felipe had warned the castle very clearly of his present position. "It was told to me, neither as father confessor nor as inquisitor, but as a simple guest. Promises of secrecy were neither asked nor given. It is young Don Gaspar and the lady whom I take to be his present mistress that made this accusation."

"That one again!" Don Sagesse's shoulders relaxed with a shudder.

"Is there anything in it?"

Shaking his head, the count spread his hands helplessly. "My friend, we were like children. We had always told fortunes and thought no evil in it, until Holy Mother Church taught us better. If my sister has done so again since we learned it is sin, I had not known of it."

"The method they mentioned concerned casting beans into circles traced on the ground."

Don Sagesse nodded sadly. "That was my sister's favorite way, before we were taught better."

"I had best speak with her. Not, you understand, as inquisitor, but merely as a friend come to warn her. Don Sagesse," the priest went on, laying his hand gently on the count's shoulder, "why should Don Gaspar hate you so much?"

"Some years ago, when he was coming into his manhood, he tried and tried to have his way with our young women. But we are a strict people, my friend. You know that. We have always been a strict people, at least in that. We believe that such things are for husband and wife, and them alone. I am proud to say that none of our young women would listen to him. And, when he tried to force Maria Détangere—she who was to wed my son Hernani—she screamed, and so some of our men came and drove him away. I think that is why he is our enemy."

"It may become very serious, when your enemy is lord of this region." Torn between honest concern and selfish temptation, Don Felipe added, "Perhaps you should take your people elsewhere."

"Where? We have been over there, in France. Before that, in my father's time, and his father's, we were in the empire of great King Sigismund, and he himself gave us safe-conduct. But wherever we try to live, we find enemies. I do not know why this should be. Perhaps we have indeed been cursed to wander forever, for some sin our ancestors committed. Here, at least the old lord has allowed us peace."

"I fear that Don Alfons cannot live much longer."

"True, but we have still the friendship of your Reverence, and of our good Fray Giuliano, and, I think, of some others in the village."

"May we be enough! Well, my friend, never fail in your prayers. Even in Old Testament times, God set limits to how many generations He would punish for the sins of their ancestors; and we are blessed to live under His merciful New Testament. But now, I had best see Doña Bonté."

"She is with her daughter and the wives of my sons, preparing our dinner," Don Sagesse replied, heavily but not without hope.

Don Felipe decided, "This afternoon will be soon enough."

They returned outside. Surrounded by sunlight and people, the count quickly shed all appearance of concern for anything beyond the new construction. But not, the priest thought, before Doña Pilar noticed the crease between her uncle's eyebrows. Or perhaps it was in the priest's face that she read something. Or it might have been that their simple departure for private conference touched her fears. Whatever the reason, Felipe found her gaze fixed anxiously upon him, but as soon as he met her eyes, she lowered them.

Prudence should have made him ignore it, for both their sakes. For once in his life, he defied prudence. "Daughter," he murmured to her—although another priest served her as confessor now, he had done so once, and he sensed it would be wholesome for both of them to remember it—"might I speak with you privately...at your convenience?"

He was amazed how soon she found it convenient. In the hour when the men were already at their siesta while the women, who ate later, were still taking their food, she came to him where he reclined on brightly woven cushions in the shade of his host's new colonnade.

"Don Felipe," she said, sitting smoothly on her knees before him.

"Doña Pilar." Now that she had come to him, he felt himself embarrassed, wondering what he had contemplated saying to her. "Have you finished your meal?"

"I have. Sir, my uncle has told my Aunt Bonté that you must speak to her upon a grave matter. Must you speak to me, also?"

"My lady...with you, there is no question of 'must.' I merely wished... I thought that you would wish to know at first hand of the matter." He drew a deep breath, watching her anxiously. She sat intent and motionless save for the natural blinking of her eyes. Kindest to say it clearly and quickly. "Doña Bonté has been accused of telling fortunes with beans tossed into circles drawn on the ground."

"Accused by whom?" Pilar asked with that sort of quietude which often accompanies very deep feeling.

"By Doña Violante de Barcelona, whom I take to be the current lover of Don Gaspar de Monsecors y Tequilador de la Castel de Agapida."

"You speak well to call her his 'current' lover," Doña Pilar remarked with dry scorn. "This accusation—how serious is it?"

"First, Doña, you must understand—" (you above all others, he added in his thoughts)—"I have not come this time as inquisitor. Whatever the simple priest and beneficiary of Nuestra Señora de Agapida may learn here this month need never come to the attention of the tribunal of Ainsa. Even if it does, fortunetelling is not in itself, unless accompanied with certain other beliefs and circumstances, the most serious type of heresy. Even if I were here as inquisitor, there would not be any danger to your aunt's life."

"But, because we are who we are, any such threat to one of us throws all of us under suspicion." She bowed her head briefly. When she looked up again, it was to speak as a practical woman rather than one complaining against fate or injustice. "What are these other beliefs and circumstances that can make it more serious?"

"Evidence that belief in false gods or wilful entanglement with the powers of evil is involved," he answered frankly.

She seemed to relax. "Long ago, when we were completely ignorant, we used to read fortunes and believe them. I do not think we ever understood what powers showed them to us. Since we learned to be better Christians, we have given it up. Only, sometimes, some of us may toss beans or look at the palms of hands for some *gadje* who wishes it. For us, it is like a game—like the tossing of dice, when if they roll to the right number for a man, his fortune is that he wins the money. When we toss beans for the *gadje*, our fortune is that we win a little of their money. The temptation is great, Don Felipe, and sometimes one or another of us still falls to it, even though we no longer completely remember how to read the beans. I do not think that any of us ever understood that the Evil One had any hand in it."

"And your aunt was one who fell to the temptation? You need not answer, Doña Pilar. I hope to learn it from herself."

"I prefer to tell you. Two young women came from the castle. It was a month ago or more, soon after Don Gaspar brought his Doña Violante here. They were scarcely more than girls. From what you say, I believe they must be her handmaids. They bedeviled all of us to read their fortunes and tell them how well they would marry. At last my poor Aunt Bonté did it. She promised them each a fine husband, took their maravedís, and thought that would end it."

He nodded reassuringly. "From what you tell me, Doña, there is neither heresy nor mortal sin in this. Venial sin, yes, for it smacks of some deceit and charlatanism. But that is easily absolved. If your aunt's account agrees with yours, all that remains will be to see that none of you give them any such grounds for attacking you again."

"Yes. Don Felipe, from my heart, I thank you.... Is there anything else you would say to me?... Would you hear my Confession again?"

"Do you find Fray Giuliano a good pastor?"

It was her turn to nod. "Even as we tell him our sins, he respects us as if we were holy saints."

Not that the Calé women would have any great sins against purity or chastity to confess: in such matters, they put to shame all too many Old Christians—even the monks, nuns, and popes themselves (rest their souls) Don Felipe remembered from the days of his youth, before the reforms of Torquemada and Cisneros.

"In that case, Doña Pilar," he said, "I have nothing more to speak of with you."

He took pride in having hidden his regret that he could find no further legitimate reason to keep her; and yet, as she rose...did he glimpse some slight hint that she, also, regretted how soon their conference must end? Knowingly and consciously, he had offered her the opportunity to warn her aunt of all that he had said. If it were not for that, would Pilar herself have found excuses to prolong their talk?

"Perhaps, Don Felipe," she said, almost as though reading his thoughts, "we may find another hour...to speak of the Faith? Father Giuliano teaches us well, but he has much to do...and you were the first who opened my eyes. Before you, I had known only Don Fadrique, and sometimes passing monks and friars, but they always kept us at a great distance."

"Doña Pilar," he said solemnly, "it would give me great pleasure to speak with you on matters of our holy Faith."

She kissed his hand and departed. He lay back, wondering whether he stood gazing down into a slippery abyss or up into a dazzling firmament, and marveling that he felt no alarm, but only a deep anticipation which seemed both pleasant and as natural as the ripening wheat or the hatching of a clean, brown egg.

* * * *

Several months went by. During that time, they exchanged letters: one letter apiece, written by their own hands—Fray Giuliano taught reading and writing to any of his flock who wished to learn, and Doña Pilar Labaa had so wished. Don Felipe would not willingly have told anyone how carefully—as if casually—he laid her letter up in his Divine Office, marking the day of its arrival.

Late that fall, he visited Agapida again. Three times within a single year…it astonished himself. This time he braved the roads with Gubbio as his single attendant, and, while he did not in any sense disguise himself, neither did he make any show of his priesthood, riding in completely secular garb, neither too rich nor yet too sober—for he would not attract robbers, and yet his soul throbbed with spring despite the nearness of winter.

He went directly to the Calé settlement, letting no one else, not even Fray Giuliano, learn at once of his arrival. At need, he could put it forward that his experience with Don Fadrique had taught him the need for keeping watch on his vicar, and that secrecy was always useful in such work.

He found that the Calé loved their new pastor just as well even knowing that he need never be aware of their report. This gratified but failed to surprise Don Felipe. His true concern lay elsewhere.

Doña Pilar and he had enjoyed two long conversations during his last visit, both centering on spiritual matters and both in the presence, if not under the scrutiny, of other people—one in her uncle's courtyard and one beside the stream, in view of the cookfire of some cousins who still lived in their old tent. This time, with the chill wind of November for their excuse, they soon managed to slip away together into a small cavern she had made her own, not far from her uncle's house. Here were a threadbare but still colorful carpet; some old cushions; two ancient blankets hung up like tapestries; a little hearth with kettle, cups, and firewood waiting near; and, on a flat stone covered with a red cloth embroidered in designs of yellow, orange, and green, a small oil lamp and a tiny printed volume of the *Handbook* of Erasmus, a precious gift from Fray Giuliano.

Someone must have seen her bring him here; but no one had protested. She was, after all, a mature widow held in honor among her people; and he, the graying inquisitor who had delivered them from a parish priest notable for corruption even in this generally corrupt age of the world.

She mulled a hot herbal draught for them against the chill. They sat awhile, drinking it from little red cups and talking of the size and strangeness of the earth, and whether or not the kingdom of Prester John might be reached by penetrating deeply enough into the lands found by Pereira, Vespucci, and others.

At length, when the pounding of his heart was such that he thought she must hear it as well, he brought out the gold ring with its carnelian the breadth of his little fingernail, bearing the carven likeness of Juno's head—the ring his mother had given him when, still a boy, he had been sent away to Rome. Now, handing it to Pilar, he said, "Doña, will you be my wife?"

She replied slowly, "You are a priest." But she seemed to take his question as though she had half expected, even awaited, it; and this enheartened him.

"True," he assented. "I am a priest. But neither a monk nor a friar. I have looked into this point with some care, Doña. In the time of the Apostles, even bishops were allowed one marriage. Secular priests, like myself, were not forbidden wives until more recent centuries. The ban is no divine law, but merely a changeable rule of the Church."

"Is that not enough?" She slipped her hand into his. Her fingers were trembling. He held them tightly, trying to still them. She went on: "If we were to marry, could they not burn you?"

"Burn me?" Smiling, he shook his head. "Hardly! When priests marry in private, there is no suspicion of heresy and no work for the Inquisition. Even if one were found who flaunted his marriage with a great public show, the Holy Office would sentence him but lightly."

"Nevertheless, for you to take even so much risk…" She swallowed and averted her face a little. "Don Felipe, I will be to you as…Béatrix de Córdoba was to Don Fadrique—"

"My lady! Do not insult us both!" He kissed her hand. "I will never make you an outcast among your people."

"I am barren." She spoke in a low, halting voice, her head bowed. "With care—"

"No! For your safety, there must be witnesses. Your own people must know that you are my true and honored wife."

She lifted her face to him, such a smile beaming from her eyes as saints might wear upon first beholding Heaven. He would never know, nor greatly care to know, whether she had offered concubinage merely to test him.

After giving each other a single kiss upon the lips, they left her cave at once, to seek out her uncle.

The following afternoon, Don Felipe sent Gubbio to tell Fray Giuliano that they had come and were allowing the Calé to host them this time, but would visit the village tomorrow. While the Italian was absent, Felipe and Pilar wed each other according to a mix of her people's customs and his, in the presence of her uncle and as many other Calé as could squeeze into the courtyard of Don Sagesse. Let Gubbio think what he wished—that his master was finally following the example of good Pope Alexander, or that he was carefully sparing his servant full knowledge—Felipe de Granada and Pilar Labaa were husband and wife in the sight of God, themselves, Holy Church (however grudgingly), and the Calé community.

Gubbio might have been just as happy to be left out of the secret, for, whatever he thought upon his return—noticing dark glances, involuntary brief smiles, and the way in which Don Felipe's bed was made in the rearmost cavern and Doña Pilar's in the one adjoining, while the servant was banished for once from in front of his master's door to sleep beneath Florello Montagnard's roof—he kept his own Italian counsel and manifested none of his usual shrewd curiosity.

As for the Calé, unwieldily though their number was for containing a secret, they seemed to regard their trust with the enthusiasm of children and the skill born of generations of keeping silent where prudence or custom demanded. A people who were able to live their lives never speaking the names of any of their beloved dead, nor alluding to certain courses of nature—Fray Giuliano had told Don Felipe that he observed Calé parishioners to blush and look down on hearing that Gospel passage in which Christ speaks of what is taken in through the mouth and passes out of the body into the drain—such a people could well hold their tongues between their teeth at need.

Once, during the marriage night, he murmured to her, "Other women have thought themselves barren, and yet borne children safely. Sarah, Elizabeth, Saint Anne..."

He felt the resigned shaking of her head, her long, loosed hair rubbing like fibers of damask over his shoulder. "My marriage gave me many nephews and nieces, no sons or daughters."

Nevertheless, to hold one another was enough. How simple, after all, and how glorious was this sacrament of married love...the oldest sacrament of all, the one sacrament enjoyed by Eve and Adam while yet in Eden.

Not until morning did he think of Morayma, and then it was only briefly, and with drowsy gratitude to her for having preserved him all these years from the coarse sacrilege of performing this act outside the marriage bed.

His one regret was that he and Pilar could come together so seldom. But, though she would have gone back with him willingly to his house in Ainsa, where none but *gadje* eyes would watch them, he would not expose her to even the appearance of being to him as Béatrix de Córdoba had been to Fadrique Osorio. They must continue to live most of their lives apart, she among people who knew her to be an honorable wife, he among people who thought him still completely celibate.

CHAPTER 24

THE DREAM OF THE MOST DEADLY GAME

Through the dark wood he wandered, when one came and seized him by the shoulder. Familiarity had rendered her face, though mannish, no longer unpleasant in itself—dreadful only in whatever scenes it might portend. She did not smile.

"Rosemary," he greeted her heavily. "What Hell do you show me this night?"

She replied, "Haven't you figured it out yet? Hell begins on earth. What's the point in worrying about other planes of existence before you clean up the one you're on?"

"How?" he demanded. "Are we not caught here in some limbo, powerless to change any course of events? When you free me, will I not return to my own life, far in time or place or both from whatever horrors you have shown me, and remembering little or nothing of them? How, then, am I to help purify my own plane, save by furthering the fear of another among my fellows?"

She looked him full in the face, and now she gave him a grim smile. "I don't know. One of our founding sages said that if we didn't hang together, we'd all hang separately. Damn good trick, isn't it, 'hanging together'?"

Somehow he followed her meaning, despite the strangeness of her words, but before he could make reply, they heard the baying of hounds, and a second woman ran staggering between the trees, to fall in exhaustion a few paces from where they stood.

He thought at first that she was his ancestress, but no—when she lifted her head to stare wildly about, he saw that her skin was dusky and her eyes held none of Raymonde's calm. He saw also, now, that his first impression of a white robe had been in error, for this woman wore rags in many colors, bloodied like Joseph's coat, and a gold ring in one ear, though her other lobe was torn away. And the burden she bore in her arms was no martyr's palm, but a little child over whom she hunched like any desperate mother.

"The earth must be cleansed," a new voice said behind Felipe. Turning, he saw a tall man at his back, a man of pale skin, blond hair, and gray eyes, who wore a gamma cross banded around the sleeve of his stark tunic. Tears ran freely down his cheeks, but he spoke righteously. "We must be men. No taint of the subhuman races must be left alive to pollute our own superhumanity. We must be brave supermen and exterminate them all."

"Do it yourself!" snapped Rosemary. "As far as I'm concerned, they're family."

Don Felipe looked again, and found Rosemary at his other shoulder; it was a youth, bearing a long gun of the future, to whom the gray-eyed man had been speaking.

"I cannot, sir," the youth replied with a sob. "I know they are subhuman, but they are so…lovable!"

The gray-eyed commander laid one hand on the youth's shoulder and said in deep sympathy, "I know, lad, I know, but we must be brave men and purify the world for our descendants. Now do your duty like a man, and I will not report you for insubordination."

Wiping his eyes with his banded sleeve, the youth raised his gun, took aim, and fired upon the kneeling woman, who fell with a cry, shielding her child even in death.

But now the gamma-cross men had vanished, and a nobleman's hunting party had just burst into the clearing to fire the shots.

Beneath the woman's body, the child continued to wail. Laughing, the hunters shot again and again, piercing the corpse until at last the wails ceased.

Don Felipe covered his eyes and turned away from the scene. "At least those men of the future felt pity. At least they did not laugh!"

"They might have felt pity," said Rosemary, "for all the good it did."

The hunters had bound the woman's wrists and ankles to a long pole and were carrying her away like the carcass of a deer. One of them stuffed the infant's corpse into his bag and followed. Their laughter faded into the chorus of a hunting song.

"I do not wish to follow them," said Don Felipe.

"Neither do I," his guide agreed. "Too bad we don't have to." Turning, she led him through a door in the wall that he now found had been at their backs.

They stood in a cloistered walkway, the longest he had ever beheld. Looking between its columns he saw, in the open courtyard, the two trees of Eden—of Life and of Knowledge—their branches heavy both with blossoms and with fruits in all stages of development, some appearing luscious beyond endurance, others prickly and rotten on the bough. Around these trees cavorted apes and monkeys of all sizes, plucking and swallowing the fruits with abandon, afterward changing, some into men and women, others into strange twisted creatures like gargoyles or demons.

"In here," Rosemary grunted, pulling him by one sleeve through a doorway at their other hand.

Into a catacomb like those of Rome, or so he thought at first. Its end he could not see, for the dark winding; its only illumination came from the strange, steady light in Rosemary's hand; yet their steps echoed as though on scrubbed tile. He began by counting his steps, but at a certain point found himself counting "ten thousand" over and over, with no recollection of having reached that figure from "one."

"In here," his guide repeated, throwing open another door.

Light, laughter, and delicious aromas flooded the passage. Drawn to them like nail to lodestone, Felipe entered a banquet hall bright with roaring fireplace and candles enough for a cathedral. They stood in many-branched silver candlesticks on the long table, among its platters of steaming meats. A cloth white as milk draped the board, and laughing men in curious attire ate from golden plates and drank from crystal goblets through which the red wine shone like rubies.

Still more candles clung in sconces to the walls, casting shadows up from dozens or hundreds of trophies, so that the dark ghosts of antlers, tusks, and muzzles danced spiderlike over the ceiling. Among them was a curiously regular shadow, like the outline of a perfect semi-circle. Searching downward with his eyes, Don Felipe saw that it came from the single golden earring of the woman whom he had watched hunted down...

There was her head on the wall, mounted like any other trophy, and the head of her babe beneath hers, so that they resembled some glassy-eyed portrait of the Madonna and Christ Child. Ah, Ihesu! Sweet Ihesu, Mary, Joseph! Was she not Pilar's own brother's wife, Calixta Aranse?

"Oh, God!" Felipe cried, staring again at the platters. *What do they eat?"*

"Somebody wrote a story," Rosemary remarked, "about a human being as 'the most deadly game' to hunt. Funny, huh? Of course, these men never thought of Gypsies as human."

One of the feasters threw a goblet at the fireplace. It soared across the long room, to strike with a smash that woke the sleeper. Remembering nothing else of his dream, he lay awake a long while, listening for another crash.

CHAPTER 25

THE LONG ARM OF THE CHILD

Fernando Lepecheur, Pilar's oldest nephew, brought her letter: "My Lord Don Felipe, come at once or you will come too late."

With great effort, the priest held his voice calm. "What is this?"

"Don Gaspar." White with exhaustion, the boy was swaying on his feet. At Don Felipe's gesture, Gubbio set a chair for Fernando, who tottered into it and went on, "He threatens to drive us away. All. Forever. They say...my grandparents and the old people...it is like those times beyond the mountains, come down on us again."

The inquisitor of Ainsa had received his vicar's letter late the evening before, and it had troubled him all night. Fray Giuliano wrote that old Don Alfons was dead at last, after lingering longer than anyone expected. Barely in time for his father's funeral, Don Gaspar had returned from his latest journey to Barcelona, this time bringing a middle-aged man in place of his usual lady of questionable virtue. As zealously, even piously, as if his own virtue were not in question, Don Gaspar spoke of finally carrying out certain laws of the kingdom aimed against the Calé, honored but not executed in Agapida since their passage.

Already determined to lay aside all other business and set out for Agapida, Don Felipe had arisen while the morning was still dark. Young Fernando's arrival at earliest dawn trebled the urgency.

Fray Giuliano's messenger, none other than his own servant Pablo Savarres, was still asleep on the bed Don Felipe had caused to be readied for him beside the warm hearth. Without waking Pablo, the inquisitor turned the Calé youth over to his good cook Diego Sos to feed and find bedding for. In less time than it might take to mumble a rosary, Don Felipe, his servant Gubbio, and his personal guards Armiento and De Sotra were galloping on fast horses toward Agapida, having left instructions for the fiscal and scrivener to gather two or three trustworthy familiars and follow with all possible haste.

Don Felipe's party arrived to find the Calé settlement empty of people, as of anything that could easily be carried away. Where tents had stood, only long-smothered places in the browning grass marked their former sites. As for the houses, some few were burned and still smoking, the rest ransacked, with heavy breakage. In the little courtyard of which Don Sagesse had been so proud, some columns were charred and others splashed with blood; some herbs dug up and others trampled down; and bones strewn around ash-covered spits showed where at least one pig and several fowls had been roasted and devoured, no doubt by the mob that had done the other damage.

Sending Armiento and De Sotra to tell Fray Giuliano of his coming, and directing Gubbio to make thorough investigation of Don Sagesse's caverns, the inquisitor hurried alone to Pilar's little cave. He found it stripped and bare—gone were the carpet and cushions on which they had celebrated their love whenever he could come to Agapida these last two years, the blankets they had sometimes used to cover themselves and sometimes hung back upon the cavern walls, her little kettle and cups, and all her books—her Erasmus and every volume her husband had brought her to join it.

He saw, however, that she must have taken all this away herself, for her little stack of firewood remained undisturbed, and her tiny lamp still rested on its flat rock. Nature had made this cavern difficult to notice from outside, which must have saved it from the mob.

Wondering why she had left her lamp, he picked it up. It was dry, its oil drained out or burned away; but, in the dim daylight that seeped around the corner concealing the entrance, he saw that a small leaf of paper had lain beneath the lamp.

He carried both items outside. The paper proved to be a page torn carefully from one of her books: a love sonnet of Francesco Petrarca's, done into Spanish. He remembered the long afternoon when they had helped commit it to one another's memory.

She had found means to leave him one last message...in such a way that no one else who might find it first could know its meaning or prove anything from it against the priest. He kissed the paper and laid it up in the pocket nearest his heart.

He must have lost himself then for some moments, for when next he became aware of time and the world, his face was wet with tears, his fist clenched painfully around the tiny lamp, and his servant standing beside him, softly calling him over and over by name.

"Too late," Don Felipe repeated. "We are too late."

"We would have been too late," the Italian pointed out, "even if we had started the moment Pablo Savarres brought you the message from your vicar. Who could have foreseen that Don Gaspar would act as quickly as this? He must have been preparing his final orders even as Fray Giuliano sealed his letter and sent Pablo off to us."

"Only last night. They must have roasted their pig only last night. Fray Giuliano's flock—my own parishioners, in God's sight—the people I freed from the tyrannies of my first vicar—and they have done this...

celebrated this driving out of those whom they should have welcomed as fellow Christians."

"They had to obey Don Gaspar, did they not?" said Gubbio. "You may shoulder the ultimate responsibility for their souls, but their secular lord still has some power over their poor bodies."

"And pig, I suppose, is good no matter where roasted and eaten," Felipe added bitterly.

After a pause, Gubbio asked gently, "Did you love her very much?"

"She is my wife." What reason, any longer, even to pretend to keep the secret from his lifelong servant? "She is still my wife. Ah, God!" He stared around, but the trampled ground and hard rock hid their trail. "Where have they gone?"

* * * *

Fray Giuliano greeted them with tears streaming from his own eyes. "Almost a full quarter of my flock, gone!" he almost babbled. "And they the best quarter! Forgive me, your Excellence. I could do nothing. Nothing! At least…at least there was no blood. They shed no blood. But who could have thought… Some of the best of my villagers were with that mob, screaming and throwing gobbets of mud along with the rest, even at these people who have been their fellow churchgoers for almost two generations! Thank God Pablo and his wife did not go out with them, nor Rodrigo de Sangrada, nor Maria and Isabel Pacheda… But so many! When Don Gaspar came with his soldiers and others from the castle, who would have thought so many of my own best people would fall in with the rabble?"

Himself so greatly in need of comfort, Don Felipe sought to comfort his vicar. "In part, it is fear that drives them, fear for their own safety if they should seem to go against their prince of this world. God will forgive them." He felt his jaw harden. "It is Don Gaspar de Monsecore y Tequilador de la Castel de Agapida who has led these little ones astray."

"I warned your Reverence we would have trouble with him," Gubbio remarked.

Without turning, Don Felipe told him: "Go and make sure our horses are being well stabled."

As Gubbio left them alone, Fray Giuliano repeated, "Almost a quarter of my flock! Forgive me, my lord—if your Excellence had been here—"

"Tell me what you can about this new companion of Don Gaspar," the inquisitor cut in. "This middle-aged man he has brought back with him…from Sodom, I take it?"

"He is called Pedro del Niño. I have seen him only once—a man with the face and the belly of a tavern sot, for all that he wore silk and velvet in the company of his new patron."

* * * *

Fray Pablo and the Dominican fiscal arrived that evening, bringing with them four good familiars and also Don Martin de Villaréal, Don Felipe's personal secretary, who after carrying out his master's instructions had felt too anxious to wait at home.

Don Felipe took them all in his entourage, along with his two personal guards, vicar, and manservant, when he went to the castle that night by torchlight and demanded entrance.

They had to shout twice before a guard responded. "My master has ordered us to admit nobody after dark."

"The Holy Inquisition orders you otherwise. Man, it is a matter of Faith!"

Results were not immediate, but Don Felipe allowed them the space of a Miserere; and by the time his murmuring lips reached "Amen," the portcullis was inching upward.

The dozen men rode through into the castle courtyard, but did not dismount until Don Gaspar's soldiers came to hold their stirrups.

"Who…" The officer in charge coughed nervously, bowed to the inquisitor, and tried again. "Who have you come for?"

"We will begin by speaking to Don Gaspar himself."

The mutters that rose from Don Gaspar's men had the sound of involuntary protest against an anticipated blow. Who in Agapida, village or castle, could fail to know of the inquisitor's friendship for the banished Calé?

"Your Reverence," said the officer, "forgive me—I cannot, in loyalty—"

"You must choose, man, between mere human loyalty and loyalty to Holy Mother Church!"

"I…" The officer fell to his knees before Don Felipe. "May your Reverence forgive me , I…" He bent to kiss the inquisitor's foot. Almost, Don Felipe might have pitied him, but for thinking of what part he must have played in helping drive the Calé from their home. Had he relished carrying out his orders last night? Struck any of Pilar's—of Don Sagesse's people? Knocked them into the dust, stolen their belongings before their eyes? Even—oh, God!—attempted to rape…

"Up, you cringing coward!" It was Don Gaspar's voice, but the young lord himself remained invisible until some of the familiars moved forward so that their torches pricked out his face, his long-fingered hands, and the shining of his jewels, where he stood on the steps to the keep. "I will see them," he went on, his words filled with smug defiance, "in my great hall. All of you, come with them!"

"Follow!" Don Felipe told Micer Garcias and Don Enrique de la Santa Cruz, whose torches were those that had illumined Don Gaspar. They obeyed, and the inquisitor strode after them, leaving the rest of his people to fall in behind. Caught between awe of the Holy Inquisition and fealty for their secular lord, the men of the castle flanked them with careful, almost completely silent respect.

On the dais, Don Gaspar already sat at his ease in the high-backed chair, with arms and cushions, that had been his father's and grandfather's before him. Two wax candles in tall holders dropped their light on him, one from either side, and he kept his fingers idly occupied in toying with a tiny, delicate knife. As they entered the hall, he began, as if permission were his to grant them: "Come, my reverend lord. Speak to me."

Stepping between Garcias and Santa Cruz, Don Felipe closed the distance, to stop a pace or two from the dais and level his forefinger at the young lord. "Don Gaspar de Monsecore y Tequilador de la Castel de Agapida, you are under grave suspicion."

Don Gaspar looked up, a flicker of surprise seeming to cross his face. This was not, apparently, the attack he had expected. "Am I indeed? Of what? In what way does cleansing my land of wandering rogues constitute heresy?"

"Wandering rogues?" With difficulty, the inquisitor kept his voice calm. "These people are your fellow Catholic Christians, who had lived quietly among you for two generations—"

"My father was in serious error to allow it!" the young man cut in. "They were those same wandering Egyptians against whom our laws warn us."

"Your discourtesy toward a servant of the Holy Office has not gone unmarked," Don Felipe resumed. "Nevertheless, I will tell you this much: your cruelty to fellow Christians does not constitute the most serious charge laid against you."

"What, then?" Don Gaspar seemed genuinely puzzled, though strangely unworried. "We are all of us sinners, but I have always been true and devoted to Holy Mother Church in all my sinning."

"I do not wonder that you hesitate to confess so heinous, secret, and unnatural a crime in the presence of your own soldiers." Ordinarily, no competent inquisitor should have given even this much hint of the nature of the charge; but he was desperate to learn as much as he could, as quickly as he could, of the Calé's enforced departure, and where they might have gone.

Don Gaspar's frown cleared suddenly. He laughed. "Ah, is that it? Well, Don Inquisitor, you are off the scent completely. Grant me a private interview, and I will soon show you your error."

"Speak here, or I order your arrest at once."

Their eyes locked, old inquisitor and young castellan. Another tense silence filled the hall. At last Don Gaspar said, as if swearing some casual oath, "By the Holy Child of Daroca! If your Reverence truly wishes to discuss these things so openly, let us call in all the village and hold a public debate."

Don Felipe stiffened as though struck. Pedro del Niño…why had he never suspected until this moment? Struggling desperately to hide his emotions, he said in tones of measured command, "God Himself prefers mercy wherever possible. I will grant you your private audience."

"Your Excellence—" began the fiscal. Don Felipe stilled him with a wave of his hand.

"We will need one torch to light our way," Don Gaspar observed with mock courtesy. "Let your Reverence choose the bearer."

Don Felipe glanced around at his people and beckoned Gubbio, as the one man among them who had already been with him during his days as Ordinary to the bishop of Daroca, and who had proven his ability to keep secrets when he chose. The Italian nodded, took Ramon Armiento's torch, and stepped forward. The fiscal put his hand on little Fray Pablo's sleeve and made as if to follow, apparently assuming that as officers of the Inquisition they were to be included in the audience; but Don Felipe motioned them back.

At Don Gaspar's directions, Gubbio lit their way through muffled passages and up drafty stairs to a windowless door. Its hinges were obviously on the inside, marking it as a door that could be barricaded against invaders rather than one fashioned for a prison cell. Discerning some seepage of light from beneath this door, Don Felipe instructed his servant, "Wait here outside."

Don Gaspar lifted the latch, stepped aside, and, with a bow and a smirk, waved for Don Felipe to enter.

He found eight wax candles burning at once—one at each corner of the bed, and one in each corner of the room. In this prodigality of light, a figure sat sprawled on the bed: a man with the belly of a tavern sot, his boots still on his feet, a goblet in his hand, and a bottle gleaming beside him on the bedclothes.

Don Felipe stood regarding him in silence. Was this truly the same person who had remained in his memory all these years as a guilty and terrified young boy?

From behind the churchman, Don Gaspar spoke with smug satisfaction. "He flinched at my mention of your Holy Child."

The man on the bed, who had been staring back at Don Felipe, his eyes shiny smears in the candlelight, nodded and took a long drink from his goblet. "I knew him again," he said on lowering it. "He has not changed so much. Would you have known me again, Bishop's Ordinary of Daroca? Pedro del Niño, who was Pedro Choved in his boyhood, before his last living parent disowned him."

Don Felipe replied, "I do not think that I would have known you again, not even in daylight. Man, man! Are you not ashamed to have squandered the discipline given for your penitence and wholesome correction?"

Pedro del Niño laughed coarsely and refilled his goblet from the bottle by his side. "Wholesome correction! You call it wholesome correction for a boy to be disowned and banished from his home, turned out to live on his own?"

"Neither Holy Church nor the secular arm did that to you, Pedro Choved, but only your widowed and outraged mother."

"I loved her." Del Niño drank again. "Once.... Listen to me, Don Priest. I have had years to think of it. You told me there were witnesses. You lied. I swallowed your lie when I was a frightened child, but now I am a grown man, and you cannot frighten me again. For years I have searched my memory, and there were no witnesses. We had made sure of that. No mortal eyes saw us. No, there was one way and one way only anyone else could have known. Some holy churchman broke your so-called Seal of Confession."

Don Felipe heard a sharp indrawing of breath. It was his own.

Del Niño lowered his goblet the better to frown at the churchman. "It must have been that damned old Franciscan. But stand there and deny to my face that you were the one who came acting on what he told you, you and old Fray Potbelly, or that you knew he broke the famous Seal in telling it!"

To say anything at all would be to renew, even compound the old sin still further. Don Felipe stood silent. Unfortunately, his very silence revealed his awareness of the justice in Pedro Choved's accusation.

Don Gaspar said, "He thought he could threaten us. He thought that you and I..." A laugh. "...were playing at sodomy!"

Pedro del Niño looked at the inquisitor again and chuckled, showing a mouthful of blackened teeth. "Then we must find us a new woman or two, eh? Well, Don Priest, and if I had ever done such things, do you think I would confess them to any of you lying priests? As soon go to an honest alcalde and confess cutting throats!"

"Then you have cut yourself off from the sacraments," Don Felipe said in great bitterness of spirit. "You cast off every hope of salvation—"

"What will you do to him, Don Inquisitor?" Don Gaspar cut in sarcastically. "Will you arrest my good friend for heresy and hear us cry aloud to all the world how it came to be known who killed the Holy Child of Daroca?"

Don Felipe saw himself defeated. In committing mortal sin so many years ago to save one innocent people, he had condemned another, equally innocent people—for had this weapon not fallen into Don Gaspar's hands, would even the new lord of the castle of Agapida have braved the inquisitor's displeasure? He had thought the punishment due for that sin paid in full by his eleven years' imprisonment, but now he saw that when he risked his soul to save his friend, he had planted the loss of his wife. Was he to win her back at the cost of yet more souls?—all those humble souls, their faith but recently restored in the sacrament of Confession after Don Fadrique's abuses, who would be shaken to the very roots of their faith and perhaps lost forever were they shown proof of even one solitary instance in which the Seal of Confession had failed to hold.

Toward Pedro Choved he had no right to feel anything else than deep and guilt-ridden grief. Don Gaspar, however... Ah, cursed wretch! to rend two whom God had joined together! Swallowing his rage, he turned to the young lord. "Tell me, at least, where they have gone."

The young lord waved his hand. "Over the mountains to the north. I think I heard some of them talk of trying their welcome in French lands again. Will your Reverence abandon everything to chase after them?"

Salvaging what dignity he could, Don Felipe replied in as even a tone as he could muster, pretending not to notice the younger man's mockery: "My work lies here. You have satisfied me for now that your sins, though scarlet, are not heretical. See that you give me no notorious cause to suspect either of you again."

What Pedro del Niño had already said concerning his disbelief in the sacrament of Confession would have given any other inquisitor grounds for suspicion if not accusation—Don Felipe was asking only that the pair of them avoid any scandal so open and obvious as to force the inquisitorial hand. They knew it, and smirked; but, having won, allowed him to retreat quietly, pretending to the world that they had merely succeeded in laying his suspicions to rest.

Secretly, he found his defeat all the more bitter in that, even had he won the interview, he could probably have learned nothing more. Chances were that Don Gaspar had stated, for nothing but the simple asking, as much as he knew about where the Calé had gone. Having found in Del

Niño his weapon for defying the inquisitor and achieving his old aim, why should he not have told this discouraging truth?

For many years, Don Felipe was to send scouts and messengers in search of the Calé. At first Pilar's nephew, Fernando Lepecheur, who had escaped his people's fate by bringing her husband the news, served as one of these scouts; but the boy failed to return from his third journey beyond the mountains. Hoping that he had found and rejoined his people, but fearing that he had not—else why would they not have accepted Don Felipe's offer of safe conduct and a new home nearer his own town of Ainsa?—the inquisitor arranged to have Masses sung for him…for all of them…in perpetuity.

Part of the priest, and that a very large part, ached to do the very thing his enemy had proposed in cruel jest: leave everything behind, take horse, and ride alone over the mountains in search of his wife and her people. Time and again, especially late at night or in the toils of some tedious case, he formed the resolution to do it. If he were as vigorous as he had been only a few seasons earlier…but, though upon his first visits to Agapida he had felt like a youth just entering the springtime of life, now he felt weak and aged beyond his actual years. Accepting the blow as the final—he hoped—repayment for that mortal sin of his true youth, he bowed his spirit beneath the weight of the work God had apparently given him to accomplish, offered unremitting prayers for his wife and her people, and let her absence slowly become a deep and tender scar.

In Heaven, surely, as God was merciful, they would come together again.

CHAPTER 26

THE DREAM OF THE BARREL

He did not recognize the city, but it seemed to be nowhere in Spain. The air had much that same chill he had found in Ireland, and faint mist blurred the details of upper stories and roofs.

People filled the street. Some wore bright colors trimmed with lace; others dark and unfrilled stuff; and the poor, as always and everywhere, went patched and drab, even in their holiday best. That it was a holiday he guessed by their mood. Some chattered in merriment, while others strode in sedate anticipation, their eyes shining and mouths twitching upward at the corners. Only a few looked grave, and most of them walked with heads lowered and shoulders hunched, as if trying to escape their fellows' notice. Don Felipe doubted that their precaution was necessary, for no one glanced at him, despite the great difference between his garments and theirs. He was clad in the Italian fashion of his youth, and all their clothing—bright or sober, rich or poor—was as simple in its cut as so many Doric columns. He surmised that he was seeing distant descendants of his own contemporaries. He felt no surprise when Rosemary, in her even simpler tunic and trousers, pushed through the crowd to join him.

"Where are we this time?" he asked, and merely nodded when she replied,

"Lancaster, England, 1628. For now."

As they followed the happy throng, he grew aware of a series of ringing thuds. At first he thought them a clock, but as he counted thirteen, then fourteen and fifteen strokes…and they had been going on for some time before he began to count…he understood them to be blows, perhaps of a heavy hammer or mallet. Unless they were some giant heartbeat. They had the regularity for it.

Still flowing with the crowd, Felipe and Rosemary emerged in an open place where he saw, to his horror, a stake raised high on a great mound of faggots, and a man already chained to it.

"No!" he exclaimed, for a moment remembering only his waking custom. "Never have I attended the place of burning!" He struggled to turn back, but the crowd pressed him in on every side. They still hardly glanced at him—they seemed impersonal as the ocean—but their merriment mocked his efforts. The sound of blows, whether hammer, clock, or heartbeat, pierced through their jollity without drowning or diminishing it. They paid no more attention to it than to the inquisitor.

At his shoulder, Rosemary said, "Don't you want to see one of your own get his martyr's crown, or palm, or whatever?"

He managed to work around and face her. "A Catholic? They would burn a Catholic? In Catholic England?"

"Henry the Eighth changes all that."

"*What*? The Defender of the Faith?"

"Just until he wants to divorce your own Fernando's daughter for not giving him a son," she answered tightly. "You'll hear about it in a couple of years, your time, when it happens."

"And this is what his apostasy will bring about!" Don Felipe looked again at the stake. He could not quite make out the features of the martyr to be.

Rosemary shrugged. "Catholic, Protestant, Jewish, Islamic—you're all Thunder God exclusionists."

Ignoring her, he squinted harder at the man chained to the stake. "But it—it is El Santon!"

"If you've seen one," his guide remarked Delphically. "Look to the right of the pyre."

He did so, and finally located the source of the ringing blows. A black-haired, swarthy young man was bending over a carpenter's table, hammering boards together.

"What is he making?" Felipe asked.

"You tell me," Rosemary replied.

The victim screamed. Looking back at the pyre, Felipe saw it speck-led with dots of orange fire, like a rosebush breaking into bloom. The mob burst into a tumult of ecstasy which drowned out the carpenter's blows, but not Rosemary's voice. "Thunder," Felipe heard her say—or, perhaps, think, her mind directly into his. "One more burnt offering and a little thundershout for that Big Old Whitebearded Thunder God in the Sky."

The pyre with its flame-blossoms, the carpenter working as if noise-lessly at his table, and the roar of the crowd all blended into a kind of veil, behind which everything shimmered, wavered... When it steadied again and the veil lifted, the city had changed. Now it looked Spanish... definitely Spanish or, perhaps, Portuguese, though he could not have named it. Old Moorish buildings glowed as if with sunset in the light of the pyre—for, against all custom, the place of burning had been set in the town square—and the people of the crowd, while clad still more strangely than their predecessors, now wore the mark of Iberia, the strains of Gothic, Moorish, and Hebrew blood mingled together for centuries, with traces of even more exotic elements. Don Felipe fancied he saw more children of Ham among the paler faces than there were in his own lifetime, and more Calé…so not all the efforts to drive out Pilar's people were to succeed.

He thought he might have felt at home among them, were it not for the bloodthirsty joy that warped their shouting faces. He forced himself to look once again at the object of their derision, who had begun to writhe.

To Don Felipe's eyes, the victim remained El Santon; but Rosemary observed, "Still Arrowsmith, only this time he's an English Protestant who made the mistake of honeymooning in Spain. The Inquisition got them both, him and his bride."

"I do not understand."

"Of course, some historians say this Arrowsmith is really the first one, the Catholic martyr of 1628, and English folk memory changed details around to ease the collective Anglo conscience."

At his table beside the pyre, the carpenter hammered on. Somehow, in spite of the distance and the crowd between, Don Felipe could see great tears falling upon the wooden staves where he bent over them.

"I still do not understand," the inquisitor repeated.

"Neither do I, but I think maybe it's a smack of how God sees things. Past, present, and future all mixed together."

"But if this burning is not really to happen…"

"Who says things aren't real just because they don't actually happen?"

Again the martyr screamed—a shriek so piercing that it shot pain through Felipe's own body from head to heels. "I can watch no more of this," he protested, turning his back to the stake and finding himself at the cathedral doors.

Rosemary pushed them open and walked in at his side. The great doors closed behind them, like huge boulders rolling back into place, and for a moment all was murky to Don Felipe's eyes. Bit by bit, he made things out. First the candles. A tiny orange flame here, another there, several more yonder…casting their glow over altar and congregation… how could it have appeared so dark at first? Hundreds of ducats' worth of candles illuminated some ceremony of singular importance. Some royal wedding…or funeral…or both at once? He seemed to catch glimpses of bride and groom before the altar, and in momentary confusion he thought he heard that they were that same pair of English Lutherans seized honeymooning in Spain…but looming much larger and clearer than they was the royal catafalque.

"Let's see…" Rosemary said, as if consulting unseen notes. "Fifteen ninety-eight and fifteen fifty-two. Obsequies of El Rey Felipe Dos and Mr. William Gardiner. Two desecrations. Your choice which one is worse."

"Those people sitting on benches," said Don Felipe.

"The civil judges, with their wives and other attendants," Rosemary replied dryly.

"Their benches are draped with black cloth. I see other benches, but none of them are so draped."

She nodded. "Watch."

He looked at the altar, where Mass was commencing. All seemed in order there, at least. Moving his gaze back to the congregation, however, he beheld confusion. The judges and their wives sat quietly enough in their draped benches—looking, indeed, more like statues than living flesh—but the inquisitors' benches prickled with pointing hands. They, who ought to have set the people an example of how to attend Mass, had their heads together buzzing like wasps.

At length they pushed one of their underlings out of his place and sent him scuttling to the benches where sat the city magistrates. They, who had also been staring and pointing at the judges' black drapery, now commenced pointing at the inquisitors as well, arguing with one another until they became a second wasps' nest.

Mass was continuing, but not without small hesitations on the part of priest and servers as they glanced down from time to time at the various groups of benches. It was becoming difficult even to hear, let alone follow, the solemn Latin phrases.

Four or five officials squeezed themselves out of the magistrates' benches and scurried over to those of the judges, pointing to their black drapery. The noise from below rose until it completely drowned the holy chanting. Someone shouted, "Never! To the jail with them!" and some ten or a dozen of the judges' attendants clambered from their places to seize the four or five magisterial messengers and haul them, kicking and protesting, from the church.

"This is worse than tobacco at the altar," Don Felipe observed to Rosemary.

"They don't like that black draping. They want it taken off. Something about precedence."

"They are right," the inquisitor agreed. "The initial blame lies upon those judges. Yet to protest it in this fashion…"

A man whose clothing suggested that of a secretary left the inquisitors' benches and approached the judges. Met by a wall of raised fists, he hesitated, looked around, and finally climbed to the royal catafalque itself. From here, he turned and cried an inquisitorial excommunication down upon the city judges unless they left the cathedral at once.

The ghostly bride and groom looked around in distant annoyance at the wasplike people below. The priest had given up and stood in silence before the altar, head bowed and shoulders—Felipe thought—shaking a little, his acolytes crouching near his feet to stare wide-eyed at the tumult.

The secretary, having returned to the inquisitors, had gone from them a second time toward the judges with a paper in his hand, and suffered a second repulsion, climbed the catafalque once more and shouted out that the judges were all excommunicate and must leave the premises before the Mass could continue. A man in the judges' benches stood up and shouted back that they declared all the acts of the tribunal null and void, and were at that very moment drawing up the proper instrument to deprive the inquisitors of citizenship.

Someone from the magistrates' benches went to the inquisitors hoping, as nearly as Don Felipe could make out by the movements of his hands, to calm them; but their faces waxed more wrathful. One of them stood and thundered, "Not though Saint Paul himself were to come down from Heaven and order us to act otherwise than as we do! Not though it cost us our souls!"

From a chair of honor, a high churchman rose and called out, "Let the Mass continue, under pain of excommunication for the officiating priest!"

But the officiating priest had disappeared, no one knew where. In the confusion, no one had seen him slip away. Don Felipe hardly knew whether to blame him for deserting a half-said Mass, or applaud him for escaping and leaving it unfinished in the presence of so many who cared less for God's heavenly than for their own earthly privileges. Besides Don Felipe and the pagan Rosemary, and the now-visible, now-unseen bride and bridegroom, one person alone in all that riot appeared to take any interest in seemly decorum, and he was a quiet, not unhandsome young man who stood as near the sanctuary as permissible, keeping his nose buried in a small book.

The inquisitor looked at him again, and asked Rosemary, "Who is that?"

"Gardiner," she replied.

For one moment, Don Felipe had thought him to be El Santon, reading a pamphlet from his own press. But Juan de Calamocha was outside, undergoing his passion. Don Felipe had come into the cathedral so as not to witness his agony.

"Let the Mass continue!" the high churchman cried out once more, and pointed his forefinger at the inquisitor. "Under pain of excommunication!"

"They're calling you," said Rosemary, and Don Felipe found himself, unvested as he was, standing before the altar, with Host and Chalice waiting before him.

Had the Consecration yet taken place, or not? He could not remember. Desperately though he searched his mind, he could find no recollection of how far the original priest had come, or at what point he had abandoned his post. Hands trembling, keenly aware of his secular garb—which must be long out of fashion—Don Felipe bowed over the Elements and said a provisional Consecration over the Host.

He genuflected to the Body of Christ. He stood again, lifted It from Its poor gold paten, and raised It high above his head. The Elevation, at least, would have as much dignity as he could humanly lend it, no matter whether the buffoons on their benches were watching or not. By their continued hubbub, he thought not. In his opinion, that this Mass should continue was scandalous. Nevertheless, since he had been commanded to finish it, he would do so with as much—

A blow struck his arms, so hard that it numbed them. The Host fell. Aghast, he tried to catch it. His arms swung like staves of wood, and a knife pierced his left hand. The pain doubled him over, half on the altar—but danger to the Body of Christ outweighed any personal grief. Calling all his will, he jerked himself up and around.

He saw Gardiner—the hitherto quiet young man—in the act of casting the Host underfoot and stamping on it.

That unthinkable sacrilege silenced the whole cathedral. They who had squabbled so long and loud about their worldly privileges now stood or sat frozen, mouths agape like wounds. The bridegroom shielded his bride's face from the terrible sight. Blood flowed from the remains of Sacred Flesh where They lay mangled on the sanctuary floor.

Rosemary stood frowning, arms folded tightly across her breast. Even she, Pagan though she called herself, seemed to disapprove.

Staring at the man, Felipe whispered, "Why?" Then, his voice breaking out despite himself, "My God! You have assaulted God Himself!"

As though his cry were the release, a roar burst from the assemblage. Contorted faces howling for vengeance, they surged forward, arms straining toward the desecrator like the spines of some vast hedgehog. Don Felipe threw himself down on the floor, striving to cover the broken Host with his own body lest the mob trample It themselves in the rush of their zeal. He saw more than felt Gardiner's knife still transfixing his hand, its point coming through the palm. He desperately feared that it might scratch the Sacred Flesh.

"Stop!" Rosemary shouted above the noise of the mob. Once again they fell silent, arms frozen in midreach, faces turning to watch her. A head or more taller than almost everyone else present, she strode up to the sanctuary steps, halting just short of Felipe's hands. "All right," she said, gazing steadily at Gardiner. "Why did you do it?"

He answered: "To awaken them to their foul idolatry."

"Idolatry?" cried Felipe. "How is it idolatry to worship the very Body of the One True God?"

Rosemary stooped and yanked the dagger from his hand. Some of his blood spurted down to mingle with Christ's Flesh before he could prevent it. But his guide had straightened again and returned her gaze to Gardiner. Balancing the dagger between her hands as if testing its point with one finger, she said, "By stirring them into frenzy. Lot of good that does."

"I knew that it must cost me my life."

"You'll be lucky if it doesn't cost the life of every English Protestant in this country." Turning to Don Felipe, she went on, "Your call, inquisitor. Who gets him? Due process of law, or the mob? The mob would be quicker."

He looked at them and shook his head. "Let Gardiner's blood not be upon their heads."

"I'd call that academic," she remarked. "But suit yourself."

Seizing the offender by one arm, she marched him in a straight line to the doors, the mob parting for them like the Red Sea for Moses, though not without many curses and much shaking of fists.

Don Felipe remained to gather up the Sacred Fragments as best he could and lock Them safely in the Tabernacle. It seemed to take him a very long time. When at last he finished and looked up, the cathedral was empty of everyone save Rosemary, who stood in the doorway beckoning.

"I turned him over to the justice of 1552 Portugal," she told Don Felipe. "Come watch it."

"I should prefer to stay here and pray for—"

"Great-grandfather, this time you haven't got the choice." Seizing his arm as moments ago she had seized Gardiner's, she led him outside.

Blinking against the glare of sunlight, he gasped. The stake had been made into the fulcrum of a long lever, from one end of which the sacrilegious wretch dangled in chains, while executioners worked the other end to lower him nearer the flames and raise him again, prolonging his agony. His garments already burned away, the red-hot chains were scorching their patterns into his naked, blistering skin. Blackened, and cracked with stripes of blood, soon his nakedness would be invisible. The crowd laughed, jeered, hooted and mocked, relishing a poor sinner's pain in the free assurance that all was for the greater glory of God.

Yet—he saw with sudden shock—if they themselves were not sinners, they could not have enjoyed watching the sufferings of Satan himself.

"I die one of God's martyrs!" Gardiner screamed. The crowd howled him to scorn, and the executioners dipped him again into the fiery bath, so that his words became animal shrieks.

Beside the pyre, the carpenter still labored at his craft, unnoticed by the crowd. His tears, where they fell upon his staves, looked bloody; and when he raised his hammer, Don Felipe saw that a great chunk had been torn out of his arm, leaving the upper bone bare and glistening for about the length and breadth of a Communion Host.

It seemed that Felipe was gripping Rosemary's arm, rather than she his, for he felt his fingers squeezing as deeply as torture cords into flesh. Try as he would, he could not loosen them.

The lever broke. Like a man falling through thick water, the man-sized lump of bleeding charcoal toppled into the flames. The Carpenter plucked him out unburnt and clothed in white, put a palm branch into his hand, and set him on a platform, narrow across the front but stretching back out of sight, where a radiant multitude waved similar branches. El Santon was among them, and also...

"Raymonde!" Felipe exclaimed, pointing to one who stood embracing Gardiner. "There is my ancestress!"

Rosemary made a peculiar double grunt. "Uh-huh. So she's your 'ancestress' all right, but I'm still waiting to be your 'descendant.' And, incidentally, hers."

He looked in perplexity at the woman of the future. The whole scene had changed around them, save for the Carpenter working at His table; and, with the scene, Felipe's own past...or, rather, he seemed to have a sort of double memory, glimpses of different lives, one of them filled with strange and impossible things.

"Valencia," Rosemary told him. "July 26th, 1826."

He saw the twisted columns of the Silk Exchange, the old church of Los Santos Juanes, and many structures such as part of him knew quite well but the other part not at all. No longer moblike, changed even more in temper than in costume, the crowd had grown sober and solemn; all watched quietly and many with half-hidden disapproval.

"Cayetano Ripoll, schoolmaster," said a heavy voice, "for heresy and the teaching of heresy, you are sentenced to the flames."

He nodded. Vague memories showed him that he had indeed committed these sins, though even now he felt no guilt for them.

Someone put a cord around his neck and began, from behind, to twist it tighter...tighter.

"Don't worry," Rosemary said. Inconsequentially, he thought. His throat completely constricted, he could no longer expel his last breath, and was drowning in the stale air trapped in his lungs…a long death it seemed, with the world moving very slowly beyond the tears that half veiled his sight.

The Carpenter picked his handiwork up at last and brought it forward. It was a barrel, large enough to serve as coffin for a grown man, and having its outside painted with large and bloody tears. "These are your flames," the Carpenter said softly. "Behold the final fruit of this thing you have wrought in My Name."

He raised the barrel and slipped it down over the dying man.

Rosemary said, "Technically, great-grandfather, your Inquisition isn't responsible for Ripoll's death. It's already dead itself, and the bishops are acting on its behalf. But this is what it all comes down to."

He heard no more. All was darkness.

CHAPTER 27

THE LAST ACT OF FAITH

Don Felipe woke before the predawn dark, to look through his window and see a clear vista of stars, promising well for the feast day. Unable to sleep again, he thought he felt a rustle near his feet, and kicked at it, then propped himself up in his bed to sit huddled in blankets with his hands pressed together for warmth. He considered summoning Gubbio. A cup of steaming water would have been pleasant to hold beneath his nose, simultaneously warming his fingers and clearing his inhalations; but in pure forgetfulness he might sip, and an inquisitor's failure to take Communion at early Mass on this day could be a source of scandal to any common folk who might hear of it, so he let his old servant snore on outside the door.

The bedding rustled again. Truly, he thought that he had been less troubled with vermin in the secret cells than here in his own bed in Daroca (where he had finally returned as senior of the tribunal's two inquisitors). Strange how, as the years passed, he caught himself from time to time in curious nostalgia for those long days and longer nights of solitary confinement, with no other labor or responsibility than to worry about his trial and the state of his conscience.

He must check yet again with his few charges still under present investigation, to be sure that their cells remained free of rats. Completely free of mice was but an impossible dream anywhere in this sinful world.

This morning he remembered more than usual of his night's dreaming. A barrel painted over with flames...and it had been the coffin for some poor wretch no more guilty than Saint Peter...and someone had said that to this the Holy Office must come at last...

At length the stars quietly began to disappear. Soon the procession would be assembled: the penitents for reconciliation, each with his or her new godparent to assist at the rebirth of spiritual life; the hapless unregenerates who must at last be pruned away and let fall to the secular arm...three of these today, and one of them poor El Santon—since his father's death, the only Juan Delgado de Calamocha, who had fallen under scrutiny time and again until at last he exhausted all their efforts.

An unsigned pamphlet, traced to his press thanks to certain peculiarities of the typeface, had appeared making the claim that Holy Church had herself preserved the heresy of Arius—that Ihesu was merely a created demigod—by transferring it from God's Son to His Mother, the most Blessed and Glorious Virgin Mary. Since this was seen as touching on the Immaculate Conception, which the Dominicans in the Council of Faith still opposed (and therefore, Don Felipe guessed, were privately somewhat less than outraged by the statement in question), that case had ended with the master printer sentenced to abjuration *de levi*.

Then, when the Lutheran heresy began spreading out plaguelike from northern lands, someone reported having heard Maestre Juan liken Holy Church to the Titan Saturn devouring his children lest one of them overthrow him and reign in his place. Since no such statement could be found in any printed work from his press, and there was but a single witness, it was quietly decided that the erstwhile El Santon de Aragon suffered from some species of lunacy, and it did not even come to his arrest.

Next he issued a pamphlet, this one boldly bearing the name of his shop—virtually a signature to the text itself—which included the argument that, even as "an eye for an eye and a tooth for a tooth" was to be interpreted as forbidding any person to demand more redress than essential for perfect balance, so the law of the tithe had been meant to prevent the Church from ever impoverishing her children by demanding more than a tenth from them. This time, with the evidence in print, he had been arrested and imprisoned awhile. But, since the pamphlet had been aimed primarily at the State, the passage going on to argue that no secular authority should ever demand more in taxation than the spiritual demanded in tithes; and since El Santon had already at least once been set down as insane, his case was suspended and himself quietly released through the back door.

At last, however, came the time when they could no longer either ignore or release him but, for the spiritual welfare of the populace as a while, must excise his notorious heresies from their midst. As though further emboldened by each successive escape, he had begun proclaiming, both aloud and in print, that Ihesu had not suffered and died to ransom His people—for such a ransom, such a debt, could only be cancelled and forgiven, never paid—but that, rather, God had chosen to comprehend what His poor creatures suffered by enduring human agonies Himself, in His own Person, and thus, in that way, hallowing and sanctifying them.

From some fragment buried as deeply within the layers of his memory as any surviving record of his own imprisonment must be buried within the secret records of the Daroca tribunal, Don Felipe seemed to hear a soft voice saying, "I believed that this Lord of the Old Testament was hard and cruel because He had not yet learned compassion by passing through the Virgin's womb, by tasting for Himself the full measure of human pain through enduring the torture of the cross." Unable to find any episode, framework, or speaker for these words, he buried them once again and sadly agreed to Maestre Juan's arrest.

Juan had succeeded in identifying the latest charge against him by including it in a list, running to four full pages, of more than a score of various propositions, some heretical and some of such sound orthodoxy as to lay the man still further under suspicion for doubting them.

"Juan, Juan," Don Felipe had asked him in one interview, "how have these Lutherans led you so far astray?"

"Lutherans? My lord, do you think me a Lutheran? I am a good and loyal son of Holy Mother Church!"

"So you were baptized, and given almost enough instruction for a priest." (Indeed, the inquisitor thought, the newly baptized printer had soon stored up more clerical knowledge than many a parish priest enjoyed.) "Is this the use to make of all your excellent learning?"

"Why has God given us minds at all, my lord, if not to ponder these things?"

"Why, to assist our wills in choosing the true Faith and cleaving to it."

"But do you not see, my lord Don Felipe? Our God—the one and only True God—is so great, so vast! and we are so small, so infinitely small, so very limited. Each of us can grasp no more than a few infinitely tiny scraps of the Glory of God, and clothe those few poor scraps of vision each in his own pitiful words, and so fashion of them one more little door into Heaven—but all our doors lead at last into that same Glory of God!"

The inquisitor blinked, seeming to hear that same unidentified voice from deep in his forgotten past cry exultantly: "And upon the surface of this great Immensity of God we crawl, specks infinitely tiny, and we *must* use many religions and creeds if ever we would glimpse even the tiniest Atom of the Essence of God!" But this was heresy or, at the least, demonic temptation—for the demons, like the sirens, could speak in voices sweet as those of angels when it served their foul purpose. Shutting his mind to it, Don Felipe objected, "Surely you would not pretend that all these so-called 'doors'—which are, in other words, so many heresies—are equally righteous and safe?"

"Equally safe? No, my lord, hardly equally safe! And their righteousness I do not pretend to judge. I say only, my lord, that each of us must enter by whatever door he finds best suited to his own size and shape, and may God have mercy on us all!"

"Juan, Juan!" The inquisitor shook his head mournfully. "Could you not at the very least exercise the great virtue of prudence? Keep these heretical temptations to yourself—privately seek out some good spiritual counsellor to help you resolve your doubts—but refrain from publishing them to the scandal of the whole Church and downfall of your fellow Catholic Christians?"

Lowering his gaze, Juan had slowly plucked off the spectacles which he, like his old master printer of Calatayud, now wore in his turn, wiped them on his sleeve, returned them to his face, and heaved a soft, deep sigh. Then, raising his head again, he said, "We must let these things out of our hearts, my lord, even if it should prove that they are weeds. Otherwise, they will choke us and stifle us."

Juan, Juan, alas! my poor San Juan de Calamocha! Felipe's heart had wept. You will force us at last to burn you! And with that thought had come the dim memory of another voice, too hard and grim to sound like that of a tempter, saying: "Don't tell me that a lot of so-called martyrs didn't goad their so-called persecutors into doing it."

To Don Felipe's comfort, however small, the one-time El Santon was spared formal torture in any degree. There was neither purpose nor need—out of his own mouth he had condemned himself—the Council of Faith did not so much as raise the question, simply condemning him, in varying measures of regret, to relaxation with the customary plea for mercy to the secular arm.

When Don Felipe's junior inquisitor, Fray Estevan de la Clemencia de la Madre de Cristo, remarked, "This is what comes of giving common laymen too much instruction in the Faith," Felipe determined to take upon himself the duty of informing Maestre Juan of the sentence at the customary hour, on the eve of its execution. It had only remained to hope and pray that the unfortunate man be reconciled and mercifully strangled before his pyre was lit.

Bits and pieces of last night's visit rose again in Don Felipe's memory, almost as clear as if he could step from his bed back into El Santon's cell and lay his hand once more on the shoulder of the condemned printer.

"Must I die, then?"

"My poor friend, too often has Holy Mother Church held you safe from the secular arm, only to see her great mercy abused and betrayed."

"Has pointed me out to the secular arm for burning—No! Let me recant!"

"Yes! Save your soul. Your body you can no longer save—but save your soul, which is by far the most important part, and your body will live again at the Final Judgment."

"Don Felipe! Don Felipe! My only sin has been searching too desperately for God!"

"But what need for all this mad searching? Has not God Himself revealed all necessary truth through His Blessed Son, and has not Holy Church preserved and interpreted it for you, as for all of humankind?"

A little of the old defiance had flashed back into the condemned man's face. "Are we babies, to accept our beliefs from our mothers' lips, chewed to pap for us to swallow whole?"

"Yes, my friend, in the eyes of God we are all of us indeed babies and infants. But call His revealed truth, not 'pap,' but rather pure and wholesome milk from our mother's breast. Poor man, poor man, your sin is not even limited to searching for God along paths which He Himself has forbidden. Why have you chosen to spew forth your poison in print, thus endangering other, simpler souls?"

"Children indeed, are we? Then let me go home, Don Inquisitor. I no longer wish to play these childish games!"

"Then repent this one more time. For the spiritual welfare of her other babes, Holy Church can no longer risk the false mercy of saving you from the secular arm. But spare your flesh the torture of the earthly fire and your soul the eternal torments of Hell. Be reconciled, and go to God's judgment a clean and forgiven spirit, to sit in Heaven side by side with that Good Thief who received his blessing from Christ's own lips."

For a moment, Juan El Santon had seemed to waver. Alas, in the very teeth of despair his pride had visibly wrestled down his terror. "Say, rather, go a forsworn and cowardly spirit," he had answered at last. "A soul more likely to be damned for betraying the God of its own conscience than blessed for groveling one more time—and to no earthly purpose!—before the God of hypocrisy and murder. No, this time I will *not* renounce my own poor thoughts and words!"

That was the moment when, unable to lay his hand on the wretched man's head in blessing, Don Felipe had gripped his shoulder in simple human sympathy. What the two brothers, standing by in silence, might have made of the gesture, the old inquisitor hardly cared, even now. Let them question him about it—only let them question him, if at all, then at once—he had his answer ready. He had made one final attempt to reach the poor sinner, to try whether a compassionate touch might succeed where words had failed.

But where and how, he berated himself, did my words fail? What argument of mine finally sealed the poor man's doom? Lord, hold not against Your misguided Morisco-Lutheran child the failure of a bumbling old would-be spiritual adviser!

Was it truly too late for El Santon? Might he not yet repent in time? Might not that pair of brothers, one Dominican and one Franciscan, young though they were, have brought him sometime during the night to repentance and salvation? Or, if they too had failed, might not the elation of this day's ceremonies strike a holy response from that sensitive soul, once—however tenuously—still ardently and eagerly Catholic? Or at least when his final hour approached, and he saw his fellow sufferers, both of whom had been successfully reconciled in their cells, being mercifully strangled at their stakes beside his?

The cathedral bell tolled four strokes, each one seeming to raise a tremor that was still vibrating as the next stroke began. Surely, Don Felipe mused, an overfine imagination must magnify the tones of the bell at this hour, else how had he—or anyone else in Daroca—slept through the tolling of the night's earlier hours?

If the imagination of an inquisitor, who would spend this day in pomp and princely dignity on the scaffold of honor, were wrought up to such a pitch, what of the poor wretches…

The door opened and Gubbio came in, still stretching, his yawn visible in the light of his candle—a waxen one, as befitted a holy day. Opening his eyes wide enough to see his master sitting up in bed, he nodded comfortably and started laying out Don Felipe's finest garments.

"Old friend," the priest said suddenly, "tell me: the penitents…the reconciled and, perhaps even more, the condemned…is this not *their* day? The day of their rebirth, either in this world or in the next… Is it not they who most shine in the eyes of the people?"

Gubbio shrugged. "Maybe in the streets. And this evening in the burning-field, they'll naturally have the attention all to themselves, even if they should happen to be strangled before the flames reach them. But in the square, my Don, that is where all eyes will rest on your Resplendence and the other great ones beside you."

Coming over to the bed, he folded the covers back and bent to help his master out into the day. As he yawned again, his breath flowed over Don Felipe like a draught of wine.

"Do you not, then, take Communion today, Gubbio?"

"Forgetful in your age, are you, my Don? Once a year is plenty for sinners like me, and thank God for His mercy in that, I say! It might be one thing for high churchmen like you to stand fasting at early Mass, but workers like me need something in the belly to help our poor flesh bear up beneath all that grace hitting our souls."

"It was not so much forgetfulness, old friend, as hope that someday, perhaps today… But no, you are right. Frequent Communion touches too near presumption." He almost added, "when indulged in by simple souls," but his Italian had never been notable for simplicity. "No," he finished aloud, "the safest customs are best, for body as well as soul."

Gubbio winked.

* * * *

The day turned out cloudless, though not overly hot: perfect weather bespeaking the perfect grace of Heaven as it fell over the public Act of Faith. Surely the grace of Heaven fell. Surely the young priest Fray Benedeto drew it down through the holy ceremonies at the altar raised out of doors beneath God's own blue vault, to flow outward from thence over them all—Don Felipe and his new junior inquisitor, along with the local dignitaries, hidalgos, and secular officers in their high places of honor, common folk come in throngs from town and countryside for many miles around, penitents and condemned standing in consecrated patience with their godparents at their sides.

Yes, they were the center of it all, these penitents. Surely it was upon them that God's grace fell most strongly from the altar. Godparents and commoners, nobility and secular officials, churchmen and even representatives of the Holy Office could receive only the backwash, the overflow. It was these lambs, whether in sanbenito or other garment, for whose benefit the entire ceremony existed.

How else could they have stood there, so meekly and quietly, if not sustained even more than the rest of the assemblage by the vast outpouring of grace from Heaven? Those sentenced to live…yes, the mere desire to live on in the greatest comfort possible to them might in itself have been enough to hold them quiet and obedient. But the three condemned ones—what else save God's grace could have kept *them* from raising riot? Don Felipe's eyes located Maestre Juan, standing upright and still in his yellow sanbenito and miter painted over with flames and demons, his eyes closed and arms crossed on his deeply heaving chest. In his place, thought the inquisitor, had I no hope of Divine forgiveness and Heaven at last, I should kick and scream until dragged away. What had they to lose? Even if brutally beaten down…a well-hurled stone or expert jab of the pike might prove still swifter than merciful strangulation at the stake, so why not court death at the hands of soldiers or mob? What had the condemned, considering this world alone, to lose?

"Their dignity, perhaps," said an almost mocking voice near Don Felipe.

Finding his eyes shut like those of El Santon, the inquisitor opened them to behold, perched at his feet, somewhat in the fashion of a jester, on the very edge of the scaffolding, the dark man of Saint Patrick's Purgatory.

Felipe blinked. The sun continued to shine from a sky cloudless and benign as ever. The holy chant proceeded as smoothly, the entire assemblage watched in unbroken awe, not a single cough cut the sanctified silence…and not a single head appeared to have turned at the stranger's voice. No one else except the senior inquisitor alone seemed to have noticed the impudent new presence.

"After all," the dark man went on, "how much would violent resistance benefit them at this juncture?"

Yet they stand when they should, the inquisitor thought. They turn and move when so directed. Why not simply sit down and do nothing more of their own exertion?

"On the other hand, without hope, why not simply play along and spare themselves at least a few gratuitous kicks and fisticuffs?"

You *are* a demon of Hell! as I sensed so many years ago. Else why torment my holy meditations with doubts better befitting youth than age—better befitting poor El Santon than myself!

"Torment?" Unruffled, the dark man cocked one brow in the direction of the penitents and the condemned.

The inquisitor gazed at them again, marveling anew at the depth of their patience. What else could lend them such quiet dignity, save Divine Grace? Or… Juan's words came back to him: "I no longer wish to play your games." Had not the demon of the Purgatory echoed this in his "play along"?

My God! I have been blind! All these years, I have been blind!

"Don't overreact," said the dark man. "Your hypothesis stands as much chance of accuracy as does mine. My present status eschatologically speaking carries with it no particular claim to infallibility."

"But we are children! We are truly *all of us* no more than tiny little children before God, playing out our silly little mystery plays to murderous endings! This is what the great Dumb Ox of God meant in laying down his great *Summa Theologica* as 'all straw'! And I have been one of those who force other children to play their parts to the death, according to the rules of the childish bully!"

"Then leave," said a woman's voice beside him.

"What good would that do anybody?" said another woman's voice at his other side.

Jerking his head from side to side, he saw them both: the one dark and delicate, somewhat smaller than himself, lovely as an angel and clad in flowing white, with the martyr's palm in her hand; the other plain of face, larger than most grown men, and wearing simple tunic over trousers. Raymonde! Rosemary! As he felt their names, all the memories flooded back, to every drop of flame and gout of blood.

Raymonde went on, answering Rosemary's question, "It would show them that one enlightened soul refuses to play any longer at being wicked. Great-grandson, you would turn yourself into a living symbol of God's truth."

"He'd probably turn himself into a temporarily living bonfire," said Rosemary. "How much would that help those poor wretches down there today, and how long would anybody else remember the grand gesture?"

"That," remarked the man of the Purgatory, "might depend on what historian, if any, set it down for posterity."

Ignoring him, Don Felipe concentrated on the women. Never have I seen or remembered either of you outside my dreams. Am I again dreaming?

"No," the dark man replied almost before the question was asked.

Felipe considered the scene around him. All seemed much as it had before any of the three appeared, save that beyond them it wavered and shimmered as though the very sunlight had a strong and rapid pulse. As yet, no one else seemed to have seen or heard any of his strange companions, not even the churchmen standing close on either side, whose positions the women had somehow usurped without displacing them. Nor did anyone else save the ghostly three show signs of having heard Felipe's own words. For this, even in his agitation, the inquisitor felt profound relief.

Dying, then?

Rosemary snorted. "If you were, great-grandfather, I'd say go ahead and make a big production of walking away from it all."

"I believe," Raymonde told him, "that you are suffering a moment of Enlightenment. Accept it worthily."

"When in doubt," the dark man suggested, "compromise."

Don Felipe pictured himself turning deliberately, walking past his fellow dignitaries without a glance, descending the steps, and proceeding, not to the table of refreshments beneath the scaffold of honor, but out of the square itself. Would the crowd part for him in awed silence? Or would it be required of him to push his way through?

Or suppose he were to collapse here and now, disrupting the Act of Faith with a feigned seizure? The disruption would be slight and soon over. He had seen it happen several times, although more often among the penitents and condemned than among the dignitaries.

And, in the end, Rosemary was right. It would change nothing, not one thing, for the unhappy children under sentence. So, in the end, he did nothing.

* * * *

Nothing save visit the burning-field late that evening, after a light supper and an hour of troubled rest.

Never before had he come outside of town to that place where the secular arm carried out its executions. He knew of persons who considered themselves blessed for attending the burnings after missing the Act of Faith itself, and of many more who called themselves doubly blessed for attending both Act and burnings. But such piety had always lain beyond his personal comprehension. Even today, though he thought of defying the propriety befitting his office and forcing himself, in penance for his life's work, to follow that part of the crowd which streamed from square to burning-field, he could not do it. The condemned had suffered at their stakes while he supped and rested in physical comfort far from the scene of their agony.

The stench of scorched human flesh still choked the air, but that of fear and bloodlust had largely dissipated along with the crowd. Charred remains clung to the stakes, barely visible but no longer recognizable, by the fading glow of the embers, as human bodies.

Which of the three had once housed the soul of San Juan de Calamocha? Had the earnest soul repented at last and earned strangulation before burning? Or had he followed his Ihesu in suffering the uttermost? The inquisitor decided not to ask.

His otherworldly companions, whether dreams or visions, had long departed; but this time the women remained in his wakeful memories. The burning-field seemed less grisly—in some way, less real—than the terrible sights of his lifelong dreams. And yet, in another way, it was worse: filled with great, and solemn, and forever unfillable emptiness. Juan El Santon was gone.

He was gone. Human power could never restore what it had so easily destroyed. They had forced him out of the game he no longer wished to play, and already Don Felipe ached for the man's earthly presence, the curious gadfly innocence of his small, searching heresies.

Had good, hard-pressed Pope Alexander felt this way after yielding at last to the harsh necessity of burning Fra Girolamo?

But there should have been some other way! Surely nothing—*nothing*—could in God's sight be worth *this*! Could I not—somehow—have argued my Council into voting him a harmless madman, this time for good and all—quietly releasing him and leaving him to chase his theological notions in peace, only confiscating and burning his pamphlets from time to time as need might demand?

Were not poor San Juan de Calamocha's dreams and visions, if all could be said, far more wholesome than mine? Yes, even to that curious little Purgatorio of his youth…and he had gone so much farther, might have gone so much farther yet… And who is to say that his dreams were less involuntary than mine have ever been?

Or, ah, God! have I become another Fray Junípero, so hardened in my zeal for Thy Glory as to ignore the infinitely greater claims of Thy Mercy

"God help me," the inquisitor murmured, safely beneath his breath. "I can follow my vocation no longer."

Fortunately, the dark man's compromise lay clear before him. Retirement to a life of prayer and meditation had always been an honorable choice, and one that no fellow churchman, not even another inquisitor, could question. Having failed to quit his life's work dramatically, he did so quietly; and, as soon as making the decision, felt how appropriate was the official name for retirement upon half pay: "jubilation."

CHAPTER 28

THE DREAM OF TWO PROPHETS

He stood in the porch of a great, white temple, looking down over a river, its banks marginated with buildings that seemed now to be of Italy, now of some outlandish village striving to establish itself in the heart of a strange, dense wilderness. Finding Rosemary on one hand and Raymonde on the other, both present with him at once, he guessed he was about to witness an intermingling of past and future events.

"Where are we?" he asked them.

"Milan," said the one. "Easter Day, by the reckoning of Rome, in the year of our Lord 1300."

"Nauvoo, overlooking the Mississippi," said the other. "New World state of Illinois, June 1844."

He blinked, trying to reconcile the images, and turned to the temple's interior. It was at best half finished, but at an altar of purest marble, presiding over a congregation wherein people of old illuminations seemed to stand side by side with inhabitants of the unimaginable future, a priest in antique vestments was singing High Mass.

His ears told him, with a shock, that the priest was a woman.

"She is Mayfreda," his ancestress told him, "pope of that Guilielma who was called the very Incarnation of the Holy Spirit."

"Could be why they brought her here," said Rosemary. "I think Mormon scripture makes a big deal of the Spirit, too."

"The Gulielmites." Don Felipe closed his eyes for a moment, trying to remember...had not one of his teachers in Rome mentioned this heresy? "Gulielma of Milan...but she died in...in..."

"In peace," Raymonde said, sounding, for the first time since Don Felipe had met her, very slightly envious. "In 1282, in her bed, in peace, and even in the odor of sanctity. To her followers, she was another face of God."

Rosemary grunted. "What if she was right?"

Don Felipe reacted unthinkingly, by making the Sign of the Cross at her.

"Oh, crackerjack!" snapped Rosemary. "I'm not possessed, I'm not a devil, and you can't make me one by wishful thinking...great-great-grandfather. I'm just used to asking questions."

"Like you, great-grandson, we were born of mortal flesh," added Raymonde. "And even martyrdom brings only a simple palm. It does not bring the answer to every question."

Popess Mayfreda began reading from a gold-bound book held by a female acolyte. "Listen!" Felipe exclaimed, holding up one hand. "The suppressed gospels of the Gulielmites?"

Rosemary shrugged. "I wouldn't know 'em from the *Silmarillion*. You act eager enough to hear 'em, considering your people suppressed them."

"I listen from old habit, because it was once my duty to understand heresy," he answered, but before he could hear any great amount, there came a roll of thunder and the scene changed around them.

Now they stood within a chamber, not large, yet so plainly and sparingly furnished as to seem larger than it was. Floor, walls, and ceiling were of rough wood, and there were iron bars on every window. The thunder continued to roll, loudening and diminishing but never stopping.

The popess sat on a low, narrow cot, speaking earnestly with a tall and handsome man in early middle age.

"Interesting," Rosemary observed. "As I recall, Joseph Smith had his brother with him."

"And it was another woman, Andrea Saramita, who perished at the stake with Gulielma's apostle pope," said Raymonde.

Don Felipe went nearer, trying to overhear the man and woman; but the thunder rose again. He could make out neither Joseph Smith's words nor Mayfreda's, only those of his ancestress and pretended descendant.

"My point is," Rosemary was saying, "if these Guilielmites had come along in the right time and place, maybe they could've done as well as the Mormons."

"Are you saying that it was a true revelation?" Raymonde inquired.

"I don't give a hang about revelations! Give almost any religion—no matter how righteous-mad it makes people at first—a generation or two, and it'll become as respectable as any other religion."

Don Felipe felt he could not, even now, permit such a statement to pass uncontested, but even as he turned around to challenge it, he understood that the long wave of sound was no longer thunder, but an angry mob. Hardly had he recognized this, when they broke into the chamber—tall, rough men with soot-smeared faces, brandishing long guns.

Those in front aimed their weapons at the prophet and popess. Sheets of flame exploded from the tips of the gunbarrels in a blinding roar, and Don Felipe woke.

Only a flash of lightning and clap of thunder. Close...so close that when dawn came they would no doubt see at once where the bolt had fallen…but for now, he could place this latest dream alongside all those others in the secret archives of his mind, and fall asleep again listening to the storm as to a friend.

How if he were to spend some part of his jubilated years in writing them down? *The Apocalypses of Don Felipe de Alhama de Karnattah…* and where should he hide them? to rest safely concealed until well after his death, and come to light only when the world was safe for many doors to God.

CHAPTER 29

THE RANSOM

Midmorning, and the sun of mid-September, shining from an all but cloudless sky, filled Don Felipe's garden with a glow more rich than if the place had been enclosed in stained glass. Contentedly drowsy in his cushioned chair, his back resting on a sun-warmed column, the jubilated inquisitor closed his eyes for a moment, opened them when his book slid off his lap to land with a thump in the bed of overgrown basil. He blinked a little in tranquil surprise at observing how much the shadows had shrunk during that momentary closure of his eyes; but were not such things to be expected in a man's age?

Recovering the small volume, he sat turning it over and over in his hands. A duodecimo of approved devotions, totally above suspicion, but bland as porridge, both in content and manner of serving it up: uniform, mechanical letters, each formed by a pat of metal that might almost as well have been cast into gunshot; and all these lifeless little letters crowded together page after page with no grace of illumination either in pictures or margins, this particular volume having not even woodcut nor engraving, nothing save spaces for initials which had never been filled in.

Don Felipe's parents had remembered the days before printed texts, when each word had to be copied anew in every volume. Then, books had been true books, every letter the personal touch of a human hand. Thoughts so transmitted, from one person directly to the next, had been as good as spoken. Felipe could still sense it when he picked up a hand-copied volume.

I have grown up with printing from a press, he mused, and old with it. Is this not part of the dulling and cheapening—the coarsening—of our age? When thoughts are shot as if from guns upon paper, page after identical page, what becomes of the soul behind those thoughts? (Ah, Juan, poor Maestre Juan El Santon! But let me not remember you on this tranquil day.) Once, readers treasured each precious volume. When books become cheap, who will read them with awe or even attention, who will absorb the meaning of their words? Will people not come to read books as rapidly and mechanically as they print them? And, as the next step of logic, to write them with equal speed and inattention? Is this not, indeed, already taking place? What will become of literacy itself, when nothing remains worth reading?

In my parents' age, a reader took time to linger over a book, to hold it in a cloth, to turn each leaf with care, and, when finished for the nonce, to lay the volume tenderly away in its proper place. Then, books were worthy of such treatment.

He had begun to wax nostalgic, not so much for his own past, as for that of his parents, as he imagined it to have been. But the things Raymonde had shown him allowed him to imagine only so far before they rent the rosy veil his reverie threw over the far past. The thoughts of those days might have been less hurried, the study more intense, the pace of life less cluttered; but no murder or massacre could ever have been less terrible by mere virtue of taking place in some more graceful age. War had always been war, blood and fire had always been blood and fire, and those who instigated them had always stained their own souls, no matter what cause they believed themselves to be championing.

In many ways, he regretted the memories that had never long left him again, after flooding his wakeful mind that day of his last Act of Faith, five years ago. Before that, when between dream and dream he had recollected nothing of them, he had at least been able to play his active part in the world, to believe that his times and his role in them were of some value. No, more: he had come at last to look upon his era as God's crowning accomplishment and the cornerstone upon which he, Felipe de Granada, was helping to build all that would follow in glory. Now, with the dreams ever before him to remind him that horrors were equally real in all ages, even to reveal heretical practices of one generation as papally approved traditions of another...all this, and he still could not judge with certitude whether the dreams of his lifetime were visions from God, delusions from the Devil, or mere freaks of his own troubled brain. Why should God allow Albigensian Raymonde to appear as a martyred saint, or permit Pagan Rosemary to lie concerning her supposed descent from Don Felipe's own loins? Even that vision of Saint Patrick's Purgatory could have been false or diabolical as easily as true, and so the dark man's occasional appearance with Raymonde and Rosemary neither validated nor invalidated their revelations.

And yet some of them had clearly proven true—that terrible dream of Alhama, and the occasion shortly after his last Act of Faith when Rosemary showed him the coming sack of Rome in time for him to warn Gamito so that the Jewish family escaped the city before the Spanish and German armies reached it.

He knew it behooved him to share all this with his spiritual director, for even those priests who served in such capacity themselves might prove incapable of weighing their own experiences. But where to find a spiritual director not only of sufficient wisdom, but of safe discretion, and who would not laugh such wild visions as old Don Felipe's out of court half heard?

Meanwhile, and in spite of all, he could not give his ladies up lightly or ungratefully, for had they not brought him from active life into contemplative, from Martha's part into Mary's? Could this result from any work of Satan?

Returning to the book in hand, he considered filling in its blank initials himself. His fingers were still steady. He could send Gubbio for colors and a few fine brushes. Though on half pay from the Holy Office, he had still his savings with the bankers, both here in Aragon and there in Rome. A good share of these funds, along with all the monies due him from Nuestra Señora del Pilar de Agapida, he had been returning to good Fray Giuliano for his new Franciscan houses, where Masses and prayers were continually offered for Pilar and her people; but he nevertheless had a few coins to spare, especially now that his diet had become frugal as any monk's, and his household reduced to manservant, secretary, cook, and one or two dayservants.

Turning the duodecimo's pages, however, he shook his head to the notion of coloring in its capitals. It would not be the same: it would no longer be one mortal creature offering small bouquets to another, but merely one man indulging his own vanity. Perhaps, had this text been worthy enough that he could think of passing it along to someone else…

But enough, for now, of reading…in so far as he had done any reading. Devotions as insipid as those of the colorless duodecimo, he could pen for himself, even as he had penned them during his years of imprisonment. Lifting his lap desk into place, he prepared pen and ink, brought out an old leaf of paper, and began filling it with meditations that not even Fray Tomás de Torquemada could have faulted… Pity that Spain was hardly safe even to think of committing to paper *The Apocalypse of Don Felipe de Granada.*

After perhaps ten minutes, dipping his pen while idly pondering whether or not to insert some pious adjective, for no conscious reason he flicked the leaf over and found, instead of virgin blankness, writing on the other side.

He needed a moment to know it for his own writing. Time had changed his manuscript style. Time indeed…was it half a century? All those years had changed more than his handwriting, more than Felipe himself: they had changed the world around him. Yet this leaf rested in his hand almost as fresh as when it had come from the papermaker's drying line, and the words he read upon it brought his youth back so vividly that it seemed he should have been able to step into it again as easily as walking from this side of his garden to the other.

It was the romance he had barely begun, in an idle moment at the outset of his churchly career, as secretary to the bishop of Daroca. It was the knightly tale of Florindo, survivor of Roncesvalles, and the fair Zorinda. He thought that he could almost remember how he had meant it to continue. Zorinda, of course, had been modeled upon his lost Morayma, Hamet's sister, the lady ideal of his first youth. Where were they now? With Gamito he had managed to keep up communication over the years, but of the Moorish family neither the Christian friend nor the Jewish one had ever learned another word.

Well, God—or Allah, if the lady preferred, though the canny old inquisitor would never have whispered such words aloud, even in privacy—God, however named, grant that Morayma, her brother, her husband, and all whom they loved had somehow achieved long and happy life in spite of the age and the Spaniards' betrayals. Meanwhile... Florindo, Don Felipe supposed, must have been meant as an idealized portrait of himself, the young knight who would win on paper the Moorish maiden whom the young student had been forbidden in life. He found little resemblance now. From the few lines before him, Don Florindo the knight had been a perfect mirror of all chivalric honor, virtue, and courage. Don Felipe the priest had sinned against the holy sacrament of Confession, betrayed his first love by taking another to wife (although *that* he could never regret), and preferred prudence to bravado along every step of his path. Yet Age could look with tranquil and faintly amused tolerance upon Youth.

To eyes washed with a foreglimpse of Eternity, all earthly things were straw, even those efforts most aspiring to touch divinity. In these days, with even Erasmus denounced and forbidden—at least here in Spain, where once his books and others had flowed freely—perhaps approved devotions had even more chaff about them than did simple, silly romances. Dipping his pen again, Don Felipe set himself to finish the sentence left so long half complete.

Words came with surprising rapidity, though shaping themselves into a more whimsical episode than whatever adventure the very young priest had no doubt contemplated; and Don Felipe was nearing the bottom of the page when Gubbio came in with the announcement, "Master, you are wanted."

"Old friend," Felipe answered, chuckling as he laid down his pen, "I cannot readily believe that, especially at this hour of the day."

The Italian clucked his tongue. "A few thin years out of the world, and already your Serenity forgets that for most poor, worldly souls this is as good an hour for business as any."

"As you, my man," the priest returned mildly, "appear to forget that these days prayer and private meditations are my business, which it behooves you never to interrupt save in most dire emergency." More amused than angered or embarrassed, Don Felipe cast an unblushing glance at the tale of Florindo and went on, "Who, in what emergency, could want the assistance of an aged and jubilated inquisitor, long retired from the world?"

Gubbio grunted. "Not as aged as that, my master. I am your senior by a year and more, and I can still swing a stout enough staff when I so desire. As to what the lad's business might be, that you must ask him yourself. I can keep him till dinner if your Tranquility demands it, but he is a sullen young lump and in half an hour I may like it better to accompany you to High Mass, than stay here with him bumping around underfoot."

"Do you raise my curiosity in this manner, you rascal, and then offer to leave it to bedevil my meditation for the rest of the morning? I will see him in...I believe that I will see him here."

Gubbio's eyebrows rose like shaggy white flags. "In your private garden?"

"Is this some wild beast, to trample everything underfoot?"

"As your Eminence wishes." The old servant shrugged, bowed, and departed.

Don Felipe replaced his paper—not quite as if hiding it—returned his lap desk to the flagstones at his feet, folded his hands upon his lap, and waited. The sun warmed his bones; the water plashed pleasantly in the fountain; and the flowers, though little more to his tired old eyes than blurs of color, had never shone more bright.

In a few moments Gubbio was back with the visitor, a shortish, not overly scrawny lad of perhaps fourteen or fifteen, wearing travel-stained clothes and a travel-stained face.

"Don Felipe de Granada?" the lad began in a voice that, even while seeming not yet entirely deepened, held no tone whatever of awe and only the scantest of respect. "Also known as Don Felipe de Nuestra Señora del Pilar de Agapida?"

"I am he. And you are..."

"Juan."

"Juan." With a nod, the old priest accepted the single name, at least for the present. "Well, Juan, I was led to believe that you came seeking me out on a matter of some urgency."

For the first time, the boy's stiffness showed a crack. Lips trembling, he said, "One whom you once...perhaps...held dear, is held captive by bandits. They demand ransom."

Felipe's heart lurched. "Who?"

"You do not know," Juan replied accusingly. "You cannot so much as guess."

"Is it so difficult to conceive that an inquisitor may count more dear friends than one in his life?"

"And more dear loves than one?"

Don Felipe found the crucifix round his neck digging deeply into his right palm. All who had ever known of his boyish worship for Morayma must either be long dead or far from Aragon, and he had thought his secret marriage with Pilar well wrapped in layers of discretion. But he had never been Morayma's lover in more than aspiration, and the name he whispered was that of Pilar.

"So you remember," said the youth. "Or have the gift of guessing. Or both."

"Young man, never was I one of your damnable licentious clerics! In all my years, *she* was the only one. Though how you know of something held private among her, myself, and her own people so many years before your birth… But no matter now! What ransom do they demand?"

"Wait one moment," Gubbio interrupted. "Our young friend here named no names. Your Reverence did. Before haggling over terms of ransom, how can we know, first, that they really hold the lady you think—or, for that matter, anyone at all—and, second, that this rapscallion is not one of them?"

Don Felipe sat back shakily. "Old friend, you speak bald reason. Where his own heart is concerned, even an experienced inquisitor may lose his head. Lad—Juan—what proofs can you show us?"

For answer, the youth took a small bag from around his neck and half flung it down in the churchman's lap.

Opening it with trembling fingers, Don Felipe drew out a packet sealed with horsehair and unstamped wax. He broke the seal and unwrapped the paper. A stone tumbled out—a carnelian the breadth of his little fingernail, carved with the head of Juno. He caught his breath and read what had been written on the paper with a scratchy pen and sooty ink:

"My own, three of us have returned alive from over there beyond the mountains. One you do not yet know, and my unhappy uncle is crazed with grief and age. Our captors ask 3,000 sueldos. Your ring does not leave my finger, the stone only will I part with."

Gathering himself with a deep breath, the old inquisitor returned his gaze to the boy before him. "You are the one whom I do not yet know?"

Juan nodded.

"And the name of her uncle"

"You say you loved her, and you do not remember? He was once a great man among us, a count by *gadje* reckoning, when our number was greater."

"I remember names well enough, and I have one particular uncle in mind whom I guess to be the one she mentions. I know, however, how reluctant your people have always been to call their dead by name, and I fear to break that custom by choosing the wrong name." Don Felipe paused, the fact sinking in:

Dead. All dead. The Calé he had known in Agapida, those clean and honest souls, and all but one of the children born to them since the vengeful young Don Gaspar drove them away…

Calixta Aranse…wife to Pilar's brother…Calixta and a babe of hers… So that evil dream had also been among the true ones?

Tears pressed into his eyes. Forcing them back, he went on, "Do *you* know his name, Juan?"

The boy scowled and muttered, "Uncle Sagesse."

"Sagesse. Don Sagesse Labaa." Feeling one tear slip out despite his efforts, Don Felipe nodded and squeezed the carnelian more tightly in his hand. "How do we know, Juan, that they are still alive—she and Don Sagesse?"

"Would they have left the ring on her finger if she were not? Would I have uttered their names if they were not?"

"Alive and wearing my ring she may have been when you left the bandits. How can we be sure that is still the case?"

"If they had wanted the ring more than the ransom, would they have let the stone come away with me?"

Gubbio barked a dry laugh. "Best either rack the lad or recruit him, my Don."

Juan transferred his glowering stare momentarily to the servant. "She would not thank you for treating one of her people worse than the bandits have treated us."

Although Juan's gaze had returned almost at once to Don Felipe, it was Gubbio who answered the boy. "Do you call it worse, then, to be tortured than murdered?"

"I call it worst of all to be tortured *and* murdered."

"Have done with this!" Don Felipe exclaimed. "Will they accept the sum in jewelry and merchandise?"

"Yes, if there are no tricks."

"Master!" cried Gubbio. "You do not consider paying?"

"I do not *consider* it, Gubbio. I mean to *do* it."

"At least take this business to the alcalde—"

"If they see any soldiers," Juan cut in, "they will hide. You will never see them then, not unless they attack by ambush. And no doubt they will kill her and Uncle Sagesse both."

"How many of them are there, boy?" demanded the inquisitor.

"Seven that I saw, with their old chief to make eight, and I do not count their miserable women. There could be as many again that I did not see."

Gubbio said, "The alcalde must know of such a swarm."

"Perhaps he does," Don Felipe replied. "Perhaps his men have tried and failed so far to track them. Be that as it may, I will give them all that they ask."

"And trust this… this 'Juan' to guide us?"

"And trust Juan to guide us." Although, as a matter of principle, Don Felipe chose not to assure Gubbio in the boy's presence that they could report the bandits to the alcalde as soon as they had Pilar safe. Pilar and Don Sagesse, whose mind might have been crazed, but whose native nobility of soul could not have been destroyed by whatever tragedy had struck his people.

* * * *

Gathering the ransom—jewels, wines, fine cloth goods that Felipe had been saving for garments to be made whenever he found a worthy tailor, three hundred odd dineros and a hundred or so Castilian maravedís in coin, even (despite Gubbio's grumbles, but with every assistance from that good and loyal cook Diego Sos) their entire store of spices—was the work of two hours, interrupted only by a hurried meal. Taken all together, it might, as Gubbio complained, have been sold for considerably more than the amount demanded. Don Felipe cared nothing for that, as long as it brought his wife back to him after all these years apart.

They packed and saddled the animals without delay. Don Felipe would not even pause to hear High Mass at midday in the church of San Martin, as was his usual practice. He did, however, celebrate a dry Mass that evening in the common room of the adequate hostelry where they stopped for the night. Gubbio held the book, while the innkeeper, his wife, their Morisco servant, and a pair of merchants also stopping at the inn stood looking properly honored to hear Latin prayers recited by a former inquisitor. Juan stood farthest back, making no sound, his face deep in shadows.

The Morisco came to table remarkably clean for a man whose daily labor included seeing to the stables, and one of the merchants declined his bowl of pork tripe on the plea that he had taken a temporary vow of abstinence from all meat. These things would have provided evidence enough, even without certain other small things Don Felipe's trained eye noticed, for Fray Junípero and others among his former fellow guardians of the purity of the Faith to commence investigations. As for Felipe, his mind again moved back to his boyhood—as if seeking refuge from present anxieties—and found there only harmony in the three religions living side by side. The people about him had heard the Missa sicca with every outward token of piety. It was all that he himself, in his prime, would have required. Possibly the fault lay with his earliest inquisitorial instruction, from mild old Fra Guillaume. Which manner of instruction... had he himself not tried to pass it along, in his turn, to his own successors?

In any event, he had long left all that behind him. Moreover, tasting the tripe caused him a twinge of envy toward the man who refused it. Although it appeared to please everyone else's tongues well enough.

Unable to sleep, the old priest rose again long before dawn and said Mass privately, seized with longing for all the grace he might wring from God upon this day's efforts. Doubts were rising in his brain as to the rectitude of passing over so many small signs of possible heresy. Raymonde and Rosemary might applaud such willful blindness, but Raymonde and Rosemary might have been sent by the Evil One to tempt him into the errors of false mercy. Could this present crisis, falling upon him in his age, be divine punishment for years of concentrating on the notorious errors while turning blind eye and deaf ear to petty telltales, of seeking his own benefit more than God's in prosecuting—when confiscations were needed—the dead and those who had fled, of finally seeking to escape into contemplative life rather than amending his active career? He half promised God to make full report, after all, at the nearest tribunal so soon as he should have Pilar safe.

And yet, to have Pilar safe again... Could this chance, if it came out well, be called in any sense punishment? Would it not be the greatest earthly reward possible or conceivable?

But if, after all this, we should only lose each other again?

Ah, God, show me Thy will—send me Thy unmistakable sign!

* * * *

They were on their way again at earliest dawn, munching bread and cold bacon as they rode. By midday they were in the mountains. Presently Gubbio demanded, "Well, Juan, how much longer?"

"Maybe half an hour," the boy replied, sounding strangely defiant, "maybe half a day. This is *their* territory. It is for them to find us."

"Then where in our Lady's name are you leading us?"

"The good God knows. They brought me blindfold to those stones we passed back there, that look like the face of an old woman, and told me when I came back to wander away from the path and let them do the rest."

Gubbio stopped his mule with a jerk. "If this is so, I for one go not a single step farther! Let them come and find us at the old woman's face, if they want us."

Juan twisted sharply around in his saddle to glare at the old servant. "They told me to wander off the path! Turn back now, even to those stones, and we risk her life! and the old uncle's as well."

"Gubbio, Gubbio," Don Felipe interposed. "Turn back and wait for us if you wish, but Juan and I will go on as the bandits instructed him. Let me ride in front, since it appears that our exact route no longer matters, and give Juan the reins of our pack mule."

They rearranged themselves, Gubbio grumbling the entire time; but, when after ten or twelve paces Don Felipe looked back, he was satisfied to see his servant still tagging doggedly along at the end of their small procession.

Perhaps half a rosary later, they heard the harsh cry: "Mouth to the ground!"

It seemed to come from somewhere above. Don Felipe squinted up, but could see nothing.

"To the ground!" the voice repeated.

The priest glanced around. Juan was already lying prone on the rocky soil, Gubbio scrambling out of the saddle to follow his example.

Returning his gaze to the rocks ahead and above, the inquisitor said, as loudly as he could without breaking dignity: "I am an old man and a priest, come to ransom Doña Pilar Labaa."

"Mouth to the ground!"

"For the love of God!" Juan exclaimed. "If you would see her alive…"

Don Felipe's heart beat to the point of pain, but still he sat in his place. "What proof have we that you are even of the band that is holding that lady and her uncle, Don Sagesse Labaa?"

A small explosion sounded, and gunshot pocked the earth some yards away, startling the mules. Gubbio's ran. Juan, still hanging to the reins of both his own mount and the pack mule, was jerked to his feet. Don Felipe kept to his saddle with difficulty.

"Hold them, curse you!" bawled a second strange voice.

Gubbio rescued Juan, who might otherwise have been dragged away before releasing his beasts, and together they got them under control. Felipe found his habitually placid Blanca—the third of that name—easier to calm. Indeed, he envied her ability to recapture quietude. Attempting to emulate it, he looked up again and told the unseen bandits: "You see what such unseemly and useless threats may cost you. Already one mule with her saddlebags has escaped us. If you would have what remains, bring the lady and her uncle out to us safe, unharmed, and in good health, and we will make our exchange with no further trouble."

Two men stepped into view. Both held handguns and wore blades. With quick darting of his eyes, Don Felipe glimpsed two more, one on either side, letting their heads and the muzzles of their guns be seen above the rocks. Whichever had fired would have had time by now to recharge his piece.

The taller of the two bandits in full view laughed—it sounded more like amusement than cruelty—and said, "Old man, how much trouble can you make for us? Ours is the advantage in numbers, arms, and age. We could take all you bring, leave you dead, and keep the woman for ourselves. What stops us? Your Holy Orders?"

With effort, Don Felipe held his back straight and his voice steady. "Play such tricks too often, and who will trust you and others of your trade far enough to bring you ransom for anyone?"

This time the bandit's laughter was unmistakably amusement, free and honest. "Old priest," he said, "your manner pleases me. Come on, then. It will be simpler and quicker to take you to the lady than to bring her here."

Gubbio, looking round cautiously, climbed into Juan's empty saddle. Juan remained afoot without protest, silently leading the pack mule. The shorter bandit led the way, the taller dropped back to stride along beside the priest, and the other two presumably followed with their guns.

Don Felipe found that in other circumstances it might have been not impossible to like the man at his side. Perhaps forty lean years of age, he bore himself with the grace of a noble; he seemed almost as well-washed and laundered as a town merchant; his beard looked no more than two days old; his ready grin displayed a set of strong if tobacco-stained teeth with a single upper canine missing; and his brown eyes, only slightly bloodshot, showed both dignity and humor.

"Should we not go blindfold?" the priest inquired.

"You do not like the view, Don Priest?"

"I do not wish to be killed for knowing the way."

"Ah! No fear of that," the bandit answered with another laugh. "We are guiding you as through a maze. It will take the rest of the day, but one might find worse ways of passing an afternoon, and this should give Pedro time to catch your missing mule, eh?"

Looking behind, and seeing two bandits still bringing up the rear, Don Felipe guessed that Pedro must be yet a fifth man. That left, by Juan's original count, no more than three still at their camp, wherever it was, to guard the prisoners. Don Sagesse was at least Felipe's own age, but a man could be old and still strong—witness Gubbio—and Pilar would be barely fifty. "You give me your word," he demanded of his guide, "that the lady and her uncle are not only unhurt, but in comfort?"

"When I left, they were in as much comfort as any of us."

"Neither bound nor chained?"

"Penned up a little, but in bodily comfort for all that, I promise you. Papa Mano does not mistreat guests who can draw wealth to us as the lodestone draws iron."

"'Papa Mano'? Then you are not yourself the leader of your people?"

"I am Papa Mano's lieutenant. You may call me Tiberio," the bandit explained, making half a bow as he walked. "I do not say whether or not it is my real name, but you may as well call me by it as by any other."

"Well, Tiberio: if you spend the rest of this day bringing us to those whom we have come to ransom, does this not mean we may find ourselves constrained to pass the night beneath your roof?"

"'Beneath our roof'!" Tiberio laughed heartily. "Well, you have my word that you will not be any worse for it. Will you pay for your lodging by hearing our Confessions, Don Priest? And singing Mass for us?"

"Why not? It cannot do you much harm, though I fear that neither will it do you much good."

The hours passed less slowly, Felipe suspected, for himself than for Gubbio and Juan, or even for three of their guard-escorts. All of the bandits save Tiberio appeared to be men of a taciturn sullenness rivaling Juan's, and even Gubbio had rarely shown so little inclination to speak. Only the priest and Tiberio exchanged conversation.

At last, late in the afternoon, they reached the bandits' camp. Two ragged women tended a goat and stirred a small iron pot above a little fire of very dry wood. Four men in various states of age and beardedness sat among the rocks jesting and drinking. Gubbio's mule, stripped of her bags and harness, stood tethered to graze on sparse mountain grass near the mouth of a cave.

"Hey! Papa Mano!" Tiberio shouted joyously. "Look what we bring you! Not only ransom, but a priest to hear our confessions and sing Mass for us!"

One of the oldest bandits raised his head from his drinking bowl and stared at Don Felipe. The priest stared back. He knew those blue eyes, that straight nose... if he could but peel back the years, shave away the silver beard and smooth the brow of its wrinkles...

The bandit recognized him first, if only by a heartbeat. "Don Felipe de Bivar y... whatever! 'Priest' you said, Tiberio? By God's holy backside, this is no 'priest' you have brought us—it's a damned inquisitor!"

Gripping his saddle, Don Felipe replied: "As who should know better than you?—Manuel Urtigo!" He spoke calmly but quickly, to make his statement before the impending tumult.

"Inquisitor?" said Tiberio, the first by a syllable to repeat the word. Some whispered it, but most barked and spat.

"Yes!" cried Gubbio. "Maltreat us at peril of the displeasure of the Holy Office!"

"Put up thy sword, old friend," Don Felipe told him, not wanting these rough men to hear the edge of desperation in his servant's voice. "Did the Holy Office not prove, years ago, that this same Manuel Urtigo had kept his Catholic faith pure and true? Scarlet and mortal his other sins may have been even then, but they were not among those that the Inquisition may judge. Where are they whom I have come to ransom?"

"Take him to them!" shouted Urtigo. "Let him spend these next hours thinking about all that we can do to him!"

"Wait!" said Tiberio. "I have given him my word that he will not fare any worse for passing the night with us."

For the length of an Ave Maria, the old chief and his lieutenant stared into each other's eyes like dogs locked in a test of will. At last Urtigo said, "He will not fare any worse for spending the night. Nothing but my command stops us from doing to him at once whatever we may save for later. Take him! Take them all!"

Further revelations trembled on Felipe's tongue. He bit them back just in time.

"Your Excellency," Tiberio murmured, with a not ungentle pressure on the priest's elbow, "you must get down and come on foot." Half apologetically, he helped the old churchman dismount and led him past Gubbio's mule toward the cave, pausing at its mouth to strike flint and steel to a small clay hand-lamp that waited in readiness on a little ledge. Three more bandits followed, one bringing Juan and two Gubbio.

The tunnel smelled of the needs of sinful flesh. Don Felipe held his handkerchief to his nose and wondered how much suffering such an atmosphere must cause the Calé. The passage was not, however, excessively rough underfoot, nor excessively long. Presently a tiny flame appeared at the tunnel's end. As they neared it, Don Felipe saw that there were also bars. Behind them, something moved with a swishing of cloth and audible intake of breath.

"Pilar?" he exclaimed.

"Felipe! Ah, my own, is it you!" Her voice held anger—but not, he thought, directed at him.

Gubbio attempted another ill-placed threat involving the vengeance of the Holy Office. Don Felipe cut him off. None of them said anything more until after Tiberio and his men had opened the makeshift cage long enough to push the new prisoners in with the old, shut the door and secured it again with a large if rusty padlock, and departed.

The instant the last bandit was out of sight, Pilar seized Juan by one arm and said in low, fierce passion, "You fool! What do you mean by coming back? By bringing *him* back?"

"Could I leave you, mother? Could you truly ask *that*?"

"So now you will lose *both* parents, and maybe your own sweet life as well!"

"*Both* parents?" Don Felipe caught the bars to help hold himself on his feet.

"She did not even tell you? Felicitas! You did not so much as tell him? Yes, my husband—when I told you I was barren, I spoke the truth as I thought it to be, but I was mistaken—this is our daughter! This young fool who could have lived, but chose instead to throw away both your life and her own!"

All these years... Rosemary had spoken the truth.

"No," Felipe answered, shaking his head. "Not her own. She will live... at least long enough to bear one child. This I know. This I know from visions... visions I never fully understood until this moment. Felicitas? Not 'Juan'—Felicitas! My daughter."

Don Sagesse spoke. "Our last daughter. The last of all my tribe."

"What happened?" said Don Felipe, speaking more to his wife than to the poor, broken old count of the Calé.

"It was a village of lawless men," Felicitas took it upon herself to answer. "Beyond the mountains. 'Lutherans' you would have called them, I think. Their own priests stopped them in time to leave a few of us alive. Alive and hiding. The *gadje* here on this side of the mountains are better. They at least offer us a chance to be ransomed."

"A trap for your father, you mean, little fool!"

"No," Don Felipe interjected. "Stop blaming her. Do you think I could have rested without coming for you myself?"

"She was to tell you that she is your daughter, not that I was still alive! That letter—she even showed you that, I suppose—it was written only to fool them into letting her go. She was to have destroyed it and kept only the jewel, to show it to you and prove who she is."

"I bless her for bringing me this chance to save you, or at least to see you once more, to hold you in my arms once more, whatever the price."

Gubbio mumbled something beneath his breath.

Ignoring him, Don Felipe went on, "As for their intention to trap me—had you told them my name?"

"Them? Never! I had told Felicitas whom to find, that was all."

"I thought as much. They did not even seem to know me for a man of the Holy Office until their leader recognized me. We have an ancient score to settle, Manuel Urtigo and I. Had it been otherwise, I think they would have accepted the ransom and let us go."

Gubbio grumbled, "Pity it is not otherwise, then."

"And I rejoice in this chance to settle it!" the inquisitor said firmly. "Although not the tenth part as much as I rejoice to find you again, my love, my wife. And... can this truly be our child? My daughter... you looked younger as a boy, by several years."

"She was born half a year after they drove us from Agapida, that time you were not there to stop them. You cannot think I would ever have married another, as long as you might still be alive."

"And searching for you. Oh, God, if even one of my messengers had ever found you!"

Gubbio muttered, "I would God they had, and none of us be here now."

"Shame!" Don Sagesse cried unexpectedly. "Is it not shame for a priest's man to complain against the fate Christ hands him?"

"God graciously allows us to bear our fate more easily by complaining about it... does He not, master?"

Don Felipe hardly heard his servant and Don Sagesse. Holding Pilar tightly, he said, "If there is any honor among thieves, they will let you go. At need, appeal to Tiberio. He is, I believe, the most nearly honorable among them. In Rome I have a friend from my earliest boyhood—one Gamaliel Ben Joseph—a rabbi of the Hebrew people. My visions warned me that Rome would be sacked, in time to warn him of it in a letter before it happened, these two or three years ago. My warning saved him and his family. Only last year I had word through my Italian bankers that they were living once again in the city, alive and in good health and comfort. Even if Gamito has passed on into the bosom of Abraham since my last news of him, his family should remember me, what I have done for them."

"And you, my husband?" said Pilar.

"And me?" Gubbio put in. "Master, what about me?"

"If we survive, Gubbio, we shall go to Rome along with my wife and family. If you survive, old friend, and I do not, my last command is that you serve them with all the faithfulness you can find within your bones.

And that you arrange for Diego Sos to join you, if he so chooses, and Don Martin also."

"But what if these bandits know me?" Gubbio's voice dropped to a barely audible whisper. "Oh, Mother Mary, what if the villain remembers my face, too?"

"Pray that we both escape," Don Felipe told him. "For if I escape, you will, also. If God grants me justice this time against my ancient enemy…" He lowered his own voice still further. "But even if not, you had no direct part in Manuel Urtigo's case. He may ignore you. Provided, of course, that you play your canny old self, and never let it slip to them that you might ever have enjoyed any connection with the Holy Office beyond that of an inquisitor's personal domestic."

"For these scoundrels, that could be enough! I wish we had burned the devil when we had him!"

"No, old friend," Felipe admonished his servant, "never wish that evil had been done in place of good, not even when it seems to our weak and selfish sight that the results might have been more to our own comfort. Such a wish, uttered within hearing of any knowledgeable soul less well acquainted with you than I, could smack of heresy."

"Still the scholar of godly things," Pilar murmured huskily, sliding her hand over her husband's wrinkled cheek to pinch his ear with gentle fingers. "Still and ever. Win free, my love, and I promise that we will all of us go to Rome together."

* * * *

Manuel Urtigo's last threat had seemed to promise them the night, crowded together. Yet it could have been little more than half flown when Tiberio came. "Your Excellency," he announced, with a bow that might have been reverential in earnest, "they are waiting for you, and pray do not hold me in any way to blame."

"Why, then, do you bring the summons?"

The bandit lieutenant set his lamp in a convenient niche before making a self-deprecatory shrug. "Papa Mano insisted on this in token of my loyalty. You understand, your Excellency?"

Don Felipe stood. "Whether I understand or not, Tiberio, it is for God to pass the judgment on you. But I admonish you to choose your master well. I have seen terrible sins committed in the name of loyalty."

Tiberio bowed his head and, turning the key in the padlock, answered only, "We have guards at the entrance."

His caution was hardly needed. Wooden bars would have presented little obstacle to five cramped prisoners, were it not for the bandit camp just outside, at least part of which seemed never to sleep. Felipe pressed his silver rosary—the last thing of value, save his garments and his crucifix, that he had about his person—into his daughter's hand, and stepped forward to go with the lieutenant.

Halfway along the tunnel, Felipe said, "I am no longer a young man, and the body has certain needs, especially pressing in the old, which dignity dislikes fulfilling in the presence of the other sex... you understand?"

Tiberio nodded slowly. "A fig for Papa Mano's command! If your Excellency pleases to turn aside into that little corner to your left, we can say, if we must, that your lady delayed us with clinging and weeping."

"Your mercy, Tiberio, may perhaps in God's sight outweigh your readiness to lie." Don Felipe turned aside. He had wondered how the Calé, with that wonderful delicacy which held them from so much as hinting in company of this particular need, had fared during their days of imprisonment. Surely the outlaws had made some provision, perhaps led them out singly to some private place from time to time, and Papa Mano's 'command' had applied only to this night.

After Don Felipe finished adding his part to the foulness of the cavern's air, he gave Tiberio a quick priestly blessing before they went on again. Nourishing the bud of friendship could do no harm.

At the mouth of the tunnel his steps faltered, if only for a moment. Ten paces from the opening stood a stake.

He glanced at Tiberio, who bowed his head again, replaced his lamp among the stones, and blew out its flame, almost as if that might hide the shame from his prisoner. It did not. The moon was but a crescent, and the bandits' campfire small; but its glow sufficed. A thick chain wrapped the stake as though in readiness and, while the brush and faggots piled round its foot were scarcely enough to roast a lamb, more fuel waited in a tall stack at a little distance.

The thought flooded his brain, Is it for this that I have never in all my life, outside involuntary dreams, witnessed a burning? The emptiness of his stomach was as if a mountain peak had been pulled out from under him, the base of his skull felt like something squeezed to bursting by pressure from beneath. Was this, then, what they felt at last—all those relaxed to the justice of the secular arm?

But it was not for a descendant of El Cid and Aguilar, as also of the holy heretic martyr Raymonde, to show fear in the presence of his enemy. Walking away from Tiberio's touch on his arm, Don Felipe strode forward to face Manuel Urtigo, once the scourge of Axtilan and before that the monster of the rape of Alhama, who still sat in the same rocky perch he had filled that afternoon.

"Well, Don Inquisitor," Urtigo said, sneering, "and how do you like it, hey?"

Most of the bandits and some of their women laughed as if their Papa Mano had made a fine joke. Don Felipe noted with a trace of satisfaction that not all of them laughed. It was a beginning, especially with Tiberio among the silent ones.

"I can look beyond this, 'Papa Mano,'" the inquisitor replied in a voice of purpose, "to the hope of Heaven. Can you say as much? however your pitiful earthly life may end."

Some of the bandits looked thoughtful, but 'Papa Mano' said quickly, "Ah! No fear for that, Don Inquisitor. When my time comes, we send someone out to bring us a priest who knows how to hold his tongue. No fear that it will ever be you. Hey, lads?"

This time the laughter was a little less loud, a little more ragged than before.

"Make sure, then," Don Felipe told them, "that death does not take you by surprise. As I have heard can happen in the life you have chosen."

Urtigo grunted. His next speech had a rehearsed sound, down to its heavy sarcasm. "I apologize to your Reverence that we cannot risk too much fire. Begging your blessing, we will have to roast you slowly. Bit by bit. The little flames licking up to your knees, like fawning little puppies..." He licked his dark lips. "First they take off your fine clothes— puff! puff! puff! They pop your skin open, sputter in your blood, we give them a little more wood to keep them company—as much as we dare—they start reaching above your knees. The chain heats up, brands your skin while it waits for its little fiery friends... ahhh! You will still be alive to see the sun come up, but I think by then you will not much care. Hey, lads?"

And now only a few of them laughed, although those few laughed loudly.

"I perceive, 'Papa Mano,' that you have witnessed these things before now. I suspect that you have watched them as often as you could, and with great relish. This does not surprise me. But: have you taken no wholesome warning at all from them?"

"Have you, Papa Inquisitor?" The bandit leered. "Holy Mother Church tells us to enjoy seeing heretics burn, hey?"

Tiberio protested, with a glance at Don Felipe, "Not to enjoy it, no— but to take warning by it, as his Excellency says. To see Hell in it, and—"

"Mouth in the ground, Tiberio!" the chief interrupted in a way that showed why no one else, before his lieutenant, had ventured an opinion in the debate between Manuel Urtigo and his prisoner. "Well, Don Inquisitor," Papa Mano went on, "we are merciful, too. We offer you the same mercy you offer us, when you have us. Recant and confess, beg our merciful pardon, and we will strangle you quick. That way your lady in there will get only your stench, not your screaming."

Pilar and Felicitas, Gubbio and Don Sagesse. Don Felipe knew that his daughter would survive to bear at least one child... but the circumstances of her life? and of her child's begetting? He knew nothing of the fate of the others. Nevertheless, he would endanger them all the more if he betrayed his concern for them any further than he had already done by bringing their ransom in person. Drawing himself up, he answered only, "What can such as you, Manuel Urtigo, possibly call upon me to recant and confess?"

"Confess that your 'Holy Inquisition' is a stinking monster!"

"Confess any such thing at the demand of a murderer? In a few moments—to spare your people the full warning of what may someday befall them, in their souls if not also their bodies, unless they repent—I may perhaps agree to some such proposition. But now, at this moment, while still in full possession of my reason and free will, I tell you, Manuel Urtigo, that we of the Holy Inquisition have labored hard, long, and with any sacrifice for the glory of God and the truth of His Holy Catholic Church, as we understand it in this age of our frail human history; and in thus blaspheming against the Holy Office, you have betrayed yourself at last as an accursed heretic!"

"And who reports me, hey?" Urtigo half screamed, waving one hand furiously. "Chain him! Chain him up to the stake and light our fire under him!"

"No!" Tiberio cried, and a thin murmur seconded him. "He is a brave old lad. Let him finish what he has to say."

Some of the bandits started toward Don Felipe. The rest held back as if to see what would happen. Tiberio took a step forward and drew his sword partway. Those who had started to obey Papa Mano stopped and looked back at him.

Don Felipe seized the word first. "Once, Manuel Urtigo, we found you guiltless and innocent of heresy. We mounted you upon a fine horse and set you free with honor. This alone proves that we are capable of error, or, at least, that we lack foresight." Trying to take advantage of the hesitation he sensed in Urtigo's band, he looked around at them and said, "Any and all of you who, having heard this man's heresy, fail in your duty to God and Holy Church of bearing witness against him, make yourselves fautors of his heresy and partakers in his guilt."

"What would your Excellency have?" Tiberio asked in tones of mild protest. "We are hunted outlaws. We cannot approach a tribunal without putting ourselves in danger of our very lives. Besides—forgive me, these are not my own words—but I have heard that you yourselves make them heretics, with what you do to them in your secret prisons."

"Where have you heard such a thing? What can you know of the Holy Inquisition's secrets?"

"Hah!" cried Manuel Urtigo. "Have I not been there? Does Papa Mano not know by his own experience how you could make a heretic out of the sweet Ihesu Himself?"

This time the mutterings, even a few exclamations uttered aloud, were on Papa Mano's side; but Don Felipe hardly heard them. "And you have spoken of these things?" he whispered, thunderstruck. Then, seeing whatever slight moral advantage his enemy might have enjoyed over him until now dissolve away, he raised his voice to a cry: "You have broken your Oath of Silence!"

If Don Felipe had once, while still young, broken the Seal of Confession in order to save a friend from false accusation, Manuel Urtigo had, in full maturity, broken the equally solemn Oath of Silence, apparently for no other reason than to rouse his followers.

"You and your forced oaths!" Manuel snarled, as if having had to think out his reply. "First you torture us to make us speak, and then you do it again to make us keep silent. You with all your subtle new tortures that leave no marks! You and your oaths forced in blood!"

Once only had Manuel Urtigo been tortured—at least by the Inquisition—and that no farther than *in conspectu tormentarum*. Never had he been denied food, drink, bedding... he had waxed fat and healthy during his half-year in the secret cells, and that almost entirely at the Inquisition's own expense. Never had the Holy Office, to Don Felipe's personal knowledge, introduced into Aragon any torture that was not already old in the secular justice of Spain's other kingdoms.

"You may have broken the Oath of Silence in spirit only," cried the inquisitor, "by telling falsehoods of your experience. Or you may have broken it both in spirit and in letter. Whether you have uttered truth or falsehood, I do not say, for *I* will not break the sacred Silence. But this I say: that in the eyes of God and Heaven, if not of this sinful world, you are a murderer many times over!"

"So are most of us, your Excellency," Tiberio said, loudly enough for Papa Mano to hear and bark an appreciative laugh; but Don Felipe thundered on:

"You are the murderer of my own father and mother, of both of my brothers—the one hardly more than a child—of the wife of my elder brother and of her infant child in her arms, and of my sister, a helpless maid! Yes, you slew them all, my sister with your own bloody hands and the others, if not in person, then by command! My sister you raped before slaying—"

"What else are women for?" Manuel Urtigo interrupted. "Hey, lads?"

Some ragged laughter. Not much.

"Following which, you broke her neck with a cruel blow to her chin," Don Felipe continued, "breaking skin and flesh so that her blood gushed forth. Your men stood by and cheered you on—'Bravissimo, Manuel!' Even the one who had just lost a thumb to some defender's blade."

One of the old bandits standing near his chief's rock uttered a low cry.

"My mother also," the inquisitor added, "I think, from the way in which her blood soaked her bed, you must have raped. All those of you here present who have laughed at the raping of women, if you have ever loved a woman—bride or mistress, sister or mother—think of her raped, then murdered and lying in her blood!"

"Alhama!" moaned one of the bandits. The same one, Felipe guessed, who had cried out at mention of the severed thumb.

"That was war!" Urtigo protested. "That was when we helped reconquer Granada gloriously for their Most Catholic Majesties!"

"True!" Don Felipe agreed. "And for that reason, beyond the touch of mere human justice. Nevertheless, the family of Bivar y Aguilar—my family—was Christian, Catholic. Had they not sent one son to Rome for schooling? so that I alone, of all my family, survived. Even Jews, even Moslems, were among those spared and taken prisoner by the Castilian army that day, but you and your men, Manuel Urtigo, destroyed a Christian family with great murder—an entire household of good Catholic Christians, descended in direct line from El Cid! In my father's library, you broke the head from a marble bust of Tully and thrust into its place the head of my younger brother, a boy half grown, whose life you had severed for the mere joy of murder!"

"How does he know?" exclaimed the bandit who had spoken once to moan and again to breathe the name Alhama. "Holy Inquisitor, *how do you know these things?*"

"They were revealed to me even at the time, miles away in Aragon as I was, in a vision sent by Almighty God, Who beholds all things, from Whom nothing is hidden!"

"They are true?" cried Tiberio. "Enrico, are they all true?"

"To the smallest detail," the old man who obviously remembered Alhama answered with a groan.

"God!" Tiberio ejaculated with something between a gasp and a sigh. "Your Excellency knew all this, and yet you let him free?"

"Rightly or wrongly," the inquisitor repeated, "we found no heresy in your 'Papa Mano.' The Holy Office is not for the wreaking of personal vengeance, nor the punishment of mere murder. Such sins as Manuel Urtigo has committed in battle and warfare, remain for God's judgment alone."

"Brothers!" shouted Tiberio. "I say that we free the old priest and his people, and burn Papa Mano instead!"

A great outcry went up. The cheers all but drowned the protests— Tiberio's party must have long been gathering strength, the lieutenant waiting like a young ram to topple the old leader.

Manuel Urtigo rose to his full height and stood a moment, bawling back at them. His words were unintelligible, his face darkened and contorted like that of a demon. Then, all at once, he clutched his head and crumpled.

The camp gradually quieting as it watched, he slipped... slowly, as it seemed... fell, lay still at the foot of his rocky throne. Two of his older men and one of the women hurried to him, touched him, turned him over. The woman laid her hand on his brow and shook her head.

"Bring me candles and water," Don Felipe said clearly, "such oil as you have and a little salt. And free my companions, and let my servant bring my stole and my book from our saddlebags. I will give this man, my ancient enemy though he is, Extreme Unction before we go."

"And the ransom, your Excellency?" Tiberio asked.

Not until that moment, hearing the respect in the new leader's voice, did Don Felipe expel a sigh of relief. "Let us say, my friend Tiberio, that you and your fellows shall keep fully half of it."

They answered with another cheer. Don Felipe folded his arms and nodded, waiting for what he needed to give his ancient enemy the last sacrament. He could sense both Raymonde and Rosemary standing at his sides, and even Rosemary, he thought, might this time be smiling.

CHAPTER 30

THE DREAM OF THE TUG-OF-WAR

"What place is this?" he asked.

"Hospital," said Rosemary.

He looked around. They stood in a passageway, painted in bright pastels, adorned only with framed pictures, stretching into infinity. All angles were stark, most lines straight. The light, which flowed through a honeycombed ceiling, resembled that of the sun when behind high clouds, casting a harsh glare over all things.

"It is as clean," he remarked, "as even Moors could ever wish." He spoke doubtfully, for, although Moors would have appreciated its cleanliness, they would have made of it something artistic and lovely, with graceful arches and twining curls painted over the walls in rich colors.

"Clean?" Rosemary snorted. "The dirt's just invisible. People can still pick up more disease bugs in hospitals than anywhere else. In here," she went on, pushing one of the largest pictures.

He saw that, after all, some of them—those in frames that touched the floor—were not pictures, but doors. This one opened to her shove. He followed her in.

The chamber was large, but held four beds only, one in each corner. It could have held three times that number. White screens partially shielded each bed from the others, so that he could see only one, the one to his immediate left, clearly and entirely. In that bed, a man lay, half covered with rumpled bedclothes. He wore a light sleeveless tunic that, but for its dark though faded colors, might have appeared part of his sheets. His head alone, resting restlessly on a pillow covered with white cloth, and his arms could be seen uncovered. His face was ruddy and had once been round, but now was drawn with long suffering. His hair had been black and now was more than half silver. His eyes were closed, but Don Felipe thought he did not sleep. A woman sat at his bedside, both her hands upon one of his.

"Dying," said Rosemary. "Alzheimer's. All they really have for it where we are right now is a name and a few research clues."

"Al-... Is it Moorish?"

"No. It's memory. It makes you forget. Everything, eventually."

A second woman, dressed in crisp white trousers and pale yellow tunic, came to the other side of the bed and held a handleless drinking vessel to the man's mouth, trying to slip a tiny, bent white tube between his lips. He moaned and twitched his head away. She moistened his mouth with a damp cloth and left the room.

"He's reached the point," Rosemary said grimly, "of forgetting how to swallow."

"My God! And yet he still lives?"

"They're experts in keeping people alive."

The second woman returned, bringing two similarly clad assistants and a pole as tall as herself. It rolled on its own small, wheeled platform; and had near its top a crosspiece from which swung a clear membrane pouch or bladder filled with water or another fluid. A long, clear tube dangled from this bladder, like a very thin intestine but much more stiff.

The first woman moved away to the foot of the bed. The three rolled the pole to its head, took the hand she had relinquished, and started jabbing and prodding at it with a large needle.

The man twitched, jerked, thrashed, made strangled little cries in his throat. The woman at the foot of the bed turned her back on the scene and buried her face in her hands.

"Why do they torture him?" Don Felipe cried.

"They want to help him," Rosemary answered. "They've already given him pain blankers. With needles, the only way he can still take them. That hurts him, too. Now they're giving him basic nourishment."

Never had Don Felipe relished the duty of witnessing even *in conspectu tormentarum*. Now he too turned away, staring at the far wall, which seemed to be one huge window, glazed with marvelously large panes of glass that glinted behind complicated coverings made of many blades of very thin metal. He became aware of murmuring outside, as of seawaves dashing against the hospital. The more he tried to close his ears to the man's incoherent protests, the more clearly he heard this outer tumult. The more he recognized it as the rumbling of a mob.

"Right to life!" the voices were chanting, over and over. "Stop the killing! Respect life! Respect life! Everyone has the right to life! Everyone!"

An explosion silenced them, but only for a heartbeat. Then someone shouted, "Dirty cocorkian!" and thunder followed. With a shock, Don Felipe understood that it issued, not from any stormcloud, but from the throats of the mob. It was dull cheering. Stunned, he hardly understood why, he turned back to the man in the bed.

The first woman, she who had sat beside the sick man, her hands on his, now said: "No." Turning, she looked at the people of the hospital and told them, "No more. It's hurting him too much. There's no hope, so let him die."

They looked back at her, nodded, and slowly took away the pole with its pouch, tube, and needle. The second woman lingered longest, straightening his pillow and coverings, stroking his hand and head, moistening his lips once more with the damp cloth. Last, she laid one hand on the first woman's shoulder for the space of a Gloria, as though to comfort her.

Her assistants wheeled the pole to the door; but, as they opened it, the mob burst inside, thrusting them back to the bedside.

"Murderers!" shrieked one woman at their head, pointing her finger at them... or was it a hand gun? "Euthanasiasts! Co-corkians! Atheists!"

Other limbs of the mob began beating at the hospital people, trying to force them to return with the bladder and jab its needle somehow into the victim's arm after all. When the hospital people collapsed or fled, several of the mob caught up bladder and needle and scrambled toward the bed as if to insert it themselves.

The man moaned in agony. Don Felipe looked at him again, and it was Ihesu, lying atop the bed with arms extended on His Cross. Blood welled forth from the nails to pool on the floor. Another great splotch of Holy Blood reddened the bedclothes where His feet must be. He moaned again.

Don Felipe found himself on his knees, with no memory of kneeling.

And yet the sight was... horrible, grotesque. He thought that he had never fully understood... Ihesu—the Son of God, God Incarnate—in His suffering had been as misshapen, as painful to behold, as any victim of stake or torture chamber. What, truly, did he—did all Christians—worship when they worshipped the Crucifix? God? Or pain? Ah, Ihesu, Mary, Joseph—had Holy Church made a false god out of suffering? Was it idolatry to worship God's agony and, with it, whatever suffering they themselves could cause their fellow mortals?

Rosemary still stood, but her hand gripped his shoulder.

The woman who had sat beside the dying man stepped forward between bed and mob... and she was Mary, God's Mother. "No," she told them, tears flowing down her face, but her voice steady and quiet. "It is finished. Let him die."

She who led the mob shouted, "Only God has the right to let people die!"

"And is God not attempting to take my dear one?" the Holy Mother replied. "But by your actions you believe neither in God nor Heaven, or you would not bend all your power so furiously to deny our Heavenly Papa that same right you claim to champion on His behalf, of gathering souls to Himself."

"Is this what it will be," Don Felipe whispered, "to die in future centuries? This—this tug of war between God's manifest will and man's medicine? Is the stake not almost better?"

He woke rejoicing that he lived in his own century, when physicians could still do so little to prolong life beyond God's limits.

CHAPTER 31

THE DEATH OF DON FELIPE

"I am very old," he mused tranquilly, dozing in the sun-washed court-yard. "So old that at times I grow confused as to which of my friends are still in this world and which already in the next."

"The line isn't as hard and fast as people think," said Rosemary.

He looked up and saw her standing beside his chair. "Great-grand-daughter," he greeted her pleasantly, gesturing at the nearby bench. "Can you sit and chat awhile? With prudence, we can still talk freely, here in Rome."

"We always could talk freely, here in your head." She extended one hand to him. "Come on, Great-grandfather. We can talk while we walk."

He accepted her hand and stood, allowing her to draw him along. His step felt easier than it had for several winters. That was fortunate, for, when they entered the colonnaded portico, he found that it stretched away before them an interminable distance.

"Anyway," Rosemary said as though reminding him, "you've been in Rome almost fifteen years."

"So many? They have seemed only a few."

She nodded. "The effect of age."

The carved stone pillars to their right, looming up each one in turn, cut their view of the courtyard into sunny panels, while casting slanted shadows upon the wall to their left.

Each time that he looked out between two columns, he saw a different scene: himself, Gamito, and Hamet playing as boys in the hills around Alhama de Karnattah… himself at his studies in Rome, in his little stu-dent's room, making his decision to turn priest… himself interviewing, as Gubbio looked on, that seemingly sincere young cleric Don Fadrique Osorio, who had proved so poor a vicar but made—they said—a fairly decent end in the reformed monastery to which he had been sentenced… the long years in the secret cells, with their strange tranquility like that of a hermit father's desert retreat… that day when, after long prayer and meditation, he had accepted the rare solitary inquisitorship of little Ainsa… his first meeting with that excellent New Christian cook Diego Sos, who had become a better servant to him, in some ways, even than Gubbio, and still cooked faithfully for the family here in Rome… his marriage night, and all those other precious and holy hours spent enhanc-ing and bringing to ever greater perfection the Oldest Sacrament of all…

that strange hour when, after a night of sickenss and fever dreams which had nothing to do with either Rosemary or Raymonde, his good secretary Don Martin had brought him the appointment to chief inquisitorship of Daroca... himself in attendance at the quiet deathbed of that quiet, faithful little scribe Fray Pablo de María... his last pastoral visit (never guessing it to be the last) with good Fray Giuliano, growing gray and perhaps just a shade less lean in service to Nuestra Señora del Pilar de Agapida, still grieving for his lost Calé but soberly rejoicing in his new Franciscan houses... the evening Diego Sos and Don Martin had saved a starving pup from the streets, to nurse back to health... the hurried, half-secret journey from Spain to Italy... the reunion with his dear Jewish friends in the Eternal City... his daughter's marriage to a man almost as greatly to her liking as her parents had ever been to each other's... the birth of his first grandchild, followed so shortly by the peaceful passing of its other grandfather, Sagesse Labaa, aged before his time but who had recovered in his last years some measure of sanity... news and rumors of the new Ecumenical Council his present holiness, Paul III, had called to meet in Trento...

"I shall somewhat regret," Don Felipe mused, "the chance to watch this Tridentine Council unfold. But for my age, I might have wished to journey north in the hope of witnessing a little of it in person."

"It's going to make marriages like yours heretical," Rosemary reminded him.

"I did not say that I would agree with all its changes. Never, never could I regret union with my dearest Pilar! Only mourn that we lost so many years together... that I could not watch my daughter grow to womanhood.... I would have reached my century mark in 1555. Ten years yet. That will be the same year that the then-reigning pope will decree a 'ghetto,' as you call it, for the Jews of Rome."

"Glad you're finally taking my word for things."

"You told me that, did you not, in order for Gamito and his family to be warned again?"

"And then you bought this house from them."

"As you warned us in time before the sacking of Rome in... the exact year escapes me, but I think I did not yet fully trust all of your revelations at that time. Nevertheless, I warned them, and, thank God, reading the signs of the times, they took the warning and fled as they would have fled a plague, first taking the precautions that allowed them to return and build their life here anew."

"Made a regular habit of taking property off their hands, didn't you?" Rosemary observed, alluding to his purchases before the expulsions of 1486, 1492, and this year just past.

"At a fair price," he remembered with satisfaction. "Always at a fair price."

"Fair and then some. You've been a good friend to them."

"Gamito was my oldest remaining friend.... I could have fallen under suspicion a second time, back there in their Catholic Majesties' Spain, had I ever given voice to my hope of our meeting again in Paradise. Yet I fear that certain members of Gamito's family suspected my motives, comfortably though we have lived while charting out the safest route for them and their offspring through the centuries."

"They'll forget your game plan in a generation. They don't believe it now by more than a quarter."

He sighed. "Well, we have done our best. For the rest, they must shift for themselves, even as we all and every one of us need ultimately do."

In a shorter time than he would have thought possible, they stood at the end of the elongated courtyard. Here the colonnade stopped and, with it, the courtyard sunlight. Beyond, the cloistered walkway lengthened into grayer and grayer shadow, ending in a dark fleck the size of a baby's smallest fingernail.

"Have you seen my grandchildren?" He inquired, with all the pride befitting a nonagenarian grandfather, as he and his guide entered the sunless part of the walkway. "Two thus far. Two very fine young sprigs."

"She's going to have five in all. The one that ties you to me isn't born in your lifetime. Grandmother Pilar midwives the whole lot of 'em, though."

"Pilar. Pilar, my beloved.... And you, great-granddaughter? Have you borne... Are you to bear children?"

She shook her head. "A couple of godchildren, though. They turn out fine. Don't worry," she added. "My not having children doesn't stop *your* line. Not with five grandchildren to get it going."

"Abraham," he remarked. "I appreciate, now, the emotions of Father Abraham."

"Not afraid of flattering yourself, are you?"

"Have not the figures of the Old Testament been given to us as types of experience, human as well as divine?"

"Whew!" said Rosemary. "The time comes—may already have started by 1545—when religious thinkers insist the Bible is one hundred percent solid history. Turning any poor old agnostic with a grain of sense off the whole subject."

"How does one meaning preclude the other?" His guide had never, in all these years, lost the power to puzzle him.

"Well, if you know how Father Abraham felt, I know how the angels felt, all those years he wouldn't believe them."

Already, they had reached the walkway's end. The dark fleck, once the size of a baby's fingernail, was grown before them into a simple and unadorned wooden door, having neither lock nor latch nor handle, its lintel not quite as high as Felipe's forehead.

He looked sadly at his descendant. "Great-granddaughter, are you doomed, like Virgil, to remain forever outside, guiding wanderers to the very gates of Heaven, yet never yourself gaining admittance?"

"You're talking about Dante's Virgil, not the real one," she replied, putting one hand to the door and pushing it open.

He staggered a pace or two backward. Light poured through the open doorway, true; but no beauty. Or, rather, beauty in the colors, but none in the scene they formed.

A wide plain stretched before him, tilting upward at a dizzy slope to a far horizon so high it left little space for the firmament. The parched ground, studded here and there with bushes and shrubs—startling for the spiny luxuriance of their foliage—lay scored everywhere with yawning crevasses of depth beyond guessing. To left and right, brutal fencing walled the enclosure: heavy upright posts with something like dark spiderwebs, each filament thick as a man's wrist, between them, black against the thin line of smoky sky. Most of these webs held human shapes spreadeagled at their centers in the place of spiders; only here and there one of the webs showed a ragged hole and seemed otherwise empty.

In a direct line with the doorway, on the apex of the slope, a buttressed stone wall completely blocked the sky. The sun, if it existed here, must lie behind that fortress: the light bathing this landscape was a shadowless diffusion, at once glory and gloaming, mournful and lurid.

And all this slope swarmed with creatures almost as grotesque as the denizens of Hieronymus Bosch's most fantastic canvases. Many skeletal, some few puffed and bloated, almost all twisted with agony or unnatural exertion until the once human form could be recognized only in patches, they writhed and trundled with no visible purpose save to drive one another by means of whip, spiked wheelbarrow, and stranger devices.

Stabbed with fear, Don Felipe searched the scene and gradually made out that, though the few tormented the many and though their roles seemed fixed and unchanging, those who wielded the whips and other implements appeared no more demonic than their victims. Wringing some courage from his observation, he cried, "God grant that this is Purgatory!"

"You see it the way you can understand it," said Rosemary. "I see the death camp at Dachau. Don't worry. We're heading for the convent at the back of it." Stooping low, she ducked through the doorway into the purgatorial vision.

With reluctance, he bowed his head and followed, as he had done so often in the dreams of his lifetime. Pointing at the stone fortress, he tried to ask in a full sentence if it were truly a convent, but all that he heard from his own mouth, in a kind of croak, was the word, "Convent?" Suspicions of some perverted Rabelaisian abbey tumbling through his mind, he coughed to clear his throat and added, more successfully, "A convent of what order?"

"Carmelites. That's on the original plane, after the war. Here, it takes in everybody."

Walking briskly, she wove in and out among the gargoylish beings. Busily and multitudinously as they swarmed over the plain, they did not cram it; open spaces abounded between them. The boundaries of such spaces, however, were in constant flux and change, as the creatures fled one another, formed and reformed into Laoccoönian groupings, or floundered in individual anguish. This made it a delicate task to find a clear path through the loose-knit throng, and Felipe followed close on his descendant's heels.

The denizens of the plain ignored them, neither purposely molesting them nor offering to turn aside. Thus, occasional blows caught one or other of the pair. Rosemary paid them no attention. Finding them little worse than the buzzing of gnats, Don Felipe soon learned to do likewise. As for the slope, that proved far more steep in appearance than in feel; since it was both solid and gritty underfoot, walking would have been easy enough had the plain been emptier of twisted humanity. The noise, however, fell on him fiercely. All or most of the unhappy creatures chattered, jabbered, shrieked, and wailed constantly. He would have thought it impossible for himself and his guide to hear each other shout in the midst of this din, until Rosemary spoke again, in a normal voice, and somehow he understood her clearly.

"Even these poor floaters," she remarked, "can come inside whenever they're ready."

He began to observe degrees in their deformity. At last he glimpsed one arm straighten a little before his eyes. "Then this *is*, indeed, Purgatory!" he exclaimed in triumph.

"If that's what you want to call it," she replied.

"But... look!" Hand trembling, he pointed at a group he had just noticed a little to their left.

One of the most misshapen whip wielders, even as it stood flaying the victims before it mercilessly, was using its other hand to peel its own face. Half the forehead and the cheek below lay bare already, one round white eyeball staring out from flesh like butchers' meat. As Felipe watched ahast, it dug its long talons into its chin and began slowly rolling the first long strip from the other side of its face.

"Guard," Rosemary explained, giving it a glance. "Dehumanizing himself."

"An alternative hypothesis," another voice put in, "concerns the pangs of conscience and self-chastisement for actions known to be wrong."

From somewhere—in his horrified fascination with the spectacle of a creature skinning itself alive, Don Felipe had not seen where—the dark man of Saint Patrick's Purgatory had joined them.

"Why, then, not simply drop the whip?" Don Felipe asked him as their little group pressed on.

"Obstinate perversity, perhaps. Or possibly inertia. The human heart has even more convolutions than the human brain. Yet another theory proposes that those who perpetrate such deeds make themselves victims along with those whom they persecute."

The three had almost reached the convent door. Looking up, Felipe saw Raymonde waiting there.

"It is the Golden Rule," she said, joining their conversation even as she opened her arms in welcome. "The way one treats others *is* the way one treats oneself."

"Great-great-grandmother." Nodding, Rosemary reached around her and, with one forefinger, gave the door a nudge that sent it swinging inward.

The contrast with the outer yard was complete. At a great table laid with gold, lace, and crystal, stretching to infinity beneath marvelous trees and a dome of incredibly pure light, an immense multitude shared graceful good fellowship. Pilar's people Don Felipe saw there, and Gamito's, Hamet's and El Santon's; pink skins, yellow, and all shades of brown; Adamites, Taborites, and priests of Baal; persons representing every guided dream of his life, as well as many in attire he had never glimpsed before… each one a distinct individual, yet clearly a companion to all the others.

And, rising over and infusing all their happy conversation, the overpowering immanence of GOD.

"But where is Juan El Santon himself?" Felipe cried, searching the table with an anxious gaze. "Surely that earnest soul cannot still be among those in the outer confusion?"

"This is but the first of Heaven's many mansions," Raymonde reassured him. "San Juan de Calamocha has already passed far beyond here."

"Heaven, then, is not where we instantly know the answers, but where we may without burning or bloodshed discuss the questions!"

"And Purgatory," Raymonded added, "is the state of learning how to talk of all these things with neither violence nor anger nor bitterness."

"As for the question of how we can mingle here freely," the dark man remarked, "without reference to our chronological timeframe, I have long suspected—I may of course be in error, for even now I discern problems with the theory—that within one's initial step through the portal lies the entire space of time between personal death and the general resurrection, from whence we can dip back into history as sent."

"If you will excuse my absence from you for a while," Don Felipe replied, "I see one beckoning me."

THE END

www.ingramcontent.com/pod-product-compliance
Lightning Source LLC
Chambersburg PA
CBHW021224250626
47155CB00008B/2927